RELIQUARY

Aug 16

RELIQUARY

SARAH FINE

Published by 47North, Seattle

www.apub.com

Amazon, the Amazon logo, and 47North are trademarks of Amazon.com, Inc., or its affiliates.

ISBN-13: 9781503935259
ISBN-10: 1503935256

Cover design by Faceout Studio

Printed in the United States of America

For Amber, who simply understood

CHAPTER ONE

The night before everything fell apart was the best of my life—the last purely happy, uncomplicated hours I would ever have. Looking back, I'm amazed by how lies can soothe the soul, quell every fear, blind you to reality in the most pleasant of ways. Not forever, of course. And only if you really want to buy into the illusion. But back then, I did. Even as the truth sharpened its knives and hunted me down, I refused to see it.

I was too worried about whether I'd made enough deviled eggs.

"We really could have had this catered," Mom said, stopping to rub my back as I balanced each egg half on the platter and then sprinkled them all with paprika.

I blew a lock of curly hair off my forehead. Outside I could hear laughter and the faint caress of Lake Michigan against the shore. "How many people are out there?" I asked, ignoring her comment. "Should I do another dozen?" *It's my engagement party and I want to feed people,* I had said. *Just appetizers and beer. I'll be done with plenty of time to spare.*

Ugh. My mother was right. Again.

Her soft hands closed over my wrists. "We'll have plenty. But Mattie, you need to be on the deck with Ben, not stuck in the kitchen. Your guests want to congratulate you—that's the whole point of the party! Let me finish this up." She held up my hands and glanced at my fingernails, short but coated with a bright-orange polish that set off my mustard-yellow dress and strawberry blond hair. "You'll ruin these if you keep this up." Smiling, she grabbed a dishrag and wiped a smear of mayonnaise off my ring finger, and the diamond that now lived there sparkled in the light. "Look—you've already done all the prep on the peperoncini wraps and bruschetta. I've got this covered. Go."

I glanced out to where my fiancé (*fiancé!*) was standing, a bottle of beer in one hand, flashing that smile that could melt glaciers. His hair ruffled in the breeze off the lake, the sun glinting off golden strands. I bit my lip and stared. Seriously—how had I gotten so lucky? "You sure, Mom? I feel terrible leaving you with all this work."

She chuckled and shook her head. "Honey, that's my job."

My mind skipped through memories of all the times she'd rescued me from my own ambitious schemes. Like when I'd taken on decorations for the senior prom (DIY string chandeliers are harder than they look, damn you, Internet!), or the time I'd decided that I *totally* had time to make three hundred cupcakes for my sorority's homecoming party despite the fact that I had to cheer in the actual homecoming game. "I guess I'm the queen of biting off more than I can chew." I sighed. "Sorry."

She pulled me into a hug, brushing my unruly hair off my face. "It's just one of your many charming qualities." She inclined her head toward Ben, and when I turned, he was watching the two of us, his honey-brown eyes full of affection and invitation. "And clearly Ben thinks so, too."

"Remind him of that after he takes a look at the supply closet at the clinic, okay?" I nodded as he beckoned me to come outside. "I might have tried to install a new shelving system while he was fishing with Dad yesterday." Ben had told me that it was my practice, too, even though he was the vet and I was just the lab tech and assistant. I'd wanted to show him I could pull my weight. And I could . . . but unfortunately, the new shelving system could not.

I explained the catastrophe that had once been Ben's tidy closet. Mom just said, "We can get Dad over there to take a look at it tomorrow morning. He gets a kick out of fixing other people's messes." One of the reasons my dad was the most popular real estate agent in Sheboygan was that he actually seemed to enjoy patching holes and installing crown molding, and it certainly helped with sales.

"You guys are the best parents. I don't deserve you."

Mom handed me the egg platter. "Pay me back by making sure Grandpa's having a decent time, okay?"

"You got it." I grinned. "I'm a ray of sunshine. I even dressed the part." I kissed her cheek and scooted through the open sliding door to the deck, where I set the platter on a table already crowded with food.

A warm hand closed over my arm. "Finally," Ben said, his voice full of gentle teasing.

I leaned my head back and let him kiss me, savoring the taste of beer on his lips. "Mm. I think I read somewhere that anticipation is a fine aphrodisiac."

He laughed, and it accentuated the adorable dimple in his right cheek. "Is that what this was? I thought maybe you were avoiding me because of the supply closet."

"You weren't scheduled to go in until tomorrow!"

His arm slid around my waist, and he pulled me against his muscular body. "I had to go pick up some eyedrops for Barley." His aging golden retriever was falling apart at the seams, but Ben was determined to give him a good life for as long as possible. "And it's okay, really. It'll be easy to fix."

I buried my face against his shoulder. "You are amazing."

He tipped my chin up. "And I'm marrying an amazing woman. Come on. Your friend Chelsea's just gotten here, and I know you haven't seen her in a while. Also, a couple of your aunts and uncles have already asked me when you'll appear. We need to greet your guests."

Your guests.

I laced my fingers with Ben's and looked out over my parents' sprawling backyard, crowded with my extended family and everyone from my mother's book club to my preschool gymnastics coach. Chelsea, my best friend from college, lifted her glass and grinned from her spot at the makeshift bar next to the pool.

"They're not *all* mine," I said quietly. Feeling lame, I waved toward Franz, one of a handful of Ben's patients (or, rather, the family members of Ben's patients) I had invited to beef up his part of the guest list.

Ben laughed as Franz waved back enthusiastically, looking a little lost and desperate as he stood among a group of my parents' church friends. "I'm really flattered he decided to come," Ben said. "He's much more comfortable surrounded by books and wine." A professor of anthropology at University of Wisconsin–Sheboygan, Franz had invited us over to his home a time or two, where I spent the evening playing with his dachshund, Lemmie, and Ben and Franz huddled in his library discussing lofty topics they claimed were too boring for me to sit through.

"I'm glad he came, too." I bit my lip. "But he's not your family. We could have invited Asa, you know."

Ben's grip turned to iron. "You can't be serious."

"Come on, Ben. He's your *brother*."

"Listen, even if we could find him, and even if he were sober enough to show up, trust me—you don't want my brother here." His jaw clenched over the tremble in his voice. "And I don't, either. He's a criminal. A lowlife. He's—"

"Ben, he's the only family you've got left." My heart ached for him. His mother had taken off when Ben was only a toddler, and he and Asa had been raised by their father, who had died a few years back. "Weddings bring people together!"

"But with some people, that's more of a curse than a blessing."

"You don't think he'd be happy for you?"

"Mattie, the last time we saw each other, he threatened to kill me."

"*What?*" My eyes went wide. "You never mentioned that before!"

He bowed his head and shrugged. "It was a long time ago, and I don't like to talk about it. But Asa's just . . . he's messed up. He's got rage inside of him. And he's always been jealous of me. Do you think it would help if he got a good long look at all of this?"

I leaned my head on his shoulder. "I just wish you two could find your way back to each other. Family is important."

"I'm building a new family, Mattie. And there's no one I'd rather do it with." He shoved his left hand in his pocket, and I knew his fingers were running over his lucky agate. Just one of the odd, endearing habits that had made me fall deeper in love with him. I watched his face as he took a deep breath and closed his eyes. And when he opened them, he smiled down at me. His hand rose from his pocket to stroke my cheek. "You are so beautiful," he murmured.

I shivered with sudden pleasure. His touch was like a drug to me, and I was the happiest of addicts. As his fingertips trailed down my throat, my entire body tingled, and my hands balled in the fabric of his shirt, barely keeping me from sliding my palms up under it to feel his bare skin. "Do you think anyone would notice if we disappeared for a few minutes?"

My old bedroom was a few steps away, and I was already envisioning myself on the bed. His grip on my hips would be bruising and delicious. My body was already slick and soft and hot. It felt like I was one deft touch away from having an orgasm, right there on the deck. Ben's hand spread across my back, steadying me, and he glanced down at my flushed cheeks with an appreciative grin. "What were you saying about anticipation?"

"Screw it. Or, wait, screw me. That would be even better."

"If someone doesn't bring me a damn plate of food, I'm going to starve!" said a gravelly voice to my left.

Ben released me instantly and clasped his hands behind his back, like a little boy caught stealing. My reaction wasn't much better—I slapped my hands over my warm cheeks and turned toward the source of the complaint. "Grandpa! I-I was just coming to find you."

Grandpa looked up at me from his wheelchair. Dad had parked him in the corner of the deck so that he could look out over the lawn. His wide-brimmed straw hat shaded his watery, red-rimmed eyes, and his gnarled hands were clawed over the armrests. "Yes, that much was obvious."

Great. Grandpa had probably heard every word of my scheme to sneak in a quickie with my boyfriend (fiancé!). I blushed from my forehead to my toes. Could I just control myself for once in my life? "What would you like, Grandpa? Summer roll? Deviled eggs?"

"Surprise me."

Grabbing a plate and a napkin, I listened to Ben doing his best to make nice—and to Grandpa having none of it. I scooped up a few appetizers from each platter and turned just in time to see Ben reaching out to shake Grandpa's hand. When my grandfather didn't let go of the armrests, Ben saved face by giving Grandpa's hand a friendly pat.

Grandpa jerked away like he'd been burned, first glaring at the back of his liver-spotted hand and then up at Ben. "What the hell do you think you're doing?" he snapped.

Ben blinked down at his fingers, the shock on his face similar to my own. "I'm . . . sorry?"

"You should be," Grandpa growled. "Don't think I don't know what you're up to, boy."

"Try the eggs!" I said, rushing forward with the plate and nearly tripping in my strappy sandals. Stepping between my gaping fiancé and the tight-lipped old man who for some inexplicable reason had chosen the occasion of my engagement party to lose his mind, I put the plate in Grandpa's lap because hey, snacks can fix nearly anything. (Despite everything that's happened, I still believe that.)

"Mattie, I think I'm going to . . . um . . . I'm going to go make sure Franz is having a good time," Ben said.

I threw him an apologetic look over my shoulder. "I'll be there in a few."

Grandpa didn't touch the food. His hands were shaking as I knelt next to him, my sunny skirt fanning around me. "Grandpa," I said gently. "Are you okay?"

"Don't take that tone with me," he said, though his voice had lost its edge. "My hospice nurse uses the same damn voice when I dare to express an opinion about anything other than whether I would or would not care for raisins in my oatmeal." His tremulous fingers clutched at mine, and he sighed. "Never get old, Mattie."

"I won't." My chest squeezed with regret. Just a few weeks ago, the doctors had announced he only had months to live. He looked okay— apart from the rattling cough that kept him up nights and the fatigue and pain meds that made him groggy during too many of his waking hours—but lung cancer was taking him down. After the doctors' verdict, my parents had shipped him all the way to Wisconsin from his home in Arizona so they could take care of him until the end. They'd said it was the best thing for him, and to my surprise he hadn't objected. But he didn't seem too happy about it—especially because everyone was tiptoeing around him like he was going to keel over any second. I tried to take a different approach. "Hey. In exchange for not using the you're-a-crazy-old-man voice, I want to know what just happened with Ben."

He grunted. "It was nothing."

"Nothing? You refused to shake my fiancé's hand! I mean, if you overheard us just now, that was as much my fault as—"

"Mattie, how much do you know about him, really?"

"We've been together for three years!"

"That doesn't mean you know his secrets."

I frowned. "How about you tell me what you're getting at?"

Grandpa rubbed at his chest as he looked over at the lawn, where Ben was mingling like a pro. "Ask *him*."

Frustration began to creep in. Seriously, he had to pick this night to get all protective of my virtue? They'd spoken for two minutes. What could have gone that wrong that fast? "Grandpa, what did he say to you that has you this upset?"

"Find out everything you can about him. You owe it to yourself." He turned back to me, his chin trembling. "You and I haven't spoken much since your grandma died."

I looked away, ashamed. "I'm sorry. I should have written more." Or called. Or visited.

"Come have lunch with me tomorrow?"

"I have to work."

"Tuesday, then."

"Okay." I'd have to arrange with Jan, our practice manager, to cover the waiting room during what was usually her lunch break, but that wasn't anything a box of Girl Scout cookies couldn't fix.

"Mattie?" Ben called from the lawn. "The girl cousins are here." His tone said, *Help*.

My aunt Rena's four teenage daughters were a handful. I stood up and smoothed my skirt. "I'd better get down there before they stick one of their iPhones in Dad's speaker dock and turn this into a rave."

Grandpa squinted up at me. "Are you speaking English?"

"Never mind." I rubbed his shoulder. "Enjoy those eggs."

I floated over to Ben, the incident already behind me. This was my engagement party, and I was marrying the love of my life. Nothing— and especially not my cranky old grandpa—was going to ruin it.

I took out my dangly earrings and laid them on the dresser, listening to Ben give Barley a pep talk in the other room. The poor old dog had pooped all over our living room rug while we were at the party, seemingly too confused to find his way to the doggy door just a few feet away. Ben had taken one look, given me a kiss and a gentle shove toward the bedroom, and told me he would handle it. And he had, like he handled so many things. I smiled as I listened to the affectionate lilt of his voice and ran my hand down the front of my silky sapphire-blue baby-doll nightgown. I'd been a gymnast and a cheerleader all the way through college and was still in good shape. Those athlete's muscles had softened a bit since I'd abandoned the sidelines for the somewhat more sedentary life of a vet tech, but Ben loved my curves (and my flexibility), and I loved to show them off.

The nightie was beautiful, but I didn't expect to be wearing it for long.

I looked in the mirror and fluffed my hair, not that it needed fluffing. My curls were practically light as air anyway, a mass of tight strawberry blond spirals with their own ideas about what to do. When I'd said that they were impossible to tame, Ben had said they were just like me.

How much do you know about him, really? Grandpa's voice whispered in my thoughts.

"He's all set," Ben said as he strode into the room. "Whoa," he added as he caught sight of me standing near the dresser. His hand dipped into his pocket like a reflex. "I'm the luckiest son of a bitch on the planet."

"It wasn't luck, babe," I said, taking in his tall, muscular silhouette. Just looking at him made my chest ache. I could never get enough of him. Every touch was a temptation I couldn't resist. More than that, he seemed charmed by my kookiest ideas, and when I got in a mood he could calm me with a mere stroke of his fingers. Ben had always seemed perfect to me, from the moment we met. But was he *too* perfect? "Hey, so now that everything's official . . ."

Ben's eyebrows rose. "Yeah?"

"Is there anything you think we don't know about each other?"

"What?" he said with a surprised chuckle. "You mean like some deep, dark secret?" He took a step closer to me.

"I guess."

His smile flickered like a flame in a breeze. "If I did, would it drive you away?"

My heart did a back handspring. "Is that a yes?"

His handsome face, so electric when he smiled, turned to stone. "Do you *want* to be driven away? Is this a cold-feet thing?"

"No, of course not. I just thought we should get everything out before the wedding. No surprises."

"Everyone has their dark side." Then he smirked. "Like you, whenever you see a recruitment ad for the army."

"They're fighting for our country, and we repay their sacrifice with a broken-down system and inadequate health care! Wait—you're trying to turn this around on me, aren't you?"

"What do you expect me to say, Mattie? It sounds like you want me to confess to stuff that could upset you, and I'm not so eager to do that." His gaze slid down my body. "Especially not while you're wearing *that*."

The hungry look on his face sent a rush of heat between my legs. *Focus, Mattie, focus.* "I don't want you to make up stuff. I just . . ." My arms rose from my sides, as if I were reaching for the truth. "My grandpa—"

"Is that what this is about? Oh, Mattie. He just can't picture you as anything other than his little granddaughter. He's not ready to accept you as a grown woman."

"But—"

"Think about what we were talking about right when he interrupted us, Mattie."

"Yeah, I know." The humiliating memory brought the flush back to my cheeks.

"See? I could have offered him another ten years to live, and he still would have been pissed at me."

I sagged a little at the thought that my grandpa might not even have that many months to live, let alone years. "He told me to make sure I really knew who I was marrying."

"And you don't think you know?"

I crossed my arms over my chest. "I don't want to fight," I muttered, resenting Grandpa for planting seeds of doubt in my head. "Never mind."

"Uh-uh. You can't ask me things like this and not expect an answer." He reached up and began to unbutton his shirt. "You're marrying Benjamin Michael Ward. I'm thirty-one years old and got my DVM from the University of Wisconsin." He reached up to hold the anchor pendant, which he'd told me was a symbol of hope, that hung from a thin platinum chain around his neck.

"By any measure, I live a charmed life," he continued. "A long time ago I made the decision to live in the present and to grab every moment of happiness as if it was the last, because I knew it might be." He peeled his shirt back from his muscular torso and revealed his one imperfection: the faded scar and lump of his pacemaker just beneath his skin, high on the left side of his chest. "I like to think of myself as a bionic man, but the truth is, I need to be hooked up to a battery so I don't faint at the top of a flight of stairs or while I'm trying to cross the street. See, my heart beats too slow sometimes . . . unless I'm in the same room with you, in which case it races like a goddamn Thoroughbred."

My own heart fluttered as I took in the hard edge of his jaw. "Ben . . ."

"No, Mattie," he said quietly. "I'm just getting started." He let his shirt fall to the floor. "I love animals more than anything in this world—except my beautiful fiancée. From the moment I met her, my life was changed. Everything got brighter and more exciting. Even bad days were more interesting." He came to a stop a few feet away, his fingers working their way over the lucky stone in his pocket, his talisman. Slowly, he pulled it up and held it out, concentric rings of white and coral and umber, polished by the constant stroke of his fingers. "I have a few odd habits, but I think everyone does. I have a few flaws, but I hope they aren't fatal. And there is one thing I want right now, enough to beg for it."

I had to grab for the dresser to steady myself as he closed the distance between us. "What do you want that much?" I asked, breathless.

"You, beneath me."

He reached out and pulled the warm curved edge of the stone along my upper arm, and that was all it took. Waves of pleasure rippled out from that tiny point of contact, making my muscles clench with need. I whimpered as he slid the agate along my chest and throat, following its path with his tongue until he reached my mouth. "Is that what you wanted to know?" he whispered against my lips.

I nodded frantically, needing him inside me more than I need sunshine and oxygen and french fries.

"Any other questions?" he murmured as he set the stone on the dresser.

"No." My hands were already on his skin. "I shouldn't have doubted, even for a minute."

Ben leaned back and paused, his gaze intense as he took in the love-drunk look on my face. For a split second, it looked like he wanted to say more. But he just grinned. "Perfect," he murmured. "Absolutely perfect."

He scooped me up and carried me to the bed, all my worries forgotten.

I woke with a start to the sound of tires squealing on asphalt and winced as beams of morning sunlight hit me square in the face. Cramming the pillow over my ears, I groaned. "Finn York has had his license for all of three days, and he's going to get himself killed," I said. "Do you think I should talk to his mom?" Our neighbor was a third-shift nurse at the hospital, and her kid took full advantage of it. "Ben?"

I turned over to see that Ben's side of the bed was empty, then glanced toward the bathroom, wondering if he'd simply jumped in the shower early. He wasn't in there, either. "Ben?"

Frowning at the silence, I pulled on my robe and grabbed for my phone. Usually, if Ben wasn't in bed with me when I awoke, he was in the kitchen, making me breakfast. But the air wasn't scented with coffee or bacon . . . and there were no texts from him explaining where the heck he'd gone. I told myself to play it cool, since he was probably planning something crazy-romantic in an effort to surprise me.

My self-control lasted approximately five seconds before I jammed my thumb onto the screen of my phone.

The unmistakable sound of Ben's ringtone wafted through the open window of our bedroom. It was the flying theme from *E. T.*, his favorite old movie. I grinned—he might be trying to surprise me, but he'd just given himself away. Feeling clever, I waited for him to answer so I could tell him he was busted.

It went to voice mail. I padded to the window and peeked out. His car was in the driveway, but he was nowhere to be seen. "Are you hiding?" I murmured, then hit his number again.

Immediately the ringtone sounded off again, somewhere very nearby, but I got his voice mail again. I chuckled and sent him a text.

Ready or not, here I come.

I slid on my slippers and headed for the door, fully expecting to find flowers in the entryway or pastries on the porch swing . . . nothing. I called his phone again. Maybe this was less a game of hide-and-seek and more of a treasure hunt? I pulled my robe a little tighter around me as I walked slowly up the driveway, following the soaring music to its source.

His phone lay on the road right next to our mailbox, the screen shattered. And right next to it was a long black tire mark that immediately reminded me of the sound that had awakened me a few minutes ago.

I picked up the phone and clutched it against my chest. "Ben?" I whispered, looking up and down the street. My gaze fell to the mailbox, and my stomach dropped. Something red was crusted on the side, and the hatch wasn't fully closed. With unsteady fingers, I flicked the mailbox open.

Sitting on Saturday's mail, its wire lead dangling limp, was the battery that helped keep my bionic man alive.

CHAPTER TWO

I passed the next few days alternating between panicky overdrive and periodic crying jags. Ben was gone. No one had contacted me seeking a ransom. No one had found a body. No one had seen him that morning, and though the police were analyzing the black skid marks on the road, all they could say about the car was that it was probably an SUV or pickup truck of some type. The blood splatter at the scene was confirmed as Ben's, but whoever had grabbed him had left no fingerprints, no hairs, and there was no sign that Ben had put up a struggle. Evidently, analysis of nearby surveillance cameras had captured a veritable sea of SUVs and minivans driving by around the time Ben might have been taken, because it had occurred right as parents were dropping their kids off at the elementary school half a mile from our house.

I had spent hours at the station being questioned, which had led to more than one major freak-out. Why were they focusing on me while Ben was out there somewhere without his pacemaker, taken by people willing to cut it right out of his chest? I'd talked to the medical examiner. If the forcible removal of the device hadn't caused him to bleed out, he would still be left with his own unstable heartbeat, which could cause him to lose consciousness at the worst moment. Just the thought was enough to make me burst into tears. Every. Single. Time.

My mom responded to my eruptions by trying to poke Valium between my lips as if I were a baby bird. She was sitting next to me right now, in fact, the bottle of pills rattling in her purse, as I faced off with the detective in charge, a no-nonsense woman I'd gone to high school with—Deandra Logan. As far as I was concerned, her "investigation" was a joke.

"I've been telling you over and over again," I said in a tight voice. "You're wasting time by interviewing all his clients. They loved him. There was no one who disliked him even a little." I paused, remembering what Ben had said at the party. "Except for one person. Have you been able to find Ben's brother?"

Detective Logan shrugged. "We're aware of Dr. Ward's brother." She pulled a file from somewhere in the middle of her stack and peeked inside. "Asa Ward's list of juvenile offenses is a mile long—underage drinking, drug possession . . ." She whistled. "Dealing. He served a few stints in the local boys' training school. And he has one set of adult charges from over ten years ago. Breaking and entering, assault, resisting arrest. He did just over a year for that. But there's been nothing since then."

"The way Ben described him, he sounded like a total lowlife. Maybe violent." I leaned forward, trying to get a look at the mug shot in the file she was holding, but she flipped it shut before I caught a glimpse. "They're less than two years apart, so Asa's thirty-two or thirty-three. Ben quashed my idea to invite him to the wedding—there is no love lost between them. He almost seemed afraid of him." I gave my mom a cautious look. "In fact, he said the last time they saw each other, Asa threatened to kill him."

Mom's eyes went wide, but Detective Logan sounded only mildly interested as she asked, "And when was this?"

"He said it was a long time ago, but still. Maybe he wanted to settle some kind of score?"

She shrugged. "Asa Ward has been more or less off the grid for over a decade, as far as we can tell. He certainly hasn't gotten into any trouble with the law. And there's no evidence in Ben's e-mail or phone that he was communicating with his brother. All his contacts are accounted for."

I gritted my teeth. "But why aren't you looking for the guy? Tracking down an addict who threatened Ben seems a lot more productive than talking to people like Sophie Wingate. She's a little old lady with an overweight shih tzu she can't even pick up. Why do you have to waste time interviewing her?"

"We have to cover all our bases." Detective Logan was already standing up, and so was Mom, who was gently trying to pull me to my feet.

"Mattie," she whispered through gritted teeth. "Let's let the lady do her job. I've got a nice lunch waiting for us at home, and your dad will want an update."

My shoulders slumped, and I let Mom guide me out the door and back to her car, but I had no intention of eating lunch when my stomach was stuffed full of dread. "Just drop me off at home, please. I need to be alone." The detectives had already confiscated Ben's files and his computer, and, having found nothing suspicious in the house, had said I could return there if I wanted.

Mom pressed her lips together, clearly fighting to hold back her concern, but did as I asked. "Call us if you hear anything, okay? Or if you just need to talk."

"Will do, Mom."

The postal worker had left a stack of mail on our porch steps, probably because our mailbox was still surrounded by crime scene tape. The envelope on top was addressed to Ben. Detective Logan had gone through our mail, too, and had said she'd like to review anything new that came in. But would the Sheboygan police even know good evidence if it smacked them in the face? I opened the envelope and pulled out the contents.

As I read, my skin prickled with cold sweat.

It was notice of a lien. On Ben's clinic. For over two hundred thousand dollars. It had been placed by the contractor who had renovated the building. "This is so screwed up," I muttered. Ben had taken out a small-business loan to pay the guy. I'd gone with him to the bank when he'd signed off on it.

I pulled out my phone, planning to call my dad and ask him to help me make sense of the legalese, but it buzzed in my hand. "We got Ben's bank statements just after you left," Detective Logan said. "I need your help interpreting them."

I stared down at the lien. "Something's wrong, isn't it?"

"Maybe. Are you aware that his accounts were nearly empty? From the look of it, he was living hand to mouth. You claimed money wasn't a big problem for the two of you."

"It wasn't," I said breathlessly. "I mean, he was nervous about the business, but it was going better than expected—"

"Can you think of any reason he would have made several large cash withdrawals in the last three weeks?"

I glanced down at the paper in my hand. "Paying back his contractor?"

"In cash? Hmm." Detective Logan sounded skeptical. "I think we need to schedule another little chat. Obviously Dr. Ward wasn't exactly telling you everything, but maybe going over the bank statements will help us connect a few dots."

The rage bubbled up so suddenly that I couldn't contain it. "Ben is gone, and definitely hurt, and you guys are all acting like it's his fault!"

"Ms. Carver, the signs do seem to indicate that Dr. Ward was engaged in some financial activity that was questionable at best. I know you want to believe the best of him, but are you sure he didn't fly the coop before the chickens came home to roost?"

Using my last shred of self-control, I jabbed my thumb at my phone to end the call instead of screaming curses at the esteemed detective. I immediately hit my parents' number. "You're not going to believe this," I sobbed into the phone when my dad picked up. "The detective on Ben's case just suggested that he disappeared himself! It's like they're too incompetent to find his kidnapper, so they're just going to blame it on him as an excuse."

"Oh, sweetheart," Dad said sadly. "I'm sure the truth will come out soon enough. Ben was—*is*—a wonderful man. And we'll figure out what happened to him. We want him back as badly as you do."

Someone grumbled in the background, and I clutched the phone tighter. "What was that?"

Dad sighed. "Just Grandpa being Grandpa."

"And of course he thinks the worst of Ben," I said just as Grandpa rasped out a complaint about being treated like an annoying toddler. "Dad, I'm gonna go. I can't deal with him right now."

Angrily swiping at tears, I stuffed my phone back in my purse and headed inside. It was just as I'd left it a week ago, except for occasional signs of the police search and the fact that Barley was at my parents' house so my mom could take care of him. I stood in the living room, trying to figure out how to feel less useless. Yes, Detective Logan had said they'd searched the whole house, but they could have missed *something*.

Turning in place, I tried to think of what could have happened to cause Ben to withdraw money from his accounts. What had happened to that loan money? What had he done with it? My gaze lit on our walk-in closet, where all my clothes were tossed in a pile next to his, which were neatly arranged by color and season. I was going to search his pockets. Every single pocket. Hundreds of pockets until I found a clue. Even if I didn't, at least the purposeful activity would keep me from going crazy for a few more hours.

When I got to the clothes Ben was planning on taking to the dry cleaner's, I found something. In the front pocket of a pair of black slacks was a business card. He'd last worn these pants the Friday before. I remembered telling him he looked hot as I'd headed out the door to have a girls' night with some of my friends.

ALESSANDRO'S, it said. FINE MEDITERRANEAN CUISINE. The place was on Michigan, a few blocks north of downtown. I'd driven past it plenty of times, but Ben and I had never eaten there. Still, it wasn't the earth-shattering clue I'd been hoping for. He'd probably just gotten himself some takeout.

Then I turned it over, and my heart skipped a beat.

Eniro, 10pm was scrawled on the card.

I knew for a fact that he didn't have any clients or friends named Eniro. I'd never seen the name before in my life. My hands shaking, I called Detective Logan. "Hey. Sorry I hung up on you," I said when she picked up. "I think I may have found something you guys missed. Can you check Ben's phone and see if there's a contact in there named Eniro? E-n-i-r-o."

She sighed. "Ms. Carver, we've already gone through all Dr. Ward's contacts. If there's an Eniro in there, we've already checked him out."

"But Ben might have been meeting him last Friday night. He didn't mention it."

"O-kaaay." The word was drawn out a second too long for my liking.

"This could be something important, Detective. You said you had to cover all the bases."

"Ms. Carver, forgive me, but I'm going to be blunt. Please leave the investigation of Dr. Ward's disappearance to us. Your amateur sleuthing might actually interfere with our ability to find your fiancé, assuming he wants to be found. And surely you'd be thinking more clearly if you took some time for yourself and got some rest instead of grasping at straws. I'll be contacting you to schedule another conversation in the morning. If it still seems significant once you have a chance to sleep on it, I promise I'll take a look."

The muted click on the line told me she'd ended the call. I looked down at the card again. "Yeah, right. I'm sure you'll totally take it seriously," I muttered as I headed back out to my car. "Screw sleeping on it. I'm in the mood for kebabs."

Alessandro's had a plain, boxy facade, deep and narrow with little space between it and the buildings on either side. The area seemed kind of sketchy—on one side was an abandoned house with boarded-up windows. Still, there were lots of cars parked up and down the block and plenty of people around, so I parked across the street and headed inside.

It looked like a busy Friday night, and all of the tables were full. When I said I wanted to order for takeout, a harried-looking waitress waved me over to the tiny bar at the back near the kitchens.

Trying to be subtle, I snagged a menu and perused while glancing around. There were a few other customers around me, most glued to their phones. The wall was cluttered with framed photos, most including the same elderly man with bronze skin, a bushy mustache, and a shock of white hair. There he was posing in front of what might have been the Parthenon, grinning with his arm around a curly-haired woman in an olive grove, on the deck of a boat with an octopus dangling from his fist. Was that Alessandro? Or . . . Eniro?

"It's not going to be that easy," I muttered aloud.

"I always have a tough time choosing, too," said a stocky guy leaning up against the counter. "But the lamb souvlaki's hard to beat."

I smiled at him in a vague way that said I wasn't looking for conversation. A rush of warm air fluttered my curls, and I craned my neck to peer down a side hallway with a door leading outside. The person who'd just come in from the alley didn't come into the restaurant, though—he made a beeline for the end of the hall and stood there like he was talking to someone behind the door. Finally, he went inside and the door closed.

"What can I get you?"

My attention snapped back to the guy behind the counter. He looked college age, with curly, dark hair and a large, beaky nose that kept him from being handsome. "I'll have the lamb souvlaki."

Curly scribbled the order on a pad. "Anything else?"

"Um. Yeah. Do you know anyone named Eniro?" I knew it was a long shot. It wasn't like these people knew the names of all their customers, and Ben probably hadn't been meeting someone who actually worked here.

But instead of looking puzzled, Curly furrowed his brow, and his gaze slid to the side hallway. "Eniro?" he asked in a voice barely above a whisper. "Uh . . . hang on."

He disappeared into the kitchen, and a moment later I heard loud voices in another language, probably Greek. The other waiting customers tossed me irritated looks, probably thinking I'd delayed their dinner. But after five minutes or so, Curly came out again, several paper bags in his hands. He ignored me as he rang up each order and handed out the food to the people who had been waiting, then pushed the last bag toward me. "Lamb souvlaki. That'll be ten ninety-nine."

I dug in my purse and pulled out my wallet. When I opened it I realized it was still packed with bills—fifties, twenties, a few hundreds—all gifts from the engagement party. I hadn't yet made it to the bank and had been walking around with nearly nine hundred in cash. Probably not the smartest thing. I pulled out a twenty and handed it to Curly. "So . . . did the guy in the back know where I could find Eniro?"

Curly's eyes flicked toward my purse, making me clutch it tighter to my chest. "Nah. There's no one here by that name."

"Look, I really, really need to find him. My fiancé is missing, and I think he met Eniro here last Friday. He was kidnapped three days later. Please help me."

The guy took a step back. "Wish I could. But I told you—we don't have anyone here by that name. Maybe it was just a customer. Or maybe you're wrong about him meeting someone here."

"I know. I just . . ." My throat was getting tight. This was my only clue. I was one step away from losing it. "Please."

Just then the side entrance opened again, and another person headed back into the shadows to knock at the door at the end of the hall. Curly stepped to the side to block my view as I leaned to look. "I'm really sorry. I have other customers waiting," he said, less friendly this time. He gestured at the line that had formed behind me.

For a split second I considered mentioning the police investigation and how interested the detectives might be in this place, but if the restaurant staff did have something to hide, I'd essentially be giving them a heads-up.

I took a deep breath and smiled at Curly. "Okay," I said. "I must have been mistaken."

I took the food and trudged back out to my car. I didn't start it, just sat in the driver's seat and stared over at Alessandro's. As I inhaled the scent of spiced lamb, I watched a middle-aged couple, her with capris and a mass of braids and him with twill cargo shorts and a smooth bald head, walk right past the front entrance. Just before they reached the alley, the man's gaze darted up and down the street. And then he tugged the woman into the darkness between the buildings.

"Go home, Mattie," I whispered as soon as they disappeared. I turned the key in the ignition with a wrenching twist. "This isn't your job. Go. Home."

Instead, I tooled around the block and parked on the other side of the road, right in front of the alley leading to the side entrance I'd seen from inside the restaurant. I edged down in my seat, fully aware of how ridiculous it was for me, Mattie Carver, to be on a stakeout. But the idea of going home to an empty house was unbearable.

I picked at the lamb (stocky dude was right—it was awesome) and watched four more people disappear down that alley. No one came back out. And was it me, or had each person who'd sunk into the darkness looked nervous? I chewed on the inside of my cheek as yet another person, this one a woman who looked every inch the soccer mom, from her expensive highlights to her high-end running shoes, strode right past the entrance to the restaurant and slipped into the alley. I hadn't found Eniro, but this definitely looked suspicious. This wasn't the nicest part of town, and I was parked in front of what looked like an abandoned house, but none of the people I'd seen go into the alley belonged here. They'd all looked like upstanding citizens—with money.

Like Ben.

That revelation pulled me right out of my car. With my purse slung over my shoulder and my heart drumming in my chest, I slammed my door and marched into the alley. I'd bring Detective Logan something real, something she couldn't brush off as me grasping at straws.

I reached the side entrance and pulled it open, then glanced up the hall toward the kitchen and take-out counter. Curly had his back to me. Perfect. I scooted down the hall in time to watch the soccer mom disappear behind the door at the end of the corridor.

My breath shuddered from me as I reached the closed door and raised my fist to knock. If Soccer Mom could do it, so could I, right? Still, I gasped as a little hatch slid open a few inches above my nose, revealing dark eyes. "Yes?" said an accented male voice. "Can I help you?"

"Um . . . I hope so. Can I come in?"

"Code word?"

"Code . . . ?" Wait. *Oh my God.* "Eniro?"

The door opened just wide enough to allow me to edge inside. I found myself at the top of a flight of stairs, looking up at a guy who could have been Curly's older brother. He smiled down at me. "Your nerves are twanging like guitar strings. It's practically deafening."

Strangest greeting I'd ever received. His face was half-shadowed, and it only made my heart beat faster. "Sorry. I'll try to tone it down."

He chuckled. "First time?"

"Yeah," I murmured, looking down the dimly lit stairs. "Is it this way?"

"Yup. Take a left at the bottom of the stairs." He touched my purse. "You know we only take cash, right?"

I let out a jittery chuckle. "Of course."

"Get on down there, then. And have fun." He turned my shoulders and gave me a little nudge, then pulled his hands away. "Whew! You definitely need to relax. But I guess that's why you're here."

My shoulders must have been really tense. "Right. That's why I'm here."

My grip on the railing was so tight that my skin squeaked against the metal as I descended. Was this some kind of fake massage parlor? Or . . . a sex club? Drug den? Gambling pit? Cockfighting ring? What had Ben gotten himself into? My mouth had gone dry by the time I reached the bottom of the stairs, where a curtain of beads glittered dully. A low groan issued from the room it concealed. Not wanting to stop to analyze the sound, I shoved my way through the beads, snagging my hair in the process. "Ow," I whined, my hands rising to untangle myself as the beads rattled and clacked.

"Shh!" someone said as a pair of hands pulled my fingers away from my hair. "I'll get it. Stay still."

I blinked in the dim space and sighed with relief as the pain in my head eased. My rescuer, a woman in her sixties, smoothed a spiral of my hair back into place. "There you go."

She stepped back and gave me my first glimpse of the room. It was a sprawling basement space, but instead of walls there were support columns, around which were low tables surrounded by colorful embroidered cushions. Lava Lamps sat on each table. The floor was covered in thick maroon shag carpeting, and the walls had been painted the same dark-reddish color. It was like stepping back into the seventies. But that wasn't the weirdest thing about the place.

Lounging in beanbags, slumped over the tables, leaning against the walls were the people I'd seen enter. They all looked kind of blissed-out, their lips pulled into gauzy smiles, their limbs loose. The soccer mom was seated on one of the embroidered cushions, and she was the most lucid looking of the bunch, but that wasn't saying much. Her fingers were wrapped around a mug, her thumbs stroking along its surface as her eyelids drooped. I inhaled, expecting the scent of weed, but the air smelled faintly of mildew and nothing else, no food or alcohol or incense. I looked back at the hostess, who had gotten a tray out from behind her little booth next to the door. "Go ahead and sit down," she said. "I'll be there in a minute. Unless you know what you want right now?"

Panic pulsed inside me. "Um, not yet. I can sit anywhere?"

She arched an eyebrow. "Who's going to care?"

I took in the dazed looks on everyone's faces. The middle-aged couple was sacked out at a table about ten feet away, her head in his lap, her braids spread over his thighs. He was alternately stroking a wooden spoon that lay in front of him and then caressing his partner's face. Every time he touched her, she arched up like she couldn't get enough. "I'll find myself a place, then. Thanks."

Her smile became a wary frown, and she leaned closer. "What *are* you looking for, honey?" Her gaze traveled from my sandals to my capris to my tank top to my crazy hair. "You sure you'll find it here?"

I sidestepped her as she reached for my hand. "Yep. I'm just going to . . ." I gestured vaguely to the other side of the room and started picking my way along, looking for an empty table.

As I neared the back of the room, I heard a surprised grunt. "Mattie?"

I turned toward the sound of a familiar voice to find Franz squinting at me from a beanbag in the corner, his legs spread in front of him. "Franz!" I squeaked, practically diving onto the empty beanbag next to him. "You have no idea how glad I am to see a familiar face."

Franz rubbed his eyes and set the fountain pen he'd been clutching on the carpet next to him. "What are you doing here?" he asked, his voice slightly slurred. He sat up a little straighter and shook his head as though trying to clear it. "Ben never . . ." He blinked as he saw the look on my face. "He said he wasn't going to tell you."

"He didn't. I found this," I whispered, and pulled the business card from my pocket. I turned it over to show him the writing on the back.

He cursed quietly. "You shouldn't be here."

"What is this place, Franz?"

His gaunt cheeks darkened. "This is quite awkward."

"Awkward?" It came out of me loud enough for someone nearby to shush me again. "Ben is missing," I hissed.

Franz winced and covered his eyes with the heels of his hands. "I know, and I'm so sorry."

"You're going to be sorrier if you don't tell me what the hell is happening here," I whispered, unable to stop myself.

His hands fell away from his face, but he didn't meet my eyes. "Mattie, I would never have done anything to hurt Ben."

"Did you tell the police about this place?"

Franz's face sagged. "I wasn't trying to hamper the investigation, I promise you. But Ben didn't want anyone to know he came here. It's harmless, anyway. I mean, look at us." His arm flailed toward the room's other inhabitants.

"Please, Franz. I'm so confused." Every single person there was cradling some random object—a pair of glasses, a roll of tape, a picture frame. All boring, innocuous stuff. There were no syringes, no liquor, no fumes. "Why does everyone look high?"

"Because we are," he said with a vague smile, reaching down to stroke the discarded fountain pen.

"On what?"

"You have to experience it to understand it. And to understand Ben."

My heart squeezed at the knowledge that I hadn't. "So Ben came here?"

Franz nodded. "He's the one who got me into it. He said it would broaden my horizons and, oh . . ." He traced the tip of the pen along the inside of his wrist. "He was right."

I was choking on frustration. "*What* broadened your horizons?"

He poked the pen playfully in my direction. "Magic. The best drug in the world."

I had heard of molly and meth and crank and coke, but never a drug called magic. "Ben was doing drugs?" I asked in a strained voice.

All those nights I thought he was at the clinic, working late to make sure everything was perfect, that all the accounting was done . . . had he been here, spending his money on . . . ? I stared at a fit-looking guy in a polo shirt, who was rubbing a tennis ball along his throat. "What, do you absorb it through your skin or something?"

"Ben told me you were sharper than you looked."

I glared at him, but he seemed to have no idea he'd basically just insulted me. Or maybe that Ben had. "Nice. But Ben couldn't have been on drugs. He had to be careful with his heart, and the cardiologist tested his blood every few months."

Franz leaned his head back against the wall, his long fingers toying with the pen. "But that's the beauty of magic, Mattie. It leaves no trace. When it's gone, it's gone. It's extremely difficult to overdose. You can't be tested for it. It's perfectly legal. The only bad thing about it is that it always leaves you craving more."

Addicted, basically. "So Ben was hooked on this untraceable drug called magic." Was this where all his money had gone?

Franz was *licking* his pen now. "Hmm? Oh. I think he was more than hooked," he mumbled, his eyes falling shut. "This place is just a parlor, where we can come and partake of the nectar for a few hours before heading back to our daily lives. But Ben . . . he had a supplier who catered to more advanced users."

"A supplier? Like, a dealer? Did he take magic at home? At work?"

"He once confided that it was the key to his success."

"He never seemed high, though." I'd certainly never seen him looking as loose as all the people around me now.

Franz chuckled as he sucked on his pen. I was about to jab him in the ribs when a tray appeared in front of my face. But it wasn't held by the woman who'd rescued me from the beads. The man I'd seen in the pictures in the restaurant leaned over me, his mustache twitching. "How can I help you, my sweet?" His voice bore the same accent as the bouncer at the top of the stairs.

He lowered the tray, and on it sat an assortment of things—an unsharpened pencil, a plastic pillbox, a cracked CD jewel case, a pair of sunglasses, and a row of glass cylinders that looked distinctly phallic in shape. "What would you like tonight?"

"I'm just getting comfortable," I said, my voice shaking a little. Franz was nearly passed out. And here I sat in a drug den, having never so much as smoked a joint in my entire life.

The man's eyes narrowed. "You haven't been here before."

"N-no. Not here, but I've been to other places." I could tell I was close to getting kicked out—or worse. I threw Franz a sidelong glance, but he appeared too in love with his fountain pen to process anything else. He'd pulled his shirt up and was pushing the tip of it along his pale, flabby belly.

I leaned forward conspiratorially. "Actually, I was looking for a supplier."

The man snorted. "Forgive me, dear, but you don't seem the type."

I had to play this right if I had any hope of finding Ben. I pulled out my wallet and opened it, revealing the thick sheaf of bills tucked inside. Concentrating on keeping my hands steady, I pulled out one of the hundreds and laid it on the tray. "I'm easy to underestimate," I said in a low voice.

The man's gaze was riveted on my wallet. "Apparently," he said, spinning the tray on his palm so that the glass cylinders were closest to me. On closer inspection, they were pretty much glass dildos, all different colors and sizes, some with swirls and some just tinted pink or purple. "Pick your pleasure." His thick fingers slid the hundred off the tray and into his pocket.

"That was for information," I said.

He grinned. "I think you need a hit first. Show me you can handle it, and I may consider pointing you in the direction of a supplier. They're very discriminating, and if I send them the wrong sort, there are repercussions."

Repercussions . . . like kidnapping someone? I looked down at the glass cylinders. *Do this for Ben.* I reached for a smallish one with blue swirls. *Show this guy you can handle this.*

Except I couldn't.

The moment my fingers closed over the thing, waves of hot need rolled up my arm and into my chest, shooting surges of tingling pleasure into my belly. My muscles went slack, and I fell back on the beanbag. Suddenly my clothes were too tight, and my free hand rose to tug at my shirt while the other desperately clutched the glass cylinder. My lips parted, and my eyes met the man's. He was leaning over me, watching with interest as my breath rushed from my lungs and my hips began to undulate. Humiliation swelled inside me, but it wasn't enough to make me let go. I needed this so badly. It was like being with Ben: addictive, necessary, a compulsion I could never deny. I'd always loved sex and had never been shy about it, and this feeling . . . Even though I knew the man was watching, even though it was too intimate, too private to share, even though Franz was right next to me, I couldn't stop the movement of my hand as it tilted the tip of the cylinder down, as my hand sank between my thighs. If I didn't do this, I would die.

"Go ahead," whispered the man. "Don't hold back."

I couldn't have if I'd tried. My hand pressed the tip of the cylinder to my clit, and the few layers of clothes that separated the object from my body made no difference at all. I arched back as my body buckled under the weight of the most exquisite pleasure I'd ever known. The orgasm shook me from top to bottom, and I bit the back of my hand to stifle a scream as the rhythmic clenching took over, wringing me out. I thought I heard the man chuckling, but the roaring in my ears drowned him out. The ecstasy went on and on, and I had time only to catch my breath before another tsunami dragged me under once more.

CHAPTER THREE

I came back to myself all at once, jerking up to a sitting position as the glass cylinder fell from my grasp. The room was still quiet except for the occasional moan. Franz was sleeping beside me, his pen poking up from his waistband, his mouth half-open. I stared down at my hand, which was trembling and slick with sweat. In fact, my whole body was the same, and as I shifted I could feel the damp aftermath of all that pleasure between my legs. I could barely hold myself up as I rose to my feet, bracing myself against the wall to keep from sinking back down. A quick glance at my phone told me it was one in the morning.

Clutching my purse to my chest and forcing down a sob, I made my way past the remaining magic addicts: the soccer mom, the anthropology professor, maybe teachers at the local school or someone's dentist for all I knew. The salt of the earth, who'd come here to have an untraceable high. And somehow Ben was wrapped up in it, and I'd done nothing for him except to make an ass of myself. The urge to flee was instinctual and powerful. My humiliation was so deep that it felt like I couldn't contain it. I'd completely lost control of myself. For *hours*. I focused on getting through the curtain of beads without getting snagged and then rushed up the steps. The bouncer was no longer guarding the door, which was slightly ajar.

Desperate for fresh air, I shoved it wide, then stumbled back when it hit something solid. It was the bouncer, who threw the door open, looking startled. Next to him was another man, tall and lean and hovering in the shadows.

"You okay?" the bouncer asked, rushing forward to grab my arm and steady me. He jerked as soon as he touched me. "Ow. You're not okay." Wincing, he pulled me onto the landing and yanked his hands away. "But you're not hurt."

I looked down at myself. I felt like I'd run a marathon. My whole body was shaking, and my muscles ached. But he was right—I wasn't in pain, except for the knowledge that I had embarrassed myself and uncovered Ben's secret, or part of it at least. "I'm fine," I said in a broken whisper.

The bouncer grinned and sniffed at the air. "Sandro said you went hard-core. That was some of our strongest stuff." He inclined his head toward the man in the shadows before turning back to me. "He said you were interested in a supplier."

My hope was like a shot of espresso snapping me to jittery attention. "Yeah," I managed to say. Because maybe that supplier knew something about what had happened to Ben. "I am."

"Bad idea," said the bouncer's friend. "She doesn't know what she's doing, Bart."

"Excuse me," I snapped. "You don't know me."

The man leaned out of the shadows. He was wearing motorcycle boots and cargo pants that hung from his lean hips. His black T-shirt clung to his chest. There wasn't an ounce of fat on his body. Everything about him was hard, including his face. Hollow cheeks, deep-set eyes, and a nose that held the slightest curve, like it had been broken at some point in the distant past. His mouth was curled in a condescending smile. "I don't have to. I know your type."

"Oh, really?" It was the second time tonight someone had said something to that effect to me. "Please enlighten me."

The jerk's smile became a sneer as he opened his mouth to reply, but Bart waved his hand. "Doesn't matter. Sandro said I should point her in the right direction. She's got the cash."

The jerk rolled his eyes. "It's your business, so it's your risk. And speaking of, can we get back to ours? I'm parked out in the open."

"This is Sheboygan," said Bart.

"I don't care if it's Amish country. I'm exposed. I don't like to be exposed."

Bart laughed. "Sandro said you were paranoid."

The jerk stared steadily at Bart. "When Sandro asks why I'm never coming back to fucking Sheboygan, you tell him it's because you wasted my time. See how long this place lasts without me. Maybe longer than you get to keep your job, but not by much."

Bart put up his hands. "Fine. Hang on." He pinched the fabric of my shirtsleeve and gave me a tug toward the door, like he didn't want to actually touch me.

"I'm sorry," I mumbled. I hated to admit it, but the jerk was right. I had no idea what I was doing.

"No problem," Bart said, leaning down to speak in my ear. "He's just touchy."

I glanced at the jerk, who was glaring at us from the corner. Light from a passing car slanted across his face for a moment, and there was something familiar there . . . His eyes were the exact same color as Ben's, like honey. It was a needle in my heart. "Who is he?"

Bart shook his head. "Uh-uh. You just forget you saw him." He plucked a business card from his pocket and pressed it into my palm. "This is the only information I'm authorized to give you. There's good stuff there—I promise. Slow release and long lasting."

I glanced at the card. The address was in Milwaukee. "Long lasting, slow release. Good."

"And not just pleasure." He winked. "Though maybe that's just what you're looking for."

My fingers closed over the card. I snuck one last look at the jerk, who was still staring at me. He seemed dangerous, the kind of person who could hurt people without the slightest pang of regret.

"No," I said as Bart opened the door to the alley for me, releasing me into the humid summer night. "That's definitely not the only thing I'm looking for."

My fingers slid over the clear plastic as my thoughts whirled. Sun filtered through paisley curtains over the bay window of my parents' kitchen, and through the screen door I could hear the sputtering engine of my father's riding mower. It almost drowned out the low mutter of Detective Logan's voice in the dining room as she spoke to her partner on the phone.

She had brought me the evidence bag as a peace offering. After my distraught call to him the day before, my dad had apparently gone straight to her boss, who happened to be an old golfing buddy of his. She'd showed up this morning to make nice—but I could tell she still believed Ben had disappeared himself.

Thanks to her partner's call, though, I had a few moments alone with the bag. Inside was Ben's agate and his necklace, the one with the tiny anchor pendant. The chain was broken, like it had been ripped off his neck. They'd been found by one of our neighbors down the street, possibly thrown out the window of the vehicle that had taken Ben away. No doubt the detective thought he'd done that himself, too.

But I knew better. These two things were a part of Ben, and had been for as long as I had known him. Until last night, the mere thought of them had made me smile. Now, though, as I stared down at the smooth, variegated surface of the agate, my thoughts were in a much darker place. When I'd seen the couple in the magic den last night, him stroking that wooden spoon before caressing his lover's face, her moaning at the sensation, it had dredged up my own memories of Ben touching his agate before stroking my skin. Then Franz had said Ben had a supplier that catered to more advanced magic users, and it had sent my suspicions into the red zone.

Slow release. Long acting. My eyes stung as I slowly clicked each puzzle piece into place. Had Ben used magic on *me*? I swallowed back the lump in my throat and tore open the bag. Detective Logan had told me I couldn't touch this stuff because it was evidence, but in that moment it felt like the only way to keep the dread from devouring me. The agate was cool against my fingertips, not warm like the last time, when Ben had dragged it along my skin. Even so, I felt the faint pulse of pleasure, enough to harden my nipples and tense the muscles of my thighs. I dropped it in disgust. "How could you?" I asked in a choked whisper.

With clenched teeth, I reached out to touch the pendant, wondering if that would have the same effect. *The anchor is the sailor's final lifeline in stormy weather,* Ben had said when I'd first asked about it. *It reminds me that I should always have hope, even in my darkest hours.*

He'd placed my palm over the lump of his pacemaker then, and I had shed tears because I couldn't believe I was with such a beautiful man. Now I was shedding tears because I couldn't believe that beautiful man had manipulated me. Why would he have thought he needed to? I'd fallen for him the moment I'd met him, in an exam room on my first day on the job, his arms full of a litter of puppies he was trying to vaccinate. He hadn't needed to touch me—all it had taken was a look. And the more I got to know him, the deeper I fell.

My finger resting against the pendant, I recalled the way Ben would fiddle with it every time we fought. I once joked that I needed one, too, because for once I'd like to win an argument. I let out a strained laugh and pinched it between thumb and forefinger, mimicking how he would hold it when things were tense, including the last night we were together. A barely perceptible hum vibrated along my finger and up my wrist, but it definitely wasn't the same sensation as when I'd touched the agate.

"Ms. Carver!"

I yanked my hand from the bag. "Sorry. I know I wasn't supposed to touch."

Detective Logan leaned against the doorframe and crossed her arms. "Put it back *immediately*."

I looked down to see the pendant still pinched between my fingers. "I . . . just needed to hold it for a second." I braced myself for her wrath.

Instead, her face softened. "You needed to hold it for a second," she said quietly.

I blinked at her. "Yeah. I'm sorry. Please believe me—I didn't mean to mess up your evidence."

"Of course you didn't mean to mess up the evidence," she murmured.

I frowned at her. "Really?"

She gave me a vague smile, her brown eyes soft. "Really."

I looked down at the broken chain and pendant as the strangest chill went through me, a crazy suspicion taking shape. Slowly, I tucked it back into the evidence bag and then wiped my hands along the skirt of my sundress. "Okay."

"Everything all right?" my mother asked as she came up behind the detective.

"Yeah. I just . . . need to get this evidence back to the station."

Detective Logan put the evidence into her work bag. "I'd better get going. My boss let me know I'm interviewing the contractor who placed the lien today. Even though he has an ironclad alibi." Her skepticism was back, and I sagged with relief as Mom turned to escort her to the door.

"Mattie," Mom said. "Could you do me a favor and check on our elderly gentlemen? Barley's napping in the library, and I just got Grandpa settled in there and gave him his medication. His nurse will be here in a little bit to do his nebulizer treatment. He might be a little groggy, but I think he'd be glad for the company while he waits."

I walked slowly down the hall, hoping Grandpa was in a good mood today, for both our sakes. He was lying on the hospital bed my parents had set up for him in the library, and Barley was in his own bed, sleeping in the sun. The room had a great view of the lake from its circular window, and they'd raised the head of the bed so Grandpa could look out on the waves, but his eyelids were drooping.

"Hey, Grandpa," I said quietly as I knelt next to Barley and smoothed my hand down his soft flank. I could feel each of his ribs—he hadn't been eating well since Ben had been taken, and I made a mental note to pick up some of his favorite treats from the house.

Grandpa's eyes opened for a second before dropping closed again. "Mattie," he said in a hoarse voice. "Didn't think you . . . would be speaking to me . . ."

I pulled over a chair and sat next to him. "I'm sorry I got so mad." I let out a slow breath. "And I don't know exactly what set off your alarms about Ben, but you were right. I didn't know him as well as I thought I did."

His trembling fingers patted at the railing of his bed, and I put my hand up there for him to touch. "I'm sorry," he said. "I knew it as soon as he tried to put the whammy on me."

I looked at my grandfather's craggy face. He used to be devastatingly handsome—I'd seen pictures of him and my grandma from when they got married in the fifties. They'd had a jet-setting life, with my grandfather's business taking them all over the world. Their house in Arizona had been filled with mementos originating everywhere from Guinea to Mongolia to Iceland to Chile. I'd always been fascinated by them, particularly a little locked wooden box he'd told me had been carved by monks in Thailand. It was the only thing he'd brought with him from Arizona, and he slept with it next to his bed. "A touch was all it took?" I chuckled weakly. "Are you some kind of psychic?"

"No," he said, then stifled a cough. "I could feel it on him. It wasn't natural—I knew it immediately." Another cough. "He was obviously using artificial stuff."

I glanced toward the library door, hoping Mom was still occupied with the detective. "It turns out he was on this drug called magic," I whispered. "And I think he was using it on me, too, without telling me." The betrayal was a fresh wound.

"It's more than a drug," Grandpa said. "That's all some use it for, but . . ." He sighed. "Some people have it, and some don't." His words were halting, and I was guessing his meds had really kicked in. "Like any other gift, each person gets to decide what to do with it. And those without, well, sometimes they just want a piece of it."

"Hold on. Are you saying some people have magic? Like, they produce it?"

He nodded. "Where do you think the artificial stuff comes from?"

"Um, a chemistry lab?"

He let out a rasping laugh. "Magic, in a chemistry lab!"

"Grandpa, you're talking like it's actual magic, not a drug."

"It's both. And your Ben was addicted. But he had no idea about me, thank God. Or you."

"Wait, what about us? What are you talking about?" It felt so stupid to even be asking this, but I'd experienced enough the night before to know I couldn't brush it off. "Do we make magic?"

"Heavens, no," he said, then winced. "These damn meds. Pumped my brain full of molasses."

Maybe that was why he was talking so much crazy. I chuckled uneasily. "No idea how you know so much about magic," I said. "Doesn't quite seem like your scene."

His hand flopped onto his chest, and he rubbed the spot right over his heart. "More than my scene," he said wearily. "And I've been meaning to talk to you about it."

"I'm all ears."

His face was ashen as he spit into a cloth and set it at his bedside. "I had a rough night, Mattie. Tomorrow? In the morning, maybe? Always a little sharper in the morning." His voice had faded to a wheeze.

"Sure thing." I was dying to know more, but I could hear his nurse bustling through the front door, and it looked like he needed her. "I'll come back tomorrow." Hopefully with a few leads he could help me understand. I kissed him on the forehead and headed home, more determined than ever. There was a little black dress in my closet, and we were going on a mission.

I sat in my car, holding on to the steering wheel like it could save me. The Phan Club was in a warehouse in Granville, a gritty neighborhood on the northwest side of the city. Judging from the cars lining the blocks in all directions, it was a popular place. I looked down at the card Bart had given me. On the back it just said *Nestor*, and I was hoping that he was a person, not a password.

"Go, Mattie," I whispered. "Do this for Ben." All I needed was a good lead, one that would get the police department to take his disappearance seriously and investigate, which meant connecting Ben to this place somehow. I threw my car door open and skittered down a delivery lane alongside the building the club was in. There was one truck parked right next to the building. In front of it a tan minivan had backed in next to a service entrance that was up a half flight of cement steps. I slowed down, wondering if the side entrance was unlocked, and nearly collided with someone stepping out from behind the minivan.

"Sorry!" I said, stumbling back before we hit. But when I recognized the guy on whose chest I'd nearly face-planted, I groaned. "Great. It's you."

The jerk from the night before gave me an aggrieved look. He was wearing the same outfit—boots, cargo pants, and a black T-shirt that showed off his lean physique. The light over our heads illuminated his features, revealing coppery glints in his close-cropped dark-brown hair. And those eyes . . .

He looked me up and down, from my strappy high-heeled sandals to my black minidress, which I'd bought to really wow Ben on Valentine's Day a few months ago. It was a tad edgier than what I usually wore, sleeveless with a high neckline, but the shoulders and midriff were lace cutouts. I'd thought I looked tough and sexy, but as the jerk's gaze reached my eyes, I knew he'd reached a different verdict. "You're not fooling anyone," he said quietly. "Leave now before you get into something you can't possibly understand."

"How about you explain it to me?"

He shook his head and walked around the back of the minivan again. "I've got better things to do."

I followed and nearly collided with him again because he'd stopped right behind the vehicle, which bore a bumper sticker that said, "My pit bull ate your honor student."

"Please," I said. "I'm trying to find someone, and I think he might have . . . known some people here."

The guy twirled a set of keys on his long fingers and glanced at the rear window of the minivan. It was tinted and I couldn't see inside. "Do I look like a detective to you?"

"No, but you obviously know about magic and the people who use it."

"Let's try again: Do I look like someone who has even the slightest desire to help you?"

I stomped my foot, unable to contain the frustration. "Come on! I just want to know if you've seen this guy." Before he could walk away from me, I pulled out my phone and brought up a picture of Ben. It was a selfie of the two of us from the night of the engagement party, our faces pressed close. "Does he look familiar?"

He went still as the light from my phone turned his tan skin a pale blue. I could see Ben's face reflected in his eyes. "Yeah."

My heart rose into my throat. "You've seen him? Oh, thank God. Where?"

"On TV. That's the veterinarian who went missing last week."

"Oh." I swiped away the picture before the sight of it broke me. "He's my fiancé. His name's Ben. Benjamin Ward." I put the phone back in my clutch.

"I know what his name is." He said it slowly. Deliberately.

My hope was like those trick birthday candles my parents loved to put on my cake each year. Every time I blew one out, it sparked back to life again. "Do you know of anyone who might have seen him?"

"Go home, Mattie. You're not going to find Ben here. You're not even going to make it past the bouncers."

"How do you know my name?"

"I didn't recognize you last night, but I should have. You were on TV, too, remember?"

I'd done a few interviews, pleading with whoever had taken Ben to bring him home to me. "I have to find him," I murmured. "I think this Nestor guy was his supplier, and I was hoping—"

"Get out of here!" he snapped. "You're such an idiot. You're walking blind into a cave full of people who can see in the dark. It took Bart five seconds to read how desperate you were last night, and he's small-time on his best day. Here, they'll know immediately. And—"

"Know what?"

He shook his head. "Doesn't matter. The door's going to slam shut so fast that you'll be lucky if your nose doesn't end up looking like mine."

He turned away from me and pressed up against the van, his palms spreading across the glass of the tinted window. His knuckles were heavily scarred.

"Thanks for nothing." I moved to step around him, heading for the club.

"What the fuck?" He blocked my way. "Did you hear anything I just said?"

"Sure. I won't make it past the front door. Let's see about that."

I sidestepped him, and he cursed and turned toward the back of the van again. He yanked open the hatch, and I heard a low growl. "Shh, girl, it's me," he said.

"Wait, this is *your* minivan?"

He winged something at me, and I barely managed to catch it. It was a small cardboard box with *XXX* written in black marker across the side. "To ease the pain. Take it and go."

I looked down at the box, and then at his minivan, the back of which was filled with neatly stacked toolboxes and cases, one opened to reveal several rows of small boxes with similar markings. "Is this . . . ?"

"Fuck stick. Just like the one you had last night."

Heat spread across my chest and up my neck. "I tell you I'm searching for my kidnapped fiancé, and you give me a-a-a—"

"Fuck stick?" He annunciated each word while wearing a nasty, knowing smile. "Seemed like you enjoyed it before."

He reached into the van, and I heard a collar jingling as he patted the creature inside—the honor-student eater, I presumed. I leaned to the side to see that it was a gray pit bull with light eyes and ears cut woefully short. Its muzzle was covered in ugly scars.

"I'll be back soon, Gracie," he said to it, receiving a plaintive whine in response. Then pulled two cases from the back, set them on the asphalt, and slammed the rear door of the minivan shut. When he straightened, he looked surprised to see I was still standing there. "Oh. There's no charge."

"My fiancé is *missing*. Someone took him and left his bloody pacemaker in our mailbox! He might be suffering. He could be dead."

"Bummer," he admitted, "but I have an appointment to keep, so run along now."

"Run along now'?"

He glanced around. "Is there an echo in here?"

"You are such a-a—"

"Need some help? How about—"

"Asshole!" I shrieked.

He chuckled. And then his smile fell away suddenly as he moved toward me, leaning into my space in a way that made me stumble back instinctively. But he just kept coming, backing me up until my butt hit the rear of the delivery truck. He smelled like soap and dog and . . . mangoes? He placed his hands on either side of my head, trapping me, leaving me staring at the curve of his mouth. "You did not know the real Ben."

"Did you?" I whispered.

He stared down at me. "No. I don't think I ever did."

"But you obviously think you know me."

"Let me see . . . You were a popular girl in high school, maybe a cheerleader. My guess is that your life to this point has been pretty damn painless. You like Taylor Swift, and your parents are lifelong Republicans." His smile went flat. "And you clearly don't think things all the way through before diving in headlong. I'll bet you think that's cute, when in actuality it's dangerous as fuck and annoying as hell."

I flinched at his anger, and he glanced down at my hands, still clutching the box. "You were living for that ring on your finger long before Ben got down on one knee," he said, more quietly this time. "You still wonder why on earth he chose you, and I'll bet you held back when you guys fought, because you were afraid he'd walk out and take your whole future with him. And that was terrifying to you, because you couldn't imagine anything outside of the safe little cardboard life you were raised to want. So basically, you're a small-town girl with small-town tastes and dreams, and a small-town life ahead of you." He tilted his head. "How'd I do?"

"'Asshole' was definitely the right word," I managed to say, my voice breaking.

"No argument there. Go home and take a bubble bath, Mattie. Paint your nails. Drink a glass of merlot. Call one of your girlfriends and tell her all about the asshole you met today. Then crawl into your little bed and make yourself come to take the edge off." He jerked his chin at the box in my hand. "That'll last at least a week, depending on how hard you go at it."

I glared up at him, my cheeks on fire, knowing my eyes were probably shining with tears, and hating him for it. "Well, thanks," I said. "I guess I'm all taken care of."

He pushed himself away from the truck and took a few lazy steps backward. "Excellent. I live to serve." He turned on his heel and picked up his cases, the muscles of his arms standing out in sharp relief as he hefted them. "Drive safe, now. You're a long way from Sheboygan."

He marched up the steps and kicked the side door a few times, and it quickly opened. He didn't look back before he headed inside, and the door slammed shut a second later.

Stiffly, I walked slowly toward my car, ignoring the low growl that came from the pit bull inside the minivan. But then I paused and turned toward the vehicle. The minivan was bigger than a normal car. Like SUV big. Could *this* be what had left the skid marks outside my house? Could the jerk have been involved in Ben's kidnapping?

Why else would he be so eager to steer me away from this place?

I patted the side of the minivan and was rewarded by a round of vicious barking. "I might be a Taylor fan, Gracie, but there are a lot of things your owner doesn't know about me." I stalked back to my car, a plan already forming in my head.

CHAPTER FOUR

Still seething, I slid into the driver's seat and flipped down the visor to peer at myself in the mirror. A fresh face, pink lips, hair bouncing around my face. Really, no wonder the jerk didn't think I belonged here. I looked like I was barely old enough to drink, let alone meet up with a drug dealer.

I gritted my teeth. Now I wanted to get into the Phan Club for two reasons. I was more certain than ever that the clue to finding Ben was inside. But also, if I was honest with myself, I was desperate to show that jerk how wrong he was and to uncover whatever he was hiding. Digging deep into my purse, I found a lipstick in a dark shade I'd worn only once before deciding it looked too dramatic. I wiped my mouth with my arm and put it on, going heavy. Then I fished out some eyeliner and gothed myself up. Knowing there was little I could do for my hair—it is basically impossible to make curls look badass—I twisted it into a messy updo.

And then I sat and thought about what I was about to do. The jerk had said that the bouncer last night could feel my desperation. Bart *had* seemed to know how I was feeling. If the jerk had been right, though, the bouncers at the Phan Club doors would be more like the jerk himself, and like Sandro, all doubting that I was looking for a high, assuming that I couldn't handle it, or maybe thinking that I was a snitch, and any of those suspicions might cause them to turn me away.

If I was going to get inside, I needed to lose the desperation. I looked down at the triple-X box and then peeked around to make sure I wasn't being observed. "Well, here we go," I muttered, and pulled open the lid.

Ten minutes later, I forced myself to let go of the thing. It fell onto my lap, and I had to wrap it in a piece of tissue to get it back in its box without touching it with my bare hands. The slightest stroke was enough to make me come again. My heart racing and my cheeks burning, I tucked the box under my seat and got out of my car. Gracie let out a muffled bark but quieted as I walked down the delivery lane toward the club entrance around the corner. I concentrated not on Ben, but on what I could get if I made it through the doors—more magic, more pleasure. My limbs were loose, and the beat from the pounding music was already vibrating inside me. I reminded myself that no one knew me here. No name, no shame. Smiling faintly, I slid into the line amid a group of twentysomethings wearing vinyl and chain belts. They smelled like shampoo and upscale perfume, telling me this was a thrill for them, not a lifestyle. To tell the truth, they didn't look so different from me. It made me even more suspicious as to why the jerk had wanted me to stay away.

Instead of checking IDs, the bouncer—a guy with long brown hair and a nose ring—was touching each person who entered the club, on the arm, the neck, the cheek; any exposed skin seemed to do. He sported a relaxed smile, though his eyes were sharp and assessing. He went through a couple of people and seemed to approve them. A blond woman sitting next to him stamped the back of people's hands and sent them inside. Then he got to a muscular guy with a military haircut, wearing a leather vest and pants. When the bouncer touched him, I could tell there was going to be a problem. "Not sure this is the place for you," the bouncer said, glancing at the stamp woman.

Buzz Cut stepped away from them. "Are you kidding? Come on. My money's as good as anyone else's."

The woman hopped off her stool to intercept him. She was clad in a vinyl catsuit that hugged her lithe body, and she had big, solemn blue eyes. Next to Buzz Cut, she was tiny, but she approached him without any apparent fear. As he tried to sidestep her, she took him by the hand. "You don't want to be here anyway," she said softly.

"Fuck this," said Buzz Cut. "I don't want to be here anyway." He turned and stomped away, and the woman calmly moved back to her stool.

I watched him go, eerily reminded of my brief conversation with Detective Logan this afternoon when I'd removed Ben's anchor pendant from the evidence bag.

I just needed to hold it for a second, I'd said.

You needed to hold it for a second, she'd echoed.

What the hell was going on?

No time to figure it out now—I was up, and I knew I had to play it cool. Focusing on the lingering ache between my legs, I smiled at the bouncer when he reached for me. His fingers slid down my shoulder, and the touch was enough to strum the already-taut strings of my desire. He grinned. "Someone's already warmed up. Go ahead. Have fun tonight."

"I plan to," I said, holding my hand out for the blonde to stamp. Our eyes met, and she tilted her head, giving me a curious look. My stomach tightened, but then I heard the bouncer reject another hopeful behind me, and she had to slide off her stool and have another weirdly hypnotic exchange.

I pushed through a revolving door and got my first glimpse inside of the Phan Club. It didn't look so different from the clubs I'd been to in college. A bar occupied one side of the room, but drinks weren't the only thing for sale. Instead of chipped mugs and spoons, there were rows of glowing sticks and necklaces laid out on the counter. On the packed dance floor, people writhed to the pounding music. Some were wearing the necklaces, others simply clutching them with their hands. A few people were teasing their partners, running the sticks along their bodies. It reminded me of the magic den the night before, only for the younger crowd.

I scanned the room and was relieved that the jerk was nowhere in sight.

I moved along the wall, narrowly avoiding a few grasping dancers trying to pull me into their clothed orgy. My body trembling with the temptation even as I stared in shock at some of the stuff taking place in plain view, I managed to reach the bar without losing myself again. To one side, people were stumbling along and ducking into different rooms down a long hallway. They seemed more stoned than the people on the dance floor.

"What can I get you?" asked the bartender, an Asian woman with short, spiky hair and intricately patterned tattoos down the sides of her neck.

I pulled out the card Bart had given me. "I was actually hoping I could talk to Nestor. I have a referral from Sandro."

She glanced down at the card and nodded. I wanted to lean over the bar and kiss her, simply for being the first person who didn't tell me I wasn't the right type or that I was in over my head. "I think he's in the back. I'll let him know he's got a customer."

She headed toward the hallway, but stopped as another guy walked out carrying a box of glow sticks. "Is Nestor back there?" she hollered over the music.

"Yeah," the guy said in a loud voice. "He's helping Asa get settled with his clients. He'll be out in a minute."

Asa? My stomach dropped as the bartender came back over to deliver the good news. "Oh, hey," I chirped. "I went to school with a guy named Asa!"

Her eyebrow arched. "Probably not this guy."

"It's a pretty unusual name." I took a step back when her eyes narrowed. "But you're right. That Asa was very straitlaced. Very conservative, that one! Not the kind of person to hang out in a place like this. I mean, not that there's anything wrong. With this place, I mean."

I was babbling, and I knew it. "Never mind. I'll have a glass of merl—I mean, a Bud Light. Can I have a Bud Light?"

She nodded slowly. "Coming right up."

Good lord, I was not a subtle beast. I'd managed to get myself in the door, but I was my own worst enemy. I sat there with my beer and slowly churned through everything I'd learned. People were buying and selling objects imbued with magic, this drug that could induce phenomenal pleasure with a single touch. But there was more to it than that—the bouncer outside seemed to be able to sense stuff from people, like Bart had done to me the night before, and the stamp lady had a weird ability to influence others, which maybe I'd been able to do with the detective when I'd been holding Ben's anchor pendant. Grandpa had hinted that some people produced magic naturally, while others used artificial forms . . . I laid my head down on the bar and closed my eyes, unable to get traction.

And then there was the Asa issue. Ben's older brother, a known drug dealer even as a teen, this unfindable guy who had threatened to kill Ben the last time they were together. And now someone named Asa was right down the hall, and I was betting he had honey-brown eyes and a sneer that made people feel two feet tall. He was dealing magic now, and I wondered if it hadn't been as long since the brothers had seen each other as Ben had led me to believe. I sat up straight, downed the rest of my beer, and hopped off my stool, feeling a little queasy. I needed to get Asa to spill.

I melted into the crowd near the bar and cautiously danced my way to the entrance of the hallway, where I slipped in behind a couple that was headed for a room.

"You sure you want to do this?" the woman asked her companion.

"Yeah," said the guy. "They'll never trace it back to me. I'll just put it in the office where he'll find it and pick it up, and *wham*—" He glanced over his shoulder, saw me, and clamped his mouth shut.

"It's okay," I said. "I don't judge." I smiled. *There you go. Subtle.*

Each door along the hallway had a symbol on it and a number, and the couple peeled off to go into room six, which had a rough cross carved into the door. I wondered what it meant—that guy sure wasn't here to say his prayers. All alone now, I walked slowly, leaning in to listen for murmured conversations behind the doors. I was mostly met with silence. Some moaning, but I was familiar with that now. And then . . . I paused in front of room thirteen, which had a hexagon with three parallel horizontal lines through it. Was that the jerk's voice?

"Everyone ready?" he asked. Then someone else said something, too muffled for me to hear. I leaned closer, straining to catch any hint of what was going on inside, what the jerk might be doing and who he was with, anything that would hint at his true identity or give me a clue I could use to find Ben. "This is going to take a few minutes."

More muffled words. I leaned closer and pressed my ear to the door.

. . . Which wasn't actually fully closed. The moment I put my weight on it, the thing swung open and I stumbled forward, off-balance in my strappy heels. I had the impression of shocked faces in the candle-light as my arms flailed. Then my toe caught and I went down, landing directly on top of an immense shirtless man. Panicked, I slapped my hands down to push myself up, my palms coming into contact with his bare, hairy flesh. And as soon as they did, a rush of intense sensation shot up my arms and into my chest, like my veins had been injected with liquid lightning. My mouth dropped open, but I couldn't get my lungs to draw air. My eyes were wide, but all I could see was sparks and flashing colors. My thoughts were like Niagara Falls, roaring and rushing with unstoppable speed straight over the edge, crashing onto rocks, white mist filling the space within my skull.

My head bounced off the floor as I hit the ground. Blinking and gasping, I looked up to see three faces gazing down at me.

Three very angry faces.

"What just happened?" asked the man I'd landed on. His flabby middle was sagging over his belt, and a gold chain held a pendant nestled in his abundant chest hair. "She stole it before I got to feel a thing."

"Hey, I didn't steal anything," I said.

"Shut the fuck up," a woman snapped. She had garish auburn hair that was clearly dyed and the face of a woman in her late fifties. She was looking at me as if I were a cockroach she'd love to stomp on. "Asa, I demand an explanation. Who is this? Is she a conduit?"

Asa Ward looked down at me with his deep-set honey-brown eyes. "No," he said, his voice flat. "She's a goddamn reliquary."

CHAPTER FIVE

"I'm a what?"

"Shut up," all three of them said at once.

"Did any of it get into the relic?" the woman asked.

"Hand it over," said Asa. "Let me see." He wiggled his fingers impatiently, and the shirtless man pulled the necklace over his head. Asa cradled it in his palm for a brief moment before handing it back to the guy. "Nope. Totally empty."

"You do not want to screw with me," the woman said, shooting daggers at Asa.

"I'll just be going now," I said quietly. "So sorry for interrupting." I started to sit up.

Asa pressed the toe of his boot into my shoulder. "Stay. *Down.*" He tore his gaze from my face to look at the woman. "I'm sorry about this, Mrs. Lichtel. I'll recover the magic and get it into the relic as soon as possible. I'll let you know when it's done."

"What about me?" asked the shirtless guy.

Asa patted the man's shoulder. "Go have a drink on me, Don. But stay at the bar, okay? I'm going to want you back in a bit." He glanced down at me. "I just need a few minutes."

Mrs. Lichtel nudged me in the ribs with her red pump. "And her? She stole from me. Who let her in here?"

I looked down at myself. *Something* had definitely happened, but it hadn't felt like any magic experience I'd had thus far. "I don't think I—" I gasped as Asa's boot pressed harder into my shoulder.

"I'll deal with her," he said, staring steadily at Mrs. Lichtel as if daring her to question him. A drop of sweat glistened at his temple.

"I want my magic in that relic *tonight*," she said from between gritted teeth. "Or you can kiss your commission good-bye. Your choice."

Every line of Asa's body was etched with tension. "Of course." He gestured toward the door. "Right now, though, we need a few minutes of privacy."

Mrs. Lichtel looked stunned for a moment, but then she stalked into the hallway.

"But I didn't get to—" began Don the shirtless guy, but Asa merely shoved a shirt into the guy's arms and ushered him to the door, finally taking his freaking boot off my shoulder in the process. I took the chance to look around. I was lying next to a cot, where Don had been when I'd landed on him. The only other furniture in the room was an upholstered burgundy chair in the corner and a table lined with a row of three candles. Asa's cases were against the wall.

"It turns out I didn't know you that well at all," Asa said quietly as he shut the door and leaned on it, blocking my only escape route.

I couldn't sit up even absent Asa's boot on my shoulder, but I managed to prop myself on an elbow. My head was throbbing, and I was still out of breath. My chest felt like it had been pumped full of ocean water, stinging from the salt. "Why didn't you just tell me you were his brother?"

"Because it was none of your business." He was watching me like a fox might watch a rabbit.

"Well, you'd better let me walk right out of here. I told the police I was coming, and they'll bust all of you," I said.

"No, you didn't." His voice was completely calm. "You rushed in without thinking. That's what you do, isn't it? I told you it was dangerous."

My eyes started to burn, but there was no way I was going to cry in front of this jerk. "I didn't mean to interrupt."

"No, you meant to eavesdrop."

"I wanted to know if you were Ben's brother."

"And now you do."

"Right." My voice was barely more than a whisper, because my throat was suddenly so dry. "And now I'll be going."

"Nope. You seem to have forgotten that you're in possession of stolen property."

I groaned. "Why do you guys keep saying that? I have no idea what you're talking about!"

"Don't tell me you can't feel it." Before I could flinch back, he was on his knees next to me, his long fingers around my throat. I cried out, but he shushed me as if I were his dog and closed his eyes. His brow furrowed and his mouth drooped into a frown before he opened his eyes once more. "Are you doing that on purpose?"

I glared at him. "Doing what? Let me go!"

Asa released my throat, slipped his arm under me, and deposited me onto the cot. The temptation to punch him was overwhelming. Instead, I clenched my fists and pressed them to my forehead, resting my elbows on my knees. "Just tell me what a reliquary is, you jerk. And explain what just happened."

"You touched my conduit in the middle of a transaction. We were moving the magic from a natural into a relic via the conduit, but as soon as you fell on Don, it all flowed straight into you, where it will remain until I extract it."

I shrank back so abruptly that the cot would have overturned if Asa hadn't braced his foot on the edge of it. "We can do it fast," he said. "All I need is Don back in here and your cooperation."

Sarah Fine

I rubbed my hand over my chest. "Are you saying that there's magic *inside* of me?"

He nodded. "A sweet little package of manip, meant for a corporate customer. Not a huge amount, but very high quality. It's a hefty commission and I am planning to collect, one way or the other."

"Manip?"

"Manipulation. The customer wears that necklace in the boardroom, and boom—they miraculously vote in her favor every time."

"Manipulation . . . magic? Like . . . wait. Is this actually *magic*? Like *magic* magic?" I stifled a half-hysterical giggle. "You're serious?"

"'*Magic* magic'?" He groaned. "I wasn't wrong about you after all. You really don't have a clue."

"*I* don't have a clue? Do you have any idea how ridiculous all of this sounds?"

"I don't give a shit how it sounds to you. If you hadn't busted in here and ruined my fucking night, I wouldn't have to spell it out for you! But since you did, and since you're the one who *asked the fucking question in the first place*, I suggest you listen to my answer." He rolled his eyes. "Or don't. I can pull that magic out of you whether you cooperate or not."

"Screw you, Asa." I clumsily got to my feet, that weird sloshy feeling trying to pull me back down. Somewhere in the back of my mind, a little voice told me to be scared, but I was too overwhelmed by everything else to feel it.

Asa stepped between me and the door. "You're not going anywhere until we get Mrs. Lichtel's juice out of you."

"Unless you want me to kick and scream, you won't lay a finger on me."

He shrugged. "I could just get Rhonda in here to tell you to stay quiet and cooperate."

"Rhonda?"

"The blonde at the door. You might have noticed that she's very good at getting her way. Or, hey, Mrs. Lichtel herself would probably love to play with your mind—but she won't be as gentle. She's pissed."

I looked away. "Please don't do that to me," I whispered.

"Then play nice and help me get back what you took, Mattie."

His voice was as soft as I'd ever heard it, and I looked back at him. Now that I knew who he was, I could see a slight resemblance to Ben. His hair was darker, but like Ben's, it had a wave to it, an inclination toward curly. His cheekbones were sharper, but like Ben's, they were high and defined. There was a curve to his mouth that was vaguely familiar, but I hadn't yet seen Asa truly smile—though I had seen him smirk. I stared at him, missing Ben so much that it hurt, and wishing his brother would show an ounce of the compassion Ben possessed in spades. "Can you please explain to me how I supposedly 'stole' the magic? It's the least you can do if you want me to help."

"Oh, for fuck's sake—" He put up his hands in surrender when he saw the look on my face. "Okay, okay. Whatever it takes to get you the hell out of here. Yes, we're talking about '*magic* magic,' as you put it. Some people are born with it. Most aren't."

"And *I* was born with it?"

"Nope." He gestured impatiently for me to sit down on the cot again, then slid down the door to sit on the floor. "You don't have magic of your own, but you can store it."

"In my body." It was somewhere in my chest. I could feel it in there, the slightest pressure, a kind of unsteadiness, like my center of gravity had moved.

He nodded. "Every reliquary is different. The best can hold vast amounts of magic indefinitely, and not a soul will know it's there." His eyes met mine. "Not even someone like me."

"Are you a reliquary, too?"

He shook his head. "I'm a sensor. A sniffer."

"Like that bouncer outside? He was touching people, and using that to decide if they could come in or not."

"Diego's a different kind of sensor. Intention is his specialty. Bart's one, too, but for emotion. I can't sense feelings or intentions, or not any more than a normal person can, at least."

"So there are different kinds of sensors. And you sense . . ."

He stared at me steadily for a moment. "The presence of magic."

I buried my head in my hands again. "I'm so confused."

Asa sighed. "Four types of magic, three types of human vessels."

"Okay. Sensing—"

"It's called Sensilo."

"And pleasure—"

He was getting fidgety, tapping his toe, his jaw tight. "Ekstazo. It's the juice that powers all those toys out there."

"Fine. And then there's Mrs. Lichtel. She's a manipulator."

His eyes glinted in the candlelight. "They're called Knedas."

"And reliquaries are the fourth kind?"

He groaned, like his impatience couldn't quite be contained. "Different kind of vessel. You don't have magic. Neither do the conduits, like Don. Magic passes right through him, but for a moment he gets to feel it. Probably why half of them do this job."

I thought back over what I had stumbled into. "So when I interrupted, Mrs. Lichtel was passing her magic through Don and into the necklace?"

Asa tapped the tip of his slightly crooked nose. "And then you crashed the party."

"Wouldn't have happened if you'd actually made sure the door was shut."

He arched one dark eyebrow.

"Is Ben like you?" I whispered.

"Ben is nothing like me." He pushed his way up from the floor.

"But he was using magic."

56

"Right. A *user*."

"He's drained his bank accounts. He's—"

"Not my concern." Asa rubbed his hands over his face.

"You seriously don't care?"

His hands dropped to his sides. "Not even a little, Mattie. And now that we've had our little Q&A, can I get Don in here so I can conclude my business for the night? Gracie's in the van, and I don't like to leave her alone for long."

I couldn't fault him for being worried about his dog—thus far it was the only likeable thing about him. And he clearly wasn't going to let me leave until he'd pulled the magic out of me, an idea that was about as pleasant as a trip to the dentist . . . but more pleasant than the idea of blond Rhonda or nasty Mrs. Lichtel coming in here and screwing with my mind.

"Fine," I said. "I'll wait here while you go get him." Maybe once Asa went out to the bar to fetch his conduit friend, I could find that side entrance and bolt for my car.

Asa tilted his head. "I wouldn't go anywhere, Mattie. If you do, I will hunt you down. And believe me when I say I don't stop until I get what's mine." He opened the door and leaned into the hallway, where he flagged down someone and told them to get Don.

"Ah. Here we go," he said a moment later. He pulled the door wide, and in came Don, his face flushed and sweat dripping from his fleshy cheeks.

"I was dancing," he said between heavy breaths. Don's curly hair was standing on end like he had been electrified.

Asa gestured between us. "Don, Mattie. Mattie, Don."

"And you're really a reliquary?" Don asked. "Never met one of those."

"You wouldn't know if you did," Asa said as he gestured for Don to lie on the cot. I edged to the side to make room, especially as Don stripped his shirt off again, revealing his hairy chest and the gold necklace that was supposed to be the repository of the manipulation magic that I'd inadvertently sucked up.

God, what a weird night. It was like I'd stepped into a parallel universe. How were these people walking among us, with all these special things they could do? How many other people really knew about it, like Grandpa? Last night I'd stumbled into a drug den, and suddenly I found myself wishing it were that simple. Magic was apparently real. Not only that, it was some kind of black market business for these people. And for all I knew, Ben had been the victim of a hit. Maybe the contractor who'd renovated the clinic wasn't the only one Ben owed money to.

"Mattie, I want you to sit on the floor next to Don."

Don looked up at me and grinned. "Unless you want to lie on top of me like you did before?"

"I'm cool with standing," I said as Don waggled his eyebrows.

Asa stepped between us, his back to me, and leaned over Don for a moment. He didn't say anything, but when he stepped away, Don's face was pale, his gaze averted. Asa turned to me. "You've never done this before," he said, his voice low. "If you start on the floor, you won't have far to fall."

At least he'd somehow gotten Don to behave. Reluctantly, I sank to the carpet. "What do you want me to do?"

"Just sit there and let Don do the work."

Great. I was just a piece of luggage they needed to unpack. "Is it going to hurt?"

"Did it hurt going in?"

"No."

"There's your answer," said Asa. "It's not pain magic."

"*Pain* magic?"

"That's the fourth kind," Asa said, his voice flat.

Don shuddered. "I don't mess with the Strikon," he said to me.

"Do you do this a lot?"

"I'm kind of new to it." He rubbed his belly. "I'm an accountant, actually. But this pays well, and it feels good. Pretty sweet gig, if you ask me."

Asa squatted next to us. "Okay, Don, you ready?"

"I was ready an hour ago," he said, swiping sweat from his brow. He stuck out his hand, offering it to me. "Let's do this."

"Take his hand, Mattie."

I looked down at Don's fleshy hand, really not wanting to touch his clammy skin again. Then again, I didn't really have a choice. Slowly, I slipped my palm onto his, and his fingers closed around mine. Don's eyes fell shut and he arched up a little, but then he sagged back down.

"Um, I barely feel it," he said. "Are you sure she's got it?"

Asa frowned as he looked me over. "I thought so, but it was tough to . . ." He edged closer, but stopped as I flinched back. "I'm not going to hurt you. I just need to touch you again."

"Not around the neck this time," I told him. "I didn't like that."

His fingers encircled my wrist, and he stared at the floor. "It's definitely in there." He seemed puzzled as he looked down at my other hand, still clutched in Don's sweaty grip. "Don, are you pulling on it?"

"I usually don't have to! One touch, and *zip*." He looked at me, his chest puffed out. "I'm what you call a superconductor."

Asa closed his eyes, as if trying to summon his patience. "Try pulling."

Don's face contorted as he squeezed my fingers. Sweat trickled down the side of his face and into his ear. Finally, he grunted in frustration. "Nothing."

"Fuck me, Mattie Carver, you are literally full of surprises," Asa said, staring at me. He ran his hand through his hair. "Of all people."

"What's wrong?"

"You have to give the okay or it won't transfer."

"I was perfectly willing for it to transfer! It's not like I want someone else's magical juice inside me."

Don snorted. "I like reliquaries."

Asa shot him an annoyed glance before looking back to me. "I'm not saying you were holding it on purpose. But you're going to have to consent before the magic will leave you."

"Consent." Normally, I was a big fan of that word, but this time?

"It's not going to work if you're passive. You actually have to take charge." I think he could tell I wasn't getting it. "Picture a trunk, right? That's a typical reliquary. You open the trunk; you take out the magic."

"Okaaay."

"You're more like a bank vault."

"Oh."

"And right now, you're the only one who knows the combination."

Asa was looking deep into my eyes, and it was doing funny things to me. I didn't feel like I could look away. "So I'm in control."

"You're in control."

That wasn't how he'd made it seem, threatening me with Rhonda and Mrs. Lichtel, but I decided I didn't want to find out if they could take control from me or not. "Fine. But after this, we're going to talk about Ben," I said.

Asa's nostrils flared. "Yes."

I turned back to Don and eyed the necklace, the delicate gold pendant resting on a sea of sweaty hair. "I like it when a woman takes control," he said.

I ignored him, focusing on the sloshy feeling inside my chest. I didn't feel like a bank vault—I felt more like an aquarium. But either way, it seemed I had to decide to let the magic go. I took hold of Don's wrist and closed my eyes, remembering how it had felt when the magic rushed in, liquid lightning, the taste of power like copper on my tongue. I could feel it rolling around inside me, just waiting to find its exit. All I had to do was free it. I leaned forward as I imagined tilting the aquarium and dumping all that water, all the wriggling fish, over the side.

Reliquary

The rush was immediate and electrified my muscles, a million needle pricks in the space of a second, overwhelming me. Next to me, I heard Don cry out, and I focused on pushing all the sharp tingles away, down my arms, up my wrists, along my fingertips and into his body. I regained sensation in my legs first, then my stomach and chest, then my arms. Don was writhing on his cot, still in the grip of the magic flowing through him and into the relic. But my part was done, and I fell backward, my body limp and wrung out.

I didn't hit the floor, but I collided with something almost as hard. Asa's arms wrapped around me as he caught me. His legs were on either side of mine, and the back of my head rested on his chest. I craned my neck to look up at him. "How'd I do?"

He glanced at Don. "Fucking incredible."

I let out a slow breath, regaining my scattered wits. "Now we talk about Ben."

He shook his head.

"You promised!"

"I'll do you one better." He bowed his head over mine, a startling uncertainty flickering in his eyes. "You assist me on a job . . ."

I stared up at him. "Assist you . . . ?"

"I'll help you *find* him."

CHAPTER SIX

It was a testament to how worried my parents were about me that when I said I wanted to unplug and spend the next two weeks at the spa over at Elkhart Lake, they wrote me a check for four thousand dollars, no questions asked. "I'll keep the pressure on Detective Logan. And if anything comes up, we'll let you know," Dad said. "But I'm glad you're doing this for yourself."

It hurt to lie to him and Mom, but if I told them what I was up to, Dad would be on the phone with the detective—or her boss—immediately. And Asa had said that if I brought the police into this, he'd disappear without a trace. I believed him.

I sat next to Barley in the library, petting his soft fur. It was almost time to leave. I'd already loaded my suitcase into my car. "You hang in there, okay?" I said softly in Barley's ear. "I'm going to bring him back to you."

"Hearing is the last thing to go," Grandpa said from his hospital bed. He sounded much more alert than he had been yesterday, probably because he hadn't been loaded up with painkillers yet.

I gave Barley one last scratch and moved to my grandfather's bedside. "You're not fooling me," he said. "You're not going to some spa."

"Well, it seems like we both have some secrets." It explained Grandpa's familiarity with magic, and all his cryptic comments. "Are you a reliquary, too?"

"Too?" His eyes widened for a moment. "I wondered if you were one. I couldn't tell for sure, but I've suspected."

"Is Dad one?"

"Ha! I introduced him to one of my associates once, and we did a little experiment. Jack, my conduit friend, had a relic in one hand—a tiny bit of pain magic, just enough to give a shock. And there your dad was, shaking his other hand, totally oblivious as Jack twitched. If your dad was a reliquary, it would have—"

"I know." I'd felt it. I wasn't sure if it was a good feeling or a bad one. "So it skipped a generation."

"It happens." His watery eyes stared out at the lake. "How did you find out? Yesterday I could have sworn you had no idea."

I pictured Asa's steely gaze as he pressed his boot into my shoulder and told me what I was for the first time. "Do you really want to know all the details?"

"No. You're still my little granddaughter. But it's hard not to tell your parents that you're lying to them."

My cheeks warmed. "Grandpa . . . I've been a grown-up for a while now."

"I have to keep reminding myself of that," he said hoarsely.

I laid my hand over his and lowered my voice. "Doesn't mean I don't need your guidance, though. I said I would help someone transport magic in exchange for information. Should I be scared?"

For a moment he looked totally conflicted, but then he let out a rattling sigh. "Be careful. Things were different in my day. More civilized. We had a code, and we all worked together."

"Naturals, conduits, and reliquaries, you mean?"

"We used to protect each other and work together." He shook his head. "Truly good teams are rare these days. Most are just mercenaries only out for themselves."

I thought of Asa and his minivan full of illicit goodies. Grandpa's description fit him perfectly. "How did it work back then? When you were traveling all over the world—magic was your business?"

He smiled. It seemed like talking about this had given him a little extra energy. "Yes. I called myself an international business consultant specializing in mediation. And in a way, I was. I would deliver magic to a buyer, and I would work with conduits to install the package in a relic of the customer's choosing. Commissions were good."

I played with a loose thread at the hem of my sundress. "Did you ever work with sensors?"

"Oh, of course. The bosses all have them on staff. Always part of a good security detail."

"Bosses?" I giggled. "It sounds like a mob thing."

He looked at me, and the laughter died in my throat. I'd been pushing my fears aside all morning, but deep down, I knew I'd gotten myself into something serious. And that meant Ben had, too. "I thought magic wasn't against the law," I said feebly.

"No, but sometimes what people do with it is. The Headsmen try to keep the worst under control."

"Headsmen?"

"Well, they can be women, too. Closest thing to magical law enforcement around."

"Isn't a 'headsman' an executioner?" I'd watched a BBC drama with my mom the summer before.

Grandpa nodded wearily. "They have their own agenda, which is control."

A chill went through me. Exactly a week ago, deviled eggs had been my biggest worries. And now . . . "What about magic sensors?"

Grandpa's eyebrows shot up. "Oh, those are rare. Or, they are in the business, at least. I would imagine most of them would steer clear just by pure instinct."

"Why?" Asa now seemed like even more of a mystery.

"Unless you're a conduit, you'll be affected by magic whenever it hits your skin. But if you're a magic *sensor*? Especially a powerful one?" He shuddered. "You wouldn't ever get a break. The intensity . . . I can't imagine it."

That made no sense. Asa had been *surrounded* by magic last night. The club was full of naturals. Heck, he had a van full of toys covered in the stuff! Maybe he just wasn't that powerful or sensitive? "So you haven't met many of them."

"No." He got a wistful look on his craggy face. "But the nicest young lady I ever met was one. She helped me and Jack out of a spot of serious trouble one time in Moscow. Theresa was her name. If it wasn't for her, I wouldn't be sitting here right now. I promised her I would repay her, and one day I did." He rubbed his chest like it hurt. "But that was a long time ago."

"Grandpa, did Grandma know what you were up to?"

Grandpa shook his head. "Seemed safer to protect her from it."

"And that's why you're not going to tell Mom and Dad," I said quietly. "You're going to let me go."

He took my hand. "Only if you promise to come back. And when you do, when you've found your Ben and figured out what you can really do, I have something for you."

"I'll be back," I said, my throat tightening.

"Good." His voice had faded to a whisper. "Having this power is a gift, Mattie, but it can also be a curse. Each person has to decide how to live with it."

"Well, I guess it's time to get out there in the big, bad world," I said with a strained chuckle.

Grandpa squeezed my hand. "Reliquaries are easy to underestimate. Sometimes it's our best advantage." His eyes filled with tears, and he looked away. "Get going, kid. And hurry back."

•••

I drove to the Milwaukee airport in a haze of heavy what-ifs. Last night, I had been so desperate to gather more information about what had happened to Ben that I'd agreed to Asa's offer without hesitation. He'd told me next to nothing about what we would be doing, where we would be going. I didn't even know how long we would be gone. Even as I'd packed today, I'd pushed the doubts and questions away because I'd been afraid they would crater me.

I parked in the supersaver lot and dragged my suitcase out of the trunk. Rather than getting on the shuttle that would take me to the terminal, though, I hiked all the way to the access road and stood at the corner, as instructed.

Fifteen minutes later I was irritated and scared and considering giving up when a familiar tan minivan came to a stop next to me. The tinted window rolled down, and Asa peered at my sundress with apparent amusement. "What, no picnic basket?"

I scowled at him. "Was I supposed to wear cargo pants and a T-shirt so we could be twinsies?"

"Twinsies," he said. "What a thought. Ready?" He hit a button and the side door slid open, revealing an open space between the cargo area and the front seats. Gracie was on her feet, regarding me hungrily with her pale eyes, one of which was clouded over with blindness.

I was about to get into a car with a pit bull and a felon. A guy who'd threatened to kill my fiancé. And everyone who cared about me thought I was safe and sound and *somewhere else*.

Talk about diving in headlong.

"If you expect me to get out and load your bag for you, think again," he said, misinterpreting my hesitation. He glanced in his rearview mirror and drummed his fingers on the steering wheel, but I couldn't get my feet to move.

Gracie shifted her weight and let out a bark. "Easy," Asa said to her, his voice soft. Then his gaze shifted back to me. "Are you waiting for a sweeter offer? A valet? A red carpet?"

"For all I know you're the one who took Ben in the first place." I took a step back and nearly fell over my suitcase.

"How'd you guess? And now I'm going to get rid of you, too." He smirked. "So can we get started already? I've got to get your body wrapped up and dumped in a lake before sundown."

I tucked my hand into my pocket, my fingers closing around my phone. "I can't believe I thought you would help me."

He groaned and rubbed his hands over his face. "Have it your way. Go home and spend the rest of your sad little life wondering what happened to Ben."

"Do you know what happened to him?"

"No fucking idea, though I can make a few educated guesses. The police will never find him if I'm right."

"Why should I believe you?"

He leaned toward me, his hands still on the steering wheel. "Maybe you shouldn't. And I'm not going to waste energy trying to convince you, because I. Don't. Care."

"Then why did you offer to help?"

"You have something I want, so I offered you a deal. Take it or not." His mouth was tight. "But get the fuck in the car in the next thirty seconds, or I'm gone." He glanced in the rearview mirror again.

Bart had said Asa was paranoid. He didn't like to be exposed. "I took pictures of your license plates with my phone last night," I said, wishing I'd actually thought to do exactly that. "If anything happens to me, the police will come looking for you."

He rolled his eyes. "No, they'll go looking for George Ingall of 467 Larchmont Drive in Waukesha. Give me some credit. Get in the damn van, Mattie. This is your last chance."

Gracie barked at me again, and I stuck my hand out to let her sniff it. I'd dealt with more than one pit at the clinic, and they were total love machines if you gave them half a chance. She licked sweat off my palm with her thick, wet tongue as I stared at her owner's surprised face.

"You know what I think, Asa? You don't want me. You *need* me. To do something you couldn't have done otherwise."

His jaw clenched.

"Is it dangerous, whatever it is we're doing?"

"You never know when you're going be in the wrong place at the wrong time. I'm not making any promises."

"Oh, come on," I snapped. "Stop treating me like an idiot." I took a step back and turned, making as though I were headed back to my car.

"Hey," he yelled. "I'll keep you as safe as I can, okay?"

I looked over my shoulder. "I need to make it home to my family. If anything happened to me, it would be more than they could handle."

"You're a reliquary. If you die, any magic you're carrying is lost. If the magic is lost, I don't make money, and people come after me. I like to make money, and I don't like people coming after me."

"So it's in your best interest to keep me safe."

He tapped the tip of his nose. Gracie whined and edged forward, lowering herself onto her forelegs like she wanted to play. "She likes you," Asa said quietly.

"I'm good with animals."

"Are you coming or not?" He looked up the road and then into his rearview mirror again.

My grip tightened over my suitcase handle. I knew he was right—if I went home now, I might never know what happened to Ben. I'd seen enough last night to understand that I'd stumbled onto some kind of underworld, and without a guide, I wasn't going to make it far, reliquary or not. "Okay."

I hefted the suitcase, and Gracie backtracked as I loaded it into her space, sniffing frantically at it. Before I could hesitate again, I slid the side door shut and pulled open the passenger door. Asa watched me as I hopped into the seat and buckled myself in. "So, where to?"

Asa grinned, the first time I'd ever seen him smile. It was bright and sharp as a knife. "Into the lion's den, Mattie Carver. Welcome aboard."

CHAPTER SEVEN

Asa got on 94 heading south toward Chicago, and I spent a few minutes adjusting to the incredible strangeness of being in a car with him. Gracie lounged in the back, her large, square head resting on my suitcase. Behind her, the cargo area was walled off, and Asa had hooked a net to the van ceiling to keep anything from flying over the partition and landing on her. In the cupholder was a water bottle, but it was half-full of some kind of sloshing green substance. I wrinkled my nose as Asa unscrewed the cap and took a swig. "What is that?"

"The blood of an alien hitchhiker."

"I'll bet you think you're funny."

"I'll bet you think I care what you think of me." He capped the bottle and set it back in the cupholder.

"It was a harmless question, Asa. I figured we should try to get to know each other. You're going to be my brother-in-law." I swallowed the sudden lump that had formed in my throat. "That was the plan, at least."

Asa slowed down as we passed a trooper who had pulled an SUV off the road. "Kale, celery, green apples, cucumber, parsley, ginger, and lemon juice."

"How very healthy of you," I said. I eyed his scarred knuckles and his crooked profile as we sped down the road, thinking about the few things Ben had told me—that Asa was full of rage, that he was jealous of his little brother. Ben had been close to his dad, though he'd hinted on more than one occasion that he was a demanding parent, to say the least. I wondered if Asa hadn't met his expectations, especially since I knew he'd gotten in a lot of trouble as a teenager, taking and dealing drugs, getting in fights. The opposite of his straitlaced younger brother. It seemed like a recipe for resentment. But I was hoping that somewhere in there, Asa cared about Ben more than he let on.

After asking a few more friendly questions and getting nothing more than annoyed grunts in return, I gave up. Both lulled and unnerved by the silence, I eventually dozed off, waking only to the sound of a siren. We were well into Chicago, the skyline looming off to our left. Asa had finished the green concoction and was munching shelled walnuts. I was starting to wish I'd thought to bring a bag of chips or something. "So, do I get to know where we're going?"

"Our first stop is right up the road here."

"It speaks," I murmured.

Asa snorted. "It hopes you will pull some of the same shit you did last night at the club. Think you can do it?" He took an exit and headed into an industrial area. We passed a few gritty shops with bars on the windows.

"I can try." I bit my lip as he pulled into an alley lined with "No Parking" signs.

"Gracie, stay," he said, reaching into the center console and producing a bag full of brown lumps. He pulled out one, and I caught the scent of pumpkin and cinnamon. Homemade doggie biscuits? He tossed the treat at her and she caught it, eagerly crunching it down before yipping at him. He rewarded her with a second and a third before saying, "That's enough. But feel free to eat anyone who breaks in."

She growled, and Asa gave her a scratch between her mangled, barely there ears. "That's my girl."

I was getting the distinct impression that Asa liked Gracie a lot more than he liked his fellow humans. He crammed the bag back into the console and turned to me, then pointed at a sign on a shop across the street that said, "Vang's Jewelry and Loan."

"I want you to go in there, find the shiniest and most expensive piece of jewelry in the shop, and get as much info about it as you can. Every single detail—where'd it come from, what's it made of, who fucking designed it, whatever you can think of. Anything would be helpful."

"I'm looking for a relic?"

He nodded solemnly. "Absolutely."

"And I'm supposed to buy it?"

He shook his head. "This is purely reconnaissance."

My eyes narrowed. "Is what I'm doing illegal?"

"Being a discerning customer?" He snorted as he opened his door. "Let's go."

I hopped out of the van and smoothed down the folds of my sundress. It was late afternoon, but all the cement intensified the heat, filling the alley with the scent of rotting garbage. I headed for the sidewalk as Asa lounged against the building beneath the shadow of an awning. "Aren't you coming?"

"I'll be there in a minute. I just have to make a call." He stuck his hand in one of his front pockets.

"I'm going in alone?"

"Go on," he said, waving me toward the shop. "I'm depending on you for important information."

I frowned, but jogged across the street, my purse tucked under my arm. It didn't seem like a terrible neighborhood, but it was grimy and urban and reminded me of how sheltered I was. Asa's words about my small-town self still burned in my brain, and I yanked the door of the shop open before I could pause and look back. I was going to prove him wrong.

I'd never been in a pawnshop before. Rows of guitars hung from the ceiling along one wall, and behind a counter in the back, all sorts of guns were on display. Stereo equipment, televisions, microwaves, and other small appliances cluttered the two aisles that ran down the center of the space. An Asian man with slicked-back ebony hair and a neatly trimmed goatee stared at me from his spot on a stool behind the counter. In front of him, a low glass cabinet was filled with jewelry. Target acquired. I strolled forward and managed to smile. "Hi there."

"Can I help you?"

I looked down at the jewelry in the case, eyeing the price tags. "I'm looking for a gift for my mom. Her fiftieth birthday is next week. Can I take a look at some of these?"

"Sure," he said. His tone wasn't unfriendly, but it certainly was cautious. "Anything in particular?"

I pointed at the two that were the most expensive—and the exact same price. One had a big sapphire, and the other held a small blood-red ruby. I had no idea which one was the relic Asa was looking for, but maybe if I gathered enough intel, he could figure it out. The shopkeeper unlocked the case and pulled them out, and I lifted the ruby pendant to the light. "Who is the designer on this one?"

"No idea."

"Do you know where the ruby came from?"

"Nope."

"Is this chain . . . ?"

"Gold."

"Fourteen karat? Eighteen? Twenty-four?"

"No clue."

I looked up from the pendant. "How do you know what to charge?"

"Would you pay four eighty-five for it?"

I shrugged. "Maybe."

"There you go."

The bell on the door jingled, and I glanced over my shoulder to see a tall silhouette disappear behind a row of synthesizers. The shopkeeper leaned to the side to see who it was, and I scooped up the sapphire. "This looks nice. Are these little stones real diamonds?"

Still looking toward the front of the store, he started to come out from behind the counter. "Um, give me a sec."

"I think I'm going to try this on," I said, unhooking the clasp on the sapphire necklace. "Do you have a mirror?"

He looked back at me, his brow furrowed. "I thought it was for your mother."

"It is. I want to see how it looks on . . . a neck." I held it up. Maybe if it did carry some magic, the guy would shy away from it? Or . . . want to wear it? "Could you try it on for me so I can see?" I leaned forward as if I were going to encircle his neck, and he took a big step back.

"Let me see if there's a mirror under here," he said, kneeling behind the counter. I turned to see Asa duck out the door again, leaving the bell jingling against the glass. What was he doing?

The shopkeeper popped up again, his eyes narrowed. "Hang on."

He hurried to the aisle where Asa had just been. I followed him and looked over a long shelf of records and books. "Is everything okay?"

He glanced at me like he was surprised I was still there. "What? Yeah . . ." He walked to the front door of the shop and peered out, then cursed loudly as he pounded the glass. "Vang!" he shouted as he came jogging up the aisle toward the counter again. "Ward was just in here!"

I took a step back from the counter, leaving the necklaces spread on its surface as a gravelly voice came from behind a door at the back marked "Office."

"I told that bastard that if he came back, I'd fucking shoot him!"

"Fuck," said the counter guy. "I just saw his van."

My heart skipped. "You know, I think I might get my mom a nice sweater instead," I said quietly, turning for the door as I realized what had just happened. That *bastard*.

"Hey . . . ," said the guy, the word drawn out with suspicion that only quickened my steps. "Hey! You're working with Ward!"

"Bye! Thank you! Have a nice day," I chirped as I hit the door, bursting through it and then coming to an abrupt stop.

Asa's van was *gone*. I stared at the place it had been and heard the door behind me jingle. "Stop," shouted the counter guy.

I took off running up the street with no idea where I was or where I should go. A group of guys hanging out at the corner stared at me as I sprinted through an intersection and ran up the block, footsteps right behind me. When I leaped out into the next intersection, I was lucky I didn't get crushed. The minivan came to a lurching stop right in front of me, the side door open. "Inside!" Asa shouted.

I dove on top of my suitcase as a hand closed around my ankle, but as soon as it did, Gracie, who had been crouched just behind the door, lunged across my calves. With a yelp, the counter guy let go. Asa hit the gas and the van flew forward. He blew a stop sign and hooked around a corner. I held on to the back of his seat and finally managed to get the side door shut. Sweating, my eyes burning and my ears ringing, I glared at the back of his head.

"What the hell was that?" My voice cracked over my fury. "You used me as a *decoy*?"

Asa chuckled. "'I want to see how it looks on . . . a neck,'" he said, mimicking my voice. "I swear, you are something else."

I looked at Gracie. "How can you stand him?"

She grinned at me and laid her head on my lap, drooling on my skirt. I laid my hand on her silky back and breathed. "You lied to me. You stole something, didn't you?"

"Borrowed, more like," he replied, weaving in and out of the chaotic traffic. "I plan to return it." He gestured at the passenger seat.

It was a record. CeeLo Green. It was called *F**k You!*

"Seems appropriate," I muttered. "Are you a fan?"

"What?" He jumped a curb, pulled the van into another alley between two tall buildings, and parked it behind a Dumpster. "Oh, no, we're not going to listen to it."

He cut the engine and turned, his brown eyes bright with glee. "Time to open that vault of yours, Mattie." He held up the record. "I need to make a deposit."

A few minutes later, I was dragging my suitcase up a dark stairwell, huffing like I'd run a mile, and badly needing a shower. My hair frizzed out around my face and lay heavy and damp on the back of my sweaty neck. My ankles hurt—these sandals were not jogging shoes on their best day. Gracie was waiting on the landing, saliva dripping from her lolling tongue. "You want to help me with this?" I asked her.

"Can't. She's got back problems," Asa said breezily as he jogged up the flight above me.

"Is this some kind of test?" I snapped at him.

"I'm not the one who decided to bring along a seventy-pound suitcase," he replied. "Don't worry. Only two more floors."

"Why isn't there an elevator?"

"There is an elevator, but it has functional cameras."

I bit back a curse and kept lugging the case. "This is for you, Ben," I muttered. "And you will spend the rest of your life thanking me."

I sagged with relief when I reached a landing to find Asa holding the door open. He had a small duffel bag slung across his chest. "Do you live here?" I asked.

"Nope." He headed down a hallway with walls coated in peeling orange paint and floors covered in dingy, torn carpeting. The apartment numbers indicated we were on the fifth floor. "But we're staying here tonight."

"Oh, good. I wasn't going to be surprised if you'd made me drag this thing up five flights of stairs just for a laugh."

"I never do anything just for a laugh." We reached apartment 514 and he knocked. "Daria," he called.

The door swung open to reveal one of the tallest women I had ever seen. She was wearing a red silk robe, and her long, wavy black hair was pulled back in a low ponytail, accentuating a square jaw and a prominent Adam's apple. "Asa," she said in a surprisingly sonorous voice, pulling him into a hug that seemed full of genuine affection. "It's been too long."

"I know. I had to clear out for a while." Asa pulled back and gestured at me. "Daria, this is Mattie."

Daria's pale-green eyes traveled from my frizzy hair to my swollen feet. "Rough day, honey?" she asked as she leaned down to offer Gracie her hand to sniff.

"There's room for improvement," I said, throwing Asa an irritable glance.

"Well, let's hope we can make it better. Come on in." Daria moved aside to let us into her spacious apartment, which was about ten times nicer than the hallway outside, complete with hardwood floors and funky modernist paintings of jazz musicians on the wall. Asa dropped his duffel bag next to the couch, and Gracie hopped up on it and laid her head on the arm, looking very much at home.

Daria gestured at me. "She's the reliquary?"

"Yup," said Asa. "Also an excellent decoy."

"It looks like you made the poor dear do all the work." Daria headed into the kitchen and pulled a glass from one of her cabinets.

"Yup," I said, and gratefully accepted the ice water she brought me a moment later.

Daria smiled at me and then nodded toward the CeeLo vinyl. "So that's it? Esteban had a sense of humor—may he rest in peace."

Asa looked down at the record. "No kidding. But I could feel it as soon as I walked into the place. Like it was calling my name."

"So strange that it's all that's left of him," Daria murmured.

I took a quick sip of water to calm a sudden queasiness. "Wait, so basically I'll be housing some dead guy's magic?"

Asa shrugged. Daria pulled the edge of her robe a little higher over her breasts. "Shall we get this done?"

Asa glanced at me and nodded. "We'd better. That'll give us a few hours before we need to drop it off, and I need the time."

As Daria wheeled my suitcase into a room down the hallway, I said, "I want to clean up and change first."

Asa spun the record case on his finger. "I think you'll want to wait until after."

I eyed the record. "Why?"

He caught it and held it up, the *F**k You!* on the cover facing me. "This is going to be intense."

Daria emerged from the hallway. "Where do you want to be, honey?" she asked me. "What makes you most comfortable?"

She was a conduit. Like Don. Except she smelled a lot better and actually cared about my comfort. "I'm flexible," I said.

Daria smiled. "I mean—do you like to lie down? Sit up?"

"No idea. I'm a little new to this."

Daria frowned and gave Asa a skeptical look. "Darling, this isn't newbie magic."

"She's a lot stronger than she looks," Asa said. "You'll see."

"I'm a bank vault, apparently," I added.

Daria sank down gracefully into her couch and patted the cushion next to her. "If you're sure." She still looked doubtful. Even Gracie whined and slunk off the couch, moving to stand between Asa's legs.

I sat down next to Daria, my heart hammering. Last night, the magic had lit up the inside of my skull so brightly that I wouldn't have been shocked to hear that my eyes were glowing, and this was going to be *more* intense? "Wait," I said as Asa came forward, carefully slipping

77

the round edge of the vinyl from its case without actually touching it. "What kind of magic is this?"

Asa's eyes met mine. "Emotion sensing."

Daria rolled her head around. "It's my favorite," she said to me. "Such a rush. Ready?"

I looked from Asa to the vinyl to Daria. "I guess?"

Daria put her arm around me, her large, warm hand cupping my bare shoulder. "See you on the other side." Her fingers pinched closed over the shiny black vinyl.

"Wait—I—"

When I was little, my parents took me to North Carolina, to a sandy beach with lapping waves. I was splashing in the surf, having the time of my life, when a wave crashed over me and pulled me under. I remember the water going up my nose, the sand scoring my bare skin, the world tumbling and spinning until I didn't know the sky from the ground.

That experience was awesome compared to this.

My throat closed and my chest squeezed so tight that it felt like my ribs were breaking. A massive wave of sorrow crashed over me, stinging my eyes and turning my thoughts so black that I knew that everyone I loved had died, that no one cared about me, that I was going to be alone forever. And as quickly as I'd accepted that truth, another wave pounded me: incredible anger, filling my brain with slashing knives and dreams of choking the life out of faceless enemies. But before I could sink my teeth into the hatred, it turned to joy, lifting me up so high that I was sure I could kiss the clouds until I fell just as fast, drowning in jealousy. On and on it went, shooting up and down my limbs, winding around my neck.

And then I found myself blinking up at a small brown water stain on the ceiling. My face was wet with tears, my nose was running, and my chest was heaving. The room spun as I lifted my head.

"All set," said Asa.

Daria moaned, and I turned to see she had fallen away from me. Her robe had gaped open, and I stared down at a rounded lump lying on the floor. As I squinted at it, Asa quickly leaned down, picked it up, and respectfully slipped it into her bra, filling out the cup again. Then he pulled her robe closed and gave me a hard look, as if daring me to comment.

Daria was shaking as she pushed herself upright. "Oh my God," she whispered, clutching at her robe. "You weren't kidding."

I let out a shuddery breath that ended in a choked sob. Daria let out a sympathetic noise. "Aw, Asa . . . look at her." She handed me a tissue from a box next to the couch.

Asa had the decency to look a little ashamed. He ran the toe of his boot along the tattered edge of Daria's area rug. "She's fine."

"Screw you," I whispered, then noisily blew my nose.

Asa knelt in front of me, and his eyes met mine. "You're fine, Mattie." His hand closed around my fingers, and his grip tightened when I tried to pull away. "Shh. I just need to make sure it's all there." He closed his eyes. "Damn. I don't even know how you do that," he said quietly. "It's barely detectable."

"But it's all in there?" Daria asked, eyeing the vinyl, which Asa had set on the counter.

"Yeah." Asa stood up and tugged at my hand, pulling me to my feet and looking down at me. "Now I'll bet you want that shower."

"Perceptive," I whispered.

He squeezed my hand and let it go. "Good. When you're ready, I'll take you out to dinner in Chinatown."

I looked down at my sweaty, tear-stained sundress. "Okay. Chinese food would be nice." My eyes narrowed. "Wait. You're going to take me there and pull this magic out of me, aren't you?"

He nodded. "But after, I'll buy you an entire fucking buffet of fried rice and crab rangoon, if that's what you want."

"What aren't you telling me?"

His casual demeanor dropped away like a cloak, and he gave Daria a grim look. "We're going to have to make it past some of the tightest security in the Midwest to do it."

"Where are we unloading this sensing magic?" I asked.

"It's for the mistress of the Chicago boss," Asa replied. "And we're going to deliver it without the boss knowing."

"Oh, okay. I'll wear sturdier shoes in case I have to run for my life again."

I turned on my heel and shuffled down the hallway, not bothering to ask where the bathroom was. I mostly needed to get away from Asa before I lost it in front of him. Nearly buckling with relief when I caught sight of my suitcase, I rushed into that room and shut the door behind me, then sank to the floor and let the sobs come. I don't know whether it was the emotion-sensing magic that had just been packed into my body, the fact that I was far from home in a weird place, the ache of missing Ben, or knowing that before the night was over, I would have to venture into the heavily protected lair of a mob boss and escape without his knowing I was ever there.

But right then, the one thing I needed was a really good cry.

CHAPTER EIGHT

A few hours later, I found myself in a bar on the outskirts of Chinatown, a shot of something charmingly called "liquid cocaine" in front of me. I had changed into slim black pants, a shimmery lavender shirt, and sensible flats. Asa had taken a full three hours to emerge from his room, during which time Gracie stationed herself outside his door and I paced constantly. Daria sat on her sofa, eating ice cream and watching an old Meg Ryan movie. She was bawling her eyes out—maybe an aftereffect of having that much emotion-sensing magic pass through her. I expected Asa to emerge looking like a new man. But despite taking all that time and *maybe* running a comb through his hair, he looked pretty much the same.

The pockets of his cargo pants occasionally rattled with his steps, and I'd had plenty of time to listen. Instead of driving the van, we'd walked several blocks before taking two buses and the El to get to the bar, the whole ride spent in tense silence. I'd always been a talker, so the lack of conversation had already put me on edge.

Now Asa was lounging on the barstool next to me, his long body seemingly relaxed but his eyes darting from exit to window to hallway and back again. "Drink up," he said.

"Do I have to?"

He nodded. "It'll relax you."

"I'm kind of a lightweight."

"Even better."

I lifted the full shot glass and sniffed at its contents. "You might not feel that way when I barf all over your elegant ensemble there."

He smirked. "I'm pretty good at dodging."

"How come you're not having anything?"

He stopped his constant visual scanning to look at me. "I don't drink." My eyebrows shot up, but before I could say anything, he shook his head. "Just take your medicine."

I took a sip and grimaced as it burned my tongue. "Ew! What—"

"Jäger, Rumple Minze, and Bacardí. It's a shot, Mattie, not a cup of tea." He craned his neck to look toward the exit again. "Remember the set of bouncers at the door of the Phan Club?"

"One emotion sensor, one . . . manipulator."

He leaned down and spoke quietly. "Zhong Lei has layers of them posted around his territory, and unlike Bart and Diego, these guys don't have to touch you to know what you're feeling. If you walk in radiating anxiety, they'll spot you in a second."

"You're the one scanning escape routes and fidgeting like you've got fleas!"

He groaned. "Oh my God, just drink the fucking shot."

"Could you just consider for one moment what this is like for me?" I asked, my throat getting tight. "You're a virtual stranger, and everything that's happening is so new and weird, and you're asking me to trust you with my life."

"No." His eyes were hard. "We're having to trust *each other*, because we *both* want something. Don't pretend I roped you into this. You made the decision. Own it."

I'm scared, I wanted to say. *Would it hurt you to be nice to me, just for a second?* I was right on the edge of crying again. But then I thought of Ben and how much he needed me, and the determination rose up, crowding out my tears. I lifted the glass to my lips and tossed it back, swallowing quickly. The burn was incredible, searing from my throat to my belly. I shuddered and clamped my eyes shut. "Ugh."

"Good girl. Let's go." Asa slid off his stool and poked my arm.

Clenching my teeth, I followed him out of the bar and onto the sidewalk, where we made our way beneath the big red gates that arched over the entrance to Chinatown. On any other night, I would have been thrilled to be here in the big city, the smells of ginger and garlic wafting from the open doorways of restaurants we passed, the foreign, beautiful writing that bedecked the storefronts and signs—it was like we'd stepped into a different country. Not that I would have known, since I'd only ever been as far as Canada, but still. There was so much to see. And as we walked, a lovely warmth filled my chest and made my arms feel heavy, and I found myself grinning.

Until I collided with Asa, who'd stopped dead.

He turned quickly and smiled down at me, and it was soft and friendly and such a relief that my knees felt a little weak (the alcohol helped). "How are you doing?" he asked, his voice gentle.

"I'm feeling a little woozy."

"I'd never have guessed." He took my hand. "Let's keep walking for a while. I shouldn't have rushed you. We've got time."

I stared down at his fingers curled around mine.

He winked at me. "Just to make sure I don't lose you." He tugged me into motion again. "You've never been here before?" he asked as we strolled along, past noodle shops and a bank and a karaoke club.

"No. I don't get out of Wisconsin much."

Asa simply nodded and continued to ask me questions, about where I had been, how I felt about airplane travel, whether I had a passport, and all the places I'd ever dreamed of going. I babbled, so grateful to finally be having a pleasant conversation, barely noticing as he guided me inside what looked like a cross between a recreation center and a dive bar. A few middle-aged men sat playing some kind of domino game while a waitress set small glasses of clear liquid in front of them. They stared at us as we entered, their dark eyes lingering on Asa.

As soon as the doors closed behind us, he let go of my hand and his smile disappeared. He pushed me against the wall and peered out of the doors, then pressed himself in next to me. "I thought those motherfuckers were on to us."

So his friendliness had all been fake, and I had eagerly eaten it up. Alcohol and humiliation burned red on my cheeks. "You're a real prize," I muttered.

"If you want to go outside and meet the two enforcers who just passed us on the street, go ahead." He gestured toward the exit. "No?" he asked as I took a quick step away from the door. "Then stop whining and follow me." He inclined his head toward a hallway, and one of the guys at the table directly in front of us nodded.

Asa stalked down the corridor and through a set of double doors, into a room with thick green carpeting and red walls covered in scrolls of Chinese calligraphy. People were sprawled on cushions and leaning on low tables, each caressing a single colorful domino. It was a magic den, just like the one in Sheboygan. Asa strode through the room toward the back, me tiptoeing along behind him even though nearly every occupant of the room seemed oblivious to our presence. Right as we reached another door, though, an old woman stepped from behind a counter. She couldn't have weighed more than ninety pounds. "Pockets," she said softly, gesturing at the two of us.

"Come on, Mrs. Wong," Asa replied, giving her a winning smile. "You know I'm harmless."

Mrs. Wong grunted. "Pockets," she hissed. She reached for Asa's wrist, but he yanked it away. Quick as a snake, she turned to me and grabbed my wrist instead. "Pockets?"

I totally got where she was coming from. She was just there protecting her boss, and there would be serious consequences for everyone if she couldn't do her job. "Absolutely," I said, turning out my pockets to show her they were empty. "Asa, she needs to see what you've got in there."

He caught my fingers as I tried to dip them into his front pocket. "Whoa, Mattie," he said, looking like he was trying not to laugh. "I don't think we know each other nearly well enough for that."

He let go of my hand and pursed his lips, giving Mrs. Wong an exasperated look. "Stop fucking with my friend's mind, young lady."

The old woman's eyes narrowed, but she let go of my wrist.

"Hey," I said, realization dawning.

"Pockets!" Mrs. Wong jabbed her gnarled finger at Asa.

"Fine, fine," Asa said, his tone one of weary resignation as he started laying things on her counter. A pair of latex gloves. A Pez dispenser with an alien head on the top. A thing of floss. A black cylinder, maybe six inches long, that looked like a handle of some kind, but to what I had no idea. A few jacks. A bag of trail mix and a bag of what might have been weed for all I knew. A wallet that fell open to reveal a driver's license—complete with Asa's unsmiling face and the name "Randall Waxruby."

"Randall Waxruby?" I said, then started to giggle. "Seriously?"

"Go home, Mattie. You're drunk," Asa said, giving me an amused sidelong glance as he continued to fish seemingly random junk out of the pockets on his thighs.

"Whose fault is that?" I mumbled. He set a bottle of Silly String on the counter next to the jacks. My eyebrows shot up. "You don't seem like much of a jokester."

"The things you don't know about me could fill the vacuum of space," he said as he removed a small bottle of baby oil from his back pocket and placed it next to the bag of dried greenery. "There," he said to Mrs. Wong. "I think that's it."

"Pat you down," she said, flexing her fingers.

"Wait," I said. "If she touches you, won't she be able to . . ."

But though he looked irritated, Asa raised his arms and let the old woman run her hands up his pant legs, his sides, and his back. "Want me to turn my head and cough?" he asked as she briskly felt around his groin.

"You will not hurt," she whispered as she worked. "You give her what she want. You tell no one about this."

Asa's jaw tensed as she shoved her hand under the hem of his T-shirt to touch the bare skin at his waist. "You give her what she want," she said a little louder.

Pinprick beads of sweat glistened at Asa's temples. "Yeah. You got it," he said in a tight, angry voice.

Mrs. Wong let him go, frowning, and pointed at the odd array of items that Asa had just pulled from his pockets. "You leave these things with me."

"Everything better be here when I get back." He leaned down, bracing his hands on his thighs so he could look Mrs. Wong in the eyes. "Touch a single damn thing and I'll know."

She slid her fingertip down his cheek, and he winced but didn't pull away. "But you won't care," she said.

His eyes flared. "Oh, trust me. I *will*."

Her hand dropped away, and Asa straightened and smiled. "She down in the office?"

Mrs. Wong nodded, looking startled. Asa patted the top of her head. "No worries, Mrs. Wong. I'm here to help. Come on, Mattie."

He opened the door and I darted through, finding myself in a dank stairwell. Asa joined me and headed down the stairs. "Was she one of those manipulators?" I asked as I tried to keep pace. "Like Mrs. Lichtel?"

"Nothing gets past you, does it?"

"I didn't feel a thing when she touched me. I didn't know what she was doing."

"That's why the Knedas are so fucking dangerous. One handshake and they've got you."

"But not you."

"No, not me."

"Because of what you are?" I asked. "A magic sensor?"

86

"That only helps me know what *they* are."

"Then how did you—?"

"Later," he said, wiping his sweaty face against the sleeve of his T-shirt. We'd reached a basement of sorts. He paused before the next door. "All you have to do is what you did with Don last night, okay? Open the vault and let the magic out. You don't have to say a word."

"You want me to be seen and not heard."

"Hey, you're getting the hang of this." He turned toward the door.

"I don't blame whoever broke your nose," I snapped.

He bowed his head for a moment. "I'm sure you don't," he said, then pushed the door open.

We entered a brightly lit office with a desk in the corner, heaped with file folders. Two women sat together on a couch, holding hands. Asa stepped forward and gave a quick, curt bow to the two of them. One of the women, whose long black hair hung in a silky sheet down her back, stood up. "Thank you so much for coming," she said, her voice high and lilting. "Did you bring it?"

Asa gestured at me. "She's got it. This is Mattie. Mattie, this is Zou Peizhi. She goes by Zhi."

Zhi turned to me. "As skilled as Asa is, I thought there was no way he could bring me what I needed without anyone knowing." As she looked me over, I had the sudden urge to tug at my clothes or smooth my hair. "Zhong Lei tracks my movements and watches me very closely. His guards would know immediately if anyone was smuggling new magic into his territory. He has a sensor of his own, just like Asa."

"Nothing like me," Asa said, his voice flat.

She inclined her head in apparent acceptance of his correction, then gave me a breathtaking smile. "You must be a very strong reliquary. I used to know one. A faithful friend." Her smile faded. "But after what Reza did to him, he's never been quite—"

"Is that your conduit?" Asa interrupted, gesturing at the other woman. "You the conduit?" He stepped forward as the other woman got to her feet. She was wearing a pencil skirt and a delicate, strappy top. Her face was pale, and she bit her lip as she looked from me to Asa. In her hands was a paperweight, a glass disk with a small flower inside.

"The relic?" Asa wriggled his fingers until she handed it to him. He seemed full of sudden, jittery energy as he turned back to Zhi. "You ready to get this done?"

Zhi approached her conduit, speaking in what I assumed was Chinese. The woman responded in a halting, soft voice. Asa frowned as he watched them. "She new or something?"

Zhi bowed her head. "Hualing is not my usual conduit—"

"Yeah," said Asa. "I thought it was Wu Renshu. I've worked with him before. He's good. Reliable."

"Lei sent him away because he thought . . ." Zhi clasped her hands in front of her and pressed her lips together. "There is a reason I need this sensing magic. I need to know which way the wind is blowing before it knocks down my house."

Asa looked at the paperweight. "We're here to provide, then." He beckoned to me and pointed to the couch. "Mattie, you're going to have to make sure you keep your hand on Hualing." He eyed the woman, who was fidgeting with the hem of her skirt as she waited for me to sit down. "Make sure you've got a good grip on her, and don't let go until you're emptied out."

I smiled at Hualing as I settled myself next to her. "I'm new, too," I said to her, suspecting she could understand very little of what I was saying, but hoping the friendliness in my tone would help build her confidence. "We're easy to underestimate, aren't we?"

She gave me a tentative smile and then accepted the paperweight from Asa. Zhi said a few things to her in Chinese, and then Asa nodded at me. I scooted closer to Hualing and offered my hand, then interlocked our fingers.

Hualing looked down at our joined hands, and Zhi gave Asa a questioning look. "Why isn't it working?"

Asa grinned. "Do your thing, Mattie."

I closed my eyes and opened the vault. It was easier this time, but as soon as I had tipped my imaginary aquarium, my heart started pounding. The incredible rush of emotion poured through me and into Hualing, and the woman tried to jerk her hand out of my grasp. I squeezed, but couldn't summon the words to tell her it was okay. I was too busy soaring with joy, weeping with despair, trembling with envy, shaking with rage . . .

A thin, high wail filled my ears as the wave subsided, as the gush of magic slowed to a trickle, then stopped. I opened my eyes to see Hualing in the fetal position, her hand still clutched in mine, her body racked with sobs. I let go of her and looked around, my heart still hammering.

Asa was staring down at the relic. "It's all in there."

Zhi dropped to her knees and began to rub the woman's back, murmuring to her in gentle tones.

Asa set the relic on Zhi's desk and turned toward me. "Zhi's an Ekstazo," he said. "She should be able to . . ."

Hualing's sobs turned to hysterical laughter, then she began to twitch as if she were having a seizure. Zhi snatched her hand back. "I'm making it worse," she said in a stricken voice. "This was too much for her."

"No shit. That's the risk you take when you bring an untested conduit to the party," Asa snapped. "She's broken." His voice was filled with disgust.

I slid off the couch. I was still trembling with the aftereffects of releasing all that magic, but it was nothing like what poor Hualing was going through. "Isn't there anything we can do for her?"

Asa stared at Zhi for a moment before looking at me. "Could you take her to the bathroom, Mattie? Maybe clean her up a little?"

Since the request came from him, it was tempting to push back, but Hualing looked so pathetic that I couldn't say no. Zhi directed me to a room down the hall, and I wrapped my arms around Hualing's shoulders and tugged her up. She was mumbling to herself, her face a shifting kaleidoscope of emotion. But she didn't resist as I escorted her to the large bathroom. I gently directed her to sit on the toilet.

I dampened a paper towel in the sink and wiped her pale, clammy face. Her eyes were rolling in her head. She grabbed my arms a couple of times, shaking me and shouting, but most of the time she seemed oblivious to my presence.

She'd lost her mind. *She's broken,* Asa had said. It was the touch of my hand that had transferred the magic into this woman's body. Could I have done it more slowly? Could I have controlled it better? And . . . could this have happened to me?

I took Hualing back to the office to find Zhi and Asa staring at each other across her desk. He looked pissed, and Zhi looked grimly satisfied. She smiled at me as I helped the still-shaking Hualing to the couch. "What's going to happen to her?" I asked.

"I'll make sure she is taken care of," said Zhi.

Asa grunted. "Let's get out of here, Mattie." He pushed me to the door.

"But—"

"Now." He bundled me into the stairwell without a backward glance.

"Is she going to be okay?"

"Did she look okay?" He jogged up the stairs, so quickly that I was panting by the time we reached the top. He grabbed my arm before I went through the door leading to Mrs. Wong's lair. "When we get onto the street, you do everything I say, all right? Do *not* question me."

"What's wrong?"

"What part of 'do not question me' was difficult to understand?" he grumbled under his breath. "Listen, I'll explain later, okay? It's not safe here."

"Okay. But later—"

"I promise." He yanked open the door and stepped through. It took him only a few seconds to reload all his pockets with the random crap he carried with him as Mrs. Wong watched him warily from behind her counter.

We retraced our steps and were on the street in no time. Night had slipped over the city while we were inside, but the streetlights kept the sidewalks bright. Colorful lanterns were strung in zigzags over the road, and the air was cool. A whiff of pork and onions and garlic reached me, and suddenly I was starving. But something told me now was not the time to ask Asa about dinner. He was radiating tension as he led me toward the gates, now lit with red neon.

"Come on, come *on*," he muttered. "I can feel you." His eyes darted from corner to corner, up and down. "So where the fuck are you?"

He stopped abruptly and turned, grabbing my shoulders and moving me with him. No sooner had we whirled around, though, than Asa stopped again. "Shit," he whispered.

Three men were watching us from about twenty feet away, all Asian, all elegantly dressed in black pants and sleek shirts that clung to their slender bodies. The one in the middle merely stared at us blankly. He had some sort of black leather harness on, one that folded over his shoulders and buckled over his chest. His eyes were shadowed with dark circles, as if he hadn't slept in a year. His cheeks were even hollower than Asa's. He kind of looked like a zombie.

The guy on the left, who had a wide forehead and bold black eyebrows, folded his arms over his chest and smiled smugly. "Asa Ward. I'd heard you were in town."

"Just visiting." Asa stepped closer to me and jabbed me with his elbow. "My friend here had a craving for Chinese food."

"It's true! I love dumplings," I said.

"Right," said the eyebrow guy, his gaze never leaving Asa. "You know magic doesn't leave the territory without Zhong Lei's okay, right?"

"Sure. I know the rules." Asa was smiling in the same friendly way he had when he was trying to keep me calm earlier. Before, I was too tipsy to notice that his cheerfulness didn't reach his eyes, but now it was obvious. He looked over his shoulder. "Is all this really necessary? Zhong Lei's never had a problem with me. I'm small-time."

I glanced behind us to see that two more guys were hovering maybe six feet back, close enough to make my skin crawl. "Totally small-time," I added. "He hangs out in Sheboygan, for goodness'—"

"Shut the fuck up, Mattie," Asa said from between clenched teeth.

"Your small-time days are behind you, and you know it. So what do we have, Tao?" Eyebrows asked, nudging the guy in the harness.

The zombie pointed at Asa's pants. "In there," he said in a dead voice.

Asa took a step back as the trio sauntered toward us, but froze as the footfalls of the men behind us made their presence clear. "Come on, now. It's pack in, pack out. I brought my own juice and I'm leaving with it."

Tao shook his head, his expression wooden. "No. Not this. I would have felt it coming in. He's stealing."

"Hand it over," said Eyebrows.

Asa gave me a sidelong glance as he put his hands up in surrender. "Guess you got me dead to rights." He met Tao's eyes. "Happy?" he whispered.

Tao stared at him, and for a moment his dark eyes glinted with intense emotion. Then he jerkily reached into his pocket, and his eyes fell shut in apparent relief. Exactly like Ben and his agate.

One of the guys behind us, thickly muscled and tall, laid a hand on Asa's shoulder, but Asa wrenched himself out of the guy's grip. "Get the fuck off me, you Strikon piece of shit," he snapped, sweat breaking out at his temples, glistening under the streetlights. "I'll give it to you, okay?"

The three guys in front of us stepped back, though Tao had to be guided by Eyebrows because he seemed lost in a daydream. Asa reached into his front pocket.

Tao's eyes flew wide. "It's—"

A hissing sound cut him off as Asa shoved me to the side. "Run!" he shouted.

Screaming filled my ears as I stumbled into a storefront. Then I sprinted toward the gates, fully aware I was running for my life.

CHAPTER NINE

I ran beneath the red gates and turned right, hoping to make it to the transit station we'd exited when we arrived. Heavy footsteps echoed behind me, but I could still hear shrieking spiraling into the air. I barreled into an intersection right as an arm hooked around my waist and wrenched me back onto the curb.

"Not that way," Asa barked, setting me on my feet and taking off down a side road.

Asa. I'd been so sure those were his screams I'd heard, and I was weirdly relieved to see that he was okay.

He looked back to see me still standing there. "I thought you said you could run in those shoes," he roared. "Get those little legs moving!"

I chased after Asa, who loped along Wentworth Avenue, glancing over his shoulder every few strides. I was gasping for breath—I was built more for short bursts of speed than for long dashes—and I could hear the footsteps of a pursuer coming nearer. Asa made it to a section of the sidewalk where leafy trees narrowed the path between the street and a black metal fence circling a parking lot. He paused to let me catch up, unbuttoning one of his thigh pockets. I squinted at him in the darkness, expecting to see him holding a weapon.

But it was the floss.

As we stood beneath the leaves, where the glow of the streetlights couldn't reach, he detached the side of the dispenser that was connected to the floss and lassoed it around a tree branch, then tossed the other half of the floss dispenser over the edge of the fence, leaving a thin string hanging across the sidewalk. "Duck under it," he said, breathing hard as he reached for my hand.

I looked up the sidewalk to see Eyebrows racing toward us. "Seriously? That won't stop—"

Asa yanked my hand and dragged me up the block. A moment later, I heard another scream. Eyebrows was on his knees, clawing at his throat. Asa didn't let me slow down to gape, though. He kept running, weaving down alleys, across parking lots, and through intersections. Finally, he pulled me onto a waiting bus, then shoved me into a seat and stood over me, panting and staring out the window as we lurched forward.

My whole body was shaking with adrenaline, and cold sweat trickled down my back. And I didn't have time to catch my breath, because we hadn't gone two stops before Asa tugged me up the aisle and back onto the sidewalk.

He made to tow me across the street, but I locked my knees and tore my fingers from his grasp. He rounded on me, his angular face glistening with sweat. "*Now* what?"

"No more," I said, my voice tremulous. "What the hell was that?"

His lip curled. "That was me, saving our asses." He lifted the Silly String from his pocket and looked down at the bottle. "Contents under pressure. And saturated with Strikon magic."

"So you basically squirted liquid pain on those guys?"

He nodded.

"And the floss?"

"Same." He smiled and pointed to himself. "See? Jokester. Now let's get going."

"No! I've had it with this." Everything that had happened in the last few hours crashed down on me in that instant. "Everything we've

94

done, we've done for you! I'm your decoy, your magical suitcase, your silent—"

"You haven't exactly been silent."

"Shut up! I was going to say 'partner,' but that's not what I am at all. You're using me, and putting my life in danger, and setting me up to do terrible things to people I don't even know. All I want is to find Ben, and we haven't even taken one step toward doing that!" I swallowed back a sob. "I'm done, Asa. I'm *done*. I thought you were going to help me, but you're so absorbed in your own business that you can't." I gestured toward his pants. "And you've done it again, haven't you? You've stolen something—"

"Nope. Zhi gave it to me." He was barely looking at me; he was too busy scanning the streets.

"Whatever! Let me guess—you want to put whatever piece of magic she gave you inside of me so you can smuggle it wherever you're going next."

He regarded me, and then raised his eyebrows. "Yep. That pretty much sums it up."

"Yeah? Well, fuck off!"

He whistled. "She swore!"

I charged forward and planted my hands on his chest, shoving him as hard as I could. He took a step back, an amused smile on his face, and rage exploded inside me. I cocked my arm and threw a punch. He caught my fist about a foot from his face. "Oh, Mattie. You know violence isn't the answer."

I kicked him in the shin, and he cursed and dropped my fist. I turned on my heel and stalked down the street away from him, my cheeks blazing and tears burning my eyes.

"At the risk of getting kicked again, I have to ask," he said as he fell into step next to me. "Where are you going?"

Where *was* I going? I didn't have my wallet or my phone. Asa had told me to leave them at Daria's. And he'd probably done it on purpose.

We were close to downtown, it seemed, and the streets were lined with restaurants and stores. But it was a Sunday night, so the sidewalks weren't terribly crowded.

"Mattie, I'll explain if you'll let me." I could tell he was toying with me, and it made my fists clench again.

"I don't want your explanations. I want to go *home*," I said in a choked voice. "I hate this. I hate *you*. And I hate what I just did."

Asa's long fingers wrapped around my arm, and he pulled me to a halt. "Having to run again, you mean?"

"No." I sighed. "To Hualing. You said she was broken. And I—"

"You didn't do that," he said, frowning.

The memory of Hualing's tear-stained, agonized face flashed in my mind. "I helped."

He shook his head. "There are risks, and Hualing accepted them. And Zhi never should have brought her in. She only did it because she was desperate."

I found the strength to look into his eyes. "And when Zhi said she would 'take care' of Hualing?"

"Well, I wouldn't think too deeply about that if I were you."

"And if that were me? You'd just leave me on a street corner or something, wouldn't you?"

"I don't know."

I rolled my eyes. "Thanks for your honesty. Like I said—I want to go home. None of this is getting me any closer to Ben."

"Wrong," he said softly. "While you were in the bathroom with Hualing, I was negotiating with Zhi. She'd wanted me to tuck that piece of magic into you and smuggle it out, but since her conduit was broken . . ." He shrugged. "She wanted it badly. So I demanded a bonus on top of my commission to accept the job."

"How nice for you," I hissed.

"Nice *of* me, more like. I asked if she had any information about Ben."

I gasped. "And?"

"C'mon, let's talk about it over dinner. You hungry?"

"Asa!"

He nodded toward a bar a few doors away. When I scowled at him, he leaned forward. "I think you're hangry, Mattie," he said solemnly. "And I think you should let Randall Waxruby treat you to dinner."

"You are the most infuriating man I have ever met."

He laid his hand over his heart. "I'm wounded. I just risked my ass, and I did it for you."

"For Ben, you mean."

He chuckled as his hand fell away from his chest, a dark, humorless laugh. "Right." He pointed at the bar. "Can we argue semantics while we eat?"

"Fine." Because he was correct—I had reached the homicidal zone on my hunger meter, as Ben used to tell me, and I recognized I was not at my most rational. "Lead the way. But I'm not drinking."

"Good. You'll be a cheap date, then," he said as he strolled toward the bar.

"It's not a date."

"Again with the semantics."

He got us a table instead of sitting at the bar, where a crowd was watching the Cubs game, and flagged down a waitress immediately. She came over with a little basket of popcorn. I ordered a hamburger and fries, and Asa ordered a plain salad, no dressing, no croutons, extra peppers and tomatoes, and a side of sunflower seeds. I asked for a Coke and he ordered water.

"Are you a vegetarian or something?" I asked.

"Something like that," he said, pushing the popcorn toward me. "Eat while I talk. I'm tired of having my life threatened tonight."

He did look kind of weary. Though the bar was air-conditioned, Asa was still sweating. After the waitress brought his water, he dipped his napkin in it and ran it over his face and hair, ignoring the strange look she gave him. "We have to go to Denver," he said as he flopped the napkin onto the table.

"Is that where Ben is?"

He shook his head. "That's where we have to take the magic that's in this." He reached down and unbuttoned a pocket along his calf and pulled out something wrapped in one of the latex gloves. I leaned over to see a coaster, round with a wooden rim and a cork center.

"What's in it?"

"Healing." Asa tucked it back into his pocket as he scanned the bar, the exits, the hallway behind us. "Hefty dose. Long lasting. Zhi put everything she had into this, storing it up over time. She'd been waiting for a chance to get it out. It's for her mom."

"What does that have to do with Ben?"

"It puts us in the territory of the people who probably took him."

"But you said he wasn't in Denver."

"The West is a big place." He paused when the waitress brought our food, then jabbed a finger at my fries. "I'm not saying anything else until you eat at least half of those."

I obeyed, giving him a chance to eat his own food. He ate with desperation, finishing half his salad before I'd had a chance to take a bite out of my burger. He didn't leave so much as a sunflower seed behind. Once his plate was spotless, he pulled out his leftover trail mix. When he'd finished it, he sat back and closed his eyes, wiping his face once more with the napkin. "I don't want to go to Denver unless you're carrying that magic," he said. "It's not safe otherwise."

"Safe for who?" I asked, my mouth full of burger.

His lip curled. "Touché."

"I still want to know how this helps us find Ben. And I want specifics."

"Zhi said the rumor on the street is that one of the West Coast boss's agents was sighted in Chicago last week. And in Milwaukee. Zhong Lei is furious about it. One of the reasons he's been so touchy lately."

"Because he thinks his turf is being invaded?"

"Yep, but no one could figure out what the agent was here to do. Nothing was stolen. No one was killed. No messages were delivered. No threats were made. But one man disappeared without a trace, and that man happened to be heavily in debt." His gaze streaked along the bar, and he leaned forward on his elbows. "To Zhong Lei's operation, as it turns out."

I set my burger down, my stomach suddenly threatening to rebel. "Ben was in debt to the Chinatown mob boss?"

"Who do you think controls the magic trade in this part of the country?"

"I just thought . . ." I shook my head and blew a stray lock of hair away from my face. "I don't even know *why* he owed all that money."

"Come on, Mattie. You're not dumb. He was a fucking addict, and probably worse than that."

"We don't know anything for sure," I said quietly, even as I thought about the agate and the anchor pendant. He'd used them to influence me. Who else had he done that to?

"Whatever helps you keep him up on that high horse," Asa muttered. He flinched when the full bar cheered as the Cubs scored a run, rubbing his temples before looking up at me. "But believing he was just an innocent victim isn't going to help you find him."

"So if Ben owed all this money to the Chinatown boss, how do we know Zhong Lei and his people don't have him?"

"Why take him when they could lean on him and squeeze him for every cent he's got?" Asa drained his water glass. "Plus, Zhi told me that Lei's sent a few spies west to try to figure this out. It kind of suggests he doesn't know what the hell happened."

"So who's this agent person Zhi told you about?"

Asa's eyes met mine. "His name's Reza."

Reza. Where had I heard that name before? "Wait—that was who Zhi said—"

Asa nodded. "He's a well-known operator." He scanned his escape routes again as he fiddled with his unused straw. "Never met him personally. Don't really want to."

"But you're not even sure that's who took Ben."

"No. But it's as good a lead as any."

I arched an eyebrow. "Or a good excuse to get me to go with you to Denver."

He smirked. "Mattie, you're hurting my feelings. Don't you trust me?"

"I'll think about it," I said.

"Whether you trust me?"

"Whether I'll do the job. It's been a long night." And right now all I wanted was sleep. "Can we go home now?"

Asa nodded as he waved down the waitress and paid the check. As he signed the receipt, I looked at his face, realizing that there were dark circles under his eyes that hadn't been there earlier this afternoon. "You did well tonight," he said quietly as he set down his pen. "I should have said that earlier."

I arched an eyebrow. "You flatter me, Mr. Waxruby."

He bowed his head, laughing. "*Dammit*, Mattie."

"What?"

He shoved himself back from the table and got to his feet. "Nothing. Let's go. We should make an early start tomorrow morning."

"I didn't say I was going with you."

"Yeah, but you will." He gave me a bright grin that was sharp as a razor blade. "I'm your dealer, baby. I've got what you want." He headed for the door.

I stepped outside the restaurant to find him flagging down a cab. "Hey, I didn't buy that stick thingy from you. You gave it to me."

"That's not what I'm talking about." A cab pulled up. "It's hope, Mattie. You're an addict. And I know a thing or two about addicts. You're gonna chase that high all the way to the end." He opened the door of the waiting car and gestured inside.

I glared at him, a lump forming in my throat. And then I slid into the cab.

CHAPTER TEN

I woke to the sound of a door closing and sat up in a panic. I had no idea where I was. Then it came back to me. Daria's guest room was charming and funky, like the rest of the apartment. The paintings that hung on the walls in this room were all of the Chicago skyline, but the style and colors were strikingly different in each. It reminded me of that emotion magic we'd shared yesterday—a prism of feelings.

That pretty much described this insane odyssey so far. I had no idea how to feel or think about it. But as much as I hated to admit it—and never would out loud—I knew Asa had been right. The hope that I would reach Ben again, that we would go back to Sheboygan, get married, and resume our perfect life, would drive me forward. I was nowhere near giving up on him. I needed to look him in the eye. I needed to ask him why he had manipulated me, why he had lost himself in magic, why he had hidden this whole secret life from me. And then I needed to feel his arms around me again, to lay my head on his chest and listen to his heartbeat, restored and healthy and healed. The thought of him suffering and hurting was so painful that I had to shove it away every time it reared its head. And the thought of him dead?

Rubbing away the tightness in my chest, I took a quick shower, pulled my hair back into a messy twist, and padded out to the kitchen, where Daria was slicing apples. On her table were several shopping bags from the local grocery. She smiled when she saw me. "Asa asked me to pick up a few things for your road trip."

I peeked into a few of the sacks. Raw, unsalted nuts. Dried unsulfured apricots, a package of grape tomatoes and another of washed and sliced mushrooms, a large bag of carrot and celery sticks, apples and bananas, blueberries, raspberries, strawberries, and several packages of sunflower seeds and pumpkin seeds. "No Pringles?" I poked at a few other bags. "No Twizzlers?"

Daria laughed and pushed a plate of sliced apples toward me. "Not if you're traveling with Asa."

"This is unacceptable," I muttered. At least there was coffee. I gratefully accepted a cup and sank into a chair.

Daria began to chop kale and stuff it into a blender on the counter. "He's kind of precise about what he puts into his body."

"He could stand to gain a few pounds." Asa wasn't exactly skinny, but he looked nothing like his brother. Ben prided himself on his physique and worked out every day. Both brothers had broad shoulders and lean hips, but Asa was all angles where Ben was thickly padded with muscle.

"I doubt he cares much about that." Daria tilted a cutting board and slid a few cored apples into the blender. "He's been like this for as long as I've known him."

"How long is that?"

"We first worked together . . . almost ten years ago? It's been a while."

"You must know him well, then."

Daria looked at me. "I don't think anyone could say they know Asa well."

"Everyone certainly seems to know his name. And he seems to get chased a lot."

Chuckling, Daria scooped some coconut oil into the blender, then added a few spoonfuls of some kind of seed, a bunch of chopped celery, a peeled cucumber, several sections of grapefruit, and half a mango. "He's built a reputation. I don't know how he's survived, though."

She hit the "Puree" button on the blender, and I watched its contents churn into a thick green smoothie. When it fell silent, I said, "He's lucky he hasn't gotten shot or something."

"That's not what I meant." Daria got out a large plastic bottle and poured the smoothie into it. "I'm talking about what he is." She glanced over her shoulder at me. "How did you two get together?"

I sat back. "We're not together. Not at all. Not in any universe."

Daria's brow furrowed. "Honey, that's obvious. I meant your partnership. Your *business* partnership."

"Oh." I fiddled with a crease in one of the paper sacks. "He's helping me find someone, and I'm helping him . . . do some jobs." I didn't want to tell her about Ben. I was afraid she'd be yet another person blaming my fiancé for what had happened to him. "We kind of met by accident. I didn't even know I was a reliquary until two days ago."

Daria put the smoothie in the fridge and turned to face me. "So you're basically strangers."

I nodded. "Any advice for how to deal with him? He kind of drives me crazy."

She gave me a wistful look. "Let Asa be Asa."

"Do I have a choice?"

She looked down at her hands. "Allowing someone to be who they really are, on *their* terms, instead of expecting them to be who you wish they were—that's always a choice." She looked up at me through thick black lashes. "And I have a little experience with that kind of thing."

I looked at her striking face and remembered the moment Asa had tucked her fake breast back into her bra. I smiled at her. "Some people are easier to accept as they are." I cast a glance down the hall toward Asa's room. "Some are a little trickier."

She chuckled. "Oh, honey. Give him some credit. He's survived in this business longer than most. He's figured it out. But like I said, I don't really know how he stands it."

I remembered Grandpa saying pretty much the same thing. "Because he's a magic sensor, you mean?"

Daria nodded. "Magic sniffers aren't all that common. And they usually aren't . . . healthy."

"I think we met one last night in Chinatown."

"Who, Tao? He belongs to Zhong. Most of the major bosses have a sniffer, assuming they can snag one."

"You make it sound like the bosses own them."

She popped a chunk of mango into her mouth. "The most sensitive ones are really valuable. More than any other kind of sensor. If you've got magic on you, then they can feel you coming. They can find you. They know where you hide your relics. They know if you have any juice of your own and how much. The only way to hide magic from them is . . ." She gestured at me. "But even then, if they get close enough, they might feel it in you." She shivered and ran her hands down her arms. "But there's a price to that kind of sensitivity."

"Asa didn't seem that sensitive, though," I countered. "Yesterday, this manipulator named Mrs. Wong actually stuck her hand under his shirt, and he seemed totally fine."

Daria whistled. "Maybe it seemed that way, but trust me, that had to be excruciating."

I stared down at my apple slices, which were slowly going brown. I remembered the strain in Asa's voice when he defied the manipulative old lady. "I guess it didn't look fun."

"That's what I mean about magic sniffers. It's not easy for them."

"Tao looked like a zombie. He seemed like he could barely walk under his own power."

"He's high on Ekstazo magic most of the time, I imagine, just to keep him going."

Maybe that was what he was doing with whatever was in his pocket. "Is that how Asa survives?" He certainly had a crapload of stuff in those pockets of his.

Right then a door down the hall opened, and Gracie's toenails clicked on the hardwood. Asa's voice, low and sweet in that tone he used only with her, reached me. "Go say 'thank you' to Daria. Go on, girl. I'll be out in a minute."

She came running into the kitchen. I heard the shower come on as Daria knelt to receive Gracie's wriggling gratitude. Her eyes met mine as the pit bull licked her face. "I think Asa's found his own way of surviving. But whatever you guys are doing, it involves some pretty powerful magic. Even when he makes it look easy, just think about what it's really costing him."

I thought back to the night before, to the sweat soaking his T-shirt, the circles under his eyes, the way he massaged his temples. "I think you might be right."

"But he knows what he's doing, Mattie. You just have to trust him."

A few hours later, after we'd passed the magic in the coaster through Daria and into me, Asa and I hit the road. I was feeling a little euphoric, probably an aftereffect of the healing magic, but Asa was quiet, sipping at the green smoothie as he got on the highway heading west. Every once in a while, Gracie crept up from her bed in the back to lick at his elbow, and it would draw a quick smile to his face.

"How long will it take us to get to Denver?" I asked when I couldn't stand the silence anymore.

"We'll stop in Kansas City tonight. I have business along the way."

I groaned. "You might be in fabulous shape, but my muscles are aching like nobody's business. I'm not sure I can run for my life again so soon."

His gaze was darting from the rearview mirror to his side-view mirrors every few seconds. "You probably won't have to."

A surprised laugh burst from my mouth. "Probably?"

"No promises."

Asa munched on tomatoes and blueberries and carrot sticks, and managed to look only mildly offended when I ducked into the first gas station we stopped at to get myself some Twizzlers. "These are vegetarian," I said. "Want one?"

"I'm not that kind of vegetarian."

I slid a little lower in my seat, cradling the package. "More for me, then."

As we got back on the highway, I asked, "Can we listen to the radio?"

"No."

"Why not?"

"My ride, my rules."

My ride, my rules. He must have said that to me at least half a dozen times before we arrived at our first stop, in a town called Bloomington. I sat in the van with Gracie as Asa grabbed one of his toolboxes and went into a bookstore, emerging fifteen minutes later with a spring in his step. I eyed him as he got back into the driver's seat. "Are you about to ask me to open my vault so you can make another deposit?"

"Nope. You're only for special jobs. Most of my business is dealing. There are a lot of small towns the bosses ignore, and I can move product without having to worry about them coming after me, looking for a cut."

"So you're selling . . . those sticks?"

"That's a pretty popular item, yeah."

"You must need a lot of conduits to get the magic into them."

He shook his head as he pulled out of the parking lot. "No conduits for the party items. This is surface magic, not infused magic."

"Huh?"

He sighed as he got on the interstate again. "Infused magic is what we've been working with. If you infuse an object with manipulation magic, for example, the user can draw on that power to influence others."

"Like an actual Knedas."

"Yup. Except it gets used up, depending on how much magic is put into the object."

"Okay, so how is that different from surface magic?"

"That's when the magic is just on the surface of the relic rather than inside it. And in that case, the user doesn't have the power—the power acts on them."

I thought back to Franz and his pen, the way he had been sucking on it. That must have been what all the people in the magic dens were doing with their objects. Same with the Silly String and the floss. "If you don't need a conduit for that work, how do you do it?"

"You dip the objects in the juice."

"Dip them in . . . you know, suddenly I'm not sure I want to know what you mean by 'juice.'"

He chuckled. "It could be any bodily fluid, but usually it's plasma."

"So naturals just donate their fluids on the regular?"

"They're making money off it. It's quite the commodity, depending on how potent they are. Some of the bosses have major juicing operations."

I put my half-eaten bag of Twizzlers down, feeling a little queasy. Gracie's head popped up, sniffing at the food, but Asa gently shoved her head into the back again. "Don't even think about it," he said to her, then reached into his console and pulled out her pumpkin treats. "Can you give her a few of those?" he asked me.

I took the sack and tossed the treats at Gracie—who happily caught them—then spent a few minutes watching Asa. "Do you use any magic yourself?"

He glanced at me from the corner of his eye. "No." He looked away. "Not anymore."

I bit my lip. "Did you used to be addicted?"

"Yeah. For a little while I was."

"How old were you?"

"You interested in my life story now?" He let out a bitter chuckle.

"I think it'll help me understand what's going on."

"I wasn't very old when I knew I was different," he said after a solid minute of silence. "But I had no idea what was happening to me. I would just get these feelings, like something was coming my way, and it was good or dangerous or scary as fuck, but I wouldn't know what it was."

"Magic," I murmured.

He nodded. "I thought I was crazy, and I had no one to talk to about it. My mom was long gone, and my dad . . ." His hands tightened around the steering wheel. "So by the time I hit high school, I was just trying to hold it together. I would have done anything to be normal."

I watched the muscles of his arms flex as he changed lanes. "You self-medicated."

"I guess that's what you'd call it. I just wanted to make it go away."

It felt as if I were walking on the thinnest ice. One wrong word from me and he'd clam up. And to find out more about his childhood was to find out more about Ben. "Were you around magic that much? Is it really that common?"

He gave me a one-shouldered shrug. "There's more out there than you would ever know, but that wasn't the only . . ." He shook his head as if he'd thought better about what he was about to say. "There was enough going on that I wanted to be numb."

"So you got into drugs, right?"

"Sounds like someone dug up my record."

Oops. I'd given that bit away. "It was just part of the investigation into Ben's disappearance."

"Weed, mostly," he said after a few more miles of quiet. "Some Oxy. But I kept getting deeper, and then . . ." He sighed. "Anyways, I'm clean now. I don't touch any of it."

I gave him a skeptical look. "Didn't I see you pull a bag of weed out of your pants yesterday?"

He smirked and opened his thigh pocket, then pulled out the bag I'd seen and tossed it into my lap. "Try smoking that, then. Have fun." His voice was dripping with amusement. "We'll see if we can get you some rolling papers at my next stop."

I opened the bag and gave it a sniff. It was dried kale. "You are so not what I was expecting."

Asa was smiling now. "Are you talking to my kale?"

"No, you jackass," I said, giggling. "You. The way Ben talked—"

His smile disappeared in an instant. "Oh, yes. Tell me what he said."

I flinched. "Not much, really."

"Oh no you don't. Now it's your turn. What did my dear baby brother tell you about me?"

I scooted away, my back to the window. "He just said you were unlikely to be sober."

"Don't sanitize it for me."

"He said you were . . . angry."

Asa laughed. "Can't imagine why I would have been angry, seeing as I had it so easy. Come on, this is fun. What else?"

"Asa . . ."

"Tell. Me."

"He said you were a criminal, okay?" I blurted out. "And he said you were—" My mouth clamped shut, and I stared out the window at a cornfield. Here we were, driving across the country to try to save Ben, and I was stirring up terrible memories for the guy I was depending on to help me.

"Spill it, Mattie."

"He said you were jealous of him," I added quietly.

Asa rolled his eyes. "Of course he would think that. Of course he would."

"And you weren't?"

"Jealous of him? Fuck no."

"But he was normal, wasn't he? He didn't have to deal with the things you did."

"I was glad for him," Asa said, his voice suddenly hoarse. His face was turned away, but I could see the rigid edge of his jaw. "I wouldn't have wished it on anyone, especially him. And I didn't want him involved in any of it."

"You love him."

"No."

My fingers balled in my shirt. "I don't believe that."

"Then you're an idiot."

"You can't just stop loving someone like that, Asa."

"It's easier than you think." Something sharp flared in his eyes as he turned back to me. "What else did he tell you? Don't hold back on my account."

There was something about the way he was looking at me that made my stomach go tight. "He said that the last time you were together, you threatened to kill him."

A smile spread across Asa's face. "That's what he said?"

"Are you going to tell me he lied?"

"No." He sank into his seat, looking more relaxed than he had all day. "For once, my brother was telling the absolute truth."

CHAPTER ELEVEN

We holed up in a cheap motel just outside of Kansas City after a twelve-hour day spent mostly in heavy silence. By the time we arrived, I was so desperate for fresh air that I went for a long walk and helped myself to a giant plate of pancakes at the nearby IHOP, not even caring that I was completely alone at the table. It was a relief. Riding in that van with Asa had started to feel like being trapped in a crate with a rabid wolverine.

We got separate rooms. It would have saved me a little money to share with him, but he didn't suggest it and I didn't ask. It wasn't because I felt that he would have tried something, though. We'd been together nearly constantly for the last few days, and I just wasn't getting that kind of creep vibe from him. In fact, half the time it seemed like he could barely stand me, and the other half of the time, he was laughing at me the same way I laughed at screaming goat videos on YouTube.

And I'd heard it straight from him—he'd threatened to kill Ben.

I called my mom and told her how relaxing the spa had been so far. I'd looked up the resort on my phone, so I'd already made up a schedule of massages and facials and steam room sessions for myself. I told her I'd had my chakras balanced and my lymphatic system stimulated. I crowed about how I was going to be toxin-free by the time I came home.

I held back the tears as I asked about the investigation. Mom tried to sound optimistic, but it was obvious they still had no leads. I didn't ask many questions, especially when Mom hinted that I needed to focus on my health. And when I asked if I could talk to Grandpa, just needing someone on the outside to confirm that I wasn't insane, she told me he was sleeping, but that he'd been very alert and sharp the last few days. I was willing to bet he was worrying about me.

I didn't sleep very well. I dreamed of chasing Ben down the streets of Chicago, always a few steps behind. Then I turned a corner and there was Tao, his eyes deep black pits. *It's there,* he said in a dead voice, pointing at my chest. The men on either side of him drew their switchblades. *Cut it out of her.*

I woke up in a sweat to see light filtering through my curtains. It was after seven, and Asa had said he wanted to leave early, so I rushed into the shower, packed my bags, and was knocking on his door half an hour later.

There was no answer. I lugged my suitcase down to the van, expecting him to be there, ready with a sarcastic remark, but no dice. "Where did you go?" I whispered, hating the coil of anxiety twisting tighter inside me. What if his enemies had caught up with him? No, Asa was wily and strong. He could feel people coming. He knew what he was doing. He was too wary and on guard to be caught.

He wasn't like Ben.

In the distance, I heard a familiar bark, and I walked quickly to the far side of the parking lot, where the hotel backed up to a densely wooded area.

Asa was beneath one of the trees. And he was . . . dancing?

His back was to me. Track pants hung from his lean hips. His shirt was lying on the grass next to a pair of flip-flops. They were guarded by Gracie, who was wagging her tail as she watched me come near. But she didn't bark, and Asa didn't turn around.

The early morning sun glinted off little beads of sweat across Asa's shoulder blades. His skin was tanned but smooth, no tattoos, no obvious scars. His arms rose from his sides, and his wrists flexed as he reached through the air and brought his hands back, as if he were cradling an invisible beach ball he had conjured from thin air. He took a step to the side, and his entire body leaned into the movement as he pushed the invisible ball away, then pulled it back. He looked simultaneously relaxed and entirely aware, controlled but fluid. Every little part of him, from his fingers to his feet, moved in harmony.

I stood at the edge of the lot, just watching. It took me a few minutes, but I recognized what he was doing—tai chi. I'd always associated that with old people in public parks. But Asa made it look . . . beautiful. He looked like a wave on the ocean. Like a ribbon caught in the wind. Like an arrow flying straight to the heart of its target.

"I'd never have pegged you as a voyeur," he said, snapping me out of my trance. His head was bowed, and his back was still to me. But then he looked over his shoulder. "Enjoying the view?"

My face flushed with heat. "You said you wanted to leave early. I'm ready to go."

He turned around and scooped his shirt from the grass. I looked away from his bare chest. "We heard you coming a mile away," he said. "Your suitcase wheels need some lube."

"Sorry." I glanced up to find him standing next to Gracie, his shirt where it belonged.

"I know you've been waiting," he said to the dog. "Go ahead."

Like her leash had been cut, Gracie came bounding toward me, tongue lolling, her face so joyful I had to smile. "Thank you," I whispered to her, bending down to fondle her ears and nuzzle her neck.

"You all right?" he asked as he slid the flip-flops onto his feet and walked over to us.

"I could do with a little inner peace, I guess. Does the tai chi help?"

"If you know what you're doing."

I gave him a wry smile. "No hope for me, then."

His eyes met mine. "I wouldn't say that."

"Does it help you?"

He ran a hand through his dark hair. "It's one variable in the equation, yeah."

"Variable in the equation?"

"My body is one of the tools of my trade. The most important one, in fact. I have to keep it in good shape. That makes sense, right?"

"I guess so. You don't drink, and you eat healthy. Raw, it seems like. I've never seen you eat anything cooked."

He squinted in the sunlight as he tapped the tip of his nose.

"But even with all of that, how does it help you resist manipulation?" It had been on my mind since Daria and I had talked about it yesterday morning.

The corner of Asa's mouth curled. "You want me to teach you how."

"I don't like the idea of having my free will taken away, you know?"

"Yeah. I know."

We stopped at the van to load up my heinously heavy suitcase, then went up to his room. "I'll give you a quick lesson, then I'll get ready and we'll be out of here."

He grabbed his cargo pants from the dresser and sifted through the pockets, pulling out his Pez dispenser and two of the jacks. He held up the Pez dispenser. It was olive green and had a little pointed tail. The elongated alien head was hideous, looking just as it did in the Sigourney Weaver movies, and when he pressed his thumb to the back of it, the fanged mouth opened to offer up a yellowish tablet. "Suck on this for a minute, and then focus on not doing a single damn thing I tell you to do. That shouldn't be too hard, right? You've already had plenty of practice."

I took a step back. "Before we do this . . . can you just promise that you won't ask me to do anything . . . um . . ." I crossed my arms over my chest again.

His arm fell to his side. "I don't play that way, Mattie."

I looked into his eyes, and it was all I needed to tell me he was completely sincere. "Okay." I opened my mouth, and he held out the dispenser, letting the little tab drop onto my tongue. I winced at its sour tang and tried not to think about what it was made of. It dissolved quickly, and I swallowed the acid saliva that had pooled in my mouth. "Now what?"

"Now you sit down."

I sat. It was the best idea I'd heard all day.

"Stand up."

I got to my feet. It felt awesome to stretch.

"I'm disappointed, Mattie," he said in an amused voice.

"God, I'm so sorry."

"Try harder."

"Okay." What was I trying to do? Wait. I was supposed to be disobeying him. That was the whole point of this! Except . . . everything he said made so much sense.

"I think you need to pick up my dirty socks over there." He pointed to a crumpled pair of black socks lying by his boots.

"You got it." I started for the socks, but the closer I got, the more it struck me that this was kind of gross. "Are you sure?"

"Dead sure. Pick 'em up."

I did. They smelled funky.

He reached into his bag and pulled out a small bottle of laundry detergent. "Go wash them in the sink for me."

He tossed the bottle at me and I caught it. Then I skipped over to the sink and filled it with warm water, added the soap, and scrubbed at the socks, relieved as the scent of crisp linen reached my nose. I finished up, squeezed the extra water out of the socks, and laid them on the counter. When I looked up at the mirror over the sink, I gasped. Asa was right behind me. He leaned down and took my hand, and then pressed the two jacks into my palm, closing my fingers around them. "Now tell me how you and Ben met."

My mouth opened to tell him about that first day on the job, the way Ben and I had worked together to vaccinate all those wriggling puppies, the way his smile had made my heart race, the way he'd taken me out for coffee afterward to show his gratitude, which he admitted later was just an excuse to get me to go on a date with him. But my breath caught as Asa squeezed my hand, causing the points of the jacks to dig into my skin. "Um," I said, wincing. "I . . ." Wasn't sure I should be telling him this, actually.

"Come on, Mattie," Asa said, his voice silky. "I told you all those things about myself yesterday. You tell me something." His face was only a few inches from mine. My curls were brushing his lips as he spoke, and I could feel the warmth of his breath in my ear. "Tell me about you and Ben."

He loosened his grip on my fist, easing the pain, and my wish to share all my memories returned, full force. Asa had been pretty forthcoming yesterday, but I hadn't told him much about me at all. "We used to—"

Asa contracted his fingers over my hand again, making the points of the jacks burrow into my palm once more.

"Hey," I whined. "You're . . ." I looked down at our hands, his over mine, holding my fingers closed tightly around those little metal torture devices. "You don't really want to know about me and Ben."

"Damn straight. See how it works?" He let go of my hand and stepped away from me.

I lifted my hand and looked at the jacks sitting on my palm. "It's that easy?"

"Be a love and get Gracie a snack, will you?"

I walked over to where her bowls sat, and she jumped to her feet, the stump of her tail wagging frantically. "No problem."

Asa sighed. "Not quite that easy, apparently."

I poked at his duffel bag. "Where do you keep the food?"

"Squeeze those jacks like your life depends on it, Mattie."

I obeyed, waiting for my next command.

"Now clean out Gracie's food bowl." Asa gave me a nasty smile. "With your tongue."

"What is *wrong* with you?" I asked, but Asa only chuckled and gestured at my hand, still closed around the jacks.

"You have to be sharp and alert *before* I tell you to do something, or you won't remember to resist," he explained.

"But how will I know someone is about to manipulate me?"

He shrugged. "You won't. I can feel those mindfuckers a mile off, but you can't."

"So all I need to do is walk around squeezing a handful of jacks at all times? Very reasonable." I dropped them onto the bed and rubbed at the little indentations left on my palm, feeling a little hopeless. "How did you resist Mrs. Wong, though? Your jacks were on the table."

Asa walked over to his boots and reached inside, then pulled out a small, square patch of coarse wire bristles. "Comes in handy sometimes."

"So you hurt yourself to keep your mind clear."

He slid the patch of bristles back into the toe of his boot. "It works." He gestured at the door. "Thanks for washing my socks. Could you go take Gracie for a walk while I get ready to go?"

"Of course." I grabbed the lead that was lying on the desk and clipped it to Gracie's collar. "How much time do you need?"

He smirked. "No more than twenty."

"We'll be waiting by the van." I headed out the door with Gracie by my side.

It wasn't until we were a few blocks away that I realized I probably should have asked him when the magic would wear off.

•••

We made it to Denver by dinnertime, but we agreed to off-load the healing magic before settling in for the night. Zhi had given Asa a contact for a conduit, and a few hours out, Asa gave the guy a call and set up the meeting. Zhi's mother was a patient at the cancer center in Aurora. We had to get the magic into a relic of the woman's choosing and leave it in her possession, where Zhi hoped it would prolong her mother's life—at least until Zhi could convince Zhong Lei to let her travel to Denver to visit.

I'll admit I was having less than charitable thoughts after the whole episode with Hualing, but after learning that Zhi was only trying to make it to her mother's bedside, it was hard to hate her all that much. If it were my mom, I would have done everything I could have, too.

Our conduit was an elderly African American gentleman who introduced himself as Jack Okafor. He had big hands, a sturdy body that looked strong despite his advanced age, and a short salt-and-pepper beard. Asa relaxed a little after shaking his hand. I think he recognized Jack for what he was—an experienced professional who wouldn't fall apart on the job. Jack gave me a warm smile as we introduced ourselves. But as soon as I told him my name was Mattie Carver, his eyes went wide. "Carver?" he asked.

"Yeah," I said as I pulled my hand from his warm grasp.

"Ring a bell?" Asa asked, watching him closely.

Jack waved his hands in front of him. "No, not really. Common name."

"Right," said Asa, never taking his eyes off Jack. "Well, let's get this done."

It was an easy job. Zhi's mother had the relic—a brooch made of pearls and silver. Jack and I sat by her bedside while Asa lurked behind us, standing guard. It was quick, and Jack seemed refreshed by the healing magic as it passed through him and into the brooch. I felt as I always did after—a little hungry, a little relieved to have my body to myself again.

"Anyone up for dinner?" Jack asked as we headed out of the hospital. "There's a diner right at the corner here." He gestured up the block.

"Absolutely," I said. "I'm starving."

"You guys go ahead," said Asa. "I'm going to walk Gracie and get us a place to stay. Meet at the van in an hour or so?"

We went our separate ways. Jack was a solid presence at my side as we strolled toward the restaurant. "I was hoping I could talk to you alone," he said. "You're a reliquary. And a really strong one, from what I can tell. In fact, I've only known one other who was as strong."

I stopped at the door to the restaurant and turned to him. "You knew my grandfather, didn't you? He said he had a conduit friend named Jack."

He gave me a gentle smile. "If his name's Howard Carver, then yes, I did."

Relief rushed through me, so sudden that I swayed on my feet. We headed inside, where he regaled me with stories of his adventures with my grandpa—the tough and tricky pieces of magic they'd delivered together all over the world, the fun they'd had, the money they'd made. "Howard still had a lot of good years in him when he retired," Jack finally said.

I'd polished off a turkey club and a strawberry shake, and I smiled as I twirled my straw in its glass. "I think he did it for my grandma. She really wanted to settle down."

Jack nodded. "He adored her. Missed her a lot when we were traveling. Missed his son, too. Your dad isn't a reliquary, though." He chuckled, a deep, rich sound. "Did Howie tell you about the time we tried to find out?"

I laughed and nodded. "You're the one who tried to slip him that little bit of pain magic."

"Like the static shock from hell," Jack said, his shoulders shaking. "*Zzzz—zzz-zzz.* It had nowhere to go, and Howie wouldn't let up! After that, we knew the kid wasn't going to be in the business." He looked up at me. "But here you are. How long you been doing this?"

I bit my lip. "Three days now?"

His brow furrowed. "What?"

"I kind of fell into it." I shook my head. "Actually, I literally fell into it."

The lines around his mouth deepened. "And you're working with Asa Ward."

"Do you know him?"

"He's *known*. That's all I can say."

"And?"

Jack sat back and pushed his half-eaten plate of ribs away. "Does Howie know you're here?"

"Sort of. He knows I'm looking for my fiancé, who happens to be Asa's brother." Jack was the first person in this world who I'd told, but I already felt like I could trust him.

Jack's eyebrows shot up. "Asa has a brother?"

"He's not a natural. He's just . . . his name is Ben. And we think someone working for the West Coast boss might have taken him."

Jack looked around, reminding me of Asa as he scanned the faces of the people in the diner. "And Howie let you come here on your own?"

"There wasn't much he could do about it." I swallowed the lump in my throat. "Grandpa's got only a few months to live. It's lung cancer."

He gave me an uncertain look. "Lung cancer? You're sure?"

"I don't think there's any doubt."

"Damn. I'm sorry." He folded his large hands in front of him. "If I know him, though, you're on his mind every minute of every day." He leaned forward and lowered his voice. "He wouldn't want his grand-daughter mixed up with Frank Brindle or anyone who works for him."

"That's the West Coast boss?"

Jack nodded. "Are you sure he's the one who's got your fiancé?"

"That's what Asa thinks. Apparently there was this agent who was skulking around in the Midwest—his name's Reza?"

Jack grimaced. "Reza's a Strikon. Nasty piece of work. You'd do well to steer clear of him."

"I can't—not if he took Ben."

"But why would Brindle's chief agent take your fiancé? Didn't you say he's got no juice?"

"Yeah, but he owed a lot of money to the Chinatown boss."

Thick wrinkles creased Jack's forehead. "But Reza only gets involved with big game." He scratched at his beard. "I'm having trouble understanding why he of all people would kidnap a normal from a small town outside his boss's territory. It doesn't play."

I couldn't really disagree. "That's the information we have. We got it from the mistress of the Chinatown boss."

"She just casually gave you that kind of intelligence?"

"No. We'd delivered some magic to her, and then we agreed to bring the healing magic here to her mom." Well, Asa had agreed on my behalf, but whatever. "Asa's been helping me find Ben in exchange for my assistance on jobs like the one we just did."

Jack plucked a toothpick from the dispenser on the table and twirled it in his fingers before slipping it between his lips. "Has Asa been your only source of information about where your fiancé's been taken?"

"Yeah," I said slowly.

"And you're sure that's why he's come here."

"Yeah?"

He chewed on his toothpick for a while. "Do you have any idea how valuable a strong reliquary is, Mattie?"

"What do you mean by 'valuable'?"

"I mean every boss in the world wants a good one. One who won't break. One who has control. One who can conceal the magic from anyone. That's how Howie was, and it seems like the gift runs in the family."

"What are you suggesting, Jack?"

"I'm saying that you need to be very careful, young lady. You're in the territory of the most powerful boss in the country, and you're hanging with a man whose reputation is that he'd sell his mother to the highest bidder if he had the chance."

I winced, knowing that Asa and Ben's mom had abandoned them when they were young. Ben had been only two, but Asa had been four. There was a chance he remembered her. "That's not a very nice thing to say about someone."

"Based on what I've heard, he's earned it," Jack said in a gravelly voice. "And you need to make sure he's not in this to sell *you* to the highest bidder. It's not easy to get out once a boss has his teeth in you."

"I can't just go home without even trying to find out if this is a good lead. I owe it to Ben."

"I feel you. And unlike naturals, conduits and reliquaries can evade magic sensors like Asa if we need to, as long as we're not toting magic around in our pockets." He gestured at me. "Or our bodies, as it were."

"Then I could get away from him if I needed to. Good to know."

"Always," he said as he tossed a few twenties on the table, more than enough to pay for our meal, with a generous tip on top. "Make Howie proud, girl." He reached into his pocket and pulled out a business card. "But if you need help, you call me. Anytime, okay? I owe your grandpa a favor or three."

I accepted the card with gratitude. "Thanks, Jack."

He walked me back to the parking lot, where Asa was waiting, fidgety and watchful as usual. We said our good-byes, and Jack threw me one last measured look as I climbed into the van.

Asa grabbed something from his cupholder and tossed it into my lap. It was a penny. "For your thoughts," he said as we pulled out of the lot and headed down the street.

"Just wondering what we're doing next," I murmured, slipping my hand into my pocket to make sure Jack's card was still safely tucked inside.

Asa drummed his hands on the wheel. "I checked with a few of my contacts in Vegas, and now I'm dead sure they've got Ben."

"Really?" I squeaked. "He's alive?"

Asa nodded. "One of my buyers was called to bring in heavy doses of healing and pleasure, and it turned out it was for Ben."

"Oh my God," I whispered, tears springing to my eyes. I turned my face toward the window, praying that this wasn't an elaborate lie. "Did they say how Ben looked? Did they say anything about his heart?"

Asa shifted in his seat. "I was mostly asking whether he was breathing, and he is, apparently. I didn't inquire much beyond that."

Mistrust trickled cold down my back. "So what's the plan?"

"I say we go straight to Vegas. First thing tomorrow. Quickest way to get this done, I think."

Since I'd talked to Jack, every single thing Asa said seemed sinister. I gripped Jack's card as if it could keep me safe. "And what will we be doing there?"

Asa slowed to a stop at a red light. He turned to me, the crimson light playing across his chiseled cheekbones. His smile seemed tinged with blood. "We're going to get dressed up. We're going to go to a casino. And we're going to get their attention."

CHAPTER TWELVE

I woke up to Asa banging on my door—he wanted to get an early start. Really early. It was three in the morning. We drove across the desert terrain and stopped in a tiny town called Green River. Asa's plan was to leave Gracie with an earth mother–type named Rosie who ran the local magic den. Apparently she owed Asa a favor, but she greeted both him and the dog warmly. Asa gave her a list of instructions and provided Rosie with all of Gracie's homemade dog treats, her bowls, her bed, her arthritis medication, and her eyedrops.

It was hard to mistrust a man who was clearly so devoted to his dog. I waited outside while Asa shared a long good-bye with Gracie, and stayed silent when he emerged quiet, his eyes a little redder than they had been.

Then we ditched the van. We made a quick stop in another tiny town, Richfield, at a dusty used car lot. Asa had a brief negotiation with a beefy guy named Marty who smelled like he'd just bathed in gin, and we drove away in a gray Subaru Outback with California plates. Asa made yet another stop in the town of Beaver (I kid you not), where we put all of his toolboxes except for one in storage. I peeked over his shoulder as he signed the contract for the locker. According to his ID, he was now none other than Adrian Battlebush of Fresno, California.

"How many of those do you have?" I asked as we drove away.

"As many as I need," he replied.

We arrived in Vegas just before five, and the sun was like a laser on the windshield as Asa sped into the city. He aimed his finger at a cream-colored hotel called Mistika, which was surrounded by palm trees. "That's where we're headed."

Now that we were here, a restless churning had started in my stomach. Was Ben somewhere in this city? Was he even still alive? I hadn't let myself consider the alternative, but we were so far from home, and all of Jack's questions were still spiraling in my mind. "How do you know where to go?"

"Mistika is Frank Brindle's hub. He runs a lot of his business from there."

I frowned as Asa took an exit. "So, what—we're just going to walk in there and announce ourselves? This doesn't exactly seem like your style."

"My style?"

"Yeah. You don't seem like the go-in-with-guns-blazing kind of guy. You seem more like the skulk-in-dark-alleys type."

"I don't skulk."

I gave him a once-over: the motorcycle boots, his snake hips, the shadow of stubble on his jaw, the crooked angle of his nose, his everdarting eyes fringed by thick, dark lashes. "You were made for skulking, Asa Ward."

"I don't know whether to be flattered or hurt."

"I thought you didn't care."

He smirked. "The last thing we want to do is let Reza or any of Brindle's people control the tempo. I hate surprises. I want to meet them on my terms, not theirs."

"And what are your terms?"

"We're going to ask them to give Ben back. Very politely. And we'll see what they want in return."

"Won't that depend on why they took him in the first place? When we first met, you said you had an idea of why. You said the police would never find him if you were right."

Asa sighed impatiently. "And maybe I do have an idea, but that's my business."

"Ben is *my* business!"

"Ben is a tool," snapped Asa, and then his lip curled. "In every possible way."

"Now you're calling him names. How mature."

"Oh, for fuck's sake. Can we stop talking now?" He wrenched the wheel and sped down a ramp into a parking garage, ripped the ticket from the booth operator, and muscled the car into a spot. Then he turned to me, his brown eyes glinting in the semidarkness. "I'm doing my goddamn best for you, Mattie. I'm not telling you everything, because it's safer for you if you don't know. What else do you want?"

I want to know I can trust you. "Ben," I said, my voice breaking.

"Don't you think I fucking know that already?" he shouted.

When he saw me flinch, he cursed and got out of the car, slamming the door hard enough to shake me in my seat. He stalked to the back and grabbed his duffel, then stood several feet away, waiting for me to catch up. My heart hammering, I pulled my suitcase out and extended its handle, then began to follow Asa toward a set of elevators. After several steps, I paused. "My suitcase wheels aren't squeaking," I said quietly.

Asa didn't stop walking. "I had some WD-40 in the van."

"Thanks."

"I couldn't stand the goddamn noise." He jabbed the button for the elevator, then gestured at my overstuffed bag. "We're going to the high-limit lounge tonight. You'll need something nice."

"I brought that black dress I wore to the Phan—"

"A lot nicer than that." The elevator doors slid open, revealing an interior lined with mirrors bordered with some kind of runes, which I guess were supposed to look mystical. Asa waved at a hotel map above the buttons for the floors. "There are shops on two." He pulled out his wallet and handed me Adrian Battlebush's Amex.

"Um . . . just so I'm clear, did you steal . . . ?"

"Fuck me," he muttered, running his hand over his face. "No, Mattie, I did not steal some innocent guy's identity. It's my money."

I pushed the card back at him. "I have my own. I don't really want—"

He ignored my outstretched hand. "I owe you commission on both jobs we did for Zhi. We'll take it out of that." The elevator doors opened, and he exited without a backward glance. I quickly shoved his card into the pocket of my capris and scurried out after him. The lobby was black marble, with glittering mosaics on the walls that reminded me of those tests optometrists use to check if you're color-blind. The same stylized runes popped out at me everywhere I looked. Orchids wound around trees that sprouted from tiled, humid mini-oases all through the space, making it hard to get a clear view from one end to the other. I could tell from the tension in Asa's shoulders that he hated it. Or maybe he was already feeling the magic here. Maybe it was already making him sweat.

We got adjoining rooms and rode up the elevator in silence, standing awkwardly next to a couple who were so wrapped up in each other that they didn't seem aware of us at all. I spent my time examining an advertisement for the casino's magic show. I realized I'd seen the magician before—it was Harvey Mirren, a world-famous hypnotist I'd watched a TV special on a few years back.

I'd always assumed his "victims" were just playing along. Now I suspected I was very wrong. Harvey must be a powerful Knedas, able to put huge audiences under his spell with just a look. Suddenly the walls of the elevator felt very close and tight.

When we reached our rooms, down a hallway painted with murals of misty mountains and lush forests, Asa paused at his door. "I'll come get you at seven," he said in a flat voice, then unlocked the door and slammed it behind him.

I stared at his room number, the same stylized font as the runes, and then went into my own room and collapsed on the bed, tired of trying to hold it together. I was shaking with anger and confusion. Was I really closer to Ben here, or was I just stepping into a trap? Was Asa really trying to keep me in the dark because it was safer, or did he just not want me to know what he was really up to?

I had a few hours to poke around on my own, so I freshened up my makeup and headed downstairs to shop. There were guards posted at the entrance to the shopping plaza, their eyes tracing over each guest with interest. I wondered if they were emotion sensors. If they were, they'd know in a second that I had some serious stuff on my mind, so on impulse, I stepped into a restaurant that was tucked behind one of the oases. It was early yet, so there were still seats at the long mahogany bar, and I hopped up on a stool and ordered myself a glass of red wine.

"We've got over fifty reds," said the bartender, a curvaceous brunette with heavily lined eyes. "Want to be more specific?"

"Try the Gaja Barbaresco," said a deep voice just behind me. I looked up and nearly swallowed my tongue as I beheld one of the prettiest men I had ever laid eyes on. He had these huge dark-brown eyes, the most exquisitely sculpted face, slick black hair, and olive skin. He was wearing a tailored gray suit, and he unbuttoned his jacket as he sat down on the stool next to me. My heart fluttered as he flashed a charming smile. "It has a lovely nose."

"Nose?" I absently touched mine, and my companion chuckled.

"Yours is certainly lovely, but I was referring to the scent of the wine."

My cheeks were hot. "Of course. I . . . to be honest, most of the wine I drink is of the cooler variety."

One of his perfectly shaped black eyebrows arched. "As in chilled? White or sparkling?"

"No, as in Seagram's."

He stared at me for a moment, and then it all seemed to click into place, because he threw his head back and laughed, a sound so melodious that it made me smile despite all my worries, and despite the dull pain taking shape at the back of my skull.

"You must give me the pleasure of educating you," he said, then gestured at the bartender, who immediately brought over two glasses and a bottle of wine.

"Oh—I need a separate tab, though," I said as the bartender began to walk away.

"Comp it," said the man next to me, and the bartender nodded.

I eyed my gorgeous wine tutor as he poured. "Um, hi. My name's Mattie."

"I am Tavana," he said, then tapped his glass to mine. "Lift that up and give it a swirl to release the bouquet."

I did as he suggested, inhaling the tart, fruity scent. "It does smell good."

"Good?" He made a distressed noise in his throat. "You must do better than that. To really enjoy wine, you must pay attention to nuance, Mattie. You have to open your senses so you detect each flavor note. You cannot enjoy it to its fullest otherwise." He tilted his elegant, straight nose over the rim of his glass, then inhaled deeply and closed his eyes. "Ah. Berries. Vanilla. Leather."

"Leather?"

His full lips curved into a smile. "A savory note that balances the sweetness."

I sniffed at the wine again. "Sure," I said slowly. "I think I'm picking that up. Can we drink it now?"

He lifted the glass. "By all means."

He took a generous sip, and so did I. My mouth immediately felt a little too dry, so I took another swig. Tavana's eyes were half-closed as he swallowed. "There," he said. "What do you think?"

"I think it's over my head. But it's still yummy." I drank a little more.

Tavana frowned and tilted his head. "I think I may have misunderstood your purpose for coming here."

"Here?" My heart jolted in my chest. "Oh, I'm just here to gamble."

"I meant to this bar, before the dinner hour, alone. I simply saw a lovely lady and wanted to share a pleasant drink, but it appears that sipping is not your purpose."

As he'd been talking, I'd been gulping down my wine, and I'd set my empty glass down by the end of his sentence. He chuckled again. "And there you have it."

I sagged on my stool. "Sorry. You're right—I wasn't really looking for a wine-tasting lesson."

"What *are* you looking for, Mattie?"

"To be honest, I don't really know."

"Can I do something to make your stay more pleasurable?"

"You work here?"

He nodded. "I'm a concierge of sorts. I'm just not tied to the front desk."

"Good, because that sounds uncomfortable." I glanced at the clock that hung at one end of the bar, wishing I had time for a nap, because my dull headache was taking on an edge. But I was supposed to meet Asa in less than an hour. I slid off my stool and smiled at Tavana. "Thanks so much for the wine."

He leaned on the bar, his gaze lazily drifting up my body as I took a step back. "Thank you for the company, Mattie. I hope you find what you're seeking."

I gave him a noncommittal smile and treated myself to one long look at his face, because it really was like a work of art, too pretty to touch. "Me too." I turned and headed for the shops. The guards nodded at me but didn't move in my direction. "Point, Mattie," I whispered as I walked into the first boutique I found.

Asa had told me to look nice, so I walked out twenty minutes later with the most expensive outfit I'd ever owned, hoping that I hadn't tapped out my entire share of the commission. After a quick shower, a heavy dose of Advil for my headache, and the application of some expensive product just for curly hair that I'd picked up at the hotel salon, I pulled the dress onto my body and inspected the results in the mirror. The amber material fit like a glove and shimmered when I turned. It had a deep V-neckline that rocked the girls, if you get my drift. The strappy heels elongated my legs and showed off my calves. I slid on some blush, went light on the mascara, and applied some shimmery red gloss, just in time to answer the door when Asa knocked.

Now, I had spent part of the afternoon with a guy who looked like a supermodel, so it was a testament to Asa's transformation that my breath caught as I swung the door open and saw him standing there. He was wearing slim black slacks and a suit vest that fit him like it had been tailored, clinging to his lean frame and accentuating the breadth of his shoulders. His white dress shirt and black tie were relatively conservative, but the heavy leather belt around his narrow hips sent a very different message. He'd shaved, so his face was all chiseled angles, and . . . had he put gel in his short, dark hair? "Damn," I said when I found my voice again. "You clean up nice."

"Same," he said, though he was busy looking up and down the hall instead of at me, fidgety as usual. "Ready?"

"Can we talk about what we're doing?" I asked. "Once again, I'm about fifty-seven steps behind you."

He glanced at my shoes. "And in those, you'll never catch up."

I let out a frustrated breath and winced as my head began to pound again. "You told me to look nice!"

He held his hands up. "Sorry." He took me by the shoulders and guided me back into my room, and I felt a moment of fear as he pushed me onto the bed and knelt in front of me.

He pulled a patch of wire bristles from his pocket, maybe the size of a dime. "Want to give this a try? I made it small. We could fasten it just under your big toe."

So I could avoid manipulation—as long as I was paying attention. "Yeah. Thanks."

Asa grunted and tugged my shoe off, then fastened the bristles using superglue he also just happened to be toting. "And in answer to your question—I'm going to play, and you're going to watch." He stood up, leaving me to put the shoe back on by myself.

"That's it?"

His eyes met mine. "That's it. If you get any weird vibes, tap me on the shoulder."

"Aren't vibes more your territory?"

"Just watch my back, okay?" he asked, sounding exasperated. "I need to concentrate while I'm down there."

I watched him for a moment. His edginess had only increased. He had to be tired, and he was in a place that was reportedly dripping with magic. He probably had a headache, too. Coming here was clearly not pleasant for him.

I just wished I knew he had made the journey for the right reasons. "Okay," I said. "I'll watch your back."

We set out, riding the elevator down to a lounge called Risko. "That's not a very clever name," I said as the host ushered us through the door.

"No one comes here just for pun, Mattie," Asa said, and for a second, he flashed a half smile.

I followed him as he sauntered over to the roulette wheel, where the dealer was costumed in heavily embroidered robes, long black fingernails, and a golden medallion with a dragon on it that swung like a pendulum with every spin of the wheel. Several people were clamoring to place their bets, pushing chips across a board arrayed with numbers, red and black patches, the words "odd" and "even," and a few other choices. The placard on the table indicated the minimum bet was a hundred, and there was no hint of a maximum.

"Placing a bet, sir?" The dealer looked at Asa, her eyebrows raised.

"Mm," said Asa. He pulled out his wallet and laid several hundreds on the space between the dealer and the stacks of chips she was doling out. "Let me see what I can do." He winked at her as he accepted his chips.

I moved close to watch. The table was crowded, so there were chips all over the place, and the players were elbowing each other in an attempt to place their bets—it seemed like they all wanted the same thing at the same time, either red or black, odd or even. The dealer observed the melee, muttering under her breath. I glanced at the chips. I kind of wanted to place a bet, too. And as six people all pushed their chips toward red, I knew that was the best decision ever. Definitely a winner.

But then Asa put all his chips on black. I grabbed for them. "No, put them on red!"

The dealer smiled at me, and I smiled back as she set the wheel in motion. But just as she did, Asa put his hand over mine and prevented me from moving his chips. "This is nothing like a game of *jacks*, am I right?" he asked as he pulled my hand away.

I blinked up at him. "What?"

His eyes widened as he stared at me, and then he put his foot on top of my toe and applied just enough pressure for me to feel the bite of the metal bristles.

"Oh! Oh." I shook my head. "*Nooo.* Nothing like jacks."

Asa had already turned back to the dealer, who was no longer smiling. "I've always been a bit of a black sheep," he told her as the ball settled into number twenty-two, a black notch on the wheel. Everyone except for Asa slumped in defeat.

He cashed in his winnings and moved on to blackjack, where he stared down the bespectacled dealer and walked away with a tall stack of chips, which he in turn carried over to the poker table. Now that I had my toe crimped over those painful little bristles, I could see it all—each dealer must have been either a natural Knedas or wearing a relic full of manipulation magic. They were subtly influencing the players. Not every time, and not enough to clean them out, but enough so that the house had a massive advantage.

Asa requested a glass of water from a willowy waitress and then took a seat. I stood behind him, sipping very slowly on a cucumber gin and tonic he'd ordered for me. Sweat was trickling down Asa's jaw as he sized up the other players, and I saw his gaze zero in on a fat guy right next to him. He reminded me of a bullfrog with his bulging eyes and double chin. The man was flipping a poker chip across the backs of his knuckles as he waited for his cards.

Asa grinned at the guy and spoke in a low voice. "Look at this table of stoics, eh?" He gestured at the others, who definitely had their game faces on. "They don't make it easy to spot those tells."

The bullfrog man grunted. "Easy is for pussies."

The corner of Asa's eye twitched. "You can say that again." He focused on the guy's fingers as they fiddled with the chip, which was black and inscribed with dark-red runes, same as the chips in one of the stacks in front of Asa.

They played a hand or two, and it was obvious Mr. Bullfrog was good. A small crowd had gathered to spectate, and I looked over each face, remembering Asa's request for me to watch his back. Whatever his intentions, I felt like I should at least try to do what he'd asked right now. There was something about the slight tremble in his hands as he held his cards that made my stomach hurt. My headache had subsided, and I was feeling loose from the alcohol, but I kept rubbing my toe over the bristles, on the lookout for manipulation. But with this poker game, I wasn't seeing it. The only thing I was noticing was that Mr. Bullfrog was cleaning up—and Asa's chips were dwindling.

But then, between hands, as the waitress was refreshing drinks and the dealer was cashing someone out, Asa's fingers trailed up my arm. It sent a shiver down my spine so sudden that I nearly spilled my drink in his lap. His hand closed around the nape of my neck as he tilted his head back, and then he pulled my face down to his, pausing when our lips were only millimeters apart. "Hi there," he whispered, giving me a lazy smile.

"Hi," I managed.

He slid my drink out of my grasp and set it on the table, then caught my hand and ran his thumb along my palm in a slow circle. "What are you doing later? I think I'm going to need some consolation."

He's playing, I reminded myself, wishing my heart would stop its mad gallop. So many things were wrong with this—how close he was, the heat of his hand on the back of my neck, the way one sudden move would bring our mouths together. Oh, and how I was bent over him, giving half the people at the table a view straight down the front of my dress. I needed this to stop. "It's a date," I said breathlessly. "Just—"

He grinned and let me go, and I stood up, my cheeks on fire, especially when I realized that Mr. Bullfrog was still leering at my chest. "I'd be tempted to lose, too, if I had something like that waiting for me," he said to Asa.

I scowled at him. "Hey, buddy. I'm a some*one*. Not a some*thing*."

Asa bowed his head, his shoulders shaking. "Damn straight. Except you *are* kinda something." Then he took a deep breath and raised his head, and when I looked down, I saw that he was now flipping a black chip over his knuckles, one just like Mr. Bullfrog's.

Mr. Bullfrog had noticed, too, and was looking back and forth from his own chip to Asa's, his wide mouth drooping into a frown. The frown deepened as he lost the next hand. And the next, and the next.

Asa was on a tear. He systematically knocked three of the players out before Mr. Bullfrog finally gave up. And as soon as he did, Asa announced he'd had enough and was cashing out. He smiled down at the black chip in his palm. "Thanks for the inspiration," he said, then flipped it onto the swell of Mr. Bullfrog's round belly as the man pushed away from the table.

As soon as the chip landed, Mr. Bullfrog's frown turned to a grimace. "You smug son of a bitch!" he barked—just as the dealer waved over a security guard.

Asa took a few steps back from the table and looked around, and it was only then I remembered that I was supposed to be watching his back. I'd been so riveted on the game that I'd lost track, though, and now I realized that there were a few well-dressed men standing at the bar and a nearby table, watching Asa with interest.

One of them was Tavana.

Asa took my hand. "Time to go for a walk, Mattie." He led me out of the lounge.

"What just happened?" I whispered. "Was that chip a relic?"

Asa nodded as he headed for the front doors of the hotel, walking fast enough that I was nearly jogging to keep up, and with each step, my toe clamped down on those stupid bristles. "It was emotion-sensing magic," he said. "That guy was using it to read the other players."

"But how did you end up with it?"

Asa waggled his eyebrows at me. "You helped."

Of course. Asa had used me to distract the guy, and the rest was simple sleight of hand. "You are so—"

"Oh, I am. I am indeed. Ready to jump into the fire? Not that you have a choice at this point."

"What?" He was nearly dragging me now, out to the wide plaza at the front of the hotel, where a huge expanse of glittering runes were pressed into the glazed cement. I yanked my hand away, all of Jack's warnings ringing in my head. "Asa, tell me what we're—"

"We're going to stand where half of fucking Vegas can see us. It's not complicated."

We'd reached the middle of the plaza, and Asa stopped and spun around abruptly. "I could feel your ooze the moment I hit the parking garage," he spat out.

My heart was in my throat as I turned to see Tavana standing maybe thirty feet away. He'd come to a stop, too.

Asa's hand slipped under his vest, and he pulled that black cylindrical handle thing, which I assumed was some sort of weapon, from his belt. "I must have ruffled some feathers if you decided to deal with this yourself."

Tavana smiled. "Nonsense. I hope you enjoyed the game. You really did a lovely job there. But it seems like it took a lot out of you."

I glanced up at Asa. Sweat was beaded across his forehead. It was a warm night, to be sure, but he looked like he'd just trekked across the Sahara. "Fuck you, Reza," he growled.

"He told me his name was Tavana," I said weakly.

"Tavana's his fucking last name," Asa said, looking at me like I'd betrayed him. "You met him earlier? And you didn't *tell me*?"

I shrank back. "I thought he was the concierge!"

Asa's jaw was rigid as he returned his attention to Reza, clutching that black handle thing with a white-knuckled grip. "It would look bad," Asa said, nodding toward a group of tourists, mostly elderly, who had just gotten off a bus in front of the entrance to Mistika, "if you tried to take me down right here in the middle of this plaza. You really want to do this?"

"Absolutely not. You're overreacting. Brawling in the plaza is not on our agenda this evening. Creating lasting partnerships, though—"

"Fuck you. You know what I came for."

Reza's dark eyes flared with what looked like amusement. "Oh, no. I know what *Mattie* came for. You? We had to take a leap of faith. But it seems that faith was well-placed."

Asa cursed again. "I knew it."

Reza let his eyes drift up Asa's body, just like he'd done to me this afternoon. And unlike me, he seemed to know exactly why Asa was so pissed. "We'll be happy to let you see Dr. Ward. He's a personal guest of Mr. Brindle's."

I nearly fell to the ground, the relief was so heavy. "Really?" Tears flooded my eyes. "Is he all right?"

Reza nodded. "I'll take you to him, as soon as we settle some business." His gaze settled on Asa again. "Welcome to Las Vegas, Asa Ward. Mr. Brindle is *so* looking forward to finally meeting you."

CHAPTER THIRTEEN

It had been about Asa the whole time, and he'd known it.

I wasn't sure what to think about that as I stood next to him, watching him glare at Reza Tavana with sweat running down his angular face. So many things didn't make sense.

"Reel it in, asshole," Asa snapped. "If you can."

Reza took a step back. "I can hardly help the fact that you are so . . . *exquisitely* sensitive." His voice was a caress, but it made me shudder. He was a Strikon, apparently very strong, and from the way he was looking at Asa, I was betting he was enjoying his effect on him. I couldn't feel a thing—but I did wonder if my headache earlier had come from sitting right next to Reza at the bar. "I'll try to control myself, though," he added with a seductive curve of his lips.

Asa let out a shuddery breath. "You guys went to a hell of a lot of trouble on my account."

Reza shrugged. "We are in great need." He gestured magnanimously at three men who had joined him. "I promise no harm will come to you, but I am going to have to ask that we take this inside." He glanced at a group of college-aged girls and guys who were giggling and joking with each other as they passed by, headed for Mistika. "Privacy is required, I think."

Hatred was etched in the lines around Asa's mouth. "In an enclosed space with you? No fucking way."

Reza put his hands up. "I will take my leave of you. My associates will escort you to Mr. Brindle."

"And Ben?" I asked.

Reza turned his gorgeous smile on me. "Of course, Mattie. As soon as Asa hammers out a few details with us."

I looked up at Asa to find him staring down at me. I didn't know whether to apologize to him, thank him, or smack him on the arm for not explaining things to me. "Will you do it?"

He swiped his sleeve across his face. "Yeah," he said quietly, flipping the handle thing in his palm and sliding it back under his vest.

You love Ben after all, I thought.

Reza clapped his hands, just once, like he was delighted. "Until later, then," he said to us, then strode down the street, away from the hotel.

The farther away Reza got, the better Asa looked. As we followed Brindle's men back into Mistika, Asa's strides became smoother and his shoulders relaxed. He was still grim and pale, but no longer seemed a second away from collapsing. Brindle's agents, or guards, or whatever they were—all of them were sharply dressed young men toting no obvious weapons, but they carried themselves with the same smooth confidence Reza had—led us through the main lobby and down a hallway to a restaurant called Odorajxon.

I squinted up at the sign, and Asa let out a low chuckle. "That one's not so obvious, is it?"

"I can't even pronounce it." I gave him a little smile. It was strangely good to hear him laugh, even if it was at me.

Our procession wound its way past leather booths, the now-familiar runes carved into the borders around the edges of the tables. My stomach growled ferociously, and despite the bustling noise of the restaurant, one of the agents looked over his shoulder at me. "We'll get you something to eat soon," he said with a wink.

"He can feel your hunger," Asa said, leaning down to speak in my ear.

"Wait—can you, too?"

"Nah, I just heard that little monster inside you let out a roar."

I nodded at the agent's back. "So he's a sensor?"

"But not for emotion. For . . . bodily sensations, I guess you'd say."

"Great. So if I'm feeling gassy, he'll know."

Asa snorted and looked away. "*Dammit*, Mattie," he muttered.

I craned my neck as we exited the main restaurant and entered a warmly lit hallway. My whole body felt like it had been strung with live wires—was Ben close by? How much longer until I would see him? My hope was increasing by the second.

The agents reached a room with an arched entrance and parted the thick curtains that blocked the view from the hall. Inside was a sumptuously decorated room with gorgeous murals on the walls, lush flowering plants and a fountain in the corner, several doors to places unknown, and one large booth, at which sat an incredibly fat man with bushy brown eyebrows and pitted skin. He was bald, and it looked like a helmet of shiny, peachy skin had been crammed over his skull—but the flesh at his chin and neck hadn't fit, and it sat all flabby and loose on his round shoulders. He held a tumbler of amber liquid in his hand, and when we entered, he held it up, his face brightening.

"Ah, Mr. Ward! At last," he said in a deep, gravelly voice. He beckoned to us, inviting Asa to join him in the booth. "Come and let me look at you!"

A hand closed around my upper arm, keeping me from moving forward as Asa did. One of the agents, this one with short blond hair, had restrained me. "What about her, Mr. Brindle?" he asked.

"She's with me," Asa said without turning around.

"Really, Mr. Ward," said Frank Brindle. "We'll only be discussing details, and I'm sure dear Miss Carver would be bored. Besides, I wanted to introduce you to Lila, as I'm sure you two will want to get to know each other." He gestured to one corner of the room, where a stately woman who looked to be in her late thirties stood, her shoulders straight and her reddish hair in an elegant twist, wearing a black business suit.

Asa narrowed his eyes at Lila, sizing her up. "Nope. That's not how this is going to go down. Mattie's my reliquary."

Frank's bushy eyebrows shot up. "What?" He gave his agents a stern look. "I thought she was a veterinarian's assistant."

"Oh, I am," I said. "This is my side gig."

"But Lila is the best."

Asa tugged me out of the blond agent's grasp. "Mattie's better."

"You don't know me, Mr. Ward," Lila said in a crisp English accent.

Asa glared at her as he slowly and deliberately tapped the tip of his crooked nose.

Frank cleared his throat. "Allow me to state the purpose of this little gathering, and perhaps we can discuss details later. I am in need of the best magic sniffer there is."

"Don't you have one of your own?" I asked.

He sighed, producing a ponderous, wet flapping of his thick lips. "Well, I did. But poor Wendell . . . may he rest in peace."

"Oh. My condolences," I said.

Asa muttered something under his breath, but I didn't catch it, and if Frank did, he seemed willing to ignore it. "We tried to reach out to you through your contacts but received no answer," he said to Asa.

"Did you ever stop to think that maybe it was because I wasn't interested in talking to you?"

Frank smiled, revealing his yellow teeth. "And yet here you are. Brotherly love wins the day. Imagine how fortunate we felt when we discovered the existence of Benjamin Ward, late of Rockford, Illinois, where you yourself engaged in some youthful shenanigans."

Asa's jaw was clenched, but Frank didn't seem fazed by his hostility. "And," he continued, "imagine how motivated we felt when we realized he was in dire need of assistance to prevent Zhong Lei's Strikon from paying him and his lovely fiancée a visit."

A chill ran down my spine.

"So you sent fucking Reza instead?" Asa's lip curled.

Frank rubbed his belly. "Reza was gentle."

"Reza pulled Ben's pacemaker out of his chest," I said, my voice cracking as I remembered the moment I found it.

"Ah, but he had an Ekstazo healer with him. Ben was never in any real danger." His pale-blue eyes focused on Asa. "We just needed to get your attention."

"You're lucky Mattie loves him," Asa grumbled, looking away.

"Come and sit," Frank said, flicking his fingers at a waiter, who disappeared through a swinging door on the other side of the room. "Let's discuss the possibilities for collaboration over dinner."

A moment later, several waiters came in, carrying platters laden with food. Asa sidled over to the booth like a wary coyote and sat right on the edge of the seat, looking like he was ready to flee if given the right reason. I sat across from him because he gave no indication he was willing to scoot over.

As soon as Asa was settled, one of the waiters put several plates in front of him: a few different kinds of salad, some kind of sushi-looking roll thing, fruit kebabs, and a creamy soup.

"It's all organic, vegan, and raw," Frank said as a waiter set a plate of filet mignon a few inches from the enormous swell of his belly, and another in front of me.

Asa looked startled, and Frank merely grinned. "We did want to make sure you were comfortable, Mr. Ward."

"By interrogating my contacts?"

"By inquiring as to your preferences," Frank said smoothly before turning to me. He laid his chubby hand over mine, and it was warm and reassuring. "And you, my dear? Forgive me, but we were not attentive enough to see to your needs. You are a bit of a surprise."

Asa chuckled, seemingly to himself.

I glanced over at Lila, who was still standing in the corner, as if waiting to be invited to the table. "I'll eat just about anything."

"Mattie likes fries," Asa said, picking up his fork. "And Pringles. Also, Twizzlers. *Loves* Twizzlers."

I couldn't tell if it was a dig or not, but I couldn't bring myself to be offended. "I eat plenty of other things, too."

He smirked and dug into his food. "Oh," he said between bites. "And Frank's an Ekstazo, Mattie. You keep holding his hand like that, and you'll be high as a kite before the second course."

I yanked my fingers from beneath Frank's heavy hand. "That was sneaky, Mr. Brindle."

The man chuckled good-naturedly. "Habit, my dear. I mean no harm." He took a sip from his tumbler. "Shall we talk business?" He motioned Lila over to the table, but she hadn't taken two steps when Asa looked up from his food.

"Out," he said to her. "I wasn't kidding when I said I wouldn't work with you."

Frank frowned. "I selected her especially for this job."

"I'll bet." Asa swallowed the bite of salad he'd been chewing and sat back. "You want someone to babysit me and report back, to make sure I'm still in the pocket."

"This is a sensitive matter."

"Then send me with someone I trust." Asa looked at me, then averted his gaze just as quickly.

I stared at him, an unexpectedly warm feeling stirring in my chest.

"But Frank trusts *me*," said Lila, then clamped her lips shut as Frank's eyes cut over to her. He regarded her for a moment, the conflict clear on his face. Then he waved Lila away. She scowled at me but exited quickly through the curtains.

"Now that we've lost our extra baggage," Asa said as he started eating again, "you can tell me what exactly you want." He shoved a huge forkful of salad into his mouth.

Frank grinned at him, as if taking pleasure in Asa's enjoyment of his food. "It's quite simple. I need you to go to Bangkok and collect a relic, then bring it back to me. I'll provide your transportation and accommodation."

"Mattie'll need papers," Asa said without looking up from his plate.

"I will have them waiting for you in San Francisco, along with your tickets."

Asa plucked a strawberry off the end of a kebab. "Who has the relic now?"

Frank spun a gold ring around his thick index finger. "It is currently in the possession of Sukrit Montri."

Asa swallowed his strawberry and stared at Frank. "You want me to steal a relic from the Thai boss."

"Well, it's not really his. He just happens to have it right now."

"Asa doesn't like semantics," I babbled as I took a bite of the filet, which practically melted in my mouth. I couldn't remember when I'd had a better steak.

"Mattie." Asa's voice jarred me to attention. "Jacks."

"What? Oh!" I pressed my toe to the bristles he'd pasted to my shoe, and it was a little like a fog clearing. I'd had no idea that Frank was having that effect on me, but as soon as the pain zinged through me, so did reality. "So you're saying that my fiancé's life depends on whether Asa and I can steal some relic from a boss—one like you?" I looked over to the curtains, where I could see the silhouettes of Brindle's guards hovering in the hallway.

"We don't have to put it so bluntly," said Frank with a smile.

I pushed my toe harder onto the bristles. "But it would save time if we were just honest." My heart had started to pound. "You'll let him go if we bring you this magic?"

Frank nodded. "You have my word."

Asa pushed an empty plate away and pulled his soup toward him. "And that's all you want. One job."

"It's a big job, young man."

"Kinda figured." Asa hunched over his soup and set to work.

I bit my lip. "What kind of magic is it?"

"Strikon," said Frank.

Asa paused with his spoon halfway toward his mouth. His gaze flicked to me, and then he continued eating. "Type?"

"Not really known," said Frank. "It's fairly old."

"So the natural who produced it is dead."

"Oh, yes." Frank smiled. "Long since dead. And it's apparently one of a kind. Hence my interest. I'm a bit of a collector."

"Yeah, I can feel it," Asa said quietly.

"You'd be feeling it more if I didn't keep my relics properly packaged," Frank replied. "And I have no doubt Montri does as well."

"What does 'properly packaged' mean?" I asked.

"It just means it's kept in some sort of reliquary," Asa said. "An object, not a person, though."

"You may have to be quite close to sense it," said Frank, polishing off his drink. "And you must transfer it to your reliquary as quickly as possible. It's valuable. Montri will not be happy to lose it. We'll have a private plane waiting at the airport, as exiting the city will likely be much more difficult than entering, even with a good reliquary." He eyed me. "Are you sure about this, my dear? Forgive me, but you don't sound very experienced."

"You've got my fiancé, Mr. Brindle. I'd do anything. Also, I'm apparently a vault."

"Strongest I ever met, bar none," Asa said, though now he looked a little conflicted at getting me involved.

Frank peered at me, his blue eyes intent. "Well, I suppose you do have every reason to carry out this job and bring my relic home to me."

I decided not to remind him that it didn't seem like it was *his* relic.

Asa sighed and set his spoon in his empty soup bowl. "Okay. When do we leave?"

"You leave for San Francisco tonight. You'll get your papers and tickets in the afternoon. You will depart for Bangkok on Friday at noon."

"I need to see Ben before we go anywhere," I said, my voice high and clear.

Frank pushed a button on his phone, which was sitting on the table next to his empty glass. "I've simply been waiting for you to ask. I expect you both have been so worried about him. I'm sorry this little game is necessary."

Asa stared at Frank. "All for this one relic."

Frank gave Asa a friendly, relaxed smile. "I'm very interested in the magic of this particular natural. It's important to me."

"Mattie?"

The sound of Ben's voice brought me out of the booth so fast that my half-full plate went sliding to the floor, shattering on the marble. But I barely noticed.

Ben stood near the kitchens, beside an open door leading to a small room, his fair hair tousled, his brown eyes riveted on me and shining with emotion. "Oh my God," he whispered.

With a sob, I ran to him, and he caught me in his arms and lifted me up, tilting his head back to kiss me. "I can't believe you're here." His voice broke over the words, but I couldn't speak at all. I wrapped my arms around his neck and kissed him for all I was worth. So many days of worrying, so many nights of crying myself to sleep, and here he was, looking as perfect and healthy as the last time I'd seen him. He met my passion with gusto, his arm wrapped around my waist, one of his hands in my hair. The entire room disappeared, and it was just me and Ben, a world unto ourselves.

By the time he put me down, both of us were shaking. "I wasn't sure I'd ever see you again," he said, laughing as he swiped a tear off his face.

I squeezed his hands, hungrily looking him over. "We have a lot to talk about," I told him. I'd gone over this speech in my head a thousand times as Asa had driven in silence down the highway, knowing that if I ever did see Ben again, I might be too relieved to remember it otherwise. "I found out some things about you when you were gone, some things you did—"

"I know, I know. I'm so sorry." Ben's eyes clamped shut, and his face radiated pain. "I made so many mistakes. I've spent every minute of the past week and a half praying I would have the chance to make it up to you."

"You'd better," I said in a strained voice, then laid my head on his shoulder and breathed him in.

"I never wanted you to get wrapped up in this, Mattie."

"You never should have kept it from me. Especially because it turns out that I'm a part of this world, too."

"What?"

I looked up at him. "Yeah. I only found out by accident when I ran into Asa at . . ."

I had turned to my partner in crime—but he was gone. So was Frank. Sometime during my reunion with Ben, they had cleared out and I hadn't even noticed. "He *is* a good skulker," I muttered.

"He can't even stand to be in the same room with me. I'm shocked he even came. I told them he wouldn't," Ben said, frowning at the empty booth. "But I guess they're offering him a lot of money now that he's here."

"I don't think that's why he came, Ben." I was still staring at the place Asa had been sitting a moment ago.

Sarah Fine

"How did you even find him?"

I explained how it had happened, and Ben listened with wide eyes. "And now you're going to Bangkok as Asa's reliquary?" His brows lowered. "Is he . . . treating you all right?"

"Asa's a little prickly, but I can handle him."

"'A little prickly'?" He let out a strangled laugh. "Okay."

I ran my hands down Ben's sleeves. "Can we talk about you? When I saw your pacemaker in the mailbox—"

Ben swallowed hard. "I'm okay. One of the guys had a healing touch. It was temporary, but it saved me." He sighed and stepped back.

I held his hands tight. "But?"

"Apparently, Frank has a piece of magic that could make it permanent. It's in one of his relics. He said he would give it to me." He wasn't meeting my eyes.

"Okay," I said slowly. "What's the catch?"

"It all depends on Asa," he said bitterly. "Basically, my brother, who kind of hates me, gets to decide my fate."

A tiny streak of frustration zipped through me. "He agreed to do the job, didn't he? We leave tonight!"

"Asa will get paid, Mattie. And Frank says he'll let me go once you guys are back." He pulled me to him and kissed the top of my head. "So you'd better make sure you stay safe. It's just that . . . screw it. Never mind."

I frowned, even as I held him close, relishing the planes of his muscular body, his familiar warmth after so much strangeness. "Haven't you kept enough secrets from me?"

"I'm sorry. You're so right," he murmured in my ear. "I just didn't want to put pressure on anyone. I don't want more bad blood between me and Asa, and I can't ask him for this myself."

"What are you talking about?"

"Frank promised me . . ." He took my face in his hands and made sure I was looking at him. "He told me that he would give me the relic

148

that would heal my heart permanently, but only if Asa agreed to join Frank's team."

"His . . . team?"

"Yeah. Frank's magic sensor passed away a few weeks ago, and he needs a new one. Apparently Asa is the best." Ben chuckled. "Who knew? I thought he'd be drunk in a ditch somewhere, and it turns out he's built this reputation and now all these people want to hire him." He tilted his head as my brow furrowed. "What's wrong?"

"It's just . . . Asa's not really a team player."

He rolled his eyes. "Well, that's one thing that hasn't changed. But I need this, Mattie. I can already feel the healing magic fading away, and I need to feel whole." He grimaced. "I don't think I've felt that way since I was first diagnosed with this stupid heart condition. I think it's why I got so wrapped up in the magic—it felt so good that I forgot how broken I was."

"But you were never broken. You were always perfect." I ran my finger down his straight nose.

He gave me a sad smile. "You know I wasn't. But I want to be, Mattie. For you. For the family we're going to have together. I want to live a long life and take care of you and our kids."

"I want that, too," I said softly. "That's why I'm here."

"Will you help me, then? If you got Asa to come here, you could convince him to take this job. Mr. Brindle takes good care of his staff."

"Asa *chose* to come here, Ben. I couldn't have convinced him of anything if he hadn't wanted to do it."

Ben stroked his thumbs down my cheeks. "You're underestimating yourself. Will you try to convince him? For me?"

I stared up at the man I loved, pushing down the uneasy feeling that had risen inside me. "Sure," I whispered. "I'll try. For you."

CHAPTER FOURTEEN

We rode to the airport in one of Frank Brindle's limos and flew to San Francisco on his private jet. Asa was silent throughout, but he also seemed less twitchy. Maybe now that he knew for sure what he needed to do, he was able to relax. Or maybe all that nervous energy had shifted to me. I could barely stay in my seat.

We'd found Ben. But now he was essentially a hostage, his life hanging in the balance, dependent on whether Asa and I could steal a valuable relic right from under the nose of the most powerful and dangerous man in Thailand. And on top of that, I was supposed to be convincing Asa to work for Frank so that Ben could have the healing magic he needed.

My fingertip slid over the slight indentation on my ring finger, now bare. I'd given my engagement ring to Ben for safekeeping. He swore when I returned that he'd get down on one knee and propose all over again. It had hurt to leave him, but it had only made me more determined to get him back, whole and healthy.

I rubbed the padded leather armrest of my cushy seat as we began to descend into the Bay Area. "I feel like a celebrity. Frank knows how to treat his employees, doesn't he?"

Asa, who'd been staring out his window at the glowing lights at the edge of the ocean, leaned his head back against his seat. "That's like saying a cat pampers the mice it catches."

"I don't think he's planning to eat us."

Asa pulled his gaze from the night sky and leveled it at me. "More like he's playing before he bites our heads off."

"Why would he do that? We can do stuff for him."

"Sure," he said faintly. "We're useful. Just like Wendell was."

"His magic sniffer who passed away? He seemed really sad about that."

Asa rubbed his hands over his face. Dark circles lay beneath his eyes. "No doubt. Notice he didn't mention how poor old Wendell died."

"You think he had him killed?"

Very slowly, Asa raised two fingers to his temple, cocked his thumb, and pretended to blow his brains out. "Bet you everything I own."

"But you don't know for sure."

Asa sighed, returning his attention to the view out the window. I eyed the taut lines of his shoulders and the sharp edge of his jaw, and then decided not to question him further. He obviously wasn't eager to work for Frank, and I had a feeling if I talked up the job too much, Asa would be on to me in a second.

We arrived at the airport to find another car waiting, which took us to the Fairmont Hotel in a neighborhood called Nob Hill. I spent the ride reeling from the irony—I hadn't done much traveling in my life, and already today I'd checked into two fancy hotels in two different states, flown on a private jet, and ridden in a few limos . . . but instead of sharing this experience with the love of my life, here I was with his surly brother. Asa had said he trusted me, but with the way he was acting now, barely looking at me, barely talking to me, I was starting to think he should have added "relatively speaking" to his declaration.

We had rooms on the same floor. Asa peeled off quickly, suggesting only that we meet for dinner late the next evening to talk over a plan for when we arrived in Bangkok. I was left standing in the hall with the bellboy, feeling strangely squirmy. It wasn't that I was so eager to hang out with Asa, but it felt like we had things to talk about. Or, one thing at least. Ben.

Knowing my love was safe and sound for the moment, I woke up the next morning determined to make the most of my time in San Francisco. After calling my mother and assuring her I was still having a restful time—and then frantically dissuading her from joining me at my little lakeside spa for the weekend—I set out to explore the city. I stuffed my face with a hot fudge sundae in Ghirardelli Square, amused myself for a few minutes watching the sea lions sunning themselves on the little rafts at Pier 39, toured a bakery and ate a whole sourdough pepperoni pizza, then hiked up and down the ridiculous hills of the city. I didn't want to stop moving, because then I would have to think. But just after the sun sank into the ocean, as if it were beckoning me from across the sea, luring me toward Bangkok, I started to make my way back to the hotel. It was a longer walk than I'd thought, though, and now I was going to be late. I had no idea how Asa had spent his day, but I hoped he was in a decent mood, because I was starting to get jittery as heck.

That might be why I realized I was being followed. I was nearing the edge of Chinatown when a little chill went right down my spine, and I looked over my shoulder to see a guy duck quickly into a shop. Telling myself it was nothing, I continued on, but my heart wouldn't slow down. I was maybe six blocks from the hotel, but suddenly I couldn't get there fast enough. I began to jog, glancing over my shoulder every few steps, slowing a little when I didn't see anyone behind me. It was nearly nine, and I was no longer in a touristy part of town, so it wasn't as if the sidewalks were packed. It would be tough to tail me without being spotted. I shook my head and laughed, then started to walk. "You're acting like Asa," I muttered.

I turned the corner and collided with someone coming the opposite direction. My breath was knocked out of me, and I stumbled back and had the impression of a man leaning forward to catch me.

As soon as his hands touched mine, my world exploded in a fiery burst of agony. Like my bones were its superhighway, the pain shot up my arms, across my shoulders, down my spine, and across my ribs. I tried to scream, but I couldn't draw any air into my lungs.

And then it stopped suddenly, and I found myself crumpled against a brick wall in a little courtyard, its gate hanging open. In front of me was a playground, and to my left was a long narrow pathway, maybe to another side street. A man loomed over me, tall and thickly muscled, dressed all in black, with dark eyes and ebony hair. As he leaned into the light from a streetlamp, I recognized him as one of Zhong Lei's crew who had chased us through Chicago. He was also, obviously, a Strikon. He flexed his fingers. "Make a sound, and I'll do that again," he said quietly.

"What do you want?" I asked, still trying to catch my breath.

"Information," he said with a tilt of his head. "About the job you and Ward are doing for Brindle."

I pressed my back against the wall as he took a step toward me. "No idea what you're talking about. I just spent the day at Fisherman's Wharf."

The Strikon smiled. "Mr. Zhong is a collector, you see, just like Mr. Brindle. He is interested in relics of particular value. And we can think of only one reason for Mr. Brindle to hire Mr. Ward and send him here. He is seeking something."

I glanced toward the street, wishing I had the strength to run. "Seriously. No clue."

My attacker ran his tongue along his bottom lip. "Do you really want me to touch you again?"

"No," I said, drawing my knees to my chest.

"Then tell me what you came here to find."

"A-a relic," I said.

He rolled his eyes. "Please do not insult me."

"But that's what it is! No—" My head slammed against brick as the Strikon stroked my cheek and sent a bolt of searing pain down my throat and into my gut.

"You really should be a nice girl and answer my questions honestly." He stepped back and leisurely pulled a knife from beneath his shirt. "Because I can make this hurt so much it will carve new trails in your brain, and your thoughts will be trapped in those little ruts forever, like rats in a maze. You'll never be the same." He smiled, obviously enjoying my fear as I whimpered and flinched away from him.

"It would be such a shame, wouldn't it?" he continued. "Because I know what you are. Zhi told Mr. Zhong *everything*. How would Mr. Ward feel if I broke his reliquary?"

"Mr. Ward would be pissed as hell." The voice came from the darkness to my left—a split second before Asa stepped out of it. In his hand was that sticklike black handle thing he carried with him. He did indeed look pissed as hell. And I was *really* glad to see him.

"Mr. Ward," said the Strikon, sounding amused as he twirled the knife in his fingers. "I was hoping you'd received my invitation."

Asa winced as something invisible passed between them, and I remembered what Asa had said about Reza—*I could feel your ooze the moment I hit the parking garage.* This guy probably knew Asa would sense him here.

He looked like he'd been counting on it, actually. "Come with me quietly, or there'll be more of that," he said to Asa, whose skin was draining of color.

Asa flicked his wrist, and the handle extended into a baton about two feet long. "Sorry. I've got dinner plans." He held his other hand out to me, but the Strikon stepped between us, the knife hanging from his fist—only a few feet from my face. With no warning, he slashed it forward, right at my cheek, and I didn't even have time to move.

But Asa did. He thrust his baton out and deflected the slash, stopping the blade inches from my skin. The Strikon took advantage of Asa's momentum and turned, grabbing Asa's outstretched arm and wrenching him forward. Asa hit the wall next to me with a crunch and a burst of breath, but then he ducked as the Strikon tried to stab him in the shoulder. I scrambled away as the blade hit brick, and Asa spun sharply and slammed his baton into the back of the Strikon's legs. The man staggered, but as Asa tried to sweep his feet out from under him, the Strikon recovered and delivered a hard backward kick to Asa's ribs. Blood trickled from the corner of Asa's mouth, and his face was twisted into a tight grimace as he used the baton to block stab after stab. They moved so fast that I couldn't tell who was winning, but Asa had begun to backtrack under the ferocity of the Strikon's attack, and maybe under the force of whatever painful magical vibes the guy was giving off.

I'd groped my way up the wall and gotten to my feet, but I was afraid to scream for help, because I didn't want to distract Asa for even a second. I didn't know how to help him. But then the Strikon's knife clattered to the ground, and I nearly let out a cheer. Asa bared his teeth as he sliced that baton through the air, but the Strikon blocked his arm with a bone-jarring strike and drove his fist into Asa's stomach. Asa bent double, and the Strikon kicked the baton from his hand and lunged at him. Asa landed on his back with the Strikon on top of him, the man's hands closing around Asa's throat.

Asa's eyes went wide as their skin touched, and he let out the most horrible sound. The Strikon straddled his chest. Asa's arms were free, but they were spread wide, twitching and flopping like they'd been disconnected from the rest of him. The Strikon's face split into an ecstatic smile as Asa arched back, obviously in blinding pain. He was helpless, but I wasn't. I ran forward and scooped Asa's baton from the asphalt, then held it like a bat and smacked it across the Strikon's back.

The Strikon cursed and twisted, lunging for me. I yelped and stumbled backward, swiping the baton through the air as the enraged agent powered himself to his feet. "Come here, little girl," he said between heavy breaths. "I was gentle before, but now—"

Asa plowed into his legs, and I dodged out of the way as they hit the ground again. This time, Asa was on the guy's back. Looking unsteady, Asa slammed his fist into the side of the Strikon's head. Asa's breath was harsh and his face was flushed. The Strikon shoved his hips up and rolled with Asa, slamming his elbow into Asa's solar plexus. I raised the baton to try to help, and the Strikon must have seen the movement in his periphery, because he turned to look.

It was the moment Asa needed. He threw himself on top of the Strikon again and punched the guy in the face. Asa's chin was smeared with blood, and his eyes were deep and dark as he jabbed his fist downward again and again. Veins stood out at his temples as he pinned the guy's shoulders to the ground and knocked the Strikon's scrabbling hands off his thighs. "Do you wanna see what's in my pocket?" Asa said, his voice broken by his wheezing breath. "Just so happens it's a present for you."

He punched the guy again and cursed. His fingers trembled as he unbuttoned one of his thigh pockets and pulled out the alien Pez dispenser. "Mattie," he snapped without looking at me. He extended his other hand. "Baton."

I rushed forward and slid it into his palm. Instead of hitting the guy with it, though, he flipped it upward and jammed the handle into the guy's mouth, prying his teeth open. As the Strikon continued to struggle, trying to buck Asa off, Asa lowered the dispenser to the guy's mouth and clicked the back of the alien's head several times.

The yellowish tablets fell between the guy's lips one after the other, at least six of them disappearing into the blackness of his mouth. He started to gag and thrash as Asa tossed the baton away. He pinched the guy's nostrils closed and clamped his hand under the guy's chin, holding his jaw shut. Asa's teeth gritted and his body shook, like it was taking all his strength to hold on.

Then he leaned down and said, very quietly, "Stop struggling."

The Strikon blinked up at him and went still.

Asa threw me a sidelong glance before whispering something in the Strikon's ear. After a few seconds, Asa straightened up and looked at me again. "That wasn't so bad," he said, his voice slurring—and then he slowly fell to the side. He didn't even put his hands out to catch himself as he slid off the Strikon's body.

I rushed forward and caught his head just before it hit the pavement, my heart in my throat. "Asa?"

He groaned. I cradled his head, my hands slipping into his dark hair. It was drenched with sweat, and so was the rest of him. His muscles were twitching. I leaned down to get a good look at his face, but a shadow passed over us and I looked up to see the Strikon standing right next to me. I opened my mouth to scream, but the Strikon bowed. "My deepest apologies for hurting you," he said woodenly.

He turned and walked away, marching through the gate that led out to the street.

"Wow," I murmured as I turned my attention back to Asa, whose head was in my lap.

"My baton."

I leaned over and grabbed it. Asa took it from me and pushed it straight down, making the stick part disappear into the handle again. Shakily, he stuck it in his belt. "Hotel," he whispered. "Can you give me a hand?"

"Sure." As carefully as I could, I helped him to his feet, pulling his arm around my shoulders to help him stay upright as he swayed. "But do you want to maybe go to the hospital instead?"

His eyes were half-closed. "Nothing they could do for me." He clumsily drew his sleeve across his chin to wipe away the blood. "Please, Mattie."

With my hand on his waist, the tremors in his body were shaking me, too, and it only made me hold on to him tighter as we started walking. I wanted to celebrate each time he put one foot in front of the other, because as I looked at his face, I knew it was a struggle. We passed through the gate, and I glanced over to see the Strikon standing at the curb like he had nowhere to go.

"He's not going to hurt us," Asa mumbled as I paused, unwilling to turn my back to a guy who'd been trying to kill us a few minutes ago.

"Isn't that manipulation stuff going to wear off, though?" The one tab he'd given me back in that hotel in Kansas City hadn't seemed to last more than ten minutes or so.

"Yeah." Asa's head was bowed, and I tightened my grip on him as we turned to walk the final blocks back to our hotel. "But not soon enough."

"If you say so."

We had just crossed the street when I heard an engine roar, tires screech, a horn blare, and a woman scream behind us. Startled, I craned my neck and looked back.

A block away, a bus had come to a stop in the middle of the intersection. Lying crumpled against the curb was the Strikon, his head canted weirdly to one side. A cold chill spread through my chest as I looked up at Asa. "Oh my God," I whispered. "You told him to walk into traffic."

Asa's bloodshot eyes opened and settled on me. Then he slowly brought his hand up and touched the tip of his crooked nose. "It's them or us now, Mattie. And when it comes to that, I'm going to choose us every time."

CHAPTER FIFTEEN

Asa managed to wait until we made it through the door of his hotel room to start barfing, but it was a close call. He wrenched himself away from me and dove into the bathroom, landing in front of the toilet just in time. His entire body heaved as if it were trying to turn itself inside out. Having helped out a few sorority sisters after nights of over-the-top partying, I grabbed a glass and filled it with water, then cautiously edged over to Asa as he sank to the tiles.

I knelt next to him, reaching up to flush the toilet before touching his sweaty cheek. "Hey," I said gently. "Sit up. Take a sip so you can rinse out your mouth."

He rose on shaking arms, and I lifted the cup to his lips. But the moment the water hit his tongue, he grimaced. "Nope," he said, lunging forward and retching into the toilet again.

I had my hand on his back and felt his muscles flex as he arched, as his body worked to rid itself of whatever the Strikon had done to him. "Is the magic on you?" I asked. "Should you take a shower?" I didn't know what to do for him—that Strikon had touched me, too, and I was a little achy, but otherwise fine. He'd had hold of Asa for a lot longer, though, and had seemed determined to damage him.

"I-I j-just need—" His body heaved again. "Time," he said as he sank down again. "I'll be okay."

He sounded so weak that it made my throat tight. "You can have all the time you want, but I'm not leaving you alone like this." He was soaked in his own sweat and shivering in the air-conditioned room. His eyes were so bloodshot that it looked like they might start to bleed. He had bruises on his throat, and the knuckles on his right hand were swollen. One was oozing blood.

I pressed a damp washcloth over the cut. "Thanks for saving my life, Asa."

He let out a weak croak of laughter. "Thanks for saving mine."

"Did I? You kind of look like death warmed over."

"Stop hurting my feelings."

I got up and rinsed the cloth with cold water, then ran it along his neck, smiling as he sighed and relaxed a little. "Strikon magic hurts you more than it does other people, doesn't it?"

"Yep."

"It makes you sick, when there's too much."

"Yep. But that's true of nearly all magic."

"You could have avoided him. But you came straight to us."

He cracked one eye open. "We were supposed to meet at eight thirty. You were late."

"I'm going to get you a fresh shirt," I blurted out. His was clinging to his chest and abs like someone had tossed a bucket of water on him.

I got up and went to his duffel, grabbing a clean black T-shirt that was right on top. When I returned to the bathroom, he'd stripped off his soaked shirt and was kneeling next to the tub, wiping the wet washcloth over his torso. I was torn between turning away and helping him, because he looked so fragile. I told myself to get over it and moved forward to help him up.

Being that close to him made my heart race. I knew he was dangerous; he had calmly told a man to walk in front of a bus and wasn't showing even a hint of remorse. I understood why—that Strikon could

Reliquary

have gone straight back to Zhong and gotten more men, or he could have followed us to our hotel and struck again—but still, it was the coldness with which Asa had done it that was so terrifying. And now I was pressed up against him, nothing between us except my shirt. The unforgiving lines of him, the way there was no softness at all, just the smooth sweep of skin stretched over lean muscles, all his angles, all his edges . . . being near Asa was just intense in a way I couldn't explain, on so many levels. It was a relief to help him pull the clean T-shirt over his body, covering it again.

"Are you finished puking your guts out?" I asked him.

"No promises. But I'm pretty much empty, so you can leave the wastebasket by the bed and I'll be all set."

I put my arm around his waist and escorted him to his bed. He sank into it with a groan. "What do you need?" I asked.

"Nothing," he whispered, closing his eyes. "I can take care of myself." He was lying on his back, one hand sprawled out to his side, the other lying on his chest.

I shook my head in frustration and went to the foot of the bed, where I tugged the heavy motorcycle boots from his feet, then removed his socks. Whatever was in his pockets rattled as his legs fell to the bed again. "Do you want to take off your pants?"

He chuckled, a pained, dry sound. "Why, Mattie. I thought you'd never ask." But he didn't move.

I looked down at his belt buckle and swallowed hard. "Um . . ."

"It's fine," he said, and I looked up to see him squinting at me. "I'll be fine, okay? You can go order yourself some dinner. We have a long trip ahead of us."

"I'm not hungry." I walked over to the side of the bed and sat down, and he scooted over a little to give me more space. I watched him rest for a few minutes, and some of his color seemed to come back. But in the dim light from the bathroom, his cheeks looked so hollow. "We were going to talk about Bangkok tonight," I finally said.

161

"I don't know the first thing about Thailand. Only that it used to be called Siam but that's not cool anymore. Oh, and I like pad thai. But is that the kind of thing that they serve here and call Thai food, but it's really American and actual Thai people would never eat it? Like those Chinese superbuffet places?"

Asa's expression turned pained the longer I babbled. "Shh. I'm pretty sure Thai people do actually eat pad thai sometimes, but finding out is pretty low on my list of priorities. We leave at noon tomorrow. Your passport and our tickets were delivered by courier this afternoon," he mumbled.

"Not on a private jet this time, I guess."

"Not this time. Montri monitors incoming private planes. Easier if we sneak in—in plain sight."

"How are we going to find something when we don't even know what we're looking for?"

"I'll make friends with the locals. There are ways."

"You don't sound worried."

"Right now my brain feels like it's going to dribble out my ears." I slumped. "Sorry."

"It's all right, Mattie. I've been to Bangkok before, but I know this is all new to you." His voice was gentle, like it had been when he'd played me in Chinatown, just to keep me calm. "You're doing good."

I looked down at him, searching for a sign that he was just playing me like he had before. But I swear, there wasn't one there to find. On impulse, I drew my finger down his slightly crooked nose. "You're so confusing, Asa."

"I prefer to think of myself as fascinating."

Maybe a little. "You're nicer than you admit."

"There's a corpse down the street that would argue with you if he could."

"You were protecting me."

"Shut the fuck up," he whispered.

"And you're risking a lot for a brother you claim to hate."

"Mattie . . ."

"Why didn't you stay to talk to him last night?"

He groaned. "Just because I'm doing this job doesn't mean everything's all better. It won't ever be. That might be how it works in your little world, but—"

"If it's because you're ashamed to face him after you threatened him, I really think—"

"Ashamed?" he rasped. "Fuck no. I'm not ashamed."

Asa's fingers closed over my wrist, and he pulled my hand to his face again, roughly clasped my index finger, and drew it along the bridge of his nose. "Who do you think did that to me, Mattie?"

I stared down at the place where his nose curved just off center. "Ben? Asa, he's one of the gentlest people I've ever met." I pulled my hand from Asa's grasp, and his flopped onto his chest again. "Do I want to ask what you did to provoke him?" I asked in a teasing voice, though it felt a little strained.

Asa laid his arm over his eyes, fully blocking out the light. The movement pulled his T-shirt up, revealing a stretch of bare stomach, the defined V-shape of his abs above the low waist of his pants. I resisted the urge to tug the hem of the fabric down and cover him again, and instead focused on his face as he said, "I brought him home."

"What do you mean?"

Asa sighed. "My dad had kicked me out the year before. He'd found me with . . ." He swallowed. "We'd never gotten along. I'd stayed for a bit with a friend whose dad was into magic, and he got me hooked on the nectar. It was better than weed for taking away the pain. At first it didn't take much to get me high. Hell, I could just walk into the den, and I was floating."

"Because you're so sensitive to it."

"Yeah. So I got into that scene, and started dealing. Because I could find it, you know, and the local den owner realized that. He had me stealing relics before I turned nineteen, and I was happy to do it, because I had money in my pocket again. Soon as I could, I started freelancing. Hustling. Fixing. Making whatever I could."

"Wasn't it hard for you, though? To be around magic?"

"Not Ekstazo magic. That's like catnip to me."

"You don't seem sensitive to it now."

He was quiet for a minute. "Now I know how to handle myself. Back then I was fucking lost. I needed more and more just to feel normal. And then one day, my little brother shows up. He'd seen me on the street and followed me into the den, and I found him all spread out, high as a fucking kite, his fucking letter jacket on and this stupid peach fuzz on his upper lip . . ." Asa let out a choked sound, and for a minute I thought he was going to be sick again, but then I realized it was emotion, not nausea, that was making him shake. "I hadn't seen him in months, and he was so fucking innocent, and so fucking young, and so fucking perfect. I couldn't stand the sight of him there, on that dirty floor, in that fucked-up drug den. I picked him up and took him home."

My own chest felt a little tight at the thought of Ben having followed his big brother into this unknown place, maybe just because he missed him. "You were trying to save him."

"Our dad was waiting when I got him through the door. One look at Ben and he fucking lost it."

"He didn't give you a chance to explain?"

Asa coughed out a laugh. "You never met my dad, did you?"

"No. He died before Ben and I met."

"He was a fucking bastard," Asa whispered.

"He blamed you for what had happened to Ben."

"He blamed me for *everything*." Asa's nostrils flared, and it seemed like he was trying to slow down his breathing. "Ben was snapping out of it at that point. He knew what had happened. He knew he was in trouble."

"He didn't blame you, did he?" I couldn't even imagine that. "He wouldn't have lied about it." *Would he?* Suddenly I wasn't sure anymore.

"He didn't have the chance. 'Get off your fucking pansy ass, boy.' That's what Dad said to him." Asa's voice had gone low and gravelly. "He shoved Ben. Started beating on him. I tried to stop him." His loose fingers curled into a fist. "But then he was screaming to Ben that I was trying to kill him. And Ben tackled me. Plowed into me like the fucking varsity linebacker he was."

Even then, Ben must have been thicker and more muscular than his lanky older brother. "That's when he broke your nose?"

"No. My dad got hold of me, picked me up off the floor," Asa murmured. "He held my arms behind my back and told Ben to hit me. He told him I was the reason our mom left. He said I was a fucking perverted scumbag who would drag him down, too. He said Ben had to choose."

"No," I breathed.

"I thought he would choose me. We were brothers. It was him and me. I was so fucking sure." Asa let out a shuddering breath. "But then Ben hit me so hard I couldn't breathe. I couldn't see. I was kicking and thrashing. Felt like I was choking on my own blood. Dad had my arms, though, and I couldn't . . ." Asa still had his arm over his eyes. "He told Ben to call the police. To tell them I'd broken in and threatened them."

"Oh my God."

"It wasn't hard to make the police believe their story. They had me in cuffs within seconds, even though all I could do was bleed on their uniforms."

I remembered what Detective Logan had told me—Asa had been arrested at nineteen and charged with assault and breaking and entering.

He'd served over a year in prison for trying to save his little brother from his own fate. "That's when you said you were going to kill Ben."

"I'm not sorry," Asa snapped. "I won't ever be sorry. So you can take your horror and your pity and your 'poor Ben' and your *kumbaya* 'but you're family' shit and—" He gritted his teeth, trapping his words inside.

I reached up to touch his rigid jaw. "Shove it up my ass?"

It relaxed, just slightly. "Just for that, I'll supply the lube."

I couldn't laugh; I was on the verge of tears. I felt so bad for both of them—seventeen-year-old Ben, who must have loved his brother, but had been placed in the wrenching position of choosing between Asa, whom he hadn't seen in months, and his father. And Asa, who'd only been trying to help his brother, and had gotten beaten and imprisoned for his trouble. The betrayal was so painful that I felt it stretching through the years, growing with time. Asa must have relived those moments over and over: the hope that Ben would help him, the moment he realized he wouldn't. That night had to be a thick scar on his heart.

"I don't blame you, Asa," I murmured. "I don't blame you at all."

Asa slid his arm up onto his forehead, letting me see his eyes. They were slightly redder than before. "Dammit, Mattie," he said in a broken voice before covering them again.

I reached up and stroked his fist, which loosened enough to let me squeeze his fingers. I didn't know what I was trying to do, exactly. Just let him know I was there, I guess, and on his side. Not because I was against Ben—he'd been put in an impossible position—but because I understood. Asa had needed his brother to stand with him, and he hadn't. Instead, Ben, no doubt terrified and conflicted, had rearranged Asa's face and broken his heart.

Asa didn't return my squeeze, but he didn't pull away. Still, I could feel his muscles going slack, his weight sinking into the mattress. Eventually, his chest rose and fell with even breaths, and I didn't want to move for fear of disturbing him. I sat there, gently cradling his fingers in my palm, until I was certain he was asleep.

I don't think anyone could say they know Asa well, Daria had told me. And yet, he'd just shared what had to be one of the most painful moments of his life. With *me.*

I let go of his hand. It suddenly felt like too much and not enough at the same time.

I needed to go back to my room.

I couldn't go back to my room.

Not only did I not want to leave him—I didn't want to be alone, not with these thoughts, not with all my fears, not with the journey ahead looming, not with knowing there were people out there who were hunting both of us. I slipped off my shoes, pulled the tie out of my hair, and crawled onto the opposite side of the bed. And I lay there, listening to Asa breathe, feeling the tremors in the mattress as he shifted and turned, until sleep came to claim me, too.

CHAPTER SIXTEEN

I stretched, my toes curling as I felt Ben's warmth behind me. I snuggled in, loving the weight of his arm over my waist, the feel of his body against mine.

"Stop squirming," he said in a teasing, sleepy voice.

I obeyed, and his fingers found my belly and scratched, tickling me. "Good girl," he mumbled.

Good girl? I didn't want to be good. I'd missed him so much. And I wanted to be bad. I laid my hand over his and began to push it lower.

He froze. Then he yanked his hand away, and my eyes flew open. Reality crashing down on me, I rolled quickly—so quickly that I went right over the edge of the bed and landed on the floor, conking my skull on the bedside table. My heart hammering, I slowly raised my aching head and found Asa squinting back at me, his eyes still bloodshot and hair sticking up on one side of his head. "You thought I was Ben," he said, his voice still thick with sleep.

My whole body was jangling with mixed signals: alarm along with the lingering pull of desire. My gaze darted to his long fingers, the ones I'd apparently just been pushing into the waist of my shorts. "And you thought I was . . ."

"Gracie."

"You mistook me for your pit bull."

"You mistook me for my brother. I think we're even."

"I'm not sure." My face felt as if it were on fire. How far would it have gone if Asa hadn't woken up enough to stop it? Shouldn't I have known the difference immediately? I lowered my forehead to the bed.

"Well, this is awkward." Asa's laughter sent a tremor through the mattress. "Fortunately, although I love Gracie dearly, our relationship is strictly platonic." He clutched at his head and sank into the pillow. "Ow," he said feebly.

Needing something to do, I got up and filled a glass of water in the sink, then brought it to his side of the bed. He rose on one elbow and took a sip, then drained the glass. "Thanks."

"I've got some Advil in my purse if you want it."

He shook his head. "I don't put anything like that in my body." He pressed his face into the pillow and sighed.

"You must miss her a lot."

"I hated leaving her." His voice was muffled, but I heard the sadness there.

"She's part of it, isn't she? All the things you do to keep yourself healthy." I'd seen it myself—every time he looked at Gracie, it was as if a weight were lifted from his shoulders. Every time she gave him a lick or laid her head in his lap, it drew a gentle smile to his face. Even his voice changed when he talked to her.

"She's more than that." Asa rolled to the side. "She's my girl," he said quietly. "She'd tear someone's throat out if it meant protecting me."

After what he'd told me last night, I could only imagine what that meant to him. "And you'd do the same if it meant protecting her."

"Damn straight. I nearly did, the night I found her."

I thought of the scars on Gracie's ugly-cute face, the way her ears were cut to thin strips of skin and cartilage. "Someone was making her fight."

He nodded. "It was in this little town in Kentucky. I was doing my thing, just there to swipe a relic and get out. She was in this tiny, dirty cage, waiting her turn to get torn up. She stuck her nose against the bars and whined as I passed, like she was begging me to help her, and I just couldn't . . ." His shoulders flexed as he pushed himself up to sit on the edge of the bed. "I've been in cages before. Every time, I thought I was going to lose my mind. And I couldn't stand to see her in a cage, either. It wasn't right."

"Something tells me this story ends with you and Gracie running for your lives."

"Well, that time I was carrying her," he said with a little smile. "She wasn't as heavy as she is now, though." He stretched and winced, his fingers rising to run along the purple bruises at his throat. "Still, I nearly got myself shot. I'm not sure if that was because of her or the relic I stole, though. Had to lie low for nearly a year after that."

I shook my head. "You're lucky you're so hard to catch."

"It's not luck." His arms dropped to his sides and he looked up at me. "I don't do cages, Mattie. You could paint it up with gold and fill it with diamonds, but to me it still feels the same. And I won't ever be put in one again."

He stood up, walked into the bathroom, and shut the door. I looked down at a smear of blood on his pillowcase and knew what he was trying to tell me.

Too bad it was the last thing in the world I wanted to hear.

Of all the places one could go, Bangkok has to be the most alive, the wildest, the most intense. And as I walked down the street with Asa, seeing it for the first time, the air filled with the scent of gasoline and limes and sweat and roses and spices I couldn't even name, as we passed markets brimming with flowers and fruits I'd never seen before, I felt like I'd been dropped into a brand-new world. After checking into our hotel, we set out on the main road, Sukhumvit, at least five lanes of snarled traffic penned in by high-rises on either side, flashing signs, and a train running on an elevated track. The heat raised little beads of sweat on my skin, and I was glad I'd put on just a tank and shorts for this excursion.

Asa insisted on holding my hand. "Because you're afraid I'll wander off?" I asked, even as my head was turned toward the sight of juicy dumplings arrayed on a street cart.

"No, because you're my girlfriend," he said casually, then laughed as I stopped dead right in the middle of the sidewalk. He turned to me, looking better rested than I'd seen him for a while—he'd slept the entire flight to Taipei and dozed again until we landed in Bangkok, then shut himself in his room for a few hours when we'd arrived at our hotel, probably meditating or doing tai chi or something. He'd emerged clean-shaven and looking like a tourist, wearing cargo shorts (I had to laugh), sandals, and sunglasses, which he now lowered on the bridge of his nose so I could see his eyes. "People here are going to get to know me right quick, Mattie, but they don't know you, and they don't need to. You don't want me going around telling people you're my reliquary."

"Is that bad?"

His eyebrow arched. "I told you how rare you are."

"As rare as you?"

He chuckled. "Nearly." He tugged my hand and guided me down a side street.

"Do you know where you're going?"

"No idea."

I looked up at him, his gaze darting constantly from corner to corner, face to face, his long body taut and ready while still taking relaxed strides, his nostrils flaring as he breathed in the city.

He pulled me down one street and up another for hours, until my curls were frizzing like nobody's business and sweat trickled down my back. Finally, as we reached the edge of a long string of booths shaded by awnings made of blue tarps, Asa's steps faltered and he came to a stop. "Interesting," he whispered.

We were standing in front of what appeared to be a souvenir shop. Three steps led up from the street into a long, shallow room absolutely filled with goodies. My eyes went wide as I took it all in. Carved jade or marble (honestly, they might have been plastic) Buddhas, amulets of all shapes and sizes, figurines with fanged monster faces wearing hats topped with gold spires, golden tea sets, carved wooden elephants, silky patterned kites. I was totally sucked in and wanted them all, so many tempting little treats to take home as a reminder that once in my life, I had been someplace truly foreign, someplace so far away from Wisconsin that I'd never believe it myself unless I had something to cradle in my hands and make it real again.

A scrawny old man with skin like well-tanned leather greeted us by pressing his hands together and nodding his head. I mimicked his movement, which brought a broad grin to his face, revealing a missing front tooth. He gestured toward the figurines, inviting me and Asa closer. But Asa was already busy wandering back and forth in front of the open shop, a rangy wolf on the prowl. The old man's brow furrowed, but then he beckoned to Asa and held up a pretty burnished gold charm on a chain, inclining his head toward me as if suggesting Asa should buy me a gift.

Asa glanced over at me and winked, the kind of mischievous look that made me nervous. I looked down at my sandals, getting ready to run. But Asa merely shook his head at the old man's invitation and sauntered over to a carved wooden box sitting next to the man's stool. "I want what's in there," he said to the man.

The man blinked at him. "Not souvenir."

"No, I'm sure it's not." Asa's nose twitched as he leaned closer. "Ekstazo, yeah?"

The old man took an abrupt step back. "No-no—"

Asa smiled. "Knedas, too. But whatever it is, it's pretty weak. You've been using it to pull your customers in."

"Dammit," I said, throwing the old man a resentful look.

Asa ran his hand along the top of the box. "How do you think the local Headsmen would feel if I told them about this?" he asked the man.

I wasn't sure the man understood everything Asa had just said, but at the mention of the Headsmen, the poor guy's hands went up. "No! Please!"

I'd only heard the Headsmen mentioned once before—when Grandpa had told me they were the magical brand of law enforcement. And this little man looked terrified of them.

Asa seemed pleased at the effect he'd had as he pulled a small pad of paper and a pen from his pocket. "No Headsmen? No problem." He offered the pad and pen to the man and made a writing motion. "Supplier. Password."

An hour later, after a fun little ride in a cab that seemed to be the love child of a motorbike and a Smart car, we were standing on a narrow street outside a café with bars on its windows and a winking pig on the sign out front. Asa led me inside. It was full of middle-aged white men—American and European tourists from the sound of them. They were lounging at tables, drinking tea. Some of them were also greedily eyeing the hallway leading to the back.

"Is this a den?" I whispered to Asa as we approached a glassed-in counter containing an array of fruity treats and candies.

"Sort of." He grinned at the petite woman behind the counter, who put her hands together and bowed her head in greeting. "I'd like to sample the merchandise," he said, then showed the woman a note written by the terrified souvenir-shop owner.

The woman gave him a curious glance, then led us to the back hallway and into a room filled with . . . "Oh my God," I whispered. "Are those all sex toys?"

"Which one would you like to try?" the woman asked in perfect accented English, all courtesy, as she gestured at a rack of dildos and another of fuzzy handcuffs, whips, and other stuff—I couldn't even figure out where some of them would go.

But suddenly, I kind of wanted to explore. I looked over the various toys, my heart beating a little faster, my body tightening. Asa pulled me close as I reached out to touch a pair of fuzzy black wrist cuffs. "Patience, honey," he said. "I need to concentrate, and you're distracting me."

"But—" Ben and I had never tried anything kinky, but now I couldn't get the image out of my head: me with my wrists cuffed, him standing over me . . .

Asa's grip on me tightened. "Jacks, baby," he whispered.

"Dammit!" I stomped my foot and pinched the inside of my wrist, trying to clear both the fog and the twist of need that had once again risen inside me.

The petite woman gave me a concerned look, then turned back to Asa. "Well?"

"Um . . . how about . . ." Asa turned and walked over to a Buddha statue, of all things, sitting all by itself in the corner. Benevolent and fat, the jade figurine was insanely out of place. "How about this?"

The woman laughed. "That is not for sale."

Asa gave her a polite smile. "But I could buy anything else in this room, and it's guaranteed to be absolutely full of magic?"

"Best in Bangkok. A special blend." The woman nodded toward me. "Make her scream with pleasure." She touched one of the whips. "Or pain."

I pinched myself again for good measure.

Asa rubbed his hands together, seemingly in anticipation, then leaned over and swiped a hot-pink dildo from a rack before turning back to the woman. "Except there's not a single fucking drop of Ekstazo on this," he said, tossing it into the air and catching it again, then pointing it at the rest of the rack. "Or on any of these." He put it back. "And no Strikon, either." He inclined his head toward the Buddha. "But that . . . that's different. Who loaded that thing up? That's a mindfucker I'd like to get to know. Does he belong to Montri? Bet he does." Asa pointed to another door, this one on the other side of the room, and I couldn't help but notice the tiny tremble in his hand as he stepped toward it. "That's where the real stuff is. But you save it for the locals, right? The business customers. Or the high rollers. Not for magic tourists who don't know the difference."

The woman gave him a condescending smile. "I'm afraid you are confused."

Asa shook his head. "I'm not a tourist, lady. I want the good stuff." A drop of sweat slid down his cheek.

Our host considered Asa for a moment, then pulled a key from her apron and walked over to the door, unlocking it with a quick twist of her wrist. She pushed the door open and pressed her lips together as Asa approached. It was a closet, lined with shelves containing an array of objects similar to what I'd seen in the souvenir shop. Asa ran his finger along the top shelf, touching each item in turn. "Healing, sexual, contentment—oh, that one's pretty strong . . ." He went down each tier, listing what each object contained with increasing specificity, as the woman's eyes went wide. And then he stopped in the middle of the bottom row, and he chuckled. "I hope you didn't pay too much for that one."

The woman frowned. "That is a very valuable Sensilo relic."

"Nope. Doesn't have any magic in it at all." He grabbed the thing, a little wooden elephant with a gold headdress, and tossed it to her. "Someone grifted you on that one—probably the conduit channeled it into a decoy relic during the transaction. You know what you need? A sniffer to make sure you get what you pay for."

The woman folded her arms over her chest. "What do you want?"

"Tell Montri I'm looking for a job."

And with that, Asa took my hand and led me out the way we'd come. I spent the first few minutes of our walk sucking in the fresh air and trying to rid myself of the tingling feeling low in my belly. Asa seemed to be doing the same thing, but for him, it was probably to recover from the toll of being so close to that much concentrated magic. We hiked in silence and were almost back at our hotel by the time I realized holding his hand had started to feel like a natural thing. I tugged my fingers from his grip and wiped them on my shorts.

Sarah Fine

"So let me get this straight," I said as I followed him to his room. "You spend most of your time traveling from one small town to the next, peddling magical doodads to out-of-the-way magic dens, when all the time you're such a hot property that a mobster kidnaps your brother just to get your attention, and all you have to do to turn the head of the boss of Thailand is spend five minutes in a magic shop."

"We don't know for sure about that last one, but here's hoping."

"This job has to be better paying than your usual."

He unlocked his door and pushed it wide, inviting me in. "Yeah, but I don't often have a good reliquary to drag along for the ride. That limits my options on smuggling jobs, and that's where the money is."

I sat down on his bed, glancing out at the chaotic beauty of the city. "Frank was going to send you with a good reliquary. He probably keeps her on retainer." I looked over his baggy cargo shorts and T-shirt. "Her clothes looked pretty expensive."

Asa grunted, pulled a bag of dried kale from his duffel, and began to chow down. "Money's nice, but it isn't everything."

"I thought money was important to you. Don't you want to make as much as you can?"

Asa sat down on the floor, his long legs stretched in front of him. "Money can be freedom. It can be a shield and sword. It can be a fire when you get cold. Money equals the power to protect myself." His eyes met mine. "When it stops equaling that, I stop wanting it."

I bit my lip. All day, I'd been missing Ben so much, thinking about what it might be like to be here with him. His final plea to me had been circling through my head, and I'd been trying to find a way to raise this topic with Asa. But his comments about the cage had been pretty pointed. And now he was being very clear that he couldn't be bought. I was running out of arguments.

"Something on your mind?" he asked, licking the tips of his fingers clean.

I sighed. Ben wanted me to talk about this with Asa. And I knew Asa loved his brother. But I also knew how deeply Asa had been hurt by what Ben had done, and asking Asa for more was complicated, just as Ben had said it was. Asa hadn't come right out and said he wouldn't work for a boss, but . . . "Why did you want that lady to tell Montri that you're looking for a job?"

Asa opened his mouth to reply, but a knock at the door brought us both to our feet. "Yeah?" Asa called.

"Delivery for you, sir," came a high, meek voice from the hallway.

Asa drew his baton but didn't extend it. He took a few steps toward the door, closing his eyes like he was trying to concentrate, maybe trying to sense the presence of some new and dangerous magic that had found its way to us. But then he raised his head, peeked through the peephole, and opened the door.

A young woman wearing the hotel livery stood in the hallway with a vase of orchids, gold and purple, arranged in a circular sweep that looked too perfect to be real. Asa moved out of the way so she could bring it into the room and set it on the table near the windows. As soon as she was gone, Asa plucked a thick envelope from amid the buds and pulled out a note on creamy card stock that was lined with the same runes I had seen at Mistika.

Asa read the note, and then handed it to me.

Your honored presence is requested at my home tonight at nine o'clock for an evening of celebration and discussion of new ventures.

Below that was an address. There was no signature, but the monogram on the card stock was *SM*.

I looked up at Asa to find him grinning. "This is why," he said. "We're in."

CHAPTER SEVENTEEN

The fancy car came for us a few minutes before nine, by which time I was properly liquored up and ready to roll. It had been a busy afternoon. Asa had called Frank and verified that the address on the card was indeed owned by a holding company that could be traced back to Montri. Then we'd gone shopping.

I wasn't sure exactly how it had happened, but Asa had chosen my dress. It was white except for interwoven bands of black, dark red, and white across the bust. Though the dress was strapless, it fit perfectly, not too low-cut and ending on my upper thighs. I'd spent all of high school and college wearing cheerleading skirts and leotards in front of hundreds if not thousands of people, so I wasn't self-conscious about my body. But I also wasn't eager to expose my lady parts at the wrong moment and had bought myself a pair of lacy white boy shorts. With liberal application of a shimmery body lotion (and a good bit of vodka), I was feeling pretty damn sexy.

That would have been awesome, except I was sitting next to the wrong guy. After the last two days, waking up to a frustrating case of mistaken identity and having my unsated need heightened by a nasty Knedas magic–soaked Buddha presiding over a room full of sex toys, it was especially not cool. And the fact that this wrong guy happened to look unexpectedly and ridiculously hot was making everything extra confusing. Asa was wearing a crimson shirt that looked like it had been made for him—with the top few buttons undone—and a pair of honest-to-God suspenders. Black, of course. To match his patent leather shoes and his slim-fitting black slacks. I had no idea what to make of him, so I was trying not to look at him at all. I focused my attention on a golden palace by the river, shining under the purple night sky, all steep pyramids and sharp spires.

Asa looked over at me as our driver steered us toward the waterfront. "Why aren't you talking a blue streak like normal? Do you need me to scratch your belly, girl?" His long fingers wiggled in the air a few inches from my stomach.

"Oh my God, don't remind me."

He shrugged. "Seemed to put you in a good mood before."

"It certainly did put me in a mood," I muttered, angry at myself. And at Asa. I wished I could call Ben right now. I really needed to hear his voice. "What are we walking into?"

"No idea." Asa spread his arms across the back of the leather seat. "Feels nice to be wanted, though."

I flinched away from him. "What? I don't—"

"By Montri," he said slowly, smirking.

"What am I supposed to do when we get there?"

"Whatever I tell you to."

"Great." I looked down at my pristine white heels. "I'll shed these if I need to run."

"Good plan." He nudged my foot with his. "But they do look good."

My toe scraped over the wire bristles that Asa had glued to the sole of the shoe, my protection against manipulation magic. I was starting to savor the discomfort. As I looked out the window, watching the wild, dirty, colorful city go by, I whispered, "What happens if we're caught?"

"Why do you think I avoid telling you things? You can honestly say you have no idea what's going on."

I shuddered. "Wasn't much help when that Strikon got hold of me."

Asa reached over and took my hand. "We're not going to be caught." He looked at me out of the corner of his eye. "Them or us, remember?"

I nodded.

"Do you trust me?"

I looked into his honey-brown eyes. They were a shade lighter than Ben's, it turned out. I noticed it when I saw Ben again in Vegas. At the moment the distinction seemed important. "Sometimes."

His head fell back against the seat. "That's cheating. You do or you don't."

"You really want me to pick?"

He squeezed my hand. "It's going to be us, Mattie. We'll be okay. We're going in there to scope it out. I'll talk to Montri, and you'll just be you."

"You make it sound so simple."

"You want me to make it sound complicated?"

The car slowed as it pulled to a stop in front of a set of metal gates. A moment later they swung open. We entered a compound surrounding a high-rise on the shore of the river and joined a line of other shiny black cars queueing up to disgorge their human cargo. I squinted to see who was getting out of those cars, and relaxed a little when I saw a woman wearing a little black dress and a guy in a suit. Maybe we would blend. From what I could see, the party attendees looked like a pretty international crowd.

When our turn came, Asa slid out of the car and offered me his hand. He gave the attendant his invitation and tucked me against his side as we followed the crowd along a path right next to the water. I was close enough to him that I felt the change in his body instantly. A hard shiver coursed through him, like all his muscles had seized at once. "You okay?" I whispered.

He didn't answer, but his grip on me tightened. I glanced up to see sweat breaking out at his temples. His eyes hardened. "It's here," he murmured against my hair.

"It? Like *it* it?"

Asa swallowed hard. "Yeah."

"You can already tell?" Frank had said we'd need to be close because the relic would be packaged. I glanced around. "Is it out here? Close by?"

"No. Inside."

"How can you tell the difference between it and an actual Strikon?"

He stared at the high-rise. "Relics are smaller. More concentrated. And this one . . ."

He shook his head, then stepped away from the line for the door, pulling out his phone. He punched in some sort of text, then rejoined me. But a few steps down the riverside path, he fumbled the phone as he went to put it back in his pocket, and it clattered to the walkway. As he moved to get it, his toe hit the device and it shot over the side of the path, disappearing into the black water with a tiny splash. "Well, shit," he said, then tugged me along as people crowded behind us. "I'll have to get a replacement later."

I glanced frantically back at the water. Frank had given us the phone, and it had felt like a lifeline. My grip on Asa's hand was steely. "This doesn't feel like an auspicious start," I said quietly.

"How about now?" he asked as we reached the entrance of the high-rise to find guards divesting guests of their phones and any other electronic devices they happened to be carrying.

"I think I need another shot."

He tugged me closer and nudged my chin upward. "I'll get us through this. It's you and me. Got it?"

No. It was supposed to be me and *Ben*. I clamped my eyes shut and shook my head to clear my thoughts. Asa wasn't talking about anything but getting through the evening anyway. "Got it."

We reached the guards at the door. They didn't bother me at all, because it was pretty obvious I had nowhere to carry a phone. They patted down Asa, though, and for once, he didn't have a single thing in his pockets. He just held his arms up and stared steadily at the guard who was running his hands down Asa's lean torso. From the way Asa's jaw was clenched, I was wondering if the guard was a Strikon, or maybe a Knedas. It made me hurt for him.

The crowd, men and women dressed just a notch above club attire, conversed in a variety of languages. I picked up German, Spanish, lots of Thai, and several other languages I couldn't identify at all, another reminder of how far I was from my little hometown on the shores of Lake Michigan.

We were funneled through an entryway and into a massive lounge that was open to the riverfront. I gasped—the interior walls of the place were absolutely lined with what appeared to be artifacts: shards of broken pottery framed and mounted, gilt boxes containing who knew what, little golden pots, and stout engraved figurines. I felt like I'd entered a museum, except the wide expanse of the space was occupied by comfy modern couches, chairs, and coffee tables. A warm breeze floated through from the river outside. The guests were all talking among themselves, many of them eyeing the fascinating objects on display. Waitresses patrolled with trays of fruity drinks and hors d'oeuvres. Asa snagged a small glass of red liquid for me, sniffed at it, and handed it over. "Fruit punch and rum."

"Thanks." I took a sip and reminded myself to relax, lest some Sensilo nearby pick up my tense vibe. "Do you know who these people are?"

Asa scanned the crowd. "Mostly business contacts, looks like." His eyes narrowed. "A few naturals, but not many, except for the staff. These people know what's up, though. They either buy from him or pay him for protection—oh."

"What is it?"

A grim smile spread across Asa's face. "I've got competition. Montri's got a sensor." His eyes flicked toward a hallway to my left. "That could make this tricky."

"Tricky?" I let out a weak chuckle. If the sensor was anything like Tao back in Chicago's Chinatown, he'd know if any magic came in or out. I glanced at all the possible escape routes, the hallways, the wide-open glass doorways leading to the outside space, the various doors. A guard was posted at each, some armed, some simply lounging against the walls with their arms folded, watching the guests. I was betting those were the Strikon. My heart beat a little faster, and Asa pushed my glass up to my lips. I drank half of its contents before looking up again.

"Now what? Are you going to—"

Asa put his hand on my arm as he looked across the room. "I think I'm up."

I turned in the direction he was facing to see a gorgeous woman approaching us. Her long black hair was pulled up in an intricate style punctuated by orchids and gold ribbon, and her tall, slender body was encased in a skintight sheath of embroidered red silk, matched by the wet crimson sheen on her lips. Her predatory gaze was focused on Asa as she moved through the mingling crowd, which parted to let her through, many of the men and some of the women taking the opportunity to stare hungrily at her. When she reached us, she paused for a moment, staring into Asa's eyes, and then, slowly and gracefully, brought her hands up and pressed them together, bowing her head until her chin touched her thumbs.

Asa smirked and pressed his own hands together, bowing his head slightly but never taking his eyes off the woman. I had to stomp down a strange, uneasy feeling that twisted in my stomach at the sight.

"Mr. Johnson," she said in a cool British accent, using the name Asa had used to check into our hotel and suddenly making me realize we must have been followed back there after our stop at the magic shop. "I am Maew, Mr. Montri's assistant. Thank you for accepting his invitation. He is wondering if you would like to share a private drink with him in his study before he greets the rest of his guests."

She swept her hand, tipped with long ruby-red fingernails, toward a room that lay up a few steps from the lounge, where two young men flanked a thick wooden door carved with the now-familiar runes.

Asa pressed a cocktail napkin to his sweaty forehead. "Sounds good. Just let me get my girl comfortable. She's shy around strangers."

"Of course," said Maew, giving me a sly smile. "I have already selected a companion to entertain her while you are indisposed. Ho-Jun?" She beckoned to someone behind us. "Come here and meet . . ."

"Katie," Asa said, using my hotel check-in name.

I recited it in my head a few times—I didn't know how Asa kept all his aliases straight, but between the drinks and the stress, I'd be lucky to remember my real name, let alone my fake one. "Katie Halsworth," I said.

"Ms. Halsworth, I would like to introduce you to Ho-Jun."

A man in gray slacks and a crisp white dress shirt reached our side. His tan skin had golden undertones. His killer cheekbones tapered to a narrow jaw, and his straight nose topped a soft, almost feminine mouth. But when he smiled, everything about him said pure man.

Asa squeezed my fingers. "Jacks, baby," he whispered.

I pressed my toe hard onto the wire bristles in my shoe. "Thanks." As soon as the pain zinged across my skin and up my leg, so did the threat. They'd already gotten someone to stay with me while Asa was in with the boss. I had no doubt it was Ho-Jun's job to take care of me if Asa tried to pull anything. And not in a friendly way.

"Um," I said. "Nice to meet you. But I'm fine, really, and wouldn't want to—"

"Give us a second." Asa touched my shoulder, and I tore my gaze away from my new companion. "You remember how we met?" he murmured, lowering his head until our faces were only a few inches apart.

"Yeah." Though honestly, at the moment, with Asa in my space like that, my thoughts were starting to fray at the edges.

"You were fearless," he whispered, so quietly that I knew the words were meant only for me.

"You said I was stupid."

His lips curved into a half smile. "You knew what you wanted." He leaned closer. "And I might have been *a sensor trying to do my job*, but

I couldn't take my eyes off you. Even when I should have been paying attention to other things."

I blinked up at him, confusion seeping in as his eyes bored into mine. "Huh?"

His hand slid into my hair. He was so close that his nose touched mine. My hands rose to his chest, but I wasn't sure whether I wanted to push him away or ball my hands in his shirt and pull him closer. "Stop distracting me, baby," he said. "I've got work to do."

And then he kissed me, a soft but commanding press of his mouth to mine. He pulled back quickly, a smug grin on his face. "See you in a bit."

My fingers rose to my lips as I watched him turn and follow Maew toward Mr. Montri's study. What the hell? Anger and betrayal flashed hot in my chest, but as Asa mounted the steps and I saw the little wet patch of sweat that had darkened a spot between his shoulder blades, it struck me.

He had played me again. And he never played without a reason.

Ho-Jun cleared his throat. "I know I am a poor substitute for Mr. Johnson," he said in a slightly accented voice. "But I hope you will let me keep you company. Mr. Montri's parties are always full of excellent diversions."

Diversions. I drained my punch as I thought back to what Asa had just said to me. *Couldn't take my eyes off you. Should have been paying attention to other things.* Was he telling me to create a distraction? I wiggled my big toe, brushing it back and forth over the bristles and trying not to wince as it abraded my skin. "Cool," I said, offering Ho-Jun a bright smile. "I'm kind of a fish out of water here. I've never even been to Bangkok before."

He offered his arm and led me farther into the room as even more guests crowded in. People were starting to disperse into various other rooms, though, and I could hear fast-paced club music issuing from somewhere down the wide corridor to our left. The lights had dimmed, and I sensed that the party was just kicking into gear.

And I had a master of manipulation at my side and desperately needed to stay sharp. I had no idea what Asa was up to, but seeing as he'd told me the relic we were after was right here in this space, I had a feeling he was going to make a play for it. I had to do whatever I could to help. But was I supposed to distract *everyone*? That seemed like a tall order given the sprawling layout of this place and the lack of any visible fire alarms. So was I supposed to distract someone specific . . . ? Wait. *I might have been a sensor trying to do my job,* Asa had said.

He must have wanted me to find the sensor and keep him occupied so he wouldn't notice what Asa was up to.

I glanced around the jam-packed area. Asa had looked down this hallway when he'd sensed his opposite number, but that was the only clue I had—apart from a few potentially telltale signs.

"So . . . ," I said as we headed for the dance floor. "Seems like a lot of people work for Mr. Montri. Do you each have your own specialties?" As we walked, I eyed every person we passed.

Ho-Jun laid his hand firmly over mine. "Ah, Miss Halsworth. I'm sure you will agree that such a topic is boring in the extreme, particularly when we have so many other options available to us." He gave me a slow, appreciative once-over.

Crap. If I disagreed, he'd realize I had some resistance to his magic. "Yeah. Boring in the extreme. Lots of better things to do." I beamed up at him, focusing on his handsome face and trying not to think about how his touch was making my skin crawl—not to mention my toe, which was raw from how hard I was having to press on those damn bristles. "So how about a dance?"

Ho-Jun smiled and guided me onto the dance floor. "That's better. I hope you're a good dancer."

"Oh, honey," I said. "Wait till you see my moves."

Okay, so, this was something I could do. After years of dance-squad training and more than my share of frat parties, I could grind, shimmy, and drop with the best of them. But Ho-Jun was way close, and the more he touched me, the more my thoughts went hazy, threatening to make me forget my purpose. When I couldn't take it anymore, I shifted into a hip-rolling salsa and scraped my stiletto heel hard against his ankle.

"*A-pa!*" He stumbled back and lifted his pant leg, revealing a gash that was already oozing blood.

"Oh my God," I wailed. "I'm so sorry!"

He held up his hands, looking pained. "It's all right. But I need to get this cleaned up. You stay here and dance until I return."

Feeling triumphant (okay, and just a little tipsy as the rum kicked in), I saluted him. "Aye, aye, Captain."

His brow furrowed.

"I-I mean . . . I'll stay here and dance until you return."

He frowned, but then nodded and headed back out into the hallway. As soon as he was out of sight, I did return to dancing, but I began to make my way around the floor, looking for anyone who might be this mysterious magic sensor Asa had felt. But everyone seemed to be having a damn good time. No one had that hollow-eyed stare or uncoordinated walk that Tao had had, and no one was sweating bullets like Asa always did.

How the heck was I supposed to distract someone I couldn't find?

As the minutes slid by, my frustration mounted—this was the one thing Asa needed me to do while he attempted to steal the relic that could save Ben's life. And here I was, twerking around like an idiot and wasting precious time. Just as I turned to escape into the corridor, though, Ho-Jun appeared in the archway, his dark eyes scanning the floor for me. I lurched backward, deeper into the room, squeezing myself between a few guys who seemed pretty darn happy about my arrival. I peeked under their arms to see Ho-Jun turning in place, his tapered jaw clenched.

If he found me now, I was in serious trouble.

With my heart pounding, I made it to the very back of the room and started to edge around the side, heading past a long table stocked with all sorts of goodies like I'd seen at the Phan Club, which I suspected were coated with Ekstazo magic. There was a small crowd around that table, and I slithered in between people so busy reaching for ecstasy that they barely noticed me shoving in among them. Each yard covered was precious ground. But then I neared the end of the table and caught a glimpse of Ho-Jun, still on the dance floor, twirling his finger near his head as he spoke to the two guys I'd used to camouflage my escape—he had to be describing my hair. As they all turned, looking for me, I pushed my way to the edge of the crowd around the goodie table, planning to leap back onto the floor and dance like my life depended on it.

I never made it, though—my toe caught on someone's shoe, toppling me. As I fell, I instinctively grabbed for something to keep me from hitting the floor, and my fingers closed around an arm. Instead of holding me up, though, its owner let out a cry and pitched forward. I landed on my back.

He landed on top of me.

"Sorry," I said with a wheeze as my unwilling companion raised his head.

The light caught hollow cheeks sheened with sweat, black hair practically dripping with it. "Are you all right?" the man asked in soft, heavily accented English. His eyes met mine, and I was struck by how deep the circles beneath them were.

Unbelievable. "Are you?"

He gave me a hesitant, puzzled-looking smile. "I am. Thank you for asking." He braced his hands on either side and lifted his body from mine, then helped me up, his fingers trembling. He removed several little fluorescent hoops that he'd been wearing around his arm and tossed them back onto the table, shivering as he freed himself. Just as I wondered if he was hanging out by the goodie table because it was more tolerable than anywhere else, he pointed down at my right shoe—the heel had snapped clean off. "I've damaged you, I'm afraid."

I chuckled and pulled my shoes off, carefully keeping my new companion between me and the pissed-off Knedas who was looking for me. "You probably saved me. Dancing in these was making my life flash before my eyes."

"But you made it look like so much fun."

I paused before tossing my useless shoes in a corner. "You were watching me?"

"It was very entertaining. My name is Daeng. And you are?"

"Ma—Katie."

"Makatie?"

"Um. Just Katie." I chuckled nervously. "Rum does funny things to my tongue."

His eyebrows arched as his gaze fell to my mouth. "Does it now?"

I supposed this counted as distraction, though I really needed to make sure this guy was actually the one. And I needed to do it somewhere else, because Ho-Jun had freaking disappeared, and I had no idea where he'd gone.

"May I get you another drink, then, Just Katie?"

I slipped my arm through his. "Please do, Mr. Daeng."

Daeng began to steer me out of the room, and I fought the urge to glance behind me every other step. "I haven't seen you before," he said. His fingers closed around my wrist, firm and clammy. "I could have sworn you were an Ekstazo, but you have no magic at all."

And there it was. This dude was totally a magic sensor. I pressed down the urge to whoop with happiness. "I make my own magic," I said, putting my hand over his and hoping that whatever distraction Asa needed, it didn't have to go on too long. I kind of hated to tease this guy.

Daeng stared with something like wonder at my fingers curled over his. "I can believe that. You have certainly raised my spirits tonight."

I grinned, even as I felt a certain sad sympathy right alongside my jittery thrill that I seemed to have his full attention. But I didn't get to enjoy more than a moment of that victory, because Daeng's forehead crinkled and he peered toward the main room, where I'd left Asa.

I stepped into his path, desperate to keep his eyes on me. "Should we get something to eat? Or drink? Or . . ." I glanced toward the dance floor and was horrified to see Ho-Jun standing beneath the archway—his eyes on me. "Or how about we just go in here?" I grabbed Daeng's hand and tried to pull him toward another room, this one full of Lava Lamps and soft couches. But he was still staring toward the main entrance.

"What brought you here tonight, Katie?" he asked, frowning.

"I'm just here with my boyfriend. He's a businessman. He does . . . business." I sounded like an idiot, and probably looked like one, too, as I tugged on Daeng, trying to draw his attention back to me. Ho-Jun was now headed my way, limping slightly. "But we're not that serious," I babbled as I attempted to pull Daeng toward the Lava Lamp room. "I mean. He'd like it to be serious, but I just don't—"

"Excuse me," Daeng said, releasing my wrist.

"No, wait—"

"Stop right there," said Ho-Jun, but as he reached our side, Daeng made a little choked noise and pointed down the hallway.

"Should have sensed it earlier," he said in a hoarse whisper, throwing me a suspicious glance.

Ho-Jun's hand closed hard over my upper arm. "What is it?" he asked Daeng. "Is it the sniffer? Is he trying to take something out?"

Oh God. This wasn't a pawnshop where I could just run out the door. If Asa had already swiped the relic and headed out without me, it would be a lot harder to catch up with him. Especially since Ho-Jun held my arm in a bone-crushing grip.

"Not out," Daeng said, his eyes going round. "*In.* They're coming. Very many and very fast."

Ho-Jun scowled and looked around. "What?"

Daeng took a deep breath, his whole body shuddering. And then he raised his arms and shouted, "Headsmen!"

That word was all it took to make the whole place erupt with panic.

CHAPTER EIGHTEEN

Everyone tried to make it off the dance floor at once, plowing into people who had been streaming up the hallway. Ho-Jun and Daeng had forgotten all about me and were shouting in various languages, waving their arms and shoving to get through the melee. I was carried along by the jostle of elbows and shoulders, yelping as my bare feet were trampled by hard soles. My breath burst from me in gasps as I craned my neck and tried to stay upright.

"—must have called too much attention to himself," said an American partygoer, who'd pressed in just behind me.

"Or he has something too hot to handle and they know it," said his friend.

"If they catch us here, we're fucked." The guy muscled past, pushing me against a wall as an alarm started to blare.

The intensity of the jabbing, shoving, twisting, pushing of the crowd seemed to double, everyone frantic to escape. My ears rang as I tried to keep up. We were nearly to the main lounge, where the room opened up and people were sprinting away in all directions. I had no idea where the Headsmen would be coming from, or how many of them there would be, but from the way people were acting, I really didn't want to meet them. I had no idea where to go, though, or where

Asa was. Had he finished his meeting with Montri? Would they be caught together?

My feet got tangled with someone behind me and I fell forward just as we reached the lounge. The sound of shattering glass nearby wrenched a scream from my throat. Someone had cut the lights, so I headed for the patio, flinching as several sharp cracks filled the night, punctuated by shrieking. Someone was shouting something into a bullhorn, but not in English. I heaved myself up and ran for the outside. The cement was rough against my soles as I emerged into the humid air. Flashing red and blue lights shone from either side of the building, and as I peered upriver, I could see more coming.

"There you are," Asa said as he came sprinting out of the lounge, barely slowing down as he hooked an arm around my waist and propelled me along a side path, soft leaves brushing at my calves as I ran. He was carrying something that jingled faintly with every footfall.

"What's happening? What did you do?"

"What does it look like?" His crimson shirt was soaked and he was breathing hard, wheezing every once in a while. "I'm getting us out of here."

"Are you hurt?"

"No time," he said, stopping abruptly and pressing me against a wall as he peered around the corner of the building. "Okay, come on. We're going over the wall."

I didn't bother to question him. As he ducked low and ran behind a row of cars that had been parked along the curving drive in front of the building, I followed him as closely as I could. On the other side of the cars, the red and blue lights painted the front of the high-rise. People were shouting and screaming. A few more sharp cracks nearby made me reach up and grab Asa's hand. They had to be gunshots. Asa pulled me forward, tucking us behind a security booth a few yards from the eight-foot wall that surrounded the property. There were no guards in the booth—they were probably dealing with the horde of Headsmen that had descended.

"I don't know if I can get over that," I whispered, eyeing the wall.

"Sure you can." Asa stepped back and ran at the wall, planting his foot and shooting upward. His fingers hooked over the top, and he pulled himself onto the edge. Then he reached down and wiggled his fingers. "I'm gonna help, though."

I grabbed his hand and used my feet to walk myself up the wall, but a shout from behind me nearly made me let go. They'd probably seen my white dress, like a beacon in the night. Asa yanked me up roughly, then dropped to the ground on the other side and pulled me down on top of him as shots rang out. I stifled a scream as we ran across the street, into a warren of dingy buildings that smelled like rotting garbage. I yelped as I stepped on a piece of broken glass, but Asa kept yanking on me. "Can't stop, Mattie, not n—"

Two shots cracked into the corrugated metal just above my head, and Asa cursed. I looked up to see his hands in the air as a white guy in a tan suit walked toward us, his gun aimed at Asa. He was blond, handsome but with some wear on him. He was squinting into the shadows where we'd run.

"You gonna shoot me?" Asa asked.

The man didn't lower his gun. "Step into the light," he said tersely.

I put my hands in the air and stayed next to Asa as we took a few steps forward into a slant of light from a streetlamp. As soon as the blond man saw us, he lowered his gun, his face alive with emotion. "Asa?"

"Yep." Asa let his arms fall to his sides, and so did I, but he didn't look at me. "Long time, Keenan. I'd heard you'd been stationed out here."

The lines around Keenan's eyes deepened. "What are you doing here?" He looked over his shoulder, back at the Montri high-rise, where screams and gunshots still echoed. "Were you in there?"

"And if I was?"

"We got a tip that there was major contraband—a relic we've been hunting for a long time."

I tensed, but Asa smirked. "Didn't take you long to pull this little raid together. I'm impressed."

"You called it in, didn't you?" I said quietly, a sick mixture of confusion and dread tingling across my skin. "That's what you were doing right before you kicked the phone into the river."

Keenan's gaze shifted to me as I stood there, one foot cocked upward and bleeding, my short dress torn. "Don't you usually work alone?" he asked Asa.

"She's not work." Asa's voice was tight and strained, and he leaned forward to brace his palms on his thighs. As he did, a necklace fell from the front of his shirt and hung down, glinting in the light. It looked like a locket, but a strange one—the chain was thick and sturdy, and the pendant part was nearly as big as a golf ball. "Mattie, can you . . ." He sank to one knee, and his back arched like he was going to throw up.

I threw Keenan a careful glance, but his gun was still lowered, so I rushed forward and pulled the necklace off Asa. It was surprisingly light, but had left an angry red line across the back of his neck.

Keenan stuck out his hand. "I'll take that."

I didn't move. If we didn't take it to Frank, Ben might be killed. There was no way I was giving it up without a fight.

Next to me, Asa was slowly getting to his feet. "What's it worth?" he asked.

Keenan eyed the relic in my hand. "It's priceless."

"And you know what it is."

Keenan nodded. He holstered his gun. "Of course you'd be the one to find it." His pale eyes were intense as he stared at Asa.

Asa rubbed at his chest and winced. "What's the bounty?"

"Asa?" I asked, holding the necklace a little tighter. "What are you doing?"

"Ten million," said Keenan. "British pounds, not dollars."

Asa whistled low, then stretched his arms. "I knew I was being underpaid." He casually reached down and started to unbutton the front of his suspenders, leaving them hanging over his shoulders. "Do you have the cash on hand?"

"Asa, no," I said in a choked voice. "Please."

Keenan smiled as he looked me over. "So much pain. It's personal, why you're here."

"She's engaged to my brother," Asa said. "Brindle nabbed him to pull me in."

Keenan looked surprised. "Ben? Did you two reconcile, then?"

"Nope."

"I wouldn't have thought so," Keenan said quietly. "Not after what he did to you."

I took a step away from Asa. "You said it was them and *us*," I whispered. "You said it was going to be us."

Asa wouldn't look at me, but Keenan was staring. "You actually trusted him. You feel so betrayed."

"Keenan's an emotion sen—" Asa began.

"I figured that out," I snapped. "I'm not stupid."

"But you feel that way," said Keenan. "You should know you're not the first person Asa's fooled." He let out a sigh. "And you won't be the last."

"Shut up, Keenan," said Asa.

"From the moment you meet him, you can't really help it," Keenan continued, sounding wistful. "Even though you know you shouldn't, you just want to trust him. Am I right?" His expression turned hard and bitter. "But you can't."

More gunshots rang out from beyond the wall, but whatever was going on at the compound, there was more action right here. I looked back and forth between the two men. I may not have been an emotion sensor myself, but I could still pick up the tension. The way Keenan was looking at Asa—I swear, his eyes were full of more than mistrust. They were full of . . . longing.

"Um, how do you guys know each other?"

"Do you remember the night you left?" Keenan asked Asa. "I'll never forget. No note. Nothing."

Asa stared stonily at him.

"I was sure you would come back at first. Or at least call." Keenan took a step closer. We were a triangle of betrayal now, with Asa at the apex. My heart was thundering so hard I could barely hear Keenan's next words: "It took me at least a year to realize you never would."

Asa gave me a sidelong glance before returning his attention to Keenan. "It was just another cage," he said softly.

Keenan grimaced, then quickly composed himself. "But tonight, you did call. And you've helped us find one of the four relics."

Asa stilled. "Frank didn't mention it was part of a set."

"Are you telling me Brindle sent you to steal one of the original four relics without warning you?"

"The original four." Asa scowled. "That's a myth."

Keenan shook his head. "We already found the Ekstazo relic."

"Did you destroy it?" Asa asked.

Keenan's smile was ghostly. "You can't destroy something like this."

I was beginning to sense Ben's future slipping away. "Tell me what the hell is going on!" I yelled.

"Some people call us naturals," said Keenan. "Witches, wizards, mages—so many terms to try to describe us, so many myths and only a few actual truths. And our bible is the tome of the *Essentialis Magia.*"

"Another myth," muttered Asa.

"Pages have been found," Keenan replied.

"And it talks about four relics?" I asked.

"It speaks to the original meaning of 'relic'—a body part of a saint, said to have miraculous powers. Catholicism borrowed that from us." He looked smug.

I glanced down at the pendant in my hands, a round chamber with a clasp on the side. "There's a body part in there?"

"From the original sorcerer himself, Akakios, executed by Roman invaders over two millennia ago. The faithful embalmed his body and saved four pieces, then hid them away. Blood, brain, bone, and viscera." Keenan was eyeing the relic with laserlike intensity. "These are sources of infinite power. All naturals born in the time since then are nourished by the power, passed from generation to generation, but we're only faint echoes compared to the source."

I pinched the round pendant between thumb and forefinger and shook it, listening to the contents rattle. Asa winced, and I rattled it a little harder just to hurt him. Lord knew he had hurt me. "Is that bone?"

"It just so happens it is. Strikon magic," said Keenan, taking another step closer. "But all of the originals are encased in gold."

I edged back, whimpering as the glass in my bleeding foot scraped the ground. No way could I run like this. And between Asa and Keenan, they could definitely take me down. I gritted my teeth to push away the pain.

"Brave," murmured Keenan. "But you can't escape."

I glared at him. "You don't care at all that a mobster kidnapped my fiancé? Aren't you supposed to enforce the law?"

"Yeah, but whose laws?" said Asa. "Welcome to the big world, Mattie."

I looked at Asa. "I will never forgive you for this."

Keenan smiled sadly. "I'm so sorry for your pain. I wish there was something I could do. But I need to take the relic now. We can't risk it falling back into the wrong hands."

But Asa reached out and snatched the relic from my fingers. "You get it when I get paid." His voice had gained an edge, and again, I hoped the relic was hurting him. *Bad.* "And no way are you bringing me in."

"We could iron out the details privately, tonight. No one at the office needs to know you were the source."

"Yeah?" Asa asked quietly, moving toward him as the relic dangled from his fingers. "Just you and me?"

It burned from my throat to my guts, especially when Keenan drew his gun and gave me a regretful look. "Yeah," Keenan said to Asa. "Just you and me."

As Keenan took aim, Asa pivoted and kicked the gun from his hand. Before I knew what was happening, he was behind Keenan, his loose suspenders wrapped around the man's throat. Keenan's eyes bulged and his face turned bright red as he clawed at Asa, who merely dragged him to the ground and tightened his grip. After a full minute of struggle, Keenan's arms flopped to his sides, and Asa quickly let go, leaning down to put his ear to the man's nose before sitting up again. He tossed the relic at me and dove for my foot, yanking out the piece of glass with a brutal lack of hesitation. The scream was barely out of my throat before he was pulling me to my feet.

"Is he dead?" I asked, reeling with the turnabout of the last few minutes.

"Nah," he said, putting his arm around my waist and letting me lean on him as he guided me out of the alley. "But we've got a ten-minute head start, and it'll be enough if you can move those little legs a bit faster."

Together, we limped out to a relatively busy thoroughfare a few blocks from the high-rise, and Asa hailed a taxi, giving the driver an address different from our hotel. As we pulled away from the curb, I put my head in my hands. "Did you actually call the Headsmen?"

"Yep. You were right about that. As soon as I felt this mother-fucking relic, I knew it was big. And I knew they would want it. The Headsmen seize relics that are particularly dangerous, and destroy them, which destroys the magic inside." He frowned. "Obviously wasn't the plan in this case."

"But you were never planning to give it to them anyway," I said slowly, peeking at him through the spill of curls that had fallen over my face.

He shook his head. "I called them because we never would have gotten out of Montri's stronghold on our own, and they were our escape hatch. But it only gained us a little time."

I took a close look at his face, the shadows under his eyes, the lines of strain that bracketed his mouth, the round red mark I could now see on his chest as his shirt fell open. "We have to go upload it soon so no one can sense it," I said.

Asa looked like he was biting the inside of his cheek as he glanced at the relic in my hand. "That thing is bad, Mattie. And huge. Bigger than anything I've handled before. It is *made* of *pain*. Did you hear Keenan? If he's right, this is the original source of that kind of magic. You don't want it inside your body."

I shivered at the cold sweat that had broken out across my chest and forehead. "You said I was strong."

"You are, but you're barely tested. We've only done this a few times, and I—" He cursed and slammed his hands against the ceiling of the taxi. "Should have brought fucking Lila."

"But you said I was stronger than she is!"

"Not the point," he shouted, making our cabdriver glance nervously over his shoulder.

"But Ben—"

"Fuck Ben," he snapped, running his hands through his hair.

"Why didn't you just give it to Keenan, if you don't care about your brother?"

He glared at me, his mouth tight. "I had no clue how powerful it was when I agreed to take this job. This thing could *break* you, Mattie."

"Can we get it back to Las Vegas without uploading it? What if we just packed it up and arranged for a flight out tomorrow?"

He let out an exasperated sigh. "I'll call our ride out as soon as we get to a phone, but it'll take them several hours to pull it together without Montri's contacts at the airport noticing. And when the smoke clears on that raid, Montri will know the relic is missing, and he'll know who took it. And that sensor, assuming he got out, will be able to find us. Especially with Montri's network of people all over the city. We might have until dawn before they come after us, but definitely no longer than that."

"Keenan knows you have it, too." I was still dizzy with what I had just learned about Asa. Or at least, what I thought I'd learned. I had no idea what to think of it. In some ways it didn't fit, but in others, it made complete sense. "Couldn't he bring down more Headsmen on us?"

Asa looked away. "He won't tell his people about me," he said quietly.

We rode in silence, me clutching the key to Ben's freedom, Asa's fingers white-knuckled over his own thighs. I wondered if he was waiting for me to say something, to ask him about his past with Keenan, to judge him. He'd told me so many times that he didn't give a fuck about what I thought of him, and now I was wondering if that was his armor, if he'd had to build it for himself over the years to protect whatever lay beneath.

I wondered if Ben knew. I wondered if their father had. I wondered if it was part of the reason he had been so hateful to his eldest son—Asa had said his father had called him a "perverted scumbag." It took everything I had not to reach over and take Asa's hand. As much as I hated to admit it, he had begun to matter to me.

"I'm sorry I didn't trust you," I murmured.

"It was good. Your emotions were true, and that's why Keenan fell for it."

"He couldn't sense yours?"

"I've had a lot of practice concealing my emotions. He's the one who taught me."

"So you can sense magic, resist manipulation, hide your true feelings, and withstand intense pain. Anything you can't do?"

Asa turned to me, still looking pissed off. "Convince a stubborn woman to walk away from a situation that'll probably get her killed?"

"Touché." I smiled, but he didn't smile back. "Where are we going, by the way?"

"A place where I arranged to have some supplies stashed by Brindle's contacts here."

"Who? Can they help us get out?"

"Not that kind of contacts. My guess is these people don't even know they're working for him. They just get paid to do a job for a friend of a friend of a friend."

I slumped. "Oh."

"We're going to pick our stuff up and then go to our conduit." He was radiating tension as he stared me down. "And if you're still sure you want to do this, we'll upload the magic."

I frowned as I remembered Hualing. "If this magic is as big and bad and painful as you're saying, then who . . ."

"This is a special job." Now he gave me a smile, but it was scary as heck. "And that means we have to go to a specialist."

CHAPTER NINETEEN

We arrived at a dingy self-service storage place just off Sukhumvit Road, and Asa used a code to open a tiny unit. Inside were just a few things—his black toolbox, another duffel much like the one he usually carried, and a small briefcase. He leaned over his toolbox and came up holding a first aid kit, then motioned for me to sit on the grimy concrete floor. When I obeyed, he briskly cleaned the wound on the bottom of my foot, applied some anesthetic cream, and placed a clean, waterproof bandage over it. As I rose, happy to be able to put weight on both feet again, he opened the duffel and pulled out something black and slick. He tossed it to me.

I caught it and held it up. "Um. Is this a corset?"

"Yup. There's a dress code where we're going." He yanked out a pair of stiletto-heeled, shiny black boots, then chucked another scrap of fabric at me.

"Latex hot pants? Are you kidding me?"

Asa shot to his feet and was on me with a snarl. "Listen to me, little girl," he said as he backed me against the wall. He caged me in, just like he had the first night we met, placing his hands on either side of my head. "I gave you an out. I'm only going to say it to you one more time: it's your choice. You don't want to do this, we drop the relic and head home. It's too hot to carry out, so we have two options."

Why did he seem so angry at me all of a sudden? "We agreed to this job. You chose me to be your reliquary. And we're doing this for Ben."

His eyes were dark, maybe with rage, maybe with hurt, maybe with something else entirely. I couldn't tell, but I could feel the heat. "And you don't give a fuck what happens to you in the process," he said. "That when I get you back to Ben, you might not be in any shape to recognize him, let alone go back to your happy little life together."

"But if we go home empty-handed, they'll kill him, won't they?"

"If they don't, it would signal that Brindle is weak."

That was it, then. I may not have taken any vows yet, but the night Ben had slid that diamond onto my finger, I'd known I was ready to. For better or worse. And this . . . hopefully this was the worst, and I was strong enough to take it. Because it was me or Ben, and I wasn't the kind of person who could walk away from that. "I have to do this, Asa."

"Fine." He leaned closer. "And can you do it without me?"

I thought about that. "Well . . . no. Probably not."

"*Probably* not? If I walked away and left you here right now, would you have a single fucking clue of what to do next?"

"Well, I—"

"Could you find a conduit, any conduit, let alone one who could help you? Would you know how to set it up? Would you have any idea whether the transaction was complete or not?" His words echoed sharply in the little metal room, making me cringe.

"No," I muttered.

"Then you're completely dependent on me." Our eyes met, and I glared at him, but it only made him edge closer, emanating danger. "Say it, Mattie. You're completely dependent on *me*."

I gritted my teeth. My hands were fisted at my sides.

"Say. It. Say it or we're done." He gave me a few more seconds, then shoved off the wall and turned his back, kneeling to zip the duffel. "Good luck, honey. You're gonna need it." He stood up and looped the duffel strap over his shoulder, then headed for the door, leaving the relic lying on the ground next to the corset I'd dropped.

His hand was on the doorknob when I crumbled. "I'm completely dependent on you," I said quietly, my cheeks hot.

He stilled, facing the door. "Say it again. Louder."

I cleared my throat and drew a long breath through my nose. "I'm completely dependent on you."

He looked over his shoulder at me. "Now say, 'I'm completely dependent on you, *sir*.'"

I blinked at him. "What?"

He turned the doorknob, and I put my hands up. "Fine! I'm completely dependent on you, sir! What kind of weird game is this?"

Asa let go of the door and turned around. "This is no game." He slid the duffel from his arm and let it fall to the ground. "Until I say otherwise, you will do exactly as I say. You will remember that your life and Ben's are in my hands. Now that you've decided you want to go through with this, you don't get any more choices unless I allow it. You don't get to fucking speak unless I ask you a question. You are handing yourself over to me, and trusting me to get you through it. That's the only way we do this. You got it?"

Handing myself over to him? My tongue trembled with the urge to tell him to go jump in the river, but he had me—Ben's life was at stake. "Yes."

His eyes narrowed. "Yes, what?" he barked.

"Yes . . . sir? You want me to salute?"

He reached into his bag and pulled out something small and black, then rose and approached me again. He lifted it up in the dim overhead light. It was a collar. "No saluting," he said in a low voice. "But you will show respect. Lift your hair."

"Is that Gracie's?"

"Does it fucking look like Gracie's?" He held it right in front of my face. It was much smaller than something that could have fit around the pit bull's thick neck. "Lift your hair and don't question me again."

My heart skipped a beat. He looked completely serious. I lifted my hair, and Asa fastened the collar around my neck. He toyed with the ring that hung from the front. "Good girl," he said quietly, and I relaxed a little, glad that the edge in his voice had dulled for the moment. "Now take off your clothes, and put on the outfit I chose for you."

He must have seen my eyes flare with alarm, because he stepped away from me. "I'm going to allow you some privacy."

Allow me. Like it was his to offer. And right now, I supposed it was. "Thank you."

"Thank you, what?"

I closed my eyes and swallowed, trying to push down the angry defiance swirling inside me. "Thank you, sir."

"I'll be right outside." He grabbed his duffel and headed out the door.

I sagged against the metal, my heart hammering. What the hell was going on? Shaking, I slipped off my ruined dress and examined the hot pants. They were so short that it was clear I was meant to wear nothing underneath, with a little zipper down the front that would make them fall open. "What the hell kind of dress code is this?" I muttered as I stepped out of my white lacy boy shorts and yanked the skintight latex up my legs. They fit perfectly, like a swimsuit might, but thicker and tighter. Next I eyed the corset. There was a zipper on the front, which would connect two stiff panels that were held together at the back by crisscrossed laces. I pulled the thing around my torso and zipped it up, but it was really loose. Holding it around me so it covered my breasts, I went to the door. "Asa? The corset doesn't fit."

The door opened and Asa stepped into the room. He'd changed. *Really* changed. Dressed in motorcycle boots, black leather pants molded to his thighs and lean hips, a studded black belt, and a short-sleeved black latex shirt zipped halfway down his chest, which showed off every sculpted cut of his lean muscles. "It'll fit. Turn and face the wall." His voice was flat but quiet.

I obeyed, and tensed as I felt him behind me. He briskly tightened the laces, first at the top, then at the bottom, pulling them so tight that I gasped.

"Does it hurt?"

"No," I said faintly.

"Hands on the wall, then."

I put my palms on the wall, squeezing my eyes shut at the edge that had returned to his voice. There was something about it that made me want to scream and kick, but I knew he was out the door if I did.

Asa pulled the laces even tighter, and when I winced and whimpered, he stopped. "Can you breathe all right?" His breath fanned across my bare shoulder and raised goose bumps.

"Yeah. Mostly."

He tied the strings from the corset in a bow, leaving the tails hanging down. "Then turn around."

I did, to find him kneeling at my feet, the high-heeled boots next to him. "Foot," he said, wiggling his fingers impatiently. I offered my foot and he slid the boot on. Once again, it fit perfectly, and it made me wonder when he'd taken note of my shoe size. He put the other boot on, grabbed the relic and put it in his toolbox, then rose again and moved back, taking me in. "You look good."

I did my own assessment. The boots hugged my calves. My thighs were bare, and I was wearing pants that fit more like panties. And the corset had cinched in my waist, making it look tiny between the swells of my hips and breasts, which had been pushed up to create some serious cleavage. "I have to go out in public like this?"

"You'll go out in public any way I want you to. Now shut the fuck up and follow me." He slung the duffel over his shoulder, picked up his toolbox and briefcase, and walked out of the storage unit.

I followed him, wondering if I was leaving more than just my white dress and panties behind.

•••

"Oh my God," I whispered as I looked up at the flashing neon sign. "Mistress," it said in jagged letters. We were on a side street, more like an alley, tucked into a maze of dilapidated buildings and new construction way off the main road. The door in front of us was metal, with a slot in it. Asa kicked at it, and the slot slid open, revealing a pair of dark, heavily lined eyes.

"Here to see Rose," he said.

"Have an appointment?" a feminine voice asked.

"Booked it an hour ago."

"Ah," said the woman. "Mr. Riordan. She said you bringing something very special for her." She closed the slot and opened the door, revealing a dark, cramped entryway and a set of stairs leading upward into more darkness. Bass thumped above our heads, but that was the only noise.

"I am Mistress D," she said, giving us a little bow. "Welcome to my lair." She had on skintight black leather leggings and a black bustier, and her nails were long, black, and filed to sharp points. Some kind of whip hung from the left side of her hip. She glanced at my face, then my collar, and quickly looked away as Asa took a half step in front of me.

"She ready to roll?" he asked.

"Waiting in the dungeon."

"Good," said Asa. "Take us up."

The woman bowed her head. She didn't look at me again. In fact, she seemed to intentionally not be looking at me. Somehow, despite my insane outfit, or maybe because of it, I'd become invisible.

Asa marched up the stairs, lugging his toolbox and briefcase, clearly expecting me to follow. I did, though my mouth had gone dry. We were obviously in some kind of weird, kinky club, and the mention of a dungeon had set my teeth on edge. That was where his special conduit hung out?

Mistress D opened a door at the top of the steps, revealing a long room lit with deep-purple lights. Along one wall was a set of cages and shackles. A thin woman wearing nothing more than a thong was cuffed to a rack, her bottom exposed as a man slapped her backside. Another young woman was dancing in one of the cages, wearing leather straps wrapped around her torso and nothing else, except for her sky-high stiletto boots. Compared to theirs, my outfit was pretty modest. The dancers shot us sly smiles as we passed by their cages, where they danced for a few men dressed in black lounging in chairs nearby.

We entered a hallway lined with doors. "These our playrooms," she said as we passed one, which contained what looked like a doctor's exam room. Many of the doors were closed, but I caught a glimpse of a red-painted bedroom with a large metal cage at the foot of the lush bed. My heart was kicking against my ribs, especially when Mistress D came to a stop at a room at the very end of the hallway. "And this *your* playroom," she said, pulling aside another metal slot and peering inside. "I leave you alone. But there is intercom in every room. I come to you quick."

"Good. Rose will need you after we're through," said Asa. He reached into his duffel and handed Mistress D a thick stack of Thai baht. "I won't be able to stick around, but I want to make sure she's got someone."

Mistress D smiled as she accepted the cash. "I know how take care my girls." She turned and sauntered down the hall.

Asa slipped his finger into the ring connected to my collar and drew me closer. "I'm going to explain this once," he said quietly. "Our conduit has particular needs, and she only takes jobs where her needs are going to be met."

"And she likes pain," I guessed. Of course. Why else would we be meeting her in a place like this? Don had said he would never take a Strikon job. It must be hard to find conduits willing to endure it. But a conduit who enjoyed pain? Who sought it out? She'd be perfect.

Asa tapped the tip of his nose. "And I am going to meet her needs. Got it?"

I looked into his eyes, a warm color that froze me with its intensity. "Yes, sir," I whispered.

"And when we go in there, you will keep calling me that. Call me by my name and there will be consequences."

"Okay."

"Okay, what?"

"Okay, sir."

"Good girl." He gave my collar a little tug. "Just for that, I'm going to give you one more choice tonight. Choose a name."

"Can't you just call me by my actual name?" God, this was scary enough. I was in a strange, scary place with strange, scary people. I had little idea what was about to happen—except that it involved a huge amount of pain that might drive me out of my mind—and it seemed like it would be comforting to hear my own name, especially because Asa was acting like such a stranger.

He shook his head. "You're going to trust me on this, and you're going to be grateful when it's done. Choose a name."

"Um . . ."

"Do it or I'll choose one for you."

I flinched at the sharpness in his voice. "Okay. Uh . . . Eve?" I'd always kind of liked the name.

Asa's gaze traced my face. "Eve it is." He let go of the collar and opened the door without bothering to knock first.

It swung open to reveal a simple room, not the medieval dungeon I'd been picturing. Still, what was in there scared me nearly as much. There was a metal four-poster bed with horizontal steel bars in place of a headboard. The mattress wasn't covered in sheets, but in smooth black leather, along with a few black leather pillows. It was higher than a normal bed, waist level. Like an operating table or something. And there was a metal table next to it. Apart from a few hooks arrayed in a row on the gray-painted walls, the room was empty, the floor made of smooth linoleum. In front of the bed stood a fine-boned woman, maybe in her late thirties, her long black hair pulled up in a slick high ponytail, wearing lace panties and a garter belt, fishnet stockings, and superhigh heels. Her leather bra didn't actually cover her small breasts, but rather just supported them, pushing them up and leaving them on full display. When she saw Asa, her down-turned eyes lit up for a moment and a shy smile pulled at her full red lips. She pressed her palms together and dropped her head forward, touching her thumbs to her forehead. "Welcome . . ."

"Thank you, Rose. You will call me sir," Asa said. "Eve, close the door and stay where you are." Without looking back at me, he walked toward Rose, towering over her. "On your knees." His voice was quiet, but full of command. He set his duffel, toolbox, and briefcase on the metal table.

Rose knelt immediately, letting her gaze stray up his long legs. She bit her lip as she looked at his crotch, and her hand rose like she wanted to reach for his belt. Asa caught her fingers a few inches from the front of his pants. "Look at me."

She tilted her head up. "Yes, sir?"

He gestured at his body. "Off-limits. Got it? Touch me and there will be consequences."

It could have just been me, but she looked a little intrigued by the prospect. Still, her "Yes, sir" came quickly.

"Good girl. I'm going to give you a present."

She smiled up at him as if he were sunlight, and he stroked her cheek. She leaned into his touch. My stomach tightened. I knew Asa knew how to play people, but there was something about the gentle slide of his thumb over her skin that made me feel uneasy in a way I couldn't understand.

"Eve, come over here and get on the bed."

It took me a second to get my feet moving, and when I did, my ankle buckled and I wobbled on my stilettos, which clicked like gunshots as I walked across the floor. He hooked his finger in my collar and caught me before I reached the bed. "How do you answer me?" he said softly, staring straight ahead.

"Yes, sir." I hopped up on the bed, reminding myself that this was a show. We were doing it for Rose, so she would help us do this job. All an act. All an act.

"Lie on your back," Asa said.

All an act. "Yes, sir."

Asa looked down at the beautiful, nearly naked woman kneeling before him. "I want you to tie up Eve for me, Rose. Would you like that?"

My eyes flew wide. "Um, As—?" I clamped my lips shut as his eyes lasered into mine.

"What did you say?"

"Nothing." We'd only just gotten there, and I didn't want to break down now after insisting we do this, but as Asa reached into his bag and pulled out a set of ropes, I nearly lost it. Being tied down went way beyond a simple game of pretend. "No, wait. Sir."

Asa looked up at me again. "Eve, would you like to know why we're tying you up?"

Because you're a sick bastard who's enjoying my fear? I nearly threw that bomb. My heart was drumming in my chest. But I still managed to say, "Yes, sir."

"When this transaction begins, you're going to lose control of your body. And when you lose control, you will thrash. You could easily break a bone or two. But beyond that, if I don't secure you and Rose first, you might lose skin contact midtransaction. And if that happens, we're all fucked. The magic could splinter, or be lost, or cause unnecessary damage to both of you. Do you want that to happen?"

"No . . . sir," I added when his eyebrow arched.

"Good. Rose, get to work." He pulled her to her feet, revealing that her lace panties were held together in the back by a few crisscrossing strings and nothing more. He gave her a sharp smack on the butt, and she moaned.

"How you want her, sir?" Rose asked in a quiet, sweet voice as she accepted a coil of rope.

"Cuffed, raised over her head, and secured," Asa said, heading for the foot of the bed with another section of rope in his hands.

Rose stood at the edge of the bed and smiled as she looked over my body. "She is lovely, sir."

"You may speak directly to Eve."

Rose met my eyes. "Lovely reliquary. Very nice. I like."

I tried for a friendly smile, but I could feel Asa looping rope around my ankles and securing it to the bar at the foot of the bed, and it was all I could do not to scream. I raised my arms above my head, just wanting to get this over with. "Thanks, Rose. You-you're lovely, too. Go ahead?"

She proceeded to wrap the rope around my wrists while I held them several inches apart, and then she wound the rope around the coils, creating a sort of cuff with this spiral of rope connecting it. I winced as she wrenched it tight and tied the end of the rope around one of the bars on the headboard. "All tied, sir," she said to Asa.

I tried to shift and bend my knees, but Asa had done his job, and I was basically immobile. Helpless. And my wrists . . . "Ow," I whispered.

Asa's dark head snapped up. "Ow?" He stalked over to the head of the bed, his gaze on my wrists. "Rose, this is too tight."

She bowed her head, but I could see the faint smile pulling at her lips. "So sorry, sir."

His nostrils flared. "I'm going to fix this, and then I'm going to punish you. Her hands are already turning red." His voice was a knife. "Back on your knees. Keep your eyes on the floor."

Rose dropped to her knees in an instant, and Asa blocked my view of her a second later.

I looked up at him as he loosened the coils of rope around my wrists, creating more wiggle room.

"Thank you, sir." My voice cracked over the words.

His eyes met mine, and I wanted to beg him. *Be nice to me. Please. I'm so scared.* Just a little softness was all I wanted. A little reassurance. Anything but Asa's hard edges. And I wonder if he knew that. I wonder if the choice to deny me those things on my terms was easy for him, if he knew what would happen if he did, and how it would change things between us forever. Because he leaned down and said, "You chose this."

"I know."

"I'm meeting your needs, aren't I?"

I swallowed hard. "I—"

"I think it's time for your gag." He reached over and pulled out a rubber ball connected to two strips of leather. He held it up for me to see. "When the magic enters you, you're going to scream, Eve. We don't want to disturb anyone, do we?"

"Please, no . . ."

His fists slammed into the mattress on either side of my arms, and I closed my eyes and tried to shrink into myself. "Look at me," he snapped.

I opened my eyes, and his face was right over mine. "I'm going to get you through this, Eve. Do you believe that?"

I stared up at him, at his high cheekbones and dark hair, the face I had started to look for when things went to hell. He'd brought more scary into my life than I'd ever experienced before, but he'd never left me behind. He could have easily given Keenan the relic and accepted the bounty, which was obviously millions more than he was getting for taking it home to Brindle. He could have let Keenan shoot me. But instead, here we were, because this was the only way to do what I had *insisted* on doing. Asa had taken control and made it possible. And as I looked into his eyes, that understanding broke off a little piece of me, something that would never be mine again. I could feel it cracking and splitting, and I fell with it. Fighting was pointless and stupid and unnecessary. We were on the same side, with the same goal. I needed him.

"You're going to get me through this," I said.

He nodded. "And that means you can let go. It means you trust me. It means you can focus on what you have to do, because you know I'm handling the rest." His nose was almost touching mine. "You got that?"

"Yeah," I whispered. "You're in control, sir."

Something shifted behind his eyes, primal and deep. His gaze slipped from mine and traced the line of my neck, adorned with the collar, my chest, my waist and hips, my legs, like he was taking it in, accepting all of me as his responsibility. Slowly, he returned his attention to my face. "Open your mouth."

I obeyed, and he laid the rubber ball between my lips and buckled the gag behind my head, checking the tightness by slipping his fingers beneath the strap before laying my head on the pillow again.

"Good girl, Eve," he murmured, toying with the ring on my collar as we stared at each other. I had no idea what was going on in his mind, but mine was full of pleas, for him to carry me through, to do what he needed to do. He'd said he was my dealer, and hope was my drug, and now he had me, body and soul.

Asa tore his gaze from mine and backed away from the bed. I raised my head, not ready for the moment to be over yet. Then my gaze reached his pants, where the thick bulge of his erection was obvious. Shock jolted me. A few hours ago, I'd thought I understood him, and now I was more confused than ever. Asa's eyes locked with mine again, glinting with defiance and challenge. He made no attempt to turn away or hide. He just stood there and let me look.

"Rose," he said, his voice low. "Time for your punishment."

He went over to his toolbox and opened it up, laying out his tools with the precision of a surgeon. A pair of shears, latex gloves, a set of tongs, a roll of thick red tape, the relic, and a small whip with dozens of thin leather strands.

"Get up and bend over the bed," he said to her, and she eagerly complied, leaning over until her hair tickled my thigh. "I think five lashes is fit for your disobedience."

Rose spread her arms and smiled. "Yes, sir. Thank you, sir."

Asa raised the whip, pulling the strands tight before letting them drop with a sharp smack across the middle of Rose's back. I flinched as she cried out. Red stripes flared on her pale skin as he raised the whip

214

again. It was over quickly, by which time her face was torn between ecstasy and pain. "Thank you, sir," she said again.

"Do you want a gag, too, baby?"

"Please, sir," she whispered.

He retrieved another gag, and after he buckled it, slipped his fingers under the leather strap and used it to pull her upright. He was close behind her, so close that she could probably feel him hard against her exposed backside. The sight made my breath hitch.

"You need something from me," he said quietly, reaching around to take hold of her chin and tip her head back onto his shoulder. His long fingers wrapped around her throat.

Her nod had a frantic, eager edge to it.

"Palms on the bed. Lift them even a fraction of an inch, and I stop." She complied instantly.

"You want Eve to watch, don't you, Rose? You want her to see what I do to you."

Another nod.

He twisted his hand in her ponytail and pulled her head to the side. And then, as his mouth descended on the junction of her neck and shoulder, his eyes found mine again. I whimpered as his teeth fastened onto her skin, as his hand closed over one of her bare breasts, as her squeal was stifled by the gag. Inexplicable tears stung my eyes as his other hand slid down her stomach and disappeared from my view beneath the edge of the bed. She convulsed and moaned with pleasure, her pelvis undulating. He held her there—sucking and biting at her neck, his hands claiming every inch of her—and never took his eyes off me.

I was caught, unable to tear my gaze from Asa's as Rose's muffled cries reached a fever pitch. She was writhing in his grip, coming apart only a few feet away. Her palms slid against the leather, but she seemed determined to keep them there, desperate for him to keep going.

And I was, too. Tight and wet and tingling, suddenly I *was* grateful that I wasn't Mattie right now, that I was Eve, that I was just here in this place, with no past and no future, because I couldn't find my will to resist. The need was too strong, the lure too great. I could almost feel the press of his hips to her back, the slide of his tongue along her skin, the sharp nip of his teeth, the firm stroke of his fingers. My hips rose as my muscles tensed, as my body flexed, as my own teeth dug into the hard rubber of the ball between my lips. Dimly, I knew I shouldn't be affected, that I should be able to look away, but Asa was in control, and I had surrendered, and even though he hadn't laid a finger on me, I was still about to come.

Then he stopped, lifting his head and pressing his mouth to Rose's ear. "You ready?"

She opened her eyes and nodded, her sweat-slick cheek sliding against his, adoration plain on her face.

He pulled his hands from her body and grabbed the red tape, and a few seconds later, he'd taped her hands to my thigh, palms down as she leaned all her weight on the bed. As I panted, unable to rid myself of the spiraling, tight feeling low in my belly, Asa opened his black briefcase and pulled it closer, and I caught a glimpse of what was inside—a portable defibrillator, like the one we kept in our kitchen back in Sheboygan, in case Ben ever needed it. The sight sent a drop of pure terror straight to the base of my spine, cooling the heat. Tools within reach, Asa slid on the latex gloves, picked up the tongs, and approached the relic as if it were a poisonous snake. A drop of sweat trickled down his cheek as he pried at the clasp on the pendant.

It was happening. We were going to do it right now. And these, I realized, might be my last few coherent moments. Silenced, tied up and unable to move, all I could do was stare at the man who had promised to carry me through. In the space of that minute, no one else existed for me but him. Like he felt it, he paused and looked over at me.

His mouth tightened, and he nodded. Maybe a reassurance, maybe a good-bye.

Then he flicked the clasp open. Grimacing, he used the tongs to pluck a small, knobby lump of gold from inside the pendant and quickly brought it over to Rose. "I've got everything here we might need," he said to her. "I've got you."

Rose nodded again, laying her head on my thigh, her fingers digging into my flesh. Her hair was silk against my skin. Every beat of my heart was like a bomb blast. Every thought was a prayer.

Asa lifted the edge of Rose's bra and slid the relic under the fabric.

My vision went white as agony blasted up my leg and into my chest, shredding my insides with pure annihilation.

CHAPTER TWENTY

It turns out there's only so much pain a mind can take before it simply shuts down. Like a circuit breaker, maybe. But it takes a lot of agony to get there. I honestly can't remember how long it went on. I only remember being certain that my entire body was being dipped in molten metal, that my bones were splintering and sparking, that my marrow was on fire. There was no part of me that didn't feel it, no place to run or escape, no safe corner of my thoughts where I could hide. It consumed everything, sight and sound and smell and touch, thought and wish, hope and memory.

Then it spiraled tighter, pulling itself from my limbs, wrenching itself from my spine, swirling in my chest like a whirlpool until it abruptly reached a point, like a sword stabbing straight through my heart, like all the hurt had focused on that one soft spot and was rending cell from cell, atom from atom.

And then it stopped. Gone. Done. I floated in a haze of numb relief. The absence of pain was a release unto itself. It was all I could feel, all I was aware of. Like no bad things could find me. I vaguely felt a pressure on my neck, my body being jostled, but it didn't hurt, so I didn't care.

It was the beeping that brought me back to reality.

I opened my eyes to see Asa using the defibrillator on Rose, who was lying spread-eagled on the floor, red tape dangling from her wrists, her bra cut away. Shears lay discarded next to Asa's feet. His movements were sharp and economical as he laid the pads on her now completely bare chest and pressed the button for the shock. She jerked slightly, and then the machine beeped again and Asa began chest compressions.

The second shock brought her around. Her eyelids fluttered and a tear slipped down her cheek. Asa turned her onto her side and leaned over her, murmuring softly, stroking her arm, and then motioned to Mistress D, who I suddenly realized was now standing in the doorway. As soon as the woman knelt at Rose's side, Asa got up and came over to me. His face sheened with sweat and there were circles under his eyes, but his hands were steady as they slid into my hair to unbuckle the gag.

"How'd I do?" I whispered as soon as he removed it.

"Fucking incredible." He brushed a loose curl off my brow. "But now we have to get out of here."

With a few deft pulls, he untied the ropes and freed my wrists, then did the same with my ankles. He returned to my side as I worked my jaw to ease the soreness, and held up the ball gag to show me the teeth marks I'd left. "You would have bitten off your own tongue."

"Thanks for not mentioning that possibility before."

"Part of the deal," he said. "You didn't need one more thing to worry about."

He packed up his tools and equipment, then picked up the toolbox and shouldered the duffel, but left the defibrillator on the floor, where Mistress D was helping Rose sit up. A dark bruise at the junction of her neck and shoulder stood out stark on her creamy skin. Asa ran his hand over her head and let her lean on his leg for a moment while he caressed her cheek, then nodded at the mistress, who pulled Rose away.

I watched Asa coming toward me, tall and lean and dark. The gauzy fog of numbness started to clear as I remembered the moments before I had been plunged into agony. His hips canted against Rose's backside.

His hand down the front of her panties. His mouth on her neck. His eyes on mine.

Oh God.

Asa slid his free arm around my waist and helped me off the bed. He didn't let me go after my feet hit the floor, either. Instead, he guided me out the door, down the stairs, out of the club, and into a waiting taxi, where he started to pull me close. I picked up his scent, sweat and sex, and I couldn't handle it—I put my hands on his chest and pushed him away as my throat constricted.

I reached up and clawed at the collar. "Take this off me. I need it off *now*."

Asa unfastened it and slid it into his bag without comment.

"Where are we going?"

"I got us a room at a hotel near the airport," he said as the driver sped down a wide, tree-lined road free of the high-rises we'd been surrounded by.

A room. As in *one* room? My heart stuttered. I was Mattie again, and I was engaged to a wonderful man named Ben, and the memory of watching his brother pleasure a woman—and, if I was brutally honest, wishing *I* were that woman—was crashing down on me, burying me in guilt.

"We just plugged a shitload of ancient Strikon magic into your body. I'm going to take care of you tonight."

The driver turned onto a narrow road with no sidewalks, hemmed in by thick tropical vegetation on one side and car parks and apartment buildings on the other. The hotel was maybe five or six stories, an outdoor stairwell winding up one side, rooms all lit up bright despite a dingy exterior. Asa paid the driver and got out, holding the door for me and offering his hand.

I didn't take it. God, what had happened in the last few hours? Had I only done what I had to, or had I let it go too far? Had I *cheated* on Ben? Tears burned in my eyes, and I kept my head down as I walked through the doors of the hotel. Asa caught up with me. "Mattie, it's just for one night, and you—"

"We need two rooms." What had I done? I'd laid my soul bare for Asa. Ben's *brother*. I'd surrendered completely to a man who was not my fiancé. How could that be anything other than cheating? I clamped my eyes shut, forcing down a sob. "I can take care of myself."

Asa sighed and asked the guy behind the front desk for another room, his knuckles tight over the handle of his toolbox. He tossed one of the keys at me and I fumbled it, nearly falling as I tried to bend over in my stiff corset. Asa scooped the key from the floor. "Right. You're absolutely fine," he muttered, then took my upper arm and led me to the stairs. "You're on two. I'm on four. It was the only room left."

"Good. Thanks." I needed him as far from me as he could get right now. I needed to think things through.

We reached my room and he opened the door for me, then walked in and pulled a pair of sweat shorts and a T-shirt from his duffel, along with a pair of sandals. "It's all I have for you, but I've seen you wear stuff like that before and figured it would be comfortable . . ." His voice faded to nothing as he looked me over. "Let me untie the corset for you."

"No," I whispered.

He rolled his eyes. "You're being stupid."

"Seriously? Just get out."

He scrubbed his hands over his face and ran them through his hair. "Goddammit, Mattie, you can barely even stand up, and all I'm—"

"Get out!" I shrieked, shaking all over as I pointed to the door.

"If that's how you want to do it." He stalked out the door, slamming it behind him.

I sank to the bed, letting the tears come. The last few hours had pulled me apart and rearranged me, and now I was trying to slide the pieces into place again, but they weren't fitting the way they used to. And yet I couldn't wish all of it away, because I had done it for Ben. For the man I loved. It had worked—I had this ancient magic in my little vault. Somewhere inside me lay enough pain to destroy people. To stop someone's heart, like it had stopped Rose's. Now I just had to carry it home, put it back in the relic, and give it to Brindle . . .

We had to put it back in the relic. I had to do this all over again.

I pushed that thought down a deep hole, because if I focused too closely on it, I knew I would break. With faltering hands, I yanked off the boots, then spent several minutes rolling on the bed, trying to undo the stupid knots Asa had tied at the back of the corset. By the time I succeeded in getting them undone, I was sweating and crying and aching. Something inside me felt like it had shifted and was teetering at the edge of a cliff, one stiff breeze from going over the edge. This wasn't like the sloshy aquarium feeling I'd had in the first few transactions. This was fundamentally unsteady, hard and huge and threatening. Was that my emotional state? Or the magic? What would happen if it fell? What would happen when it hit bottom?

I frowned and rubbed at my chest. "You're a vault," I whispered.

What happened if the vault got dropped off a cliff? Asa said I had control . . . but what if I couldn't hold on to it?

"Stop." I limped into the bathroom and rinsed myself off with cold water, not able to summon the energy to shampoo my hair. My limbs were leaden with exhaustion, and I had no idea when Asa would be back, banging on my door and telling me to get my little legs moving. I needed to sleep. I needed to stop thinking.

Especially about him.

I nearly wept with gratitude when I walked back into the room and saw that Asa had laid a small bag with a toothbrush and toothpaste next to my clothes. After brushing my teeth and pulling on the T-shirt and shorts, I crawled beneath my covers and focused on Ben. I imagined sitting with him on our cozy deck, looking out on our backyard bursting with summer blossoms. I'd lean against him, and he'd put his arm around me. We'd argue about what to name our first baby. It would be easy and clean and right.

Or . . . it would have been.

Should I tell Ben what had happened? Didn't I owe him honesty? I'd demanded it in the aftermath of his cover-up of what was really going on with him, so how could I possibly keep things from him with a clear conscience? But if I told him—if I told him *everything*—it would cut him deep. I'd never thought of the truth as a knife, but now I knew it was, able to sever muscle from bone, heart from heart. What had once been simple and right was tainted, and I couldn't figure out if everything I'd done had been necessary, or if I had gone off the rails somehow.

I drew my knees to my chest, wishing this strange, unstable feeling would go away. Wishing for strong arms around me, a gentle voice in my ear that would tell me things were going to be okay. But I was alone in this mess, and somehow I had to push through.

I pressed my head into the pillow and cried myself to sleep.

I bolted upright, my heart galloping, my breaths coming in sharp, strangled gasps. I put my hand to my chest, where the stab of pain was still fading. Terror pulled me out of bed. My ears rang with it. My blood pounded in my skull. I couldn't think. I could only act. I ran for the door. I had no idea what Asa's room number was, but I was going to bang on every door on the fourth floor until he answered.

I burst into the hallway, turned for the stairwell, and tripped over a pair of long legs. I glimpsed a toolbox and duffel sitting against the wall as Asa caught me in his arms. He'd been sitting on the floor next to my door. He'd changed into a T-shirt and cargo shorts, with Converse sneakers on his feet. "Whoa, there," he said in a groggy voice.

"I think it's coming out," I said, my voice cracking.

"What?" He guided me to my feet and held me by my upper arms.

"The magic. I felt a . . . a stabbing?" I couldn't slow down my breathing, and my body was tingling. My lips had gone numb.

Asa's brow furrowed, and he stuck his hand beneath the loose collar of my shirt. "Shh," he said as I struggled, needing to run, needing to flee and never stop, because something terrifying was chasing me, and it was about to sink its teeth in. "Mattie, hold still. I just need to feel it."

But I couldn't. My heart felt as if it were about to explode. "It's leaking out, isn't it? All that Strikon magic—" And when it hit, it would tear me apart from the inside out.

Asa wrapped his arm around my waist and wrestled me into my room, then pushed me against the wall, pinning me there. "Dammit. Stay still, Mattie. *Stop.*"

"Please please please—"

He clamped his hand over my mouth and bowed his head, tucking his hand beneath the hem of my shirt this time. His calloused palm pressed against my ribs. His whole body was jammed against mine, just trying to hold me still. He was shaking with the effort, or maybe with trying to concentrate despite my desperate thrashing. But a moment later, he raised his head. "It's not leaking. I think you're having a panic attack."

"No, that's not it," I said between creaky gasps for air.

"Mattie, you are so strong. I can barely feel this magic inside you, and if it was somehow trickling out, I would definitely know. When it was in the relic, I felt sick, like it was eating my bones the longer I was close to it." He took my face in his hands, forcing me to look up at him. "But now that it's in you, all of that is gone. I can barely feel it at all. That's how strong you are."

"But I can't hold it. It's going to break inside me. I know it. I can feel it. It's going to kill me."

"Then you have to focus on containing it. You have to relax and let your mind rest. Let your body do its thing."

"I can't!" My mind was reeling. Guilt or necessity, honesty or a lie to protect the innocent, the way I knew I would never be the same, the forbidden thoughts I couldn't even admit I was having. It was all in my skull, jangling around. "I can't turn it off. Everything that happened, everything I did—"

"What did you do?"

I closed my eyes because he wouldn't let me turn my head. "You know. You saw me."

"Really? I thought that was Eve," he said gently.

"Eve," I whispered. And I remembered letting Mattie go, putting her away just so I could get through everything. *Eve* had given herself to Asa. Eve had submitted and let him be in control. And he had accepted her submission, because he was strong enough, because he knew what to do, and because he was the only one who could do it.

I desperately needed him to do it right now. I couldn't carry the burden of guilt and sorrow and loss and shame for another second. "Asa?" I sniffled and wiped at my wet cheek. "Can I . . ." I let out a hitching breath. "Can I be Eve right now?" I hazarded a glance at his face, not even sure he would know what I meant.

He stepped back, allowing some space between us. "That's what you want?"

I nodded. "Only for a little while. I need . . ." My face crumpled. I needed help. I needed someone to take care of me. But accepting that from Asa felt so complicated now. He'd been right—putting this magic inside me was threatening to break me . . . just not in the way I'd imagined. "Can you just take over for a few hours? I'm so . . . I *can't*. It's too much."

He stared down at me, then let go of me and walked away. My throat tightened as he headed out the door. But he was back immediately, pulling his duffel and toolbox into the room. He came up with something in his hands, and spent a moment looking at it before turning around.

It was the collar. "Come here," he said quietly.

I walked toward him on shaky legs.

"Lift your hair."

I obeyed. "Thank you," I said as he fastened it.

"Thank you, what?"

"Thank you, sir." My breathing was already starting to slow.

He looked down at me, his eyes shadowed with something I couldn't translate. "Good girl, Eve. Now go over to the bed."

I walked to the bed, a trickle of fear sliding down my spine. *What is he going to—*

He pulled the covers back. Then he kicked off his shoes. "Get in there." He nodded at the mattress.

I paused. Asa arched his eyebrow. "Yes, sir," I said.

I'd given him control. I'd decided to trust him. I would give what he demanded in return.

I crawled onto the bed and felt the mattress dip with his weight as he joined me. He settled on his back and spread his arm out. "Now come here."

Hesitantly, I moved closer, edging over next to him as I inhaled his scent. Sometime in the last few hours, he'd taken a shower, even though he'd apparently decided to camp outside my room instead of sleep in his own bed.

He'd been unwilling to leave me alone even when I'd thought that was what I needed.

"Put your head on my shoulder," he murmured, guiding me with his fingers in my hair, stroking my scalp.

"Yes, sir," I whispered.

"You let me in," he said, "and that means it's just you and me now. Everything else stays outside the door. Every single thing. None of it gets inside, because I'm in here, and I won't allow it."

I pressed my face to his shoulder and nodded.

"So you're not going to think," he continued. "Not right now. And you're not going to worry. Or plan. Got it, Eve?"

"Yes, sir." I snuggled into his side, keenly aware of the rub of the soft leather band around my throat. I was Eve, not Mattie. Mattie had been shed like a snake skin, sick and panicked and twisted up. Eve existed only in this moment, and she was simple. She was worn out and heavy with fatigue. I sighed, so thankful that my heart was no longer in my throat.

"Good girl," he whispered, reaching over to turn out the light. "That's my good girl." His arms tightened around me, and I laid my hand on his chest, where his heart beat strong and steady. "Now get some rest. I've got you."

"Yes, sir." It came out on a slow breath as I relaxed completely, as my thoughts blanked out and I held on to him, letting him deliver me into dreamless sleep.

Asa shook me awake. "Up, Mattie, get up. Right now."

"Hmm?"

"Wake the fuck up. We have to get out." He dragged me up and smacked lightly at my cheek.

My eyes snapped open. "What's happening?"

"Get your shoes on." Asa already had his duffel slung across his chest.

I peered toward the window. It was still dark outside. But the look on Asa's face—glittering eyes, sweaty brow—told me everything I needed to know. "They've found us."

Asa nodded and yanked on my hand, and I quickly slid my shoes onto my feet and followed him to the door. He opened it a crack and paused, then jerked his head to the left. "This way." He jogged down the hallway toward the outer staircase. I ran after him, listening to the faint rattle of whatever was in his pockets. We stepped into the warm, humid night air and hurried down the staircase, but Asa stuck out his arm as we reached the ground, halting my forward momentum. From around the corner of the building, near the main entrance, came the sound of boots. Lots of them.

Sarah Fine

"Headsmen?" I whispered.

"Doubtful. Some of them have no juice." Asa wiped his face on his sleeve. "But most of them are Strikon and Knedas."

I reached over and grabbed his hand, then pointed to the back of the hotel property, which was adjacent to that dense patch of tropical trees I'd seen on the way in. "Can we sneak through there?"

Someone at the front of the building shouted, and the sound of footsteps headed our way.

Asa answered by sprinting in the direction I'd pointed. He leaped across a muddy ditch, then grabbed my arm as my foot slipped when I landed. He pulled me into the darkness of the stubby, rough-barked trees. "No good, no good," he muttered, glancing behind him, where there lay nothing but dense blackness. "Fuck, where are they?"

He pulled me along the tree line, then paused and switched directions, whispering curses the whole time. It was clear he could feel danger in every direction. Finally, he stopped and took me by the shoulders. "Mattie, they're looking for me. They don't know what you can do. What you are." He glanced at the collar, still around my neck, and his jaw clenched. "That means you can get out. I want you to—"

"Want her to what?" asked a quiet voice from the darkness.

I turned to see Daeng step from behind a tree, his face shining with sweat in the lights from the parking lot. He had a gun in one hand, aimed at Asa. With the other, he pulled a beaded necklace over his head and quickly tossed it at Asa's feet.

Asa leaped back and kicked the thing away. "Dirty trick, asshole."

"Strikon is the easiest way to disguise the presence of other magic. Have you ever noticed that? You just have to be strong enough to bear it." He took a step closer. "Or perhaps you know that already. Where is the relic?"

"Gone," said Asa. "Too hot to keep."

Daeng aimed his gun at my head. "Liar," he said to Asa before looking at me. "My lovely friend. Mr. Johnson was just saying I didn't know

228

what you could do." Daeng smiled, but it wasn't the polite, slightly sad smile I'd seen earlier tonight. "I very much hope you'll be willing to tell me, though."

"She can tie a knot in a cherry stem using just her tongue," said Asa, his hand inching toward his pocket. "And she's got a hell of a—"

The blast of the weapon cut the night. Asa fell backward with a strangled groan, clutching at his thigh, which was instantly soaked with blood. I lunged for him, but Daeng threw his arm around my neck. He pulled me against him and spoke right in my ear. "That bullet just tore his femoral artery, *Mattie*. He has about three minutes to live."

I let out a choked sob, staring at Asa, who was shaking and gasping and cursing as he tried to put pressure on his wound. The rapid pat-pat-pat of blood dripping to the leaves beneath him sounded like rainfall. "Asa," I mouthed. Horror had stolen my voice.

"I have the magic to heal him right here." Daeng guided my hand to a hard lump in the pocket of his shirt. "An Ekstazo relic." He squeezed my hand in his clammy grip. "Tell me where you put the relic you stole, and it's yours. Otherwise, we will both watch him die."

CHAPTER
TWENTY-ONE

I turned toward Daeng. "I have it."

"Mattie, don't," Asa said, his voice wretched with pain.

Daeng's eyes narrowed. "Where?"

"It's inside me."

Asa groaned. "Mattie . . ."

"One more word and I'll shoot you again," Daeng murmured, but his attention was all reserved for me. "You're lying. The relic contained the most powerful Strikon magic in the world. I would know if it were near."

I took a quick step closer to him, and he raised the gun, aiming it at the side of my head as we stood inches apart. My breaths were sharp and shallow. I could hear Asa suffering only feet behind me, and the sound made my heart feel like it had been stuffed with dynamite.

"Touch my chest and focus," I said to Daeng. "That's the only way you'll feel it. And if you shoot me, that magic dies with me, right? You want to risk that?"

Daeng released my hand, looking conflicted.

"I'm telling you exactly where it is, just like you asked," I hissed. "Why the hell do you think I would be traveling with Mr. Johnson if I weren't his reliquary?" The seconds were ticking down, each one winding my desperation and hatred tighter.

He lowered the gun to his side and shoved his clammy hand up my shirt. I guided it between my breasts, glancing down to make sure that gun was aimed away from me. "You can feel it," I said quietly, releasing his hand.

As soon as I did, Daeng's hand shifted and closed over one of my breasts, squeezing painfully and making my teeth clench. He bowed his head and let out a shuddering breath. "Oh, there it is . . ."

"Yep, there it is." And then I finally made use of that self-defense class I'd taken as a college freshman. I looped my arms around his neck and slammed my knee into his crotch.

Daeng yelped and pitched against me as I shoved and pushed to keep his gun aimed away from me. His scrabbling hand scraped down my stomach, and I frantically brought my knee up again and again, not sure if the little screams I heard were coming from him or me. The gun fell to the ground, and I kicked blindly until I made contact. It skittered across the leaves and splashed into the ditch. I scratched at Daeng's eyes and he tripped, falling to the ground. I jammed my fingers into his chest pocket and came up holding a small figurine—the relic Asa needed. Daeng grabbed for me, but I scooted backward, jabbing my foot into his face and landing a lucky shot. He grunted and rolled onto his back, blood gushing from his nose, and I dove for Asa, who was weakly clutching at his thigh.

"What do I do?" I asked.

Asa's face was white as moonlight, and his entire body was trembling. "No magic no magic no magic," he whispered, his eyes rolling. "I-I don't . . . don't . . ."

I ignored him and pushed the bottom of his shorts up, revealing the hole straight through his inner thigh, still burbling blood like a little fountain. Praying I was doing the right thing, I pressed the relic right over one of the wounds and focused on how much I wanted Asa to be okay. He cried out and arched, every muscle spasming. Terrified that I was damaging him, I pulled my hand away and looked down at the wound.

Even after only a few seconds, it was smaller, and the bleeding had slowed to a trickle. I gritted my teeth and held the now-bloody relic to his skin again, this time against the exit wound on the other side of his leg. Asa's thigh was like cold iron in my grip as he writhed, and my fingers were slick with his blood. The strangest sensation crept up my arm, slithering up my neck and into my head. Suddenly, I was keenly aware of a slice of Strikon magic lying a few feet away on the muddy bank of the ditch, and the powerful throb of Sensilo magic beneath me and behind me. It felt like a million tiny insect feet pattering along the inside of my skull, and paired with the stab of pain and the pulse of ecstasy in my palm, it was almost unbearable, too much stimulation at once. I shuddered, not sure if I needed to throw up or scream or moan with pleasure, or maybe all three at the same time. My skin tingled as a cold sweat broke out across my forehead and chest and neck.

"Take it off me," Asa said between ragged breaths, weakly trying to pry my hands from his thigh. "No more . . ."

I twisted away from Asa as I felt a surge of magic at my back and rose to my knees as Daeng barreled into me. The relic fell from my grasp as Daeng's fingers locked around my throat. His face was twisted into a hideous grimace, and his eyes were bulging. My world turned crimson and spotty as I slapped my bloody hands onto his face, trying to get him off me.

The effect was instantaneous. Daeng released his choke hold and screamed, staggering backward with his arms thrashing. I looked down at my hands.

"The blood," I whispered. Surface magic, Asa had called it. Asa's blood was saturated with his Sensilo magic, and I had it all over me. So did Daeng.

The only difference was that Daeng was already full to the brim with the same kind of sensing magic. I'd just given him an overdose. As he landed on his back and scrambled up again, his hands clawed and reaching for me, the most terrible guttural sounds rolling from his throat, I grabbed a handful of wet, bloody earth from between Asa's legs and lunged for Daeng. Short-circuited by the sensations buzzing inside my brain and along my limbs, rage devouring me, I landed on Daeng's chest and clamped my hand over his face, forcing the magic-soaked mud into his mouth. Daeng arched and thrashed, struggling like an animal in a trap, but I was relentless and savage. He'd shot Asa. He might have killed him. He had wanted to watch him die.

"How does it feel now?" I asked, baring my teeth as tears streamed from Daeng's eyes.

Hands looped beneath my arms and pulled me backward. "It's okay. Let him go," Asa said.

I struggled to get away from him, but he locked his hands around my chest and wrenched me off Daeng, who had begun to shake all over. I stared at him for a second, reddish mud smeared all over his face, his fingers twitching and flexing as Asa dragged me over to the ditch and pushed me onto my stomach, grabbing my wrists and plunging our hands into the brown rancid water. He lay on top of me as I fought him, overwhelmed and panicking at the unyielding wall of sensing magic crushing me to the ground. He rubbed my hands together underwater and then drew them up, dripping but no longer bloody. The hard tingling feeling inside my skull faded. The feeling of insects crawling on me lifted.

Panting, Asa rolled off me, and my thoughts clicked back on like a lightbulb. I turned to him, realization pounding in my veins. "You're not dying. The relic worked."

"For better or worse, you're still stuck with me." He was ghastly pale, though, and looked unsteady as he rose from the ground. Sticky blood was crusted all over his shorts and down his leg. He glanced at

Daeng, who was flopping in the grass about ten feet away, then toward the motel. "We have to run."

I looked over my shoulder. A small group of men had emerged from the hotel and were congregating in the parking lot. Asa looped his arm around my waist and pulled me backward just as one of them raised his head and squinted at the tree line.

A shout went up as he spotted us—or maybe Daeng's thrashing body. Asa plunged into the brush, and I was right behind him. He cursed and stumbled as we wove our way around thick trunks of banana trees, their low leafy fronds thwacking our faces. Behind us, I could hear yelling and pounding footsteps. Ahead of us, though, was the glimmer of passing headlights. We were nearing the road.

Asa went down with a grunt, his chest heaving. He struggled to push himself from the ground. I grabbed his sides and yanked, helping him to rise again. In the darkness, his skin was so pale it was almost glowing. It was cold to the touch, slick with sweat. The relic had healed him, but he'd still lost so much blood, and a horde of naturals was approaching quickly. Now I knew what he must be feeling, the hard tingling, the crawling sensation along his skin. Protectiveness welled up inside me as I coiled my arm around his waist and moved with him, propelling us forward.

A sharp crack made both of us flinch. "Are they shooting at us?" I whispered as I pulled at Asa, who seemed to be having trouble lifting his feet more than a few inches off the ground.

"Yep," he said with a huff as we reached asphalt. "I'd say it's time to catch our flight out of here."

I glanced up the little side street we'd emerged onto. Maybe ten yards ahead, there was a guy parking his car right next to a shabby building that might have been a bar or a convenience store, its sign lit up despite the fact that it must have been around five or six in the morning. With our pursuers still crashing through the thick woods behind us, I let go of Asa and sprinted forward, waving my arms.

The guy who'd just gotten out of his car looked at me with wide eyes as I raced toward him, blood smeared all over my shirt, my hair wild. "I need a ride!" I said, pointing to his car. "To the airport!" I jabbed my finger toward the distant sound of an airplane.

The man looked over my shoulder, and whatever he saw—probably Asa—made him scream and raise his arms up in the air. His keys dangled from one of his fingers, and in my desperation, I thrust my arms out. He yelped and threw the keys at me. They hit my chest and bounced to the ground just as Asa reached my side, looking like a blood-drenched zombie, his movements lurching and unsteady.

"Get in the car," I shrieked. The man who'd thrown his keys had run into the shabby building, and I could hear yelling inside. And our pursuers were only a few yards from the edge of the trees. I swung the back door open and shoved Asa inside, pushing his long legs as he landed on the backseat in an awkward sprawl. My heart in my throat, I dove into the front.

"Where the hell is the steering wheel?" I screamed. Then I looked over at the passenger seat, and voila. I scooted over, shoved the key in the ignition, and twisted it just as a bullet punctured the windshield.

I slammed the car into reverse and shot backward, yanking the wheel around and sending up a cloud of smoke as the car spun. Then I punched it into drive and sped forward, hunching down and expecting my world to go dark at any moment. I could hear the cracks of gunshots, could feel the hiss of bullets through the car. My breath was bursting from me in little squeaks as I reached the wide road we'd traveled to get to the hotel. I took a quick right turn and screamed again as I saw several sets of headlights streaking toward me.

"They drive on the left," Asa shouted from the back as I swerved.

"I knew that!" I cranked the wheel and looped around, forcing several oncoming cars to slam on their brakes. Then I stomped on the gas again, and the tires squealed just before we shot forward. A sharp snap made me flinch, and I cast a quick sidelong glance at the new bullet hole in the passenger window as we roared past the side street.

I was weaving in and out, streaking by cars and trucks like they were standing still. I knew the airport was to the right but had no idea how to get over there. "Why are there no freaking street signs?" I wailed, cutting in front of a taxi, whose driver laid on the horn a second later.

I wrenched the wheel to the right and pulled a U-turn under an overpass, then darted across the road toward a little sign with an airplane on it, barely avoiding a collision with a delivery truck. As more horns sounded off, along with a few sirens, I glanced behind me to see Asa lying on the backseat, a bloody phone to his ear. "Got it," he said. "We're coming in hot, so be ready."

He sat up and looked around, his eyes narrowing as he scanned the airport in front of us. "The hangar's on the southwest—" He grabbed the back of the seat as I swerved around a line of cars, one of the wheels going up on the curb.

"Which way is southwest?" I yelled.

"That way!" He pointed to my left, and I lurched onto a narrow lane, scraping the side of a building as I pulled around a slow-moving airport shuttle.

Behind us, sirens were screaming, and red and white lights were twinkling in my rearview mirror. "Oh God," I said in a choked voice, clinging to the wheel. "When did my life become a Fast and the Furious movie?"

"Up there! Up there!" Asa made a frantic wave toward a line of hangars up ahead. A sleek jet was taxiing out of the one on the very end. "That's them!" He cursed and ducked as another bullet dinged into the metal of the car.

The gas pedal was on the freaking floor as I raced toward the jet. I was terrified to slow down for fear our pursuers would catch up, but I knew I had to stop. Those two thoughts warred in my panicked brain until Asa roared my name, and I slammed on the brakes. The wheels locked and the car skidded across the concrete, barreling toward the jet. We jerked to a stop less than twenty feet away. The plane's door opened, and a set of steps flopped down. Asa had to shout at me to throw the car into park before I got out. The air was filled with the whine of airplane engines and the scream of sirens as Asa and I staggered toward the jet, clawing our way up the steps and throwing ourselves inside.

I had the faintest impression of someone pulling up the stairs and calling to the pilot to get going, but it barely reached my consciousness. I tripped over Asa's feet and landed on top of him in the aisle. His arms wrapped around me and pulled me against him. His heart was hammering against my chest, and both of us were shaking. As I felt the plane accelerate and glimpsed the outside streaking by, as my stomach swooped with our rise into the sky, I buried my face against his throat and burst into tears.

CHAPTER TWENTY-TWO

After a short flight, most of which I spent in the bathroom trying to clean myself up and pull myself together, we changed planes in Taipei, boarding a larger jet with two pilots, a flight attendant, and a security guard. Asa stared at the flight attendant as she approached him with a beautiful smile on her face. There was an eerie sort of hunger in his eyes. But then he stepped back from her abruptly as she reached out to touch his arm.

"Stay the fuck away from me," he snarled.

She blinked at him. "But-but Mr. Brindle wanted me to help you feel more comf—"

Asa turned to the security guard, who was pulling up the stairs. "Get her off this plane. She goes or I do."

I touched his arm. "Asa—"

"I will not fly across the Pacific in a tiny tin can with a fucking Ekstazo," he shouted, his voice cracking. He was still covered in crusted blood, pale as a ghost, his short hair sticking up in places. His hands were trembling in that way that made my stomach hurt.

After a terse phone call with someone in charge, the security guard hustled the flight attendant off the plane, and we were off. Asa sank into one of the couches that ran along the length of the plane and folded his arm over his eyes. His lips were gray, his face drawn. I knelt next to him. "You need to eat something. And rehydrate. Can you do that? What sounds good?"

Asa lifted his arm and peeked at me. His gaze slipped over my throat, where the collar had been until I'd quietly removed it on our flight to Taipei. "See what they have?" he asked weakly. "You know what I need."

"Got it." I walked up to the front of the cabin and smiled at the security guard, a guy about my age with sandy blond hair who looked like he might have played football in college. "Can I?" I gestured to the small galley.

"Be my guest," he said, eyeing Asa. "You guys had a rough time of it, huh?"

"Yeah. Airport traffic was brutal." I began to open each cabinet, skipping over the reheatable meals and pulling out a few bottles of water and juice, a few salads, and several packages of nuts and trail mix. With the guard's help, I carried them back to Asa. I waved the guard away, nodding toward Asa and trying to communicate that he was in a mood. Then I touched Asa's arm. "Hey. Can you sit up?"

Asa pushed himself up on an elbow, but it took some effort. I offered juice but he pushed it away. "It really might help," I said. "Get your blood sugar up."

"Or put me into a goddamn coma. I can't drink that stuff." He reached for the water and gave me a bemused half smile as I twisted off the cap for him. I watched the drops collect at the corner of his mouth and streak down his chin as he gulped at it.

"Wouldn't an Ekstazo have only made you feel better?" I asked quietly as he started to eat one of the salads. "Why wouldn't you let her fly with us?"

"It's already bad enough . . ." He looked away.

"No, what is it?"

"The relic," he said. "It was powerful Ekstazo magic. And when that stuff hits my system, it's like a line of cocaine. It fires me up, and then I'm caught all over again." He kept his eyes on his food, tossing a handful of nuts into his mouth. "So now I have the deal with the shakes along with everything else."

I thought back to the moments he'd been bleeding to death. Instead of begging me to help, he'd been muttering "no magic" over and over again. "You didn't want me to save you?"

He shook his head. "I didn't want to die. But I didn't want to be addicted again, either. I can't get trapped in it, Mattie. I can't do it. And it would be so easy."

My heart ached for him. "I feel like I should be apologizing to you, for forcing it on you."

"Don't. You were . . ." He sighed. "Fucking amazing." His eyes met mine briefly before he focused on his food again. "No one's ever fought for me like that," he murmured.

I sat on the couch across from him, swallowing the lump in my throat. "You saved me first."

This time he actually smiled.

"Asa, what's going to happen when we get back?" I asked quietly.

Asa cut a sidelong glance at the guard as he finished the salad. The guy was lounging against the wall at the front of the cabin, facing us. Asa put his dish down and stretched out on the couch, his long legs bent slightly to allow him to fit. "Come here, baby," he said, waggling his eyebrows at me. "Keep me warm."

Despite his bedraggled appearance, the timbre of his voice was authoritative, and the sound thrummed inside me, forcing me to suppress a shiver. I edged across the aisle and lay down next to him on the narrow couch. He folded me into his arms, chest to chest, and I inhaled the scent of sweat and blood, intense and earthy and dangerous. His fingertips traced up my spine, and even though I knew he was putting on an act, it made my heart pound. I couldn't help but recall what he'd done to Rose, and the memory filled my head with the dueling needs to push him away and to move closer. He wove his fingers into my curls and pulled my face close until our lips almost touched. I held my breath. Then he tilted his head, glanced up at the guard, and smiled. I looked behind me—the guy had discreetly sat down with his back to us.

Asa's hands stilled, and he looked into my eyes. "They're going to take us back to Mistika and pull that magic out of you," he whispered, holding me tight as I flinched at the thought of all that pain, all over again.

For the first time, I thought of what would happen next. "And then we're going to give this incredible weapon to an incredibly evil man. He could do so much damage, and we'll be responsible."

Asa sighed. "Brindle operates underground, and under the radar. It's not like he's going to walk into a mall and unleash it on innocent people. He'll use it as a threat, to get his way. And probably to destroy other incredibly evil men—like Zhong."

"Are you just saying that to make this easier for me?"

"It's the truth, but I'm okay with making it easier." He nudged my nose with his. "You've got enough to worry about."

"What about you?"

"I'll be at the transaction to make sure everything's good and proper. Then you and Ben are going to go straight to the airport and buy tickets home, and you're not going to look back."

"That's not what I asked."

His smile turned sad. "I'm going to take care of me."

I touched his stubbly, blood-streaked jaw. "Brindle said it was just one job."

Asa's brown eyes were somber. "He's not going to let me go that easy, Mattie. Not once he has me. And I'm not exactly at my strongest at the moment."

"Are they going to hurt you?"

"The opposite. That's why that Ekstazo was put on the flight. If I'd let her, she'd have had me amped up and under her spell long before we touched down in Vegas."

"Why?"

His fingers tightened in my hair. "So the Knedas they'll have waiting for us can do his thing without me resisting. That's how they do it
to us, Mattie. That's how they catch us and keep us."

"Magic sniffers, you mean?"

"Yeah. We can't work for the bosses, surrounded by all that juice
day in and day out, and not go insane. So the master makes sure
you're always flying high just to keep you going for as long as possible.
Remember Tao? Zhong Lei's sensor? He's on his last legs."

I remembered. His stumbling gait, his zombie gaze, the way he
stroked that thing in his pocket like he needed a hit. And Daeng, who
hadn't looked quite as bad, but had seemed sweaty and lonely and
miserable at Montri's party. I bowed my head, the horror of what I had
done to him all hitting me at once. "I shouldn't have used your blood
against Daeng."

Asa tipped my chin up. "It was him or me, and I'm sure as hell
glad you chose me. But I hate thinking . . ." He swallowed hard and
looked away.

"You're terrified of being in a cage again," I murmured. "Like
he was."

"I'll figure something out."

"I'll help."

He took my face in his hands. "You can't. You need to focus on
getting yourself out of there. That's your job. I mean it. Brindle's not
going to want to let you go, either."

"But I'm not as vulnerable."

"Hey, now." He gave me a cocky smile. "Don't underestimate me."

"Why—do you have a secret weapon in one of your pockets?"

His eyebrow arched. "You sure you wanna go there with me?"

I snorted with laughter and lowered my forehead to his chest,
knowing we were too close but unable to force myself to move away
just yet. "Asa Ward, you are so . . ."

"Oh, I am, Mattie Carver," he said faintly, his hand stroking over my curls. "I am indeed."

My fingers balled in his T-shirt, and I didn't move until I was sure he was asleep. It didn't take long, and it was a heavy rest, the kind of sleep that descends when your body has to work overtime to put itself back together. He didn't so much as twitch when I slipped from his grasp. Not when I used a wet, warm washcloth to clean the blood from his cheeks, his jaw, his throat, either, and not when I dried his skin with a soft towel. And certainly not when I lay on the couch across from him and stared at his face, sleep far out of my reach.

Ben had begged me to convince Asa to work for Frank, so that Frank would give Ben the magic he needed to heal his faulty heart.

But there was no way I could do that.

Whatever was going to happen when we returned to Vegas, I couldn't be part of helping them trap Asa. I'd seen enough to guess what it might do to him, and to guess what he might do if he lost his freedom. He was less afraid of dying than he was of losing control of himself, of his own will. I knew him well enough now to understand how hard he worked to maintain his independence, from magic *and* from people.

Ben had told me he wanted to be free, but did he know that gaining his freedom would cost Asa his? After what had happened between them the last time they'd seen each other, was he really willing to take that risk? Surely Ben wasn't even aware of the toll it might take on his older brother. He wouldn't have asked me to do it if he'd known. In fact, he would have been horrified, I was certain. Maybe he would help me make sure Asa got out along with us. Maybe the three of us would walk away, and maybe it would give all of us a fresh start.

Oh, and I needed one, on so many levels. I tore my eyes from Asa and tried to focus on Ben, but his face had gone hazy in my mind, and every time I tried to picture it, he looked more like the man sleeping across the aisle. I glanced at Asa's duffel, where I'd tucked the collar, but I refused to let myself move toward it. "Speaking of addictions," I whispered. "No way am I going down that road."

I stared at the ceiling until I fell into a restless doze, and awoke to Asa jostling my knee. "We're landing," he said, squinting out the window and frowning. "Hey," he called up to the security guard. "This isn't McCarran."

McCarran was the Las Vegas airport. I sat up and pressed my face to the window. Bright sunlight streamed down on a short runway, mountains in the distance. "What's going on?"

"We got diverted to North Vegas," the blond security guard said as we touched down.

"Why?" Asa's voice was sharp.

"Just heavy air traffic. No big deal."

I could tell Asa wasn't convinced. He was craning his neck to see where we were going as the pilot taxied off the runway and headed for a hangar. I looked out, too. The airport was set on a patch of sun-baked earth, ringed by suburban sprawl. The hangar was small, but I could already see the limousine waiting inside, the driver and another man, both dressed in black, watching our arrival as they leaned against the sleek car.

Asa had said Frank would send a Knedas to meet us, in the hopes of taking advantage of his weakness. I reached over and slipped my hand into Asa's, and though he didn't look my way, he squeezed hard enough to hurt and didn't let go. I wasn't sure if he was doing it for me or himself.

The pilot pulled the plane to a stop, and our guard headed for the front exit. "Welcome to Vegas," he said to us with a friendly smile, then opened the door.

Even over the engine noise, the gunshot was audible. Our guard toppled backward and landed facing us, blood trickling from the small, neat bullet hole right in the center of his forehead.

CHAPTER
TWENTY-THREE

"Fuck." Asa shoved me toward the rear of the plane as the pilots began to shout and more gunfire cracked against glass. He grabbed the strap of the duffel and slung it over his head, then spun toward the emergency exit. As one of the pilots began to scream and another fell, shot through the head, on top of the dead guard, Asa ripped the rectangular hatch away from the window, revealing a circular exit onto the wing.

Asa pointed out the window. "Get onto the wing and slide to the ground. Careful of the engine."

"And then what?"

"Run." He turned abruptly at the sound of footsteps, holding the emergency door in front of his torso like a shield. Stunned and terrified, all I could do was stare. As the gunman stepped into the cramped space where two dead bodies now lay, Asa charged up the aisle, letting out a bloodcurdling war cry that brought the gunman around with wide eyes. He fired off a shot, but it must have hit the door, because a half second later Asa plowed into him, sending them both back into the cockpit with Asa on top. He raised the door and slammed it down, edge first, onto the gunman beneath him. Holding down the struggling man, he did a double take over his shoulder. "What the fuck are you doing? I said run, goddammit!"

I didn't want to leave him, but I didn't want to make it harder for him to do whatever he had to do, either. Shaking, I crawled through the round exit and onto the wing. I was on the other side of the plane from the limousine. Outside the hangar was nothing but bright, dusty sunlight, but I hoped there would be a building I could run to. Inside the plane, I heard shouting and slamming. I wanted to help Asa. Instead, I slid to the ground.

Hard hands grabbed my hair and yanked me backward, under the body of the airplane. I screamed, but then my attacker thrust me upward, conking my head on the metal underbelly. Pain and sparks exploded inside my skull as I was dragged all the way under the plane and out the other side before being forced to my feet. "You will stop struggling," my attacker said between heavy breaths.

Jacks, baby. It was like I could hear Asa's voice in my head. He'd said there would be a Knedas waiting, and I was betting from this guy's calm, confident voice that he was a manipulator. But my head was hurting so much that it was easy to shrug his influence off.

Still, I stopped thrashing and glanced back at him—our supposed driver, dressed in a black chauffeur's outfit, complete with a cap on his head. And a gun in his hand, pointed at the plane.

"I take it you don't work for Frank." I couldn't think of a good reason for Brindle's people to shoot at us. "You guys managed to divert us here for this."

"Mr. Zhong would like to speak to Mr. Ward," the driver said. "Ah. Here we are." His hand tightened in my hair and he gave me a little shake.

My eyes focused on the plane as Asa's tall, lean form stepped into the doorway at the top of the unfurled steps. He had a gun, too, with a long barrel—probably snatched from the gunman who had boarded our plane. The weapon was aimed at us. "Let her go. It's me you want," Asa said as he slowly came down the steps.

"It *is* you we want, along with any relics you might be carrying. So put the gun down or I'll dispose of her." The driver pressed the barrel of his gun to my temple, drawing a whimper from my throat.

Asa stopped about fifteen feet away. "Do that and your boss is going to cut you open and pour Strikon juice all over your guts. Mattie's a reliquary."

"Mr. Zhong has many reliquaries."

"She's loaded up."

The hard pressure of metal against my temple eased. "With what?"

Asa gave the driver a ghostly smile. "Oh . . . it's an original, my friend. One of the four most powerful pieces of magic in this world." He took a step forward. "She's got the juice, and I happen to have the actual relic. I think we can agree Mr. Zhong is going to want both."

"Put the gun down and we can talk."

"You first, asshole."

"Mattie, put your hand out. Palm down," said the driver.

It seemed like a good enough idea . . . my toes curled inside my shoes. He was trying to put the whammy on me again, but if I didn't obey, he'd know I wasn't under his influence. I stuck my hand out. Staying behind me, the driver wrapped his fingers around my wrist and pressed the barrel of the gun to the back of my hand. "Shooting her here wouldn't damage this supposed magic, would it? It would just destroy her hand."

His finger curled around the trigger.

"Asa!"

"Fine," Asa said loudly, putting his hands up.

"Put the gun *down*, Mr. Ward."

Asa laid the weapon on the concrete, then straightened with both hands in the air.

"Kick it away from you."

Asa did as he was told. The gun spun off to his left.

"Now tell me where the relic is."

Something glittering and dangerous flared in Asa's eyes. "My pocket." He gave a tiny nod, and my eyes dipped to a lump in the front pocket of his bloody shorts. "Want me to bring it out?"

"Very funny. I've heard about you and your nasty tricks. Mattie, go get me the relic from Mr. Ward's pocket. Do anything else, and I'll shoot you." He shoved me toward Asa, and I took a few stumbling steps before regaining my balance.

Asa's eyes locked with mine. "Come and get it, baby."

I closed the distance between us, then slowly slid my hand inside his pocket.

He smirked. "So you *do* want to go there with me."

My hand closed over the relic—and something else. My fingers did a rapid dance over its surface as I thought about all the things I'd seen Asa pull from his pockets in the past week. It was the tiny bottle of baby oil—I was almost sure. I looked up at him.

"You *did* ask," he whispered.

I had asked him if he had a secret weapon. And what he'd given me was baby oil. "I guess I did," I murmured as I pulled the clunky gold necklace from his pocket, with the bottle of baby oil pressed between my palm and the spherical pendant.

I turned around quickly, flicking the cap open as I did. I cupped the necklace in my hands so Zhong's henchman could see it was all I had, and he nodded and beckoned me to return. My heart hammering, I trudged back over to him.

"Hand it over," the driver said as I got close.

"Here," I said, holding it out. "It's kind of ugly, but I—whoops!" I tripped over my own feet and pitched forward—squeezing the little bottle of oil as I did. It splashed onto the driver's face and hands, and I leaped back.

I expected him to scream as Strikon magic hit his skin. Or moan and cry if it was Sensilo. Instead, the guy shuddered, and his face went slack. He sank to one knee, his mouth dropping open to let out a groan.

Then he jammed his hands down the front of his pants and began to stroke himself.

That was as far as he got before Asa strode up to him and clocked him with his extendable baton. "Make sure you don't get that stuff on your hands," he said to me as the guard landed in a sprawl at his feet.

I dropped the relic and the empty bottle of oil. The guard, with a huge goose egg on his forehead from Asa's strike, had gone back to jerking off, seemingly oblivious to our presence. "Ekstazo?" I asked.

"I'd been saving it for a special occasion," Asa said with a wink as he contracted his baton. "Whoops!" he said, mimicking my voice as he slid the baton back into his belt.

He pulled a pair of latex gloves from his back pocket and carefully lifted the relic from the ground. He bagged it inside one of the gloves and stuck it back in his pocket, then knelt beside the guard—whose hands were full—and pulled a set of keys from the guy's pocket. "And now I think our work here is done. Shall we?"

He walked toward the car and opened the passenger door. "I'm driving this time. You're kind of a screamer."

I narrowed my eyes at him. "I got us to the airport, didn't I?"

He grinned as he got into the driver's seat. "Yep. Almost shattering the sound barrier—and my eardrums—in the process."

I got in and fastened my seat belt. "Where are we going?"

"Mistika." He pulled out of the hangar and slowly drove toward the exit of the airport, his eyes darting from side mirrors to rearview. "Bet you're excited to see Ben again."

I wondered if I was imagining the edge in his voice.

"I am excited," I said. But that feeling was dwarfed by dread. "Right now, though, it's just you and me."

Asa's fingers tightened over the steering wheel as he looked over at me, his eyes full of questions.

"What if we did this on our own terms?" I asked. "We have a chance, thanks to Zhong's little ambush." My mind was spinning now, hope sparking off the gears. "You don't have to go back to Frank. He wants you, but he wants the relic, too. And that was the thing he bargained Ben's life for. So I'll take the relic to him."

Asa shook his head. "You still have to go through the transaction. I'm not letting you do that on your own."

"I'm sure Frank has skilled people who've done this kind of thing before."

"Doesn't matter. For you, getting it out will be harder than putting it in."

A chill went down my spine, even as I said, "Asa, this is your out."

"I make my own outs."

"You can save your brother *and* keep your freedom!"

"Not the point," he yelled.

"Then what is?"

His nostrils flared as he let out a long breath. "Mattie, they care about the relic. They don't care about you."

"And you do," I said quietly.

"Shut the fuck up."

I suppressed a smile and looked out the passenger window. "I'm stronger than you think."

"No shit. Changes nothing."

I wanted to shake him. He was willing to risk his freedom just to make sure I made it through the magic transfer. But I was also shamefully relieved. I needed him. I didn't want to admit it, not when his life and sanity were at stake, but it had been my trust in him that had made surviving the initial transaction and its aftermath possible. Jack, the old conduit who'd known my grandpa, had said Asa would sell his own mother for a profit, but now I knew that to be completely false. If I ever saw the old man again, I would ask him where he'd heard . . .

"Jack," I said suddenly.

"Jacks?"

"No, Jack. What if we got our own conduit and did the transaction first? Then I can take the relic to Brindle."

Asa looked thoughtful. "Not a lot of conduits would take this job. But he has more experience than most."

"He told me I could call him if I ever needed anything. He knew my grandpa. He said he'd look out for me." I glanced down at my blood-smeared clothes. "But I don't have his number." It was somewhere in the luggage I'd left at the hotel. I wasn't even sure *which* hotel at this point.

"I know how to reach him," Asa said, pulling into a gas station and scanning his surroundings. "This could work."

I leaned forward and raised my eyebrows. "I'm smarter than you think, too."

He bowed his head against the steering wheel, laughing. "*Dammit*, Mattie." Then he threw open the door and headed toward the gas station's convenience store.

I rubbed my chest as I watched him go, my heart beating a little faster as I thought about the pain to come. But Asa would be there, and he would get me through it.

Then we would part ways for good.

"The sooner the better," I murmured as he ducked into the store. "For all of us."

Asa had it arranged in less than half an hour. Jack was going to meet us halfway, in a Utah town called Salina. Both Asa and I were feeling the effects of jet lag, but we hit the road immediately, terrified that Frank's people—or Zhong's—would be on our tail. The only stop we made was at a hardware store. Asa went in alone and came out lugging a paper sack full of supplies. He tucked them into the trunk and got back in the driver's seat, tossing a small red package onto my lap.

Twizzlers. "They were at the register," he said as he put the car into gear. "But seeing as there's not a single natural ingredient in them, I don't know why you'd want to put them in your mouth."

I read the wrapper. "Sugar seems kind of natural. There's salt in here, too."

He laughed and rolled his eyes. "You have really low standards."

My gaze traced over his profile. "But I know what I like."

He was quiet after that, and I leaned against the window and watched the gorgeous, harsh landscape go by, trying not to think about what would happen tonight. But the sun was relentless in its descent, and the lower it got, the harder it was to avoid those thoughts. I would have to let go and allow the pain to flood me on its way out of my body.

And it wouldn't stop, because then I would have to say good-bye to Asa.

But then I'll be on my way back to Ben, I thought quickly, pushing those dangerous thoughts away. *That's what I've been fighting for all along.*

The sun had disappeared by the time we checked into a Super 8 just off the highway. Across the road was what looked like a mall, and I got my hopes up for a Ruby Tuesday, or, even better at this point, a Gap or an Express, someplace I could pick up a decent outfit so that I could change out of my grungy, bloody T-shirt and shorts. But as we got closer I realized there were no cars in the parking lots, no signs up. A casualty of a bad economy or maybe just bad planning, it was a maze of empty buildings in want of tenants.

Nearly staggering with fatigue by that point, I let Asa check us in and usher me into a room. I didn't even protest as we both fell onto the bed. Being close to him felt natural and needed, and I was too tired to fight it.

He turned to me, his head on the pillow, dark circles under his eyes, his skin too pale for my liking. "Ready for this?"

"It has to come out sometime."

He tapped his crooked nose. "But you didn't answer my question."

I winced. "There's no other way, Asa. Don't make me think about it now, though, okay?"

He stared at me, his honey-brown eyes slightly bloodshot. "Is he worth all this, Mattie?"

"Yeah," I murmured.

"He treats you well?"

I looked away from his gaze. "He's always treated me like a queen."

"Uh-huh."

I squeezed my eyes shut. "You came after him, too. You're risking a lot for him."

"He's my little brother. No matter what he's done or how I feel about him, that won't change."

"At least you can admit it now. That's why you were in Sheboygan that night I first met you, wasn't it? You were trying to find out what happened to him. You'd seen it on the news and you couldn't ignore it. You would have come to get him even if we'd never met. Why didn't you just tell me?"

He sighed. "It was easier to live with if I didn't have to explain it to someone else. If I didn't have to say the words. Can you get that?"

"I guess I can. But you're saying them now."

"To *you*," he murmured, then rubbed his face and turned on his back. "So what's your excuse?"

"For what?"

"For not admitting the truth to me."

My heart lurched. "The truth?"

"He used Knedas juice on you, didn't he?" he asked quietly. "Before you even knew what it was, Ben used it on you. I could tell, that night when I first explained to you how manipulation magic worked."

"I'm going to work that out with him," I said, my voice sharp. "It's between him and me." Somehow, Asa knowing what Ben had done to me made the violation feel ten times worse.

A knock on the door ended our conversation. Asa slid off the bed and pulled his baton from his belt as he peeked through the gap in the thin, ratty curtains, then put the baton away and went to the door, opening it for Jack.

The old man looked like a bull as he strode into the room, his chin jutting out, framed by his salt-and-pepper beard. But he smiled when he saw me sitting on the edge of the bed. "I've been thinking so much about you, girl," he said, opening his arms.

I stepped into a brief, firm hug, which ended when he took me by the shoulders. "I hear you got some wicked magic inside you now. Should we get it out?"

A cold sweat prickled along the back of my neck. "I guess we should."

Jack gave me a curt nod. "Good. Because word on the street is that Zhong is gunning for you two after that stunt you pulled in Vegas."

Asa cursed. "It's out already?"

Jack laughed. "You can't leave that kind of mess behind and not expect a boss to come after you. Especially Zhong. He has to save face. I had three people call me about it on the drive down. I think maybe we need to move this party along so we can all split."

"Fine by me." Asa pulled out the relic, the large pendant dangling from its thick gold chain. "But get ready. Like I said on the phone, this is like nothing you've worked with before."

Jack's eyes glittered. "How would you know, young man? Talk to me again when you've been around as long as I have."

Asa chuckled and raised his hands in surrender, then grabbed a set of ropes from the paper hardware store sack. "Mattie, if you're ready. Sounds like we need to get a move on."

I pushed aside a twinge of nausea and reminded myself this whole ordeal was almost over. I'd be in Ben's arms soon. "Okay." I climbed onto the bed. "You're going to tie me up?"

He nodded. "I couldn't get you a gag, so we'll have to improvise."

Jack's eyebrows went low. "Is that really necessary?"

Asa pulled a paint stirrer from his hardware store bag. "Unless you're willing to part ways with your tongue, you're going to want one, too."

Jack accepted the stirrer and headed over to me, pulling a chair over next to the bed.

"Don't you want to lie down?" I asked.

He squared his shoulders. "I've never laid down for a single transaction, young lady, and I'm not going to start now." He leaned forward, a smile pulling at his lips. "And this isn't my first original-relic rodeo, you know?"

My eyes went wide. "What?"

Asa looked shocked, too. "You've worked with other originals before?"

Jack winked at me. "We'll talk about it on the other side. It's the best story I've got."

Knowing Jack had done this kind of thing before soothed my guilt and worry for him as Asa looped the ropes around my ankles and stomach and chest, securing me to the lumpy mattress. He leaned over me with one of the paint stirrers. "This is all I've got. But it's going to be fine. You'll be fine."

I looked up into his eyes. "Promise?"

His mouth twitched into a half smile. "You trust me, Mattie Carver. Just admit it."

"Do I have to?"

He leaned down, close enough to set my heart racing. "Yeah. You do." His voice was quiet, but it vibrated right through me with complete authority, leaving no room for doubt.

"I trust you," I whispered.

Jack cleared his throat. "Can't we just—"

"Shh." Asa gave him a cutting look. "You might have been around for a hundred years, but she hasn't." He looked down at me, and his expression softened instantly. "I'm right here, and I've got you."

I know. But I didn't get to say it, because he stuck the paint stirrer between my teeth a second later.

Jack held his own paint stirrer between his teeth and nodded at Asa, who had laid out all his supplies, including a new defibrillator, next to the bed. Asa hung the relic necklace, pendant open to reveal the lump of gold inside, around Jack's neck, and Jack tucked it into his shirt, against his bare skin. He reached over and took my hand, and Asa wound a rope around our forearms, holding us together, skin to skin.

Asa's eyes met mine. "Open up that vault when you're ready, Mattie."

Sarah Fine

I closed my eyes, my heart pounding. Inside me, I could feel that unsteady shift, the vault teetering on the edge of the cliff. I had been so focused on escaping, on surviving, that I hadn't sensed it for a while, not since Asa had taken over in that little hotel room back in Bangkok and kept all my fears at bay. But now I had to deal with it again.

Except I couldn't.

Jack's fingers squeezed my upper arm, where my biceps was bunched tight in anticipation of the pain to come. "It's okay, girl. Just relax."

But if I did, the agony would be there, all of it. Unbearable and searing, devouring me. I spat the paint stirrer from my mouth. "I can't." It came out of me high-pitched and childlike and so truthful that my cheeks burned. "I can't."

"Think of Ben, Mattie," Asa said. "Think of the moment you first see him again. Think of his face."

I clamped my eyes shut and tried picturing my love, but he kept going out of focus as the specter of agony rose in front of him. "Asa, I can't!" My breaths were coming from me in uneven gasps. "I'm trying!" I needed to get it over with, but it was like allowing myself to fall over a cliff. My body wanted to survive. I couldn't make it jump.

"Think of your future together. All the cute little babies you'll have. Once you do this, all of that's in front of you. Imagine it."

I *tried*. With everything I had. But the panic had taken over, twisting me so tight that I had no control. Tears burned my eyes as I began to struggle against the ropes. "I can't do this. Please. I can't."

"It's okay, baby." Asa's thumb stroked along my throat. "Look at me, Eve."

"But Asa—"

"Look at me," he snapped.

I obeyed him.

"How do you answer me?" he murmured.

"Yes, sir." My body was at war with itself, relief and terror twirling together in a tornado of confusion.

256

He regarded me for a moment, like he could see the storm in my eyes. "You belong to me. You know that, don't you? You made that choice back in Bangkok, and there's no going back from it. Mattie isn't mine, but you are."

Mattie isn't. But I am. I stared up at him, my thoughts blanking out, unable to think past the warm honey tint of his eyes.

"You know the truth," he said. "You can't escape from it. You're *mine.* Say it."

My lips parted. I wanted to say it. But a twinge of warning, of knowing this was another step down a road I shouldn't even be on, made my breath hitch.

Asa edged even closer, his long, lean body stretched out next to me, pulling the ropes over my body impossibly tight. I could smell his sweat, feel the heat pouring from him. His fingers wrapped over my throat, gentle but utterly dominant. "Say. It."

The words came out before I could stop them. "I'm yours, sir."

"That's right. So you're going to do as I say, aren't you, Eve? Whatever I ask you to do."

The fear rose up again, making my whole body shake.

"Asa," Jack said, sounding wary. "Maybe we should—"

"No," Asa replied, never taking his eyes from mine. "She can do this."

"I can't," I whispered. "I'm too—"

"I didn't say you could speak." Asa's voice was like a whip against my skin. But then he lowered his head until the tips of our noses touched. "But since you feel the need to do something with your tongue . . ."

His mouth was on mine an instant later, hot and possessive, his stubble scraping my chin. I moaned as I tasted a hint of salt, as he thrust his tongue between my lips. His fingers slid around the back of my neck, pulling me up as he deepened the kiss. Every inch of me was taut, straining against the ropes to get closer to him. I wanted his weight on me. I wanted his skin against mine. I wanted him inside me. My whole body was alight with that want, especially as one of his hands stroked down my side and closed around the back of my thigh, hard, awakening a new craving. He wrenched my legs apart, his fingers digging into my backside, and I wanted more. I didn't want him to be gentle. He owned me, and I wanted him to take me, to conquer me, to force me to submit. I was ready to beg for it.

And then he pulled away. His breaths sawed from him as he pushed the paint stirrer between my teeth again. "Now let it go for me, baby. Give it up to me. Everything you have."

Every part of me tingling, wet with desire, on fire for him, I had no choice but to do as he said. I felt the tipping, the moment spent on the edge, and I didn't try to stop myself as I fell. I didn't care what would happen. It was the surrender that mattered.

The agony tore its way out of me, first a slice and then a giant gash of pain, ripping through my chest and stomach, up my neck and down my legs. My thoughts were broken glass on soft flesh, obliterating hope and love and future and past. Too late I realized this would go on forever, that this was me now, every cell, every molecule, every last piece consumed with hurt.

Then, with a sudden crack and a hard jerk, my world filled with sound, the pain narrowing to the sharpest of points as it stabbed straight through me. My eyes fluttered open, my vision blurring as I took in the blood splattered on my chest, across the bedspread, against the wall.

Jack's forearm was still tied to mine. His fingers twitched against my upper arm before going still. He was no longer in his chair, and his weight was dragging me toward the edge of the bed. Asa was shouting my name as glass shattered and dust swirled in the air above my head.

I had no idea what had happened. No idea if I was dying or dead or more alive than ever.

But one truth came to me, as bright and jagged as the pain that lanced through my chest, as Asa descended on me, knife in hand, his face spattered with blood and his eyes wild.

Something had just gone very, very wrong.

CHAPTER
TWENTY-FOUR

I was too stunned to scream as Asa landed on me and hacked at the ropes holding my body to the bed. He was cursing under his breath, flinching at every cracking noise. *Gunfire,* I thought vaguely as Asa cut the final rope and yanked me right off the foot of the bed. We landed in a sprawl, him hunched over me, holding my head to his chest as my body buzzed with shock. For a moment, I could feel his heartbeat, fierce and pounding.

"Are you okay?" he said, panting, laying my head on the floor and looking my body over. He shoved his hand up my shirt and pressed his palm between my breasts. His brow furrowed. "I think we got it all out . . . ? Dammit. It's so fucking hard to tell with you."

My face was wet, and when I reached up to wipe it, the severed rope still secured to my wrist flopped against my chest. My trembling fingers came away red, but they felt strangely disconnected from the rest of me. "Is Jack all right?"

Asa's Adam's apple bobbed as he swallowed. "He's fine now, Mattie. Don't worry about him. Can you scoot over toward the door? Stay low."

"Why?" I craned my neck and started to push toward the corner of the bed so I could see the windows and door.

Asa's hands became iron around my waist, holding me where I was. "Sniper. Probably Zhong's."

"But the curtains were closed."

"The shooter would have been a sensor. And Jack would have been lit up like the fucking Fourth of July. So easy to see . . ." Asa shook his head, looking like he was going to be sick. "They'll be up here in a few seconds. We're going to have to run like hell. Can you do that?"

I rubbed at the lingering pain in my chest, and Asa frowned as he watched me. "I have to get the relic," he said. "Then we're going out the door."

"What's going to keep the sniper from shooting us?"

He left my side, commando-crawling around the corner of the bed and coming back a moment later with his elbows and chest soaked in red. His face was dripping sweat, and the bloody necklace was around his neck. "Because I'm going to use the relic against them."

I stared at the pendant. "But if you open that, what's it going to do to y—"

"Stop questioning me," he snapped. "Get to the fucking door and be ready to run on my signal."

I hated the look on his face, the circles under his eyes, the pallor of his skin, the way his neck was already red from the rub of the necklace, poisonous to him in a way it was to no one else. "But maybe I could do it," I said. "And you could run."

His eyes met mine. "You don't know how, and this isn't the time to learn."

My own eyes burned at the glitter of pain in his, and maybe he could read my fear, because he moved closer and our gazes locked. "I need to concentrate, Mattie. And that's only going to happen if I know you'll be safe."

I felt an echo of the suffering the relic caused, a needle of agony deep in my chest. He was about to turn it on our enemies—and on himself. But I knew him well enough to understand that he was going to lose it if I didn't do as he said. "Okay. You're in charge."

He reached to touch my face, but then seemed to realize his fingers were stained with blood. His hand became a fist. "Good. Go."

Dread coiling inside me, I crawled over to the corner of the bed and looked toward the door. The air was swirling with plaster dust and carried a metal tang that settled heavy on my tongue. I could see the lights from the parking lot through the thin curtains, which were now dotted with bullet holes. In my periphery, along the side of the bed, there was a dark shape, unmoving. I knew it was Jack, and I knew he was dead.

Asa edged in next to me, peering at our only exit. "I'm going to open the door."

"You want me to run to the car?"

He shook his head. "That's what they're expecting. Head for that mall across the street. Find a place to hide."

"And you?"

"I'll be right behind you."

"You'd better."

His mouth twitched into a half smile. Then he pushed me toward the door. My knees rubbed against the carpet. A bloody rope was still dangling from my forearm. My heart was an engine, revving, with nowhere to go.

Asa guided me against the wall next to the door and nodded at me. Just like in Bangkok, I wondered if it was a reassurance or a good-bye. He reached up, turned the knob, and yanked the door wide. "Stay low, and run. I've got this."

It was another leap of faith, because no sooner had he said it than the air filled with the staccato cracks of gunshots. I pushed off, my thoughts blank and dark, my eyes on the empty shells of the buildings across the street. Behind me, Asa let out a strained, strangled moan, but I forced myself not to turn and look. He'd said he could handle it.

And a moment later, I knew he had, because the night was filled with screaming, coming from the parking lot near our car. I sprinted past a

gas station on the corner, wondering how many people had already called
911 in response to the gunshots, wondering how long it might take police
to get to us. At the sound of more gunfire, I hazarded a glance over my
shoulder, only long enough to register someone sprinting across the parking lot. What if they'd gotten Asa and were coming for me?

With a quick, desperate prayer and another burst of speed, I flew
across the road and into the maze of the outdoor mall. In the distance,
a siren wailed. I darted around a corner and peered toward the Super
8, but I couldn't see the parking lot from my vantage point. I could
hear, though. Not screams—but shouts. And the squeal of tires peeling
out. Headlights flared as a car zoomed from the back of the motel and
headed straight for the mall.

I whirled around and ran past boarded-up windows covered in graf-
fiti. Some of the local kids must have had a fine time in this abandoned
place, but I hoped for their sakes none of them were here tonight.
Finally, I reached some sort of square with a dry, weedy fountain in the
center, deep in the heart of the maze. My chest was tight and pulsing
with pain as I held my breath, just long enough to hear pounding footsteps and the crunch of glass beneath boots. I glanced around, knowing
I didn't have much time to get out of sight, and spotted a window where
the boards had been pried away. The glass clung to the window frame
like jagged rotting teeth in a monster's mouth, protecting the darkness
within. With my pursuers coming closer, I pelted across the square and
carefully climbed through, nearly tripping over toppled clothing racks
that had been piled along the wall.

Quietly as I could, I wove my way through the desecrated shell,
feeling out my path with outstretched hands. I wanted to keep the
window in sight, as it offered the only source of light—the bright desert moon and stars, along with a scant glow from the gas station and
hotel across the street. But then a dark shadow blocked that out, and I
ducked behind an overturned cabinet, praying whoever was out there
hadn't seen me. The silhouette was the wrong shape to be Asa. It didn't

move in the smooth, predatory way he did. Its movements were more sudden. Like the strike of a snake.

Crack, crack, crack, scream. The gunfire erupted outside, only a few shops away. I curled into the fetal position, momentarily forgetting the silhouette outside the store, wishing the needle of pain in my chest would let up for a minute. It throbbed with every kick of my heart.

"Saw you come in here, little reliquary," said a soft voice from only a few feet away.

My head jerked up, and I found myself staring at a familiar face—it was another of Zhong's agents, the handsome guy with the slick eyebrows that Asa had downed with dental floss in Chicago. Not knowing if he was Knedas or Strikon, I threw myself to the side as he reached for me. He was quick, though, and as soon as his hands closed around my arms, my body lit up, all at once.

But not with pain. With *lust*.

My body shook with it, going tight and loose at the same time. Dimly, I was aware of the firefight outside, but I didn't care. All I cared about was whether he let go. Because I didn't want him to. Ever.

He pulled me to my feet and pressed me up against the wall. "Where is Asa Ward?" he whispered as he lowered his face to my neck. I arched into him as I felt his tongue on my skin. I stood on my tiptoes, just to bring him closer. My clothes were so inconvenient. "He has the relic, doesn't he?"

"What?" I breathed, guiding his hand to my waist.

"Asa Ward," he said, slowly dipping his fingers under the elastic of my shorts.

"I have no idea." I pushed his fingers lower. God, I felt as if I were going to explode. The only part of me that wasn't on fire with need was my chest, where pain continued to pulse.

His hand stilled on my belly, firm and resisting as I tried to move it lower. He clucked his tongue, his heartrending smile shining in the dim lights from outside. "Tell me, and I'll give you what you want. An orgasm that will change you forever."

Outside, there was still a war going on. I had no idea why there was so much shooting, but a different kind of fight had erupted inside me. I was so close to coming, that point at which you know you have to, at which you can't think past it. Except—the pain inside me was sharp, and with each throb of it, I remembered my encounter with the Strikon in San Francisco, and the way he had talked to me about what his pain magic would do to my brain. How it would change me forever.

How it would break me.

I blinked up at my handsome Ekstazo captor, his full lips and dark eyes, his bold eyebrows and ebony hair. "Why are you so interested in Asa?"

He canted his hips so I could feel the hard pressure of his erection between my legs, and the rub of it nearly sent me over the edge. "Mr. Zhong wants to punish him," he said. "And to treasure him. Funny how that works, isn't it?"

My fingers paused as I realized I had been sliding them through the Ekstazo's hair. The rope dangling from my wrist rubbed against my newly sensitized skin, clearing the fog inside my head for a moment. "So he wants to make him like Tao."

The Ekstazo's fingers slid south, his fingertips just centimeters from the edge of my panties. "He'll be taken care of. And we'll take care of you, too. I'll take care of you personally, in fact." He grinned and lowered his head to kiss me.

But it was as if his magic were beading on my skin, pulling away from my pores, drying in the heat of my anger, my hurt. I was so tired of being jerked around by magic, of it taking over my body and making it do things I didn't want it to. And the idea of Mr. Zhong doing the same thing to Asa fanned the flames. My hand slid up my captor's chest, and I moaned and tilted my head back.

Then I reached up and grabbed the end of the rope tied to my wrist. With a quick jerk, I had it wrapped around the guy's neck. If Asa could do it with suspenders, I could do it with this. As the Ekstazo wheezed and brought his knee up, hitting me square in the stomach, I clung to that rope, dragging him to the floor, where we wrestled, him punching at me.

Only instead of pain, every impact spread a tingle of ecstasy as he tried to defend himself with his magic, as he tried to steal my purpose. I wrapped my legs around his waist and my arms around his neck, keeping the rope around his throat taut, even as he sank his teeth into my shoulder. And when he broke the skin, my orgasm was instant and mind blowing. My eyes clamped shut and I screamed, undulating against my victim, shaking with pleasure even as I fought to stay alert.

It stole my strength, every ounce of it.

But it was too late for the Ekstazo. His head lolled against my arm as I shuddered with aftershocks, quickly followed by a brutal wave of revulsion. I shoved him off me, the rope uncoiling from his neck. I didn't know if he was alive or dead, only that I needed to get away from him. I staggered toward the shattered window, creeping along the wall as I listened to yet another smattering of shots. They seemed a little farther away now. Maybe I could make it to the back of the property. I'd seen a jutting ridge of hills as we'd exited the highway, so the interstate had to be close, just over those peaks. If all else failed, if Asa didn't find me, maybe I could hitch a ride. I was bloody, but damn cute. Surely someone would be willing to pick up a damsel in distress.

I wouldn't mention that I had just strangled someone.

My hand rose to rub the twinge of pain in my chest. Whatever it was—anxiety, the lingering soreness that came with letting loose such powerful magic—it had kept my mind just sharp enough to allow me to fight back, and in that moment I was grateful for it. I peeked outside the window and didn't see anyone, and the shooting had really died down.

No better time to run than now, especially since a low moan from the back of the store told me that my Ekstazo lover boy wasn't dead after all.

With the shards of glass snagging at the fabric of my shorts, I climbed through the window and looked around, trying to get my bearings. But then a sudden burst of gunfire to my left made my direction clear, and I ran to the right, staying hunched over, as if that were going to protect me from bullets. I made it back to the edge of the square. Just beyond the fountain, I could see a path that ended in blackness, but beyond the roofs of the buildings lay a dense shadow that blocked out the starlight—the hills that marked my hope for escape. I stepped into the square, but as soon as I did, a bullet hit the wall next to me.

I screamed, the terror streaking through me as more bullets crunched through wood and shattered stone, my legs moving like pistons against the ground. I made it through the square, only to see a few dark silhouettes emerge from a store right down the lane where I was intending to bolt. I stopped dead, praying they hadn't seen me yet.

Too late did I hear the footsteps coming at me from behind, and I grunted as a hard, wet body hit me, arms wrapping like steel around my rib cage. I recognized his scent a split second before he spoke. "Where the hell have you been?" Asa said, his breath coming from him in sharp gasps. The relic necklace clinked between us, the pendant closed. Sweat dripped from his jaw.

"Oh thank God," I said, running my hands up his arms, needing to reassure myself that he was all right.

"Worship me later, how about?" He hustled me into a corridor. Asa pushed my back against the wall and looked me over, his short hair standing on end. Dark, angry welts stood out on the skin of his throat. He seemed like he was on the verge of collapse. The circles under his eyes were so dark that they looked like bruises.

The sight focused my thoughts and steadied my hands, which rose to pull that poisonous jewelry over his head. He ducked his head and allowed it, bracing his palms against the wall like he was trying to hold himself up. "I thought they'd gotten you," he said.

"One of them did."

"Ekstazo." His nostrils flared. "How the hell did you get away? Did that motherfucker—"

"No." I put the necklace over my head, glad he couldn't see the color of my burning cheeks. "Stop underestimating me."

He smiled, still trying to catch his breath. "You'd think I'd know better by now."

I touched one of the welts on his neck, and he winced and pulled my fingers away. "Sorry," I said. "I guess the relic worked, though? Long enough for you to get away."

"Yep. Gave me enough of a head start." He grimaced and his back arched abruptly, and I stepped to the side as he retched.

I moved deeper into the corridor, giving him space. "Is it the relic? It didn't make you that sick before, once you'd stopped wearing it."

"Not the relic," he said, doubling over to dry heave. "Reza's here."

"What? He's working for Zhong?"

Asa wiped his mouth on his bloody T-shirt and shook his head. "No. Brindle's people are all over the fucking place. That's the shooting—Zhong and Brindle's people are firing at each other."

"Hasn't someone called the police?"

"Sure, but Knedas agents were waiting for them in the parking lot. Anyone who gets close thinks they're hearing construction sounds."

"At night?"

"Doesn't have to make sense for people to believe."

So we were in the middle of a mob war, and no one was coming to help. "Who's winning?"

A piercing scream split the night, and Asa groaned and sank to his knees. "One guess."

Reza's arrival would have changed things. "Does he need to touch people to hurt them?"

"If he's close enough, all he has to do is be able to see them."

But he could hurt Asa without any of that. He was hurting Asa just by being in the vicinity. "You have to get out of here. When they're done fighting each other, they'll come for you."

It didn't matter which side caught him. He was sunk either way.

Asa pushed himself up to his feet, using the wall for support. "Come on. We'll head for those hills behind this development." He stretched out his long arm and grabbed my hand. His grasp was cold and clammy and trembling.

I pulled my hand from his. They were chasing him, but they were also chasing the relic. The thing we'd promised to give Frank Brindle in exchange for Ben's life. "Asa, this could end here."

He leaned against the wall, gritting his teeth as another scream rent the air, closer this time. The gunfire had stopped for the time being. Maybe Zhong's people were too terrified to shoot, scared that it would lead Brindle's Strikon assassin straight to them.

"This is our chance, Mattie," Asa said in a tight voice.

"This is *your* chance. We had a plan. There's no reason not to stick to it now."

"You expect me to leave you behind?"

"I expect you to do what we agreed on. I'll give them the relic. You get as far away from here as you can." I smiled, though it was really hard. The sharp pain in my chest had been replaced with a terrible ache. My fingers rose to touch his rough cheek. "Go get Gracie. She'll be so happy to see you."

Asa cursed and folded his arm over his stomach as a piercing shriek resounded only a few stores down from our hiding place. Reza was getting closer. "We can leave the relic right here for them to find. They'll let Ben loose. You don't have to stay."

"You don't know that. If I'm here, I can explain what we had to do. I can tell them you said you were on your way to South America or something. Send them in the wrong direction."

He raised his head and leveled me with the look in his eyes. I'd never seen it before. It was somehow ferocious and pleading at the same time. "Come with me, Mattie. We're a good team. We can figure this out. Together."

Together. Suddenly, all my confused, tangled feelings for him pushed their way to the front of my brain, overwhelming and terrifying. I needed to get away from him. "I can't, Asa."

Asa's lips curled into a snarl. "Ben doesn't deserve you."

"Stop."

He swallowed hard. "Mattie." It looked like he was struggling with his words, like they were as painful as the Strikon magic all around him, like he was trying to summon the will to let them go. "When Ben told you I was jealous of him . . ."

"You said he was wrong." My heart was thrumming and my stomach was tight, and somehow the assassins all around us seemed much less threatening than what lay between me and Asa.

"That was the truth." Asa's jaw clenched. "Until—"

"Good-bye, Asa," I blurted out, my voice cracking. I squeezed my eyes closed, trying to shut the ache inside the supposedly powerful vault I carried in my chest. If I could hold the most powerful pain magic in existence, why couldn't I contain this kind of hurt? "Give Gracie a hug for me, okay?"

Asa chuckled, that dark, dry, humorless sound he made only when he was in pain. He caressed my cheek, a quick brush of his calloused fingertips across my skin. "*Dammit*, Mattie," he whispered.

And then his touch was gone, and so was he. I listened to his footsteps fading into silence.

I sank to the ground, the relic necklace clinking softly as my chest convulsed with a sob. I pulled my knees up and curled around the ache, covering my head with my arms as tears streamed down my face. I knew I shouldn't be crying. I was so close to getting exactly what I wanted. But my body thought differently, I guessed.

"Mattie. I'm glad we found you in time."

My head jerked up. Reza had knelt before me, looking dapper and smooth, as if he'd just been on an evening stroll. His dark eyes were bright. "Are you hurt?"

"N-no," I said. "I'm not hurt."

He reached for me, but I cringed back, whimpering, wishing I could control my tears. But it was all too much, all at once, and the pressure and pain in my chest were overwhelming. Reza pulled his hands back. "I won't hurt you. If I'd wanted to, I could have done it the moment I laid eyes on you. You understand that, don't you?"

I glanced at his gorgeous face, his wavy black hair slicked back from his forehead, his gaze gentle. "Please let me help you," he murmured. "That's what I was sent here to do." He offered his hand.

I took it. There was no pain. I wondered how hard he was working to control it, but I was grateful for his steadiness as he helped me to my feet. "What happens now?"

He put his arm around me, and his eyes traced the gaudy pendant nestled between my breasts. "I'm going to take you back to Las Vegas, where you will have the chance to clean yourself up before meeting with Mr. Brindle." He gave me a hypnotic smile. "And then you will be reunited with Ben, who is desperate for a report on your well-being and safety."

"What about Asa?" I asked in a broken whisper.

Reza's eyebrows rose. "What of him?" He made a show of looking around. "It seems Mr. Ward slipped away before I had the chance to greet him." His smile widened. "Another day, perhaps."

The predatory glint in his eye sent a chill through me, but it was gone so quickly that I wondered if I'd imagined it. Reza tucked my hand into the crook of his elbow and gestured toward the square. "Shall we?"

I nodded, and he led me out of the corridor and into the dusty, smoky night.

EPILOGUE

It was easier than I'd thought it would be. Frank Brindle was as good as his word. He actually seemed a little hurt that Asa would believe he'd ever intended to take him by force, though I could have sworn his friendly smile didn't quite reach his eyes. Ben and I left Las Vegas on a first-class flight a few days later, with the assurance that we'd been granted safe passage by Zhong Lei. After the firefight in the desert had killed off dozens of agents on each side, the two bosses had negotiated some kind of truce.

Our return to Sheboygan was triumphant and full of lies. With Frank's help—and probably serious nudging by some of his Knedas agents, who had been sent forth to "gather" witnesses—a story had been constructed. Ben had been kidnapped after a case of mistaken identity. He'd been locked in a trunk and transported cross-country, where, badly dehydrated and suffering from the removal of his pacemaker, he'd nevertheless managed to escape. He'd awakened in the hospital, where he'd spent several days as a John Doe before the police realized who he was.

As for me, I'd immediately emerged from my self-imposed exile at the spa to fly out to Vegas and be by his side as he recovered. We were all over the news. We smiled for the cameras. We were interviewed on the *Today* show. *Good Morning America*, too. We held hands, my engagement ring glittering bright. We didn't talk much, though. I think both of us knew we were headed for a reckoning, but neither of us felt strong enough to face it just yet.

I refused to let myself think of Asa.

I wondered if the lingering shard of pain inside my chest would ever go away, or if it was just the mark magic had left on me, how it had changed me.

A few days after the media circus died down, I went to visit Grandpa. I'd tried to steer clear of my parents' house, because I didn't want the stress of the news trucks and the reporters on the lawn to affect him. He was in his bed in the library when I arrived, and he smiled and stretched out a frail, shaking hand as I approached. I took it in mine. "I told you I would come back," I said quietly, my throat already going tight.

"That's some story you're telling," he said weakly as I pulled a chair over and sat at his bedside.

"It's more believable than the truth." I bit my lip as I took in his sunken cheeks and sagging skin. "I met someone you used to know. Jack?"

His eyes lit up. "You met Jack! How is he?"

I swallowed the lump in my throat. "We wouldn't have gotten Ben back without him."

The light in his eyes faded as he took in the look on my face. "Don't tell me. Not today."

I nodded and lowered my head to the bed rail. I wanted to tell him everything that had happened. He was the only one who understood. But maybe it was just something I needed to let go.

"Now that you know what you can do," he said after a few minutes of heavy silence, "will you go into the business?"

I shook my head. "I turned down a job, actually." Frank had taken it with a jovial smile and told me the offer would stand if I ever changed my mind. "I belong here."

Grandpa looked me over with surprise. "Are you sure?"

I bit my lip and nodded.

"Then at the very least, you be proud of who you really are, and what you're capable of."

A smile found its way to my lips. "I guess I *can* do some pretty cool stuff." Not all of it was about magic, either. I had survived. I had fought. And I'd won. "I'm actually kind of a badass, now that I think about it."

"And don't you forget it." Grandpa patted my hand. "But I'm so glad you're home safe. I was afraid . . ." He looked away, directing his gaze at my father's collection of travel magazines.

He was afraid I wouldn't make it home before he died. We hadn't made it back in time for Barley, after all. Ben's golden had died quietly in his sleep a few days before we made it home, in this very room. We'd missed our last days with him. I was so glad the same hadn't happened with Grandpa.

"I'm not going anywhere," I said, my voice thinned by sorrow. A shuffling in the doorway made me turn my head. Ben was standing there, waiting for me. I'd told him to come pick me up at six, and it was nearly half past. "I'll be back tomorrow, all right?"

Grandpa nodded, and I rose and kissed his cool forehead before moving to Ben's side.

"You okay?" he murmured, putting his arm around me as we walked to his RAV4 in the driveway.

I nodded. "I just feel bad for the stress all this has caused him."

Ben sighed and ran his hand through his sandy hair. "The stress I caused, you mean."

I turned to him as I heard the hurt in his voice. "I didn't mean it like that. I'm not blaming you."

His eyes met mine. "But shouldn't you?"

"Do you want me to?"

He put the car into gear and turned onto the street. "I want you to come back to me, Mattie. It feels like you haven't yet."

I watched the scenery go by as he made the short drive back to our little cottage. As he pulled into the drive, I looked up at the house that I'd decorated with all my fantasies of how my life would be. "I'm trying." I got out before he could open my door for me and headed up the steps.

"Mattie, talk to me," he pleaded as we reached the entryway. "I can't live like this."

He took my face in his hands and tilted my head up. I focused my gaze on the round edge of his jaw. "I'm sorry," he said with a bitter laugh. "I should be thanking you, not asking you for more." He touched his forehead to mine. "Please look at me, Mattie."

I forced myself to look into his eyes, my chest aching at the sight of their honey color. His smile was pained. "I betrayed you," he said quietly. "I violated your trust. And instead of leaving me, you saved me. You traveled halfway around the world for me. I have no idea what kind of danger you were in, but I know it must have been terrifying, and I know you did it because you love me. I don't deserve you."

Ben doesn't deserve you. I pulled out of Ben's grasp, desperate to escape Asa's voice in my head. "You made mistakes," I murmured. "I've made plenty of my own. I just . . . I want to forget about all of that."

Ben stared at me, the surprise evident on his face. "Shouldn't we talk about what I did?"

If we do, will we have to talk about what I did? It was the last thing I wanted to do. "Maybe we should just let it go and move on."

"I can't."

I looked up at him. "I'm offering you a free pass, and you're not going to take it?"

He shook his head. "Not if it means we're going to be like this. Two strangers in the same house. I want what we had before, Mattie. It was magical."

I flinched, and he cursed. "I didn't mean it like that," he said quickly, then reached out to take me by the arms. "I just meant that what we had was amazing, and I think we could rebuild it if you'll allow it."

I leaned on his chest, inhaling his familiar, clean scent. "I want to, Ben. It's just . . . a lot, all right?"

Ben's grip tightened. "Does any of it have to do with my brother?"

I tensed. "What do you mean?"

"I shouldn't have ever let you travel with him. I can't imagine how he treated you. The places he dragged you into. What he made you do."

"He did it all to save you," I said slowly. "Do you have any idea what he risked to get you back?"

Ben bowed his head. "I'm sorry."

"Someday, you need to thank him. And I think you should apologize to him, too." I ran my finger down the straight slope of his nose.

Ben's cheeks darkened. "He told you."

I nodded. "You hurt him more than he'll ever tell you."

"I didn't want to," he whispered. "My dad . . ."

"I know. He told me that, too."

"Dad was trying to protect me," Ben said. "He was tough, but that's all he ever wanted to do."

"Maybe he should have protected Asa, too."

Ben shrugged. "Maybe he tried. I don't really know. Asa never was easy. You have to know that, Mattie. He pushed Dad pretty hard."

"No, Asa's not easy." I opened my mouth to say more, about how Asa was the easiest person to misjudge I had ever met. At first glance he was mercenary and rude, callous and arrogant. But the longer you looked at him, the more you could see who he really was, the person he'd managed to become against all the odds. That person was scary and complicated and deadly . . . but also brave and decent and compassionate, even when he wasn't willing to admit it to himself. There were so many things I wanted to say about Asa, but the more I allowed his quietly thoughtful gestures and protectiveness to float into my conscious thoughts, the more my chest hurt. So I settled for "I actually don't think you know him at all, Ben."

He nodded, still staring at the ground. "Maybe that's true." He raised his head. "But I know I owe him my life. And I owe it to you, too." He pulled me close, and his eyes were shining with tears. "Will you let me spend the rest of it paying you back?"

I'd already made the choice. I'd made it in a corridor in an abandoned mall, when I'd closed my eyes so I didn't have to watch Asa walk away from me. "Yes," I whispered.

Ben let out a choked laugh. "Thank you," he said, lowering his head to kiss me.

I welcomed it. I needed it. Nothing else could erase the memories that slipped across my skin, an echo of sensations past, forbidden and confusing. I held on tight as Ben lifted me up and carried me into our bedroom. With fierce urgency, I undressed him, needing the sight of his muscular body, the weight of him pressing me into the bed. I paused to run my hand over the scar where his pacemaker had been removed. In all the chaos, lost in my own stormy sea of emotion, I'd completely forgotten about it. "Oh my God! We have to get you to the doctor," I said. "I can't believe you haven't already done that."

Ben smiled and shook his head, holding my palm over the scar. "I'm healed, Mattie," he said quietly. "Forever."

I blinked up at him. "What?"

He grinned as he pulled my shirt over my head and deftly unhooked my bra. "Frank let me have that relic. I won't ever need a pacemaker again."

I lifted my hips to allow him to unzip my skirt and slide it off. "But I thought he would only give it to you in return for Asa joining him."

Ben shook his head, his eyes focused on my body as he pulled my panties down my legs. Then his gaze met mine. "He said you had risked so much to bring him the relic that it was the least he could do."

My brow furrowed. "Really? That's kind of hard to believe."

"I know, but I wasn't going to say no." He began to kiss his way up my stomach and parted my thighs. "So I owe you my heart, too. But it was already yours."

I ran my hands up his strong back as he pushed himself into me, as we moved together. Our familiar rhythm was comforting, and I focused on it, using it to pull up the simple, easy memories of how it used to be, how we both wanted it to be again. It would take some time, but I knew we could find our way back. We were too good together not to. We were perfect for each other.

Always had been.

Always would be.

I repeated that to myself over and over until it felt automatic. I fell asleep in his arms, our naked bodies pressed together, my head on Ben's chest, clinging desperately to the normal, predictable *safeness* of our life, of him, of us.

The pain wrenched me to the surface of my easy dreams, though. I sat up, my heart hammering, each beat feeling like the slice of a scalpel. Ben was sacked out next to me, moonlight on his handsome face. Still dreaming.

I pulled a blanket around me and headed to the backyard, where he wouldn't be able to hear the little squeaks of my breath. *Panic attack,* Asa had called it. That must be what this was. I sank down on a lounger, bundled in my blanket in the cool summer-night air, and stared up at the stars, concentrating on slowing down my breathing. Tears gathered at the corners of my eyes, and I fought like hell to hold them in.

I tried not to wish for that angular face to appear above mine, crooked nose and dark hair, belonging to a man who was ready to chase away anything that threatened me. I had sent him away, because the alternative was totally unthinkable. Unmanageable. Ridiculous. It made no sense at all.

That didn't change how much I missed him.

"*Dammit*, Asa," I whispered, running my fingers across my throat.

I stayed out there for a long time, building a fence around my memories of him. He didn't ever want to be in a cage, but in my head, there was no other safe place to keep him. So I built the walls high, with razor wire along the top, trapping him along with everything else in the strange world of magic I had discovered. It didn't fit with the future I'd chosen.

By the time I was finished, the needle of pain in my chest had dulled to an ache. My breathing had slowed, and my tears had dried. Once I'd contained my sadness at what I'd lost, gratitude—for having experienced it at all, and for the man who'd gotten me through all of it—had welled up in its place. We weren't headed in the same direction, but I would always be glad our paths had crossed. And as the sun glowed weakly at the tree line, preparing to emerge and dominate the day, I got up and headed back inside.

ACKNOWLEDGMENTS

First and foremost, I want to thank the folks at 47North, particularly Jason Kirk, who advocated for *Reliquary* from the outset, along with Courtney Miller, Ben Smith, Britt Rogers, and the rest of this energetic, creative team. To Leslie Miller, my developmental editor, I am especially grateful. Lam, your patience and willingness to listen made all the difference. I'd also like to thank Janice Lee, my copyeditor, for her keen eye and precision, as well as Phyllis DeBlanche for proofreading, and Faceout Studio for their cover design.

To Kathleen Ortiz, my fierce and attentive agent, thank you for understanding my radio silence and diverting traffic when necessary. Gaby Salpeter, my assistant, gets a big virtual hug for operating as my frontal lobes as needed. And to New Leaf Literary & Media—thank you for providing all manner of auxiliary support.

Writing *Reliquary* was both exhilarating and therapeutic, and I owe gratitude to Amber Lynn Natusch and Brigid Kemmerer for excellent early feedback and cheerleading. To Brigid and Lydia Kang, thanks as well for simple friendship and hours of listening. I couldn't have made it through without your validation and screaming goat GIFs.

Thanks to my other friends, Paul and Liz, Jim (who also gave useful critical feedback about a certain scene) and Susanne, Sue and Craig, and Claudine, for providing refuge when needed and laughter, love, and reality checks at all times. A thousand thank-yous to my parents, Jerry and Julie Fine, for providing unconditional support 24/7/365, without judgment and with absolute ferocity. Of course, hugs to my babies, Asher and Alma, for simply existing and being the reason I persist.

And to my readers—this is all your fault, and I can't possibly thank you enough.

ABOUT THE AUTHOR

Photo © 2012 Rebecca Skinner

Sarah Fine is a clinical psychologist and the author of the Servants of Fate and Guards of the Shadowlands series. She was born on the West Coast, was raised in the Midwest, and is now firmly entrenched on the East Coast.